Praise for *The Map of Love*

'By general agreement (of the Booker Prize committee), the "best read" of the shortlist. A romance of the desert, it has something of the oriental exotic about it, mixed with fashionable post-colonialism'

'Political fiction that is also unashamedly romantic, a discussion of society and of ideas that is also a strong narrative – a feat that few novelists could bring off . . . Moving and entirely convincing . . . A triumphant achievement'

Literary Review

'Filled with subtlety, grace and beauty . . . *The Map of Love* is honest and intellectual. A love story, but also about the history of colonial Britain and the effects of Imperialism in a third world country. It takes on a range of topics in the way Dickens did, fusing life, art, history, class and culture into a huge, vibrant novel'

Big Issue

'Soueif is at her most eloquent on the subject of her homeland, her prose rich with historical detail and debate. Egypt emerges as the true heroine of this novel'

Independent

'Ahdaf Soueif has a talent for blending the personal and political and getting under the skin of each one of her characters'

Independent on Sunday

THE MAP OF LOVE

THE MAP OF LOVE

AHDAF SOUEIF

BLOOMSBURY

LONDON · BERLIN · NEW YORK · SYDNEY

First published 1999
This paperback edition published 2000

Copyright © 1999 by Ahdaf Soueif

The moral right of the author
has been asserted

Bloomsbury Publishing Plc, 36 Soho Square, London W1D 3QY

A CIP catalogue record for this book
is available from the British Library

ISBN 978 0 7475 4563 7

35 34 33 32 31 30

Typeset by Hewer Text Ltd, Edinburgh
Printed in Great Britain by Clays Limited, St Ives plc

www.bloomsbury.com/ahdafsoueif

FSC
Mixed Sources
Product group from well-managed
forests and other controlled sources
Cert no. SGS-COC-2061
www.fsc.org
© 1996 Forest Stewardship Council

For Ian

CONTENTS

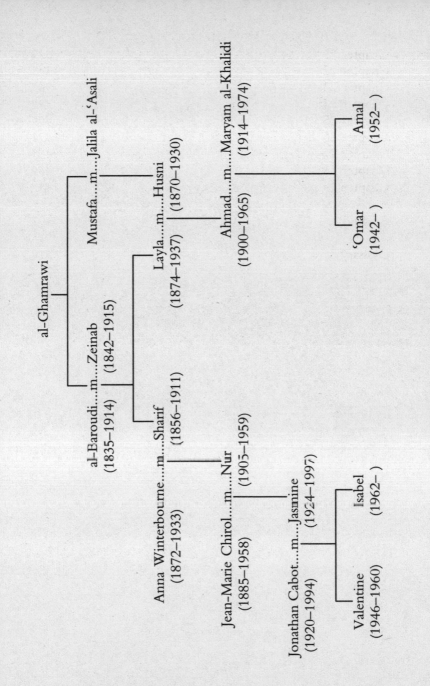

It is strange that this period [1900–1914] when the Colonialists and their collaborators thought everything was quiet – was one of the most fertile in Egypt's history. A great examination of the self took place, and a great recharging of energy in preparation for a new Renaissance.

Gamal 'Abd el-Nasser, *The Covenant* 1962

A Beginning

Even God cannot change the past.
Agathon (447–401 BC)

– and there, on the table under her bedroom window, lies the voice that has set her dreaming again. Fragments of a life lived a long, long time ago. Across a hundred years the woman's voice speaks to her – so clearly that she cannot believe it is not possible to pick up her pen and answer.

The child sleeps. Nur al-Hayah: light of my life.

Anna must have put aside her pen, Amal thinks, and looked down at the child pressed into her side: the face flushed with sleep, the mouth slightly open, a damp tendril of black hair clinging to the brow.

I have tried, as well as I could, to tell her. But she cannot – or will not – understand, and give up hope. She waits for him constantly.

Amal reads and reads deep into the night. She reads and lets Anna's words flow into her, probing gently at dreams and hopes and sorrows she had sorted out, labelled and put away.

Papers, polished and frail with age, sheets and sheets of them. Mostly they are covered in English in a small, firm, sloping hand. Amal has sorted them out by type and size of paper, by colour of ink. Other papers are in French. Some are in envelopes, some loosely bundled together in buff folders. There is a large green journal, and another bound in plain

4

brown leather, a tiny brass keyhole embedded in its chased clasp. The key Amal found later in the corner of a purse made of green felt – a purse with an unwilling feel to it, as though it had been made in a schoolroom project – and with it were two wedding rings, one smaller than the other. She looked carefully at the etchings inside them, and at first the only part of the inscription she could make out on either ring was the date: 1896. A large brown envelope held one writing book: sixty-four pages of neat Arabic ruq'a script. Amal recognised the hand immediately: the upright letters short but straight, the sharp angles, the tail of the 'ya' tucked under its body. The definite, controlled hand of her grandmother. The paper is white and narrow-lined, bound between marbled grey boards. The stiff pages crackle and resist. When she smooths them open they lie awkwardly, holding a rigid posture till she closes the book again. Some newspaper cuttings: *al-Ahram*, *al-Liwa*, *The Times*, the *Daily News* and others. A programme from an Italian theatre. Another purse, this time of dark blue velvet. She had upended it over her palm and poured out a string of thirty-three prayer beads of polished wood with a short tassel of black silk. For the rest of the day her hand smelled faintly of aged sandalwood. Some sketchbooks with various drawings. Several books of Arabic calligraphy practice. She flicked through them, noting the difference in flow and confidence. Several books of Arabic exercises, quotations, notes, etc. A locket, curious in that it is made of a heavy, dull metal and hangs on a fine chain of steel. When she pressed its spring, it opened and a young woman looked out at her. It is an exquisite painting and she studies it repeatedly. She tells herself she has to get a magnifying glass and look at it properly. The young woman's hair is blonde and is worn loose and crimped in the style made famous by the Pre-Raphaelites. She has a smooth, clear brow, an oval face and a delicate chin. Her mouth is about to break into a smile. But her eyes are the strangest shade of blue, violet really, and they look straight at you and they say – they say a lot of things. There's a strength in that look, a wilfulness; one would almost call it defiance except that it is so good-humoured. It is the look a woman would wear – would have worn – if she asked a man, a stranger, say, to dance. The date on the back is 1870 and into the concave lid someone had taped a tiny golden key. A calico bag, and inside it, meticulously laundered and with a sachet of lavender tucked between the folds, was a baby's frock of the finest white cotton, its top a mass of blue and yellow and pink smocking. And folded once, and rolled in muslin, a curious woven tapestry showing a pharaonic image and an Arabic inscription. There was also a shawl, of the type worn by peasant women on special occasions: 'butter velvet', white. You can buy one today in the Ghuriyya for twenty Egyptian pounds. And there is another, finer one, in pale grey wool with faded pink flowers – so often worn that in patches you can almost see through the weave.

And there were other things too. Things wrapped in tissue, or in fabric, or concealed in envelopes: a box full of things, a treasure chest, a trunk, actually. It is a trunk.

A story can start from the oddest things: a magic lamp, a conversation overheard, a shadow moving on a wall. For Amal al-Ghamrawi, this story started with a trunk. An old-fashioned trunk made of brown leather, cracked now and dry, with a vaulted top over which run two straps fastened with brass buckles black with age and neglect.

The American had come to Amal's house. Her name was Isabel Parkman and the trunk was locked in the boot of the car she had hired. Amal could not pretend she was not wary. Wary and weary in advance: an American woman – a journalist, she had said on the phone. But she said Amal's brother had told her to call and so Amal agreed to see her. And braced herself: the fundamentalists, the veil, the cold peace, polygamy, women's status in Islam, female genital mutilation – which would it be?

But Isabel Parkman was not brash or strident; in fact she was rather diffident, almost shy. She had met Amal's brother in New York. She had told him she was coming to Egypt to do a project on the millennium, and he had given her Amal's number. Amal said she doubted whether Isabel would come across anyone with grand millennial views or theories. She said that she thought Isabel would find that on the whole everyone was simply worried – worried sick about what would become of Egypt, the Arab countries, 'le tiers monde', in the twenty-first century. But she gave her coffee and some names and Isabel went away.

On her second visit Isabel had broached the subject of the trunk. She had found it when her mother had gone into hospital – for good. She had looked inside it, and there were some old papers in English, written, she believed, by her great-grandmother. But there were many papers and documents in Arabic. And there were other things: objects. And the English papers were mostly undated, and some were bound together but seemed to start in midsentence. She knew some of her own history must be there, but she also thought there might be a story. She didn't want to impose but Amal's brother had thought she might be interested . . .

Amal was touched by her hesitancy. She said she would have a look at the thing and sent the doorman to bring it upstairs. As he carried it in and put it in the middle of her living room, she said, 'Pandora's box?'

'Oh, I hope not,' Isabel cried, sounding genuinely alarmed.

My name is Anna Winterbourne. I do not hold (much) with those who talk of the Stars governing our Fate.

1

A child forsaken, waking suddenly,
Whose gaze afeard on all things round doth rove,
And seeth only that it cannot see
The meeting eyes of love.

Quoted in Middlemarch

Cairo, April 1997

Some people can make themselves cry. I can make myself sick with terror. When I was a child – before I had children of my own – I did it by thinking about death. Now, I think about the stars. I look at the stars and imagine the universe. Then I draw back to our galaxy, then to our planet – spinning away in all that immensity. Spinning for dear life. And for a moment the utter precariousness, the sheer improbability of it all overwhelms me. What do we have to hold on to?

Last night I dreamed I walked once more in the house of my father's childhood: under my feet the cool marble of the entrance hall, above my head its high ceiling of wooden rafters: a thousand painted flowers gleaming dark with distance. And there was the latticed terrace of the haramlek, and behind the ornate woodwork I saw the shadow of a woman. Then the heavy door behind me swung open and I turned: outlined against a glaring rectangle of sunshine I saw (as I had never in life seen) the tall broad-shouldered figure of my great-uncle, Sharif Basha al-Baroudi, and as I opened my eyes and pulled the starched white sheet up close against my chin, I watched him pause and take off his tarbush and hand it, together with his ebony walking stick, to the Nubian sufragi who leaned towards him with words of greeting. He glanced up at the lattice of the terrace and strode towards me, past me, and into the shadows of the small vestibule that I knew led to the stairs up to the women's quarters. I have not been near this house since my youngest son was nine; ten years ago. He loved the house, and watching him play, and explore while the museum guards looking on benignly, I had found myself wondering: what if we had kept it?

But this is not my story. This is a story conjured out of a box; a leather trunk that travelled from London to Cairo and back. That lived in the boxroom of a Manhattan apartment for many years, then found its way back again and came to rest on my living-room floor here in Cairo one day in the spring of 1997. It is the story of two women: Isabel Parkman, the American who brought it to me, and Anna Winterbourne, her great-grandmother, the Englishwoman to whom it had originally belonged. And if I come into it at all, it is only as my own grandmother did a hundred years ago, when she told the story of her brother's love.

Day after day I unpacked, unwrapped, unravelled. I sat on the floor with Isabel and we exclaimed over the daintiness of the smocking on the child's frock we found, the smoothness of the sandalwood prayer beads released from their velvet bag, the lustre of the candle-glass. I translated for her passages from the Arabic newspaper cuttings. We spoke of time and love and family and loss. I took the journals and papers into my bedroom and read and reread Anna's words. I almost know them by heart. I hear her voice and see her in the miniature in the locket: the portrait of the mother she so much resembled.

At the table under my window, I fit the key from the green felt purse into the delicate lock of the brown journal and turn, and I am in an English autumn in 1897 and Anna's troubled heart lies open before me:

— and yet, I do love him, in the sense that I wish him well, and were it in my power to make his lot happier and his heart more content, I would willingly and with a joyful spirit undertake anything — But, in fairness, I must say that I have tried. My understanding — in particular of men — has of necessity been limited. But within that I did strive — do strive — to be a faithful and loving wife and companion —

It is not as I thought it would be, in those girlish days — just two short years ago — when I sat by the pavilion and watched, my heart swelling with joy when he glanced smiling in my direction after a good run, or when we rode together and his leg brushed against mine.

Put football instead of cricket and she could have been me. She could have been Arwa, or Deena, or any of the girls I grew up with here in Cairo in the Sixties. What difference do a hundred years — or a continent — make?

How sadly, more than ever now, I feel the lack of my mother. And yet I could not say that Edward has changed. He has not. It is that same polite courtesy that I thought the mark of greater things to come, that I thought the harbinger of a close affection and an intimacy of mind and spirit.

We are roughly in the middle of the journal, which has already moved some way from its girlish beginnings as Anna prepared to chronicle a happy married life — beginnings touching in their assumption of order, of a predicted, unfolding pattern.

My mother is constantly in my mind. More so than my dear father — though I think of him a great deal too. I wonder how they were together. I cannot remember them together. Until she died, my memories are of her alone. And in my memory she is surrounded always by light. I see her riding — fast; always at a canter or a gallop. And laughing: at the table, while she danced, when she came into the nursery, when she held me in front of her on the saddle and taught me how to hold the reins. And it is as if my father only came into being for me when I was nine years old — and she had died. I remember him grieving. Walking in the grounds or sitting in the library. Gentle and loving with me always, but sad. There were no more dances, no more dinner parties where I would come down in my night-clothes to be kissed good night. Sir Charles came to see him, often. And they would talk of India and of Ireland, of the Queen and the Canal, of Egypt. They spoke of the Rebellion, the Bombardment and the Trial. They never spoke of my mother.

I asked Sir Charles, a few months ago, after my father's funeral, about my mother. I asked him how she and my father had been together. Had they been happy? And he, looking somewhat surprised, said, 'I expect so, my dear. She was a fine woman. And he was a true gentleman.'

Sir Charles does not speak much of private matters. He is more happy on the high road of public life. Although 'happy' is a careless word, for he is most unhappy with public life and was in an ill temper throughout the Jubilee festivities in June. Two weeks ago we were down in Saighton to visit George Wyndham and dined there with Dick Grosvenor, Edward Clifford, Henry Milner, John Evelyn and Lady Clifden. The question of whether savage nations had a right to exist came up, George arguing – from Darwin and the survival of the fittest – that they had none, and the rest of the company being of much the same mind. Sir Charles was much incensed and ended the conversation by saying (somewhat strongly) that the British Empire had done so much harm to so many people that it deserved to perish and then it would be too late to say or do anything. Edward was, for the most part, silent, I fancy because he really agreed with the younger set but was careful of offending his father. Sir Charles's only ally was John Evelyn, who declared his intention of sending his son up the Nile to 'learn Arabic, keep a diary and acquire habits of observation and self-reliance and not to imbibe Jingo principles'. I wish – if that is not too wicked a wish – I wish I were that son.

Edward visits my apartment from time to time, and he is tender and affectionate of me as he leaves. And I have long thought it was a mark of the waywardness of my character that on such occasions I was beset by stirrings and impulses of so contrary a nature that I was like a creature devoid of reason: I wept into my pillows, I paced the length of my chamber, I opened the casements to the cold night air and leaned out and wished – God forgive me – that I had not been so resilient in physical health that I might not catch a fatal chill and make an end of my unhappiness. Often, in the mornings, I had resort to cold compresses on my eyes so that no trace of unseemly anguish might be detected on my countenance when I came down to breakfast.

I have wondered whether any shadow of such turmoil came to him, for I would have been glad to soothe and comfort him as best I could, but as he always left so promptly and with such apparent equanimity, I have come to conclude that these disturbances were mine and mine only and were born of some weakness of my feminine nature, and I strove — strive — to master and overcome them. To that end I have devised various small stratagems, the most successful of which is to leave some small task uncompleted and close to hand. So when my husband rises from my bed I rise with him and walk with him to the door to bid him good night and, having closed the door, return immediately to my drawing or my book until such time as I am certain the wicked feelings have passed and it is safe for me to lift my head.

My journal is of no use on such occasions for it would merely encourage the expression of these emotions that threaten me and that I must put aside.

I cannot believe that he is happy.

2

Oh what a dear, ravishing thing is the beginning of an Amour!

Aphra Behn, c. 1680

Cairo, May 1997
Isabel gives me bits of her story. She tells me how she met my brother. A dry, edited version, which, as I get to know her, as I get to be able to imagine her, I fill out for myself. Isabel thinks in pictures: as she speaks I see the pool of light rippling on the old oak table —

New York City, February 1997
A pool of light ripples on the old oak table, picking out the darker grains of wood, then shadowing them. At its centre shines a glass bowl in which three candles float like flat, golden lilies.

'I thought maybe it's like birthdays,' Isabel says. Her voice has that slight, deep-down tremor she has noticed in it lately. She doesn't know whether anyone else can hear it. She doesn't know why it comes. She lays her fork down carefully on her plate.

'I mean,' she says, looking down, considering her fingers still resting on the fork, 'you know how when you're a kid every birthday has this huge significance?' She glances up. Yes, she still has his attention. 'You even think,' she continues, encouraged, 'that after a birthday everything is somehow going to be different, *you*'re going to be different; you'll be *new* —'

'And then?'

'And then, later —' she shrugs — 'you realise it isn't like that.'

'My dear girl – I'm sorry: my dear young woman – you can't possibly know that already.'

Is he flirting with her? He leans back in his seat, one wrist on the table, an arm slung over the back of his chair. Beyond the bowl of light, the woman he arrived with turns laughing towards Rajiv Seth. A sheet of auburn hair falls forward, obscuring her face. My brother fingers the stem of his wineglass; the back of his hand is covered with fine, black hair. She looks full at him: his face so familiar from television and newspapers. They hate him, but they cannot get enough of him. When he conducts, the line snakes around the block as though for the first showing of a Spielberg film. The 'Molotov Maestro' they call him, the 'Kalashnikov Conductor'. But the box office loves him. Now the dark, deep-set eyes are lit and fixed on her. He is laughing at her.

From the head of the table, Deborah calls out, 'Anybody want more salad?'

There is a general clinking of cutlery and shifting of plates and after a moment Deborah says, 'I'll go get the ice cream.'

Louis, her partner, groans and she flashes him a smile.

Isabel gets up and even though Deborah says, 'Sit down, sit down, I'll do it,' she picks up her plate and his and carries them into the kitchen. 'Isn't he just a doll?' Deborah whispers amid the gleaming brass pots, pans and colanders.

'He's pretty gorgeous,' Isabel agrees, not pretending not to know whom Deborah means. 'And he's approachable. Who's the lady?'

'Samantha Metcalfe,' says Deborah. 'She teaches at SUNY.'

'Is she – are they – together?'

Deborah makes a face as she leans into the freezer. 'For the moment, I guess. Why?' She straightens up and grins at Isabel. 'Interested?'

'Maybe.'

'He's fifty-five,' Deborah says, putting two tubs of ice cream on a tray. 'And –'

17

'– old enough to be your father,' Isabel completes, smiling. 'Is he really involved with terrorists?' she asks.

Deborah shrugs, arranges wafers in a blue porcelain dish. 'Who knows? I'd be surprised, though. He doesn't look like a terrorist.'

Isabel picks up the bowls and follows Deborah out of the kitchen.

When she sits down, he turns towards her. 'I wasn't laughing at you, you know.' His eyes are still smiling.

'No?'

'No, really. Really. You just looked so solemn.'

'Well –'

'So, carry on. You were telling me about birthdays.'

'What I meant was – well, for us, this is only the third time we're seeing a new century come in. And we've never had a millennium. So maybe we're –'

'Like a small kid? That's been said before.'

'What? What's been said before?' Louis leans over from Isabel's right, his high forehead catching the candlelight. He is proud of his receding hairline and wears his black hair brushed back like a Spaniard's.

'You can't do that,' Deborah cries.

'Can't do what?' asks Louis.

'Butt into a conversation like that. This isn't Wall Street. This is –'

'Why not? It wasn't a private conversation. Was it a private conversation?'

'No, no, it wasn't,' says Isabel. 'I was just saying that all this fuss about the millennium –'

'Oh, *not* the millennium,' Laura says, putting her hands to her head; 'millennium, millennium, everywhere you look it's the millennium. I thought you didn't want to do the millennium?'

'What are you doing?' asks Louis. 'I thought you were due to complete –'

'She's added on an option –' Laura begins.

'But that's just the point,' Isabel says. 'I think maybe the millennium only matters to us because we're so young – as a country, I mean. Maybe it would be interesting to see what people in a really old country thought of it.'

'It's an angle,' Deborah admits.

'India,' Louis says. 'Maybe Raji can help you there. Raji?'

The bearded head turns from conversation with Samantha.

'What does India think of the millennium?' Louis demands.

'Why don't you ask her, man?' A flicker at the corner of the dark lips, but the eyes don't smile.

'Come on, Louis, you know better than that,' says Deborah.

'Fucking inscrutable,' says Louis.

'Let's have coffee through in the living room,' says Deborah, standing up.

'What is it you want to do?' he asks as they walk into the living room.

'I thought I'd go to Egypt. See what they think of the millennium there.'

'Egypt? Why Egypt? Why not Rome? That's an old country.'

'Yes, but Egypt is older. It's like going back to the beginning. Six thousand years of recorded history.'

'Are they having a millennium there? Do you take cream?' Deborah hands Isabel a cup of coffee and waits, the small silver cream jug poised. 'Don't they use the Muslim years?'

'They use both,' he says. 'And they have a Coptic calendar as well.'

'I know they celebrate both New Years,' Isabel says, pouring herself a few drops of cream and handing the jug back to Deborah.

'Any excuse for a party.' He smiles. 'I won't have coffee, thanks. We have to be going soon.'

'I was wondering,' Isabel ventures, 'if you could give me some pointers. I've been there before, but it was a long time ago, and I haven't stayed in touch.'

19

'Oh, I think you'll find people will remember you –'

'There, you see, you're laughing at me again.'

'My dear, not at all. I'm sure you made a powerful impression. What were you doing there?'

'I did a Junior Year Abroad –'

'Don't you just adore these apartments?' Laura says, joining them.

'They're so gracious.'

'This one is beautiful,' Isabel says. 'And I love the red walls.'

They all look around the high, galleried room.

'Call me,' my brother says to Isabel. 'Do you want to call me? I'll think of a few people you can go and see. Look, let me give you my number.' He feels in his pockets. 'Do you have a card or a piece of paper or something?'

She looks in her handbag and passes him a small white notepad. He takes the cap off his fountain pen and scribbles in black ink.

'Can you read this? When do you want to talk? Do you have a deadline?'

'Yes,' says Isabel. 'Imminent.'

'OK. Call me. We'll talk.'

He turns back. 'Are you OK getting home? Can we drop you off somewhere?'

'I'm fine,' Isabel says. 'I'm on the other side of the Park. I have a cab arranged.'

The sky throws back the lights of the city, into her windows and who knows how many others. Isabel kicks off her shoes and stands looking out over the massed treetops below. If she were to open the window and lean out she would see, beyond the darkness, the lights of the Plaza and then down to Fifth Avenue where – is it her imagination or can she see a glow where Tiffany's windows are? Tempted to open the window, she puts her hand on the catch, but it is a freezing February night and she turns back to the room and switches on one table lamp. Two years on, she is still enthralled by the freedom of not being half of a couple, by the pleasure of coming home to silence, by not having to feel relieved if Irving has enjoyed the evening or to make it up to him if he hasn't – by the absence of resentment in her life.

It is after midnight and yet she is full of energy. She crosses over to the desk and checks her answering machine. Nothing. And nothing on the computer or the fax. She goes to a bookshelf and picks out *Who's Who*:

> Ghamrawi, Omar A. s of Ahmad al-Ghamrawi and Maryam, *née* al-Khalidi; *b* 15 September 1942, Jerusalem; educ Cornell Univ New York and . . . coached by . . . *Career* pianist, conductor and writer; debut with NY Philharmonic 1960 . . . tours . . . *The Politics of Culture* 1992, *A State of Terror* 1994, *Borders and Refuge* 1996 . . .

Thirty-seven years of music, and five years of words. And it is in these last five years that he has hit the news. In her bedroom, she flicks the television on and catches Jerry Springer, pointing, haranguing, '*You* had his baby – you *deliberately* entrapped him –' A fat woman with mascara running down her face along with her tears yells back, 'He needs to get *real* –' Isabel hits the mute button, goes into the bathroom and turns on the taps.

Hair caught at the top of her head with a giant black butterfly clip, a rolled-up towel wedged behind her neck, the water pale green pools shimmering amid soft hills of foam, she slings her legs over the edge of the tub, lets her arms float and settles into this, her favourite position. The automatic thought comes that it would be nice to have some music but she pushes it aside. How many times has she put on a disc only to be irritated by it after a few minutes? And then she'd have to pad out on wet feet and switch it off before it drove her crazy. She couldn't do it with the remote because of the position of the player in the bedroom. No, she would settle into the silence, and when it needed to be broken she would shift a part of herself and the soft lapping of the water would give her the sound she needed to hear.

Would tomorrow be too soon to call him?

Pharaonic toes, Irving used to say, when he was still talking about her toes – about her. Long, straight, even toes that could belong to any one of those sideways figures in the reliefs and the wall paintings, except hers were pale, not brown. She spreads them and frowns to focus on the neat, square-cut nails with their one coat of white pearl. Not chipped; good for another two or three days maybe. And besides it's winter now and who's going to see them? She lets her leg fall and slips further down into the water. Toes to go with the name. It was her father who had explained to her her name. Isa Bella: Isis the Beautiful. 'So you see,' he'd said, that summer's day, in the woods back of the house in Connecticut, 'you have the name of the first goddess, the mother of Diana, of all goddesses, the mother of the world.' She had been walking at his side, carrying a long stick with a fork at the end, engaged in a divine task: holding it out, waiting for it to tremble, to tell her she had found water, there under the grass-covered earth. And then, on the swing, as he had pushed her, and she rose higher and higher with each thrust, a chant had formed in her head 'Isa – Bella, Isa – Bella . . .'

Keeping time with small splashes in the water, Isabel drifts into memories of her father, her small hand secure in his big, warm grasp, their feet kicking up the spray as they paddle on the beach in Maine – her mother slightly apart, anxious, holding her breath almost, fearing that if she relaxed for a moment, if she let go, this child would be snatched from her as the other had been. Jasmine Chirol Cabot had never stopped mourning her son; she had held on to the birthdays, the Buddy Holly singles, the photographs. Isabel had grown up with a brother sixteen years her senior who was forever fourteen and turning for a second from the fish in his hand, from the ball in the air, from the snow-covered slope ahead, to squint into the camera. An absent brother.

22

Would tomorrow be too soon to call him?

She slips all the way down into the bath, butterfly clip and all, until the water closes over her face and she feels the tingle in her scalp as it penetrates her hair.

3

Whatever happens, we have got
The Maxim gun, and they have not.

Hilaire Belloc, 1898

Cairo, May 1997

I am obsessed with Anna Winterbourne's brown journal. She has become as real to me as Dorothea Brooke. I need to fill in the gaps, to know who the people are of whom she speaks, to paint in the backdrop against which she is living her life here, on the page in front of me.

I go to the British Council Library, to Dar al-Kutub, to the second-hand bookstalls even though they've been moved from Sur el-Azbakiyya up to Darrasa and browsing among them is no longer so pleasant. I even write to my son in London and ask for cuttings from old issues of *The Times*.

And I piece a story together.

London, October 1898 to March 1899

The light is like nothing Anna has ever seen before. Day after day it draws her back. Day after day it scatters itself on the rich carpets, on the stone or marble floors, on the straw matting. It streams through the latticed woodwork, tracing its patterns on mosaic walls and inlaid doors and layered fabrics, illuminating flowers and faces and outstretched or folded hands.

Anna looks down at her own hands, folded tight in her lap: her wedding band gleaming dull against the pale skin, her knuckles raised ridges of paler white. She unclenches her hands, stretches out the fingers and replaces the hands gently, open, on her knees.

*He is not himself. I have heard this phrase before, and now it falls
to me to use it. Edward, my husband, is not himself.*

*For seven months I followed, with Sir Charles, all news of the
events in the Soudan. For seven months I prayed for his safety
and for his return unharmed. And now he is back I hardly know
him. He is grown thin, and though his face is flushed with the
sun of the south, it is as though a pallor lurks beneath.*

*Mr Winthrop has seen him and says he has caught some
infection of the tropics and shall be well again with tranquillity
and nourishing food and, later, exercise. Upon his insistence (Mr
Winthrop's) I go out for a walk in the air each day. And I have
taken to walking to the South Kensington Museum, which is a
most beautiful and calming place and where I have come upon
some paintings by Mr Frederick Lewis. They are possessed of
such luminous beauty that I feel in their presence as though a
gentle hand caressed my very soul.*

On a low bed, pressed into a pile of silken cushions, a woman
lies sleeping. Above her, a vast curtain hangs, through the
brilliant billowing green of which the fluid shadows of the
lattice shutters can be made out, and beyond them, the light.
One wedge of sunshine – from the open window above her
head – picks out the sleeper's face and neck, the cream-
coloured chemise revealed by the open buttons of her tight
bodice. A small amulet shines at her throat. Anna glances at
her watch: she has ten more minutes.

*Today I found Sir William Harcourt in the hall, taking his leave
of Edward and Sir Charles. Sir Charles, shaking him repeatedly
by the hand, said (in his usual robust fashion) that it was a sad
day for England when a man like Sir William resigns from the
Leadership because of the conversion of the Party to Jingo
Imperialism. He spoke harshly of Rosebery and Chamberlain
calling them men of war and Sir William said it was the spirit of
the age and he was grown too old to fight it. Edward became
much agitated and retired to his chamber. He refused to allow me
to sit with him or bring him tea.*

It is now eight weeks since Edward returned from the Soudan, and, I would have thought, time enough for him to grow well again, but for all that ails his body, I now fear that worse is a sickness of the spirit. He will not speak to me about anything of consequence and barely answers when I address him on common- place matters. He will sit listless in the library for many hours and yet start if someone should enter of a sudden, so that I have learned to make some small noise before entering a room and to conduct a business with the doorhandle. He cannot bear the clatter of the teacup against its saucer –

So Anna has taken to placing folded muslin napkins under the cups. She knows he will not drink his tea, but he accepts his cup from her hand and suffers her to sit with him – no, suffers her to sit in the same room, for she cannot be said to be truly with him. She cannot, for instance, guess what thoughts are at this moment in his mind. Except that they are not thoughts of a happy – or even comfortable – nature. He sits upright in the big chair, his grey woollen dressing gown belted neatly at the waist, his hair combed back, his moustache hiding his upper lip, the lower lip drawn. His eyes fix upon some object behind her left shoulder, then move to the shrouded window, then down to the floor. They never meet her own. A muscle works, from time to time, in the clean-shaven jaw. He is waiting for this formality of tea-drinking to be over so that she may leave him.

'Edward,' says Anna, 'I have been speaking with Mr Winthrop, and he agrees that a change of air could do you good –'

'No.'

'Edward, dearest, we could go down to Horsham for a few days. You can ride, be out in the air –'

'No, Anna. I am going nowhere.' He still does not look at her, but his grip on the arm of the chair becomes tighter, and his voice, though not raised, pitches itself a note higher. 'Will you please understand that? Nowhere. If you wish to go –'

'But Edward, I have no wish for myself. I only thought –'

'Let us not talk of this. I have no wish, no strength —'

'Please, dearest, calm yourself.'

Anna puts down her cup and rises to bend at his side. She puts her hand on his, trying to ease her fingers between his palm and the armrest. When she fails, she simply lets her hand lie on his.

'You must not become agitated. We will do nothing that you do not wish. I have no desire except to help you; to help you come back to yourself. Please, dearest, will you not tell me what I can do?'

When there is no answer, Anna bends further and places her lips and then her cheek against his brow. It feels hot and slightly damp. Edward Winterbourne pats his wife's hand as it lies on his and disengages his own.

'Please, Anna. There is no need to be so concerned. It is just a matter of resting.'

Anna stands beside him. She knows he would not welcome her sitting down again. But this is not some womanly folly; they are all concerned. The servants go about their business with muffled tread. Visitors leave cards to which she replies with polite notes saying that Edward finds himself indisposed, but as soon as he is better . . . His father is concerned to the point of anger. Yesterday afternoon she had entered the library to find him speaking to the butler. When he heard her at the door he had come forward and taken her hands.

'Ah, Anna. I have just asked Wilson to take all the shot out of the guns. Just a precaution, you know. No sense in having all that lead lying around. What d'you think?'

'Yes, of course, Sir Charles,' she had agreed. 'There's no need for it.'

And when Wilson had left the room and closed the door behind him, she had allowed the fear to show in her voice and eyes. 'You don't really think, do you?'

'No, no. Of course not. Of course not.' He had paced away from her, the erect soldier's figure striding to the end of the library table. 'I hope you don't mind, my dear —' He gestured at his boots. 'I rode over suddenly, you know.'

Anna shook her head. Halfway back he stopped and struck his fist against the back of a chair.

'By God! You'll pardon me, my dear, but I feel like taking a whip to him. If he had not the stomach for it, what drove him to go? He requested that commission – he would not be denied.'

'He believed he was doing the right thing.' And also, she thought, he wanted action, adventure, purpose, a mission . . .

'I told him, though. I told him this was not an honest war. This was a war dreamed up by politicians, a war to please that widow so taken with her cockney Empire – Ah, what's the use?'

He paused, and Anna came to stand beside him. Together, they stared out of the window at the trees darkening in the quiet square. He turned to her.

'You should get out, my dear. This is no life for a young woman.'

'I do get out, Sir Charles. I go out every day, for an hour. Mr Winthrop said I must. He said I must walk in the air. I go out every day at three, and I don't come back till four o'clock. Edward likes to rest then, you see –'

'But your little face is getting quite peaky, Anna, my dear.' He had put his hand to her chin and under that gentle touch she had felt the tears rise to her eyes – as they are rising now.

'Edward, dearest, is there anything you would like? Anything that I can fetch or do?'

'I think I should rest now, for a while.'

For shame, for shame, Anna. To be weeping for yourself now, at such a time. All your thoughts should be bent on him, devoted to him. He is in need of rest, and he cannot find it.

How different this homecoming has been from that of his father when, as a child of ten, recently bereft of my mother, I lay on a corner of the smoking-room carpet, studying the map of Egypt Sir Charles had given me and listening to him tell of how they beat Urabi and took Tel el-Kebir. And I heard him talk of heroism and treachery and politics and bonds, and I felt his anger at the job he had been made to do.

But Edward will not speak and I am afraid. I have not dared voice the thought, but I am afraid we are in the grip of something evil — my husband is in the grip of something evil, something that will not allow him to shake off this illness and come to himself.

Caroline Bourke tells me that Sir William Butler, meeting General Kitchener upon his arrival at Dover, said to him, 'Well, if you do not bring down a curse on the British Empire for what you have been doing, there is no truth in Christianity.' And Kitchener simply stared at him. I asked her what he meant. What had they done beyond taking the Soudan and restoring order? And she said she did not know — but with such dark looks as left me full of foreboding. I long to ask my husband what this means, for my instinct is that there is a key here to what ails him, but I am afraid. He is so changed and now is unable to take any nourishment but the thinnest broth and some crusts of bread.

Anna stands up and walks slowly round the gallery, coming to a stop in front of an old man, his white beard and turban set off against a wall of golden brick hung with pages of white, inscribed paper. Before him, on the floor, robed in vivid reds and blues, sit the children he teaches. A sun-striped cat reclines on a green cushion watching a pair of doves pecking at the spangled mat. In the half-open doorway, the smallest of the children hesitates.

In the street, Anna starts to hurry. It is four o'clock and the light is fading fast.

I have failed him. I am constantly and repeatedly failing him. If I could but find the key to the locked door of his mind, I could sweep out all the terrors that lurk there. And he would be well again.

For I know there are terrors and they have to do with the mission he has been engaged upon, which culminated earlier this week in the signing of the Soudan Convention. An event which

has greatly angered Sir Charles and his friends so that they have
written to The Times:

Sir,
What would be said in private life, if a guardian and
trustee who had undertaken to manage the estate of a
minor, allowed the estate to run to ruin and then took
possession of it as being worthless? In 1884 we forced the
Egyptian Government to abandon the Soudan and leave
it derelict, and now, the opportunity having occurred,
we are taking possession of the country as belonging to
nobody. It is a comment on the tone of the age that we
should be doing this with the apparent approval of the
whole world, moral and religious.

It would also appear, according to the Convention
signed by Lord Cromer and Boutros Pasha, that we are
saddling on Egypt the whole cost and labour of the war
of reconquest not yet completed and making her budget
responsible for the Soudan deficits.

This invention, the British Empire, will be the ruin of
our position as an honest Kingdom.

Yours etc.

Sir Charles tells me that George Wyndham said to him plainly
that it is agreed by the Powers that the aim of African operations
is to civilise Africa in the interests of Europe and that to gain that
end all means are good.

I cannot believe George truly meant that 'all' means are
good — but he is Under-Secretary for War and is bound to
espouse more warlike principles than Sir Charles would think
right.

I wish to ask Sir Charles to speak to Edward about the
Soudan and to try to unlock — but I fear Sir Charles is too
impatient and of too volatile a temper. My father would have
been a better man for the task, for it was in his nature to be
gentle —

★   ★   ★

Dear God, dear sweet Lord Jesus, I pray constantly for my husband's mind and for his soul. He is grown weaker and cannot or will not leave his room.

*   *   *

Caroline came to visit and told me how they say Kitchener's men desecrated the body of the Mahdi whom the natives believe to be a Holy Man and how Billy Gordon cut off his head that the General might use it for an inkwell. It cannot be true, for if it were — I truly fear for Edward now.

*   *   *

Sir Charles tells me that Billy Gordon confirms the story of the cutting of the head, but is angry that the deed is imputed to him — but he will not say who did it. Sir Charles did not wish to speak of this at first, but when he learned how much I knew already, he saw that it could not be helped and that it would be kinder to allow me to speak with him, for surely there is no one else to whom I can talk of this.

Oh, how I wish now more than ever for the presence of my beloved mother! For I feel sure she would advise me on some simple, womanly way to reach my poor, imprisoned husband. I have no confidante save Caroline Bourke and she, I fear, carries my own personal interest — as she sees it — too close to her heart to be able to advise me how I can best help my husband.

*   *   *

Edward brings up everything we give him now. His stomach cannot retain so much as a cupful of thin gruel and I fancy he is attempting to purge himself of — all manner of things. I beg him to take heart, for our Lord surely watches over him as he watches over us all and God judges the actions of men but surely too He judges them by their hearts and their minds, else how can one act be held distinct from another? And surely that distinction He would make — but Edward turns away.

Meanwhile, I find out that General Gordon's sister has distanced herself from this expedition all along. She has said that if it is to avenge her brother, then she does not wish him avenged and she is certain he would most strongly have not

33

wished it himself. She says she knows the Mahdi had not wished General Gordon dead but rather had wanted him alive so that he could exchange him for the freedom of 'Urabi Pasha, the exiled leader of the Egyptian uprising of 1882. She tells anyone who will listen that her brother was among the first to come forward when Mr Blunt set up the fund to defray the expenses for the defence of 'Urabi, and that he had said, 'Here's the money, I'll wager 'Urabi pays it back himself in a couple of years.'

Each day now brings fresh horrors and Edward sickens so that I cannot bring myself to leave the house, nor do I wish it but content myself while he sleeps with a turn about the garden – the garden in which all things appear so brown and bare and dead that it would seem impossible that May will come and all will be in leaf again – and yet, today, I spotted the cheery white of the first snowdrops: the usual five, faithful to their usual place at the base of the old plum tree – and I was filled with a kind of melancholy hope –

Sweet Mary, Mother of God, I pray for my husband's soul as I pray for the souls of all the men who were joined in that terrible event –

The papers are full of it: an army of 7,000 British and 20,000 Egyptian soldiers loses 48 men and kills 11,000 of the Dervishes and wounds 16,000 in the space of six hours.

Winston Churchill promises to publish a book that tells how General Kitchener ordered all the wounded killed and how he (Churchill) had seen the 21st Lancers spearing the wounded where they lay and leaning with their whole weight on their lances to pierce through the clothes of the dying men and how Kitchener let the British and Egyptian soldiers loose upon the town for three days of rape and pillage.

The Honourable Algernon Bourke, Lady Caroline's kins-man, tells Sir Charles a heavy 'butcher's bill' was ordered for that day and communications with London were cut on a pretext so that no tempering word might find its way to the General.

Oh, I do so completely fear for my husband now, for if it is true and if he took part in those terrible deeds, he who puts honour above all else and truly thought that in embarking on this expedition he embarked on a brave and honourable task, I cannot now see how he can put it behind him – most particularly when he is so ill in body and at the mercy of the fever which burns him up for hours and leaves him, when it does, limp and so weakened that he can barely take the water that we put to his lips.

Edward Winterbourne died on 20 March 1899.

He had stood on the plain of Umm Durman and the thought that had hovered around him in 'Atbara, in Sawakin, in the officers' mess – the thought that he had for weeks held at bay – rose out of the dust of the battlefield and hurled itself full in his face in its blinding light. And once that thought had revealed itself and taken hold, the fanatical dervishes transformed themselves in front of his eyes into men – men, with their sorry encampments, with their ragtag followers of women and children and goats, with their months of hunger upon their bodies, and their foolish spears and rifles in their hands, and their tattered banners fluttering above their heads. Men impassioned by an idea of freedom and justice in their own land. But still they planted their standard and still they rushed forward with their spears and it was too late, too late to do anything but stand and fire.

I have told Sir Charles that I believe that in his heart Edward was just and honourable to the end. And that I believe that, at the end, he stood closer to his father in his convictions than he was able to say. I trust this may – in time – provide him with some comfort.

4

I mourned, and yet shall mourn
with ever-returning spring.
Walt Whitman

And what comfort was there for Anna?

There was the funeral. There was the memorial service. There were the practicalities: the solicitors to be seen, the papers to be signed. All these are chronicled in a flat, matter-of-fact manner as though by setting them down meticulously with dates and names Anna was doing her duty – what was left to her of her duty – towards her husband and her marriage.

And there was the grief, the questioning, the regrets. For months the journal in the brown leather binding is a medley of statements of fact, of fragments, exclamations –

> *If only he had died contented . . . If only he had died at peace . . .*

There are no children to be comforted, no memoirs or letters to be sorted and wept over, no heartening story to be told. There are no rituals of mourning. In the twenty-odd years I lived in England, I never found out how the English mourn. There seems to be a funeral and then – nothing. Just an emptiness. No friends and relatives filling the house. No Thursday nights. No Fortieth Day. Nothing.

The house is already silenced through her husband's long absence and illness. I see Anna wandering through it. I see her sitting in the library, her tea untouched, a book unopened on her knee –

If he had died contented . . .

There is Sir Charles's sorrow –

Sir Charles comes to see me almost every day. We sit together, mostly in silence . . .

Friends come to call. Emily, her maid, chides Anna into at least going out into the garden –

I sat in the garden for an hour today. I had not even been able to persuade him to take the air. If I had understood him better – if I had been able to make him speak to me –

Day after day she relives each scene: he sits in the library, he sits in his room, he lies in his bed. His face is pale and drawn and his eyes look past her and the words she uses are never the right words, the touch she offers is never the right touch.

If I had been able to make him speak to me –

Anna can speak to no one, can give no voice to the thoughts that weigh so much on her mind. In the early days of their grief she had asked Sir Charles, 'What should I have done?' and he had said, 'Nothing. You did everything you could, my dear.' And there it was left. For she does not wish to rouse Sir Charles's sorrow. There is Sir Charles's sorrow – and his anger. Thank God for his anger; it keeps his back straight and his step strong.

Sir Charles comes to see me often. We sit together, mostly in silence, except when he is moved to a tirade against the Empire – or rather, the spirit of Empire, for he is angered equally by the doings of Kitchener in South Africa, the King of the Belgians in the Congo, the Americans in the Filipines and all the nations of Europe in China. It is very hard, listening to him, not to feel

caught up in a terrible time of brutality and even he is helpless —
save for letters to The Times *— to do any thing but wait for*
history to run its course. But underneath all the anger, I can hear
the thought, again and again: And to think that I have lost my
son to this.

On a Monday evening, early in June, he tells her how
Arthur Balfour had persuaded the House to reward Kitchener for the campaign; how they voted him a peerage and
£30,000 and then his fellow peers left the Chamber
without speaking to him. 'It's damn hard, my dear, forgive
me. Damn hard,' I hear him say, when he feels he has run
on too much, too vehemently, the large, rough hand
resting for a moment on the thin, pale one; the narrow
edge of grief the old English soldier will permit himself to
show. And then his concern for this unhappy daughter he
is left with.

Today I walked — as I had walked so many times during his
illness — to the South Kensington Museum. I found when I got
there, however, that I was unable to look at the Lewis paintings I
had grown to love so much —

I watch and listen, helpless to help. There is no point in saying
'This, too, shall pass.' For a time, we do not even want it to
pass. We hold on to grief, fearing that its lifting will be the
final betrayal.

She must have gone into black, although she makes no
mention of fittings or dressmakers. But in January 1900 she is
persuaded to accompany Lady Caroline Bourke to Rome:

13 January
Caroline, musing over what we are to wear at the Costanzi
tomorrow, shook her head sadly over my weeds, and wondered
whether they might not be brightened by a corsage or some jewels.
I gently reminded her that it has not yet been a year since
Edward's passing and she somewhat reluctantly agreed that such

40

ornament would be unbecoming. I did say that I would not mind if she went without me, but she would not hear of it and has resigned herself to my forlorn appearance at her side. I was most sincere in my offer, for truly all the noise and glitter only serves to make me feel more — not more sad precisely, but more apart, more set aside — and the thought of relieving my mourning, even slightly, for a moment filled me with a kind of fear —

A fear that she would fail him in death as she had in life. For she had failed — there is no doubt in her mind about that. A happy man would not leave his home and go seeking death in the desert. A well-loved man would not die with horrors eating silently, secretly at his mind. If she had loved him better, perhaps he would not have needed to go to the Sudan. If she had understood him better, perhaps she could have nursed him back to health.

If I could believe that he died for a noble cause. If I could believe that he died contented —

There is the occasional kindness of friends, the silent house, and the emptiness; the absence of him who had been absent for so long. But this is a different absence. A definitive absence. No longer can she seek to draw closer, no longer can she hope for something to happen, for new life to breathe into her world. The questions that so trouble her mind are fruitless, the answers for which her heart yearns are now for ever out of reach.

A terrible thought: that in this grief I have no thought for myself. I have not once found myself thinking: what shall I do without him —

'But she's been without him all along,' says Isabel. She sits on the red Bedouin rug on my living-room floor, her great-grandmother's papers on the floor around her, the brown journal in her hand. The light of the lamp falls softly on the old paper, catches the glints of her streaked blonde hair. 'Not just when he went to the Sudan. Even when he was at home, with her –'

If I had loved him better. If I had needed him more – perhaps then I would have found the key – when he was so ill – so desperate –

'That's the trap,' says Isabel, 'we're trained, conditioned to blame ourselves. This guy was inadequate, and somehow she, the woman, ends up taking the responsibility . . .'

Later, I put more ice into our Baraka Perrier. The night air is cool and pleasant on my balcony and the darkness obscures the rubble on the roofs of the neighbouring houses. I sip my Baraka and say, 'There used to be gardens on the roofs here in Cairo. There would be trellises and pergolas and vines and Indian jasmine. Rugs and cushions on the floor, and dovecotes. And after sunset people would sit out on the roofs – imagine,' girls and boys would exchange glances across the rooftops and children would play in the cool of the evening and in the daytime the washing would be hung out on the lines, and when it came down all folded in the big baskets you could bury your face in the linen sheets and smell the sunshine . . .

'It must have been something,' Isabel says.

Yes. Yes, it was. On the bonnets of the cars parked on the street, young men sit in groups, chatting, watching, waiting for action. The latest 'Amr Dyab song, the tune vaguely Spanish, spirals up at us from the still open general store below where my children used to buy 'bombas' in the summer holidays, practising their Arabic, running up the stairs to drop them down into the street from this balcony: Beloved, light of my eyes/Who dwells in my imagination/I've loved you for many years –

'My mother is dying, I think,' says Isabel.

I look at her. I need a moment to bring myself into sync.

42

Isabel's mother, Jasmine, in the tiny space allotted to her in my mind, is a baby. My father had told me that story: Anna's daughter had given birth to a baby girl, in Paris, and had named her Jasmine. And now Isabel tells me that baby is dying.

'She has Alzheimer's. She had to go into a home. I moved in with her for a while after my father died. Then it got too bad.'

'But you go to see her?' I ask, rather anxiously.

'Yes. Sure I do. But mostly she doesn't know me.'

'That must be terrible.'

'She doesn't even know herself – mostly.'

'That must be – God! I don't know what that must be like.'

'I think . . . sometimes I think it's what she wants.'

'What? To be rid of herself?'

'She was always so worried. And when she wasn't worried, she was sad. I watched her once – she didn't know I was there, she was sitting in the living room, on the eau-de-Nil sofa, and her face . . . she just looked so sad.'

'Why didn't you go in and throw your arms round her? Couldn't you make her happy?'

'She never got over losing my brother.'

'But were you close?'

'So-so. Maybe. I was closer to my father. My mother was so intense. You could never just relax around her.'

I was standing at the window today when Sir Charles came to call, and for a moment, before I realised it was he, I saw an old man, minding where he stepped. And I was filled – God forgive me – with a wicked anger against Edward – that he should have been more careful of himself, for his father's sake –

I got to know Anna as though she were my best friend – or better; for I heard the worst and the best of her thoughts, and I had her life whole in front of me, here in the box Isabel has brought me. I smoothed out her papers, I touched the objects she had touched and treasured. I read what others wrote of her and she became so present to me that I could almost swear she sits quietly by as I try to write down her story.

If I could believe that he died for a noble cause –

What's done is done, I want to tell her. How can you reach someone who does not want to be reached? That door we spend lifetimes battering ourselves against – turn away, go out, go riding, go driving, eat, do charity work, take a tonic, travel . . .

And it is in Rome, at the Teatro Costanzi, on 14 January, that Anna, gripped by the soaring notes and by Floria's bewildered and impassioned grief, feels the answering sorrow swell and rise within her and presses her handkerchief to her mouth as the terrible emptiness fills mercifully with pain:

It was as though I had been holding myself very still, holding a door shut, holding something down; something which the music swelled and strengthened until it broke through. And for many days later, although I could not put my feelings into words, much less write them down in this journal, it was as though I felt that music coursing through my body and as it went, like a river in full flood, it churned up its bed and its banks, and I was most ill with a fever and – poor Caroline tells me – delirious and impossible for many days till one morning I woke up and – I had not quite returned to the world, but I had seen the door by which I might return.

'How long did it take her?' asks Isabel. 'Ten months?'
'Life was slower then.'
'I guess.'
She stretches, and her long, pale arms seem to catch the light of the moon high up in the clear, black sky. She yawns, brings her arms down and ruffles her hair.
'I'm keeping you up?'

I shake my head: I never sleep before two.

'It's not common, is it, for a person, a woman, to live alone? Here in Egypt?'

'No. But it's happening, more and more.'

Once upon a time I lived with a family. A husband and children. That was in England. In a house out of a Victorian novel, with stairs and fireplaces and floral cornices round the ceilings, and the sound of passing trains muffled by the lush trees at the bottom of the long garden. I learned about the seasons. I learned that the small clusters of fleshy green leaves would open into blue and white crocus, that the snowdrops appeared overnight, that daffodils should be cut but tulips shouldn't, that – with luck and care – the rose bushes would blossom twice, and that at winter's end, you could see on the bare, gnarled branches the tiny, tight buds whose pale, centred speck of green told of the leafy abundance that was yet to come.

Today, out of the window, I saw the pink carpet under the copper beech. The tree had shed all its flowers and I had not even seen it blossom. But the pink cherry was gloriously in bloom and I went out and walked around the garden and found the foxgloves in their secret places and the forget-me-nots with their golden hearts intact and then, as I looked up at the copper beech, I found, nestled in a dark corner under the spreading branches, one last cluster of blossom like a small pink chandelier and I was overcome with gratitude as though it had stayed there to say to me, Look! It is not too late.

Anna mends. The face that looks up at me as I turn from the kettle in the kitchen is no longer quite so haunted, quite so pale. The step I hear in my corridor is quicker and lighter, the rustle of the silk dress more crisp.

I walked to the Museum and I went to see the paintings. I cannot pretend to a wholly untroubled mind – nor would it be proper now to have one — but I was able, once more, to take pleasure in the wondrous colours, the tranquillity, the contentment with which they are infused. And I wondered, as I had wondered before, is that a world which truly exists?

5

Something there is moves me to love, and I
Do know I love, but know not how, nor why.
                                    Alexander Brome, c. 1645

New York City, March 1997

How can it strike so suddenly? Without warning, without preparation? Should it not grow on you, taking its time, so that when the moment comes when you think 'I love', you know – or at least you imagine you know – what it is you love? How can it be that a set of the shoulders, the rhythm of a stride, the shadow of a strand of hair falling on a forehead can cause the tides of the heart to ebb and to flow?

Which had come first, the gentle lurch as her heart missed a beat or the sight of him in the doorway? Isabel had looked down at the table: her knife and spoon lay at attention, solid and still. Drooping elegantly over the edge of the crested white plate, the corner of her folded pink napkin barely touched the shining, silver-plated steel. She closed her eyes for a moment and took a deep breath. When she looked up my brother was halfway across the restaurant, his hand raised in greeting – then his coat and briefcase were in the third chair and the menu was in his hands.

'Have you ordered? Have you been here long? I'm not late, am I? What *is* the time?' He glanced at his watch. 'I am, I guess. A few minutes. I'm sorry, I'm sorry. I couldn't get away. What will you have? Are you hungry? I hope you are. I am.'

His hands holding the menu. One hand reaching across the table to pat hers, briefly.

*   *   *

48

'You know —' he had leaned back in his seat, wiped the corners of his mouth with his napkin — 'I feel as if I know you from somewhere — before I mean.'

Watching him, her head to one side, she had smiled.

'No, seriously.' He waved his hand, a brief gesture of dismissal, as though to say, This is not a line, I am not flirting with you. 'There's something, I don't know what it is —'

'A previous life?'

He spread his hands, smiled, but the puzzled look stayed in his eyes.

My brother. As Isabel talks I can see him. She doesn't have to describe the way he walks into a room, the energy crackling off him, the heads turning to look. He walks into every room the way he walks down that long aisle through the stalls, striding, headlong, not a moment to lose. Even at the podium he gives the house the briefest of bows before turning to his orchestra: to work. And it is only at the end, when the stillness has erupted into a roar of applause and he has turned semi-dazed to face them that — after a moment — he seems to see the audience, and then there comes the big smile that catches at the heart, the sweeping bow, the great expansive gesture taking in both the orchestra and the house, the hands clasped above the head. My brother, who can make you feel special simply by recognising you across a room and who flew over at the sound of my voice on the telephone, and sat with me and held me through that long night and helped me see what I had to do; helped me be my better self.

Isabel is in love with him. And I don't blame her. She can't help it. Lots of women couldn't. And as far as I can see, it never did them any harm.

'Do you ever go back?' she asked over coffee, after he had given her names, addresses, telephone numbers.

'Where? To Egypt? Yes, of course. Not as often as I would wish. But . . .' Again the expressive hands, the rueful smile.

'Do you think of yourself as Egyptian? I'm sorry, this is

49

personal.' She had surprised herself with the question but he answered easily.

'Yes. And American. And Palestinian. I have no problem with identity.'

'You're lucky.'

'Or unlucky. Look, I have to go.' The hand raised, this time to get the bill.

'May I . . . ?' she offers, hesitant because he – and indeed:

'No, no. Of course not. Absolutely not.'

'After all, I *have* been picking your brains.'

'So what? You want to pay for my brains?' This somewhat sharply – and then the smile: 'No. That's all right, my dear. It was a pleasure.'

'Well, you must let me . . .'

'What? Let you what?' he asks as she hesitates.

'Perhaps another time *I* could take *you* out.'

A pause.

'Would you like to do that?'

'Yes,' she says quietly. 'Yes, I would.'

He looks at her, then nods his head briefly, deciding. 'Fine. Good. I'll call you.'

When she leaves the restaurant that Tuesday afternoon in March, she ties the belt of her long camel coat tight around her waist, turns up the collar, thrusts her hands into her pockets, and walks. The entrance of MOMA is lit and welcoming. She turns into the doorway and walks around aimlessly. You can do that in a museum. Not thinking, just being. When she comes to, she is standing in front of a Miró. It makes sense. The vivid blue, the bright one-eyed creatures floating, darting, alert, untethered. Out in the museum shop she buys a post-card. And now the hell of waiting for him to call.

'Mother, I've met someone. A man . . .'

Isabel is uneasy. She can't get used to seeing her mother here, in this room. There is nothing wrong with the room – except that it is completely different from any room Jasmine

50

would ever have chosen to inhabit: no flowers, no cushions, no music, no paintings, no small nonsensical bits of silver and crystal to catch the light and beam it back on to veined marble or polished wood. Nothing. Not even a photograph in a gilt frame to speak of a life beyond this place. And Jasmine is still and quiet, in a faded blue housecoat with an edge of night-dress showing white below the hem.

'I like him a lot', Isabel says. 'You know, I think you'd like him too. You probably know him – he's famous. I just wanted to tell you. He's older than me. Well, quite a lot older. He's actually in his fifties but you'd think he was forty. He *looks* forty. He's tall, and he's got black hair, greying at the temples, very distinguished. And dark, dark eyes, so dark that you think they're deep-set, but they're not.'

Jasmine's soft white hair is cut short in a boyish brush. It makes Isabel think of a new-hatched chick, she can't imagine why. She scans her memory searching for a moment when she might have seen a new-hatched chick, and comes up with a television image: an ad for – she can't remember what. They say Jasmine had got hold of some scissors and had cut off great chunks of what had become an incongruously full head of hair, and then they had tidied it up. We thought it would be better this way, they said. Isabel doesn't know whether to believe them – about her mother's cutting it off. Jasmine had always been proud of her hair. This would be easier to keep clean and tidy; no more brushing, no more fiddling with grips. She had been angry, then sad. Jasmine is even further now from the mother she knows. She wonders whether the hair feels soft or spiky. But if she should try to touch it – if she comes at all close – her mother gets fidgety, worried, frightened. Better to leave things as they are: Jasmine sitting calm and smiling in the grey leather armchair, Isabel on the edge of the bed facing her.

'Mother.' Isabel leans forward. 'Mother, dear, are you all right?'

A shadow of uncertainty passes over Jasmine's face. Her hands unfold themselves from her lap and hover above the armrests as though preparing to descend, to lever her up and away. Fine hands still, despite the sprinkling of liver spots. Jonathan, Isabel's father, had had liver spots too in his last years. The wedding band is on the left hand, the other rings are gone, the nails cut short and square. Isabel leans back and the hands touch down but the eyes are still uncertain.

'This is a lovely room,' says Isabel, trying to sound bright and reassuring. She does not add 'isn't it?' which would have thrown her mother back into confusion.

'Jonathan never really liked it here,' says Jasmine. She starts to stroke the arm of her chair.

And now it is Isabel who is confused. 'He didn't?' she asks cautiously.

'No.' An emphatic shake of the head. 'No, he didn't. Oh, he did his job. He did what he had to do. He always did that. But he never felt comfortable. He never really liked the British. He thought they rather despised Americans. He never made friends. Apart from me. But that was different, he said, since I was only a quarter British. I'm not so sure, though. He once said that he could never tell what I was thinking.'

'Was that true?'

'What?'

'That he – that Jonathan could never tell what you were thinking?'

'Oh, yes. Yes, it was true.'

'Could you tell what *he* was thinking?'

'Mostly, but then he was American – and a man.'

For a moment the old smile lights up the faded violet eyes and the ghost of vanished beauty breathes over Jasmine's face. The hand does not stop its rhythmic caress of the chair arm. Isabel feels her heart contract and turns to the window. The Hudson lies steel grey in the chill March sunshine.

'I wanted to tell you about this man. Mother?' she starts again. 'I met him at a dinner party and I've only seen him once since. He's divorced. His kids are grown-up. He's a musician – a conductor. World class. The Philharmonic and everything.

He has wonderful hands. And he writes books. I think I'm in love with him.'

Jasmine is smiling. Looking at her. Does she see her? What does she see?

'Oh, I wish Daddy was here!' Isabel buries her face in her hands. Her mother's hand strokes the chair.

Old people are starved of touch: no husband, no lover, no child to slip a hand into a hand, to plant sticky kisses on nose and cheek and mouth, to snuggle and fit into the curves of the body. I watched my grandmother – my mother's mother – in her last years: her hand, the skin drawn parchmentlike over the bones, stroking, stroking, the chairs, the table, the bed-spread.

'Anyway –' Isabel collects herself, shakes out her hair, runs her fingers through it – 'I don't know what he feels about me. When I'm with him I feel all his attention concentrated on me. I feel this – this energy between us. But I don't know if he even thinks about me when I'm not there.' She looks sadly at her mother. 'I'm not sure what I should do.'

'I've given him up, of course,' Jasmine says. 'It was the only thing to do. He's very young, you see. Such eyes! He reminds me of Valentine, of course. I don't need to be told that; I've known it all along, from the moment I saw him. Maybe that's why I took him in. I don't remember what it was, Algeria or CND or something – there were so many demonstrations that summer. But he was hurt. He was in danger and I took him in. No one could touch him then; he was on American territory – although he didn't know it. Jonathan was away and I took him in and I dressed the cut on his head. It was already swelling up into a horrid bruise. And he was so fired up with the state of the world and how he was going to change it all – he and his friends. He was so young. I sat by his bed, and later, when he was asleep, I got in next to him. I couldn't help myself. Well. There we are. I went to his place later, twice. But then I knew I had to give

53

him up. But it's been hard. It's been like losing Valentine all over again.'

'Mother?' Isabel is sitting upright now. Jasmine sounded like herself again: chatty, regretful, resigned. But – an affair? Her mother had had an affair? When? Who? Had her father known? She looks at the dimmed eyes, the cropped white hair.

'Did my father – did Jonathan know?' she asks.

'Such a sweet man!' Jasmine shakes her head. 'Such a sweet, sweet man! And so terribly in love with me.' Shakily, she pushes herself up out of her armchair, pushes her feet into pink slippers. 'I have to go now.'

'Mother,' says Isabel, sitting up straight, afraid to reach out and catch hold of a frail arm, afraid to hold on to her, 'Mother, when was this? Who was he? Did Daddy know?'

A faded copy of the old, bright smile is turned on Isabel. 'Goodbye,' Jasmine says. 'It's been so pleasant talking to you.'

6

Do you not know that Egypt is a copy of heaven and the temple of the whole world?

Egyptian scribe, c. 1400 BC

By an odd – and, I hope, propitious – chance, we have arrived at Alexandria on the same day as the new Patriarch of the Greek Orthodox Church – a church which has its seat in this city. A Mr James Barrington, who boarded as soon as we had docked and introduced himself as having been commissioned to meet me and bring me to Cairo safely (a courtesy for which I have to thank Sir Charles's letters to the Agency), kindly suggested that I might like to witness the celebrations, and the formalities of disembarkation duly dispatched, we soon found ourselves in a funny little carriage, not unlike a phaeton, with our luggage following behind and Mr Barrington perched on the box with the driver, with whom he appeared to converse most cheerfully. The two somewhat indifferent horses seemed to know their way, and responded only with a toss of their decorated heads to the occasional flick of the whip, delivered in almost desultory fashion and – I felt – more for form's sake than from any true necessity. In this manner we arrived at a tea-house (rather more in the Viennese style, I'm afraid, than the Oriental) and, the two carriages having been told to wait (I later saw our driver standing by his horse's head and most tenderly feeding him some green stuff which Mr Barrington tells me is known as 'bersim' and is similar to our clover), we settled ourselves at a window table, ordered tea and English cake (which turned out to be a plain but perfectly well-made sandcake), and waited for the parades.

I observed that there were a great many decorations about: flags and strips of gaily coloured cloth and banners – to say *nothing of the red and white rosettes decorating the carriage horses' heads and harnesses — and upon enquiring whether it was the custom to deck out the town so profusely for a Christian occasion, I learned that the Khedive (having returned from Europe) is spending the rest of his summer at Ras el-Tin Palace here in Alexandria, and His Highness having attained his twenty-sixth year three days previously, the town has been so decked out to honour him, the new Patriarch merely benefiting — as it were — from the coincidence of dates. It was a most interesting and picturesque procession that accompanied him (the Patriarch) from the Port to his Cathedral with much costume and carriages and horses and uniforms, and I could not but wonder what Emily made of it all — but she kept her usual stolid stance, moving her chair a little distance from the table we were sharing and turning it to an angle away from us. Later, when we were installed in our Pension, I made a small attempt to explain to her the oddity of Egypt's position, the country having won its independence in all but name from the Ottoman Sultan some sixty years ago though still nominally a part of his Empire, and now being ruled by the British through their Agency, and she said, 'To be sure, ma'am, three rulers instead of one, that's very odd.' In any case, she is bustlingly happy for this is a very decent Pension, belonging to a Greek widow lady who, Mr Barrington assures me, is perfectly respectable but has been left to make her own (and her little girl's) way in the world, her husband having died in some tragic circumstance which he seemed unwilling to expand upon and I cannot as yet ascertain.*

I have a bedroom and a sitting room, both looking out to the sea, and both tolerably well furnished although a little dark and ponderous for my taste. Nothing would please the landlady but she must give me the grandest room with the 'letto matrimoniale', in which she clearly invests much pride. I said that, my condition being in one essential respect similar to hers, I would not have much use for it, but she was determined. It is a rather hideous affair, all brass knobs and foliage, but very firm and clean and well fortified by curtains and hangings and draperies against any mosquito or — what I find the thought of infinitely more alarming — the flying cockroaches that Captain Bourke so kindly warned me were a standard feature of life in Africa. However, I fancy I am not really in Africa yet, for certainly this place, from what I have seen so far, seems to have more of the Europe of the Mediterranean in it than anything else, and were it not for the costume of the native Arabs and the signs in their language, you might fancy yourself in some Greek or Italian town.

I must not run on any longer, dear Caroline, but I have so many impressions of this, my first day here, and none of them as yet anything like what I had — through my own reading or through the reports of others — been led to expect that I cannot, it seems, quite feel I have captured the day on paper, and so put down my pen.

I have just read this letter once before consigning it to the post and find that I have mentioned Mr James Barrington four times (this is the fifth!) and knowing my dear friend as I do, and being sensible that her wishes for my happiness may steer her thoughts along a particular course, I take the occasion to state here that the gentleman, though certainly a gentleman (Winchester and Cambridge) and an entertaining guide, is extremely young, no more than twenty-four or five years of age, and though he may in time prove a fine friend, that is all that you must now hope for your etc. etc.

And so Anna arrives in Egypt and this, it seems, is her first letter; a little self-conscious perhaps, a little aware of the genre – *Letters from Egypt, A Nile Voyage, More Letters from Egypt*. I assume that what I have is a copy of the letter she sent to Caroline. Perhaps she was thinking of a future publication. In any case, I forgive her the mannered approach as she feels her way into my home. What else does she know – yet? And I am glad that she has broken away – that the brown leather journal is put gently aside. She did not draw a thick line under the last entry. She did not tear out and use any of the remaining pages. I flick through them, half expecting a note – a comment from later years on that early grief. But there is nothing. She simply left them blank.

I find myself curious, as I would have been with a foreign friend coming to visit: wondering what she will make of Egypt, how much she will see – *really* see. And I wish I were there to welcome her, take her in, show her around. Show her around? I, who have placed myself more or less under house arrest, moving from my living room to my bedroom to the kitchen – avoiding my children's rooms. Angry with the city – with the country – to which I had returned to find so much had changed.

Now I find myself once again in the thick of traffic, of bureaucracy and procedure, as I try to see for myself the country that Anna came to. I try to reimagine it, to re-create it for Isabel. In the glass and concrete edifice that now houses the newspaper (though the letters spelling out its name still stand on top of the ruined, gracious building that used to be its home) I go through the archives of *al-Ahram*, cranking the blurred microfilm through the reader while three women in bonnets with crochet trimmings watch me from behind one desk.

I find that pride of place, on 29 September 1900, is given to the arrival the day before of the new archbishop, Fotios, to his patriarchal seat in Alexandria. The article mentions the welcoming speeches delivered to the Archbishop while still on board his ship in the harbour and details the procession which carried him through the streets of Alexandria: the Cavalry, the Patriarchal Ceremonial Carriage, the Carriages of the Bishops and the Clerics, the Consuls of the Powers and the Foreign Nations, the People of Official Rank, the Lower Ranks of Clerics, the Leaders of the Orthodox Community and Representatives of the Community from the Regions of Egypt, Representatives of the Associations and Brotherhoods, the Learned Sheikhs of al-Azhar, Men of Letters, Professionals, Financiers and Merchants . . . all these passed in pageant in front of the teashop where a young widow fresh from England sat with her maid and the consular attaché, while her luggage waited in a hired carriage round the corner and the driver held a fistful of barsim to his horse's munching mouth and raised his head to watch the notables go by.

Alexandria
29 September 1900

Dear Sir Charles,
You have been much in my thoughts (that is to say much more than the usual much!) since the cry was heard and we all hurried on deck to peer into the horizon and make out that low-lying grey-blue shore you first saw in such unfortunate circumstances eighteen years ago.

We, however, sailed peaceably into the harbour, and I was met straight away by a young gentleman by the name of James Barrington, who had been detailed by Lord Cromer himself to find me and offer me every assistance. I know I have to thank your letters for this and I am most grateful for your kindness, for not only was the transition from ship to land achieved quite without pain, but my guide pointing out that the Court, the Government and all the Consuls – in short everybody – was still in Alexandria for the end of summer, I agreed to stay in this city for a while and see the sights. And, lest you imagine I am no longer the daughter you know but am grown fond of Society and Show, I will assure you that I felt that by insisting on continuing immediately to Cairo I would cause some inconvenience to Mr Barrington and to such others – as yet unknown – who feel it their duty to assist and chaperone an unprotected female in a strange land.

We are, therefore, lodged in the Pension Miramar, in the care of an excellent respectable Greek widow lady with a young child: a pretty little girl of about four who has taken to Emily and is constantly chattering to her in Greek, and begging her, with the most winning gestures, to dress her hair in braids and bows – a service which Emily is glad to render, since she does not consider she does enough of it where it would be most proper!

I wrote of our arrival yesterday to Caroline Bourke, and since I am sure you will be given an account of my letter, I will not say more, save that today further Jubilations were in evidence on the streets as His Highness the Khedive has been blessed with the arrival of a new baby Princess.

Alexandria seems, on the face of it, a rather jolly place and today I ventured out for a short walk on my own along the seafront, within sight of the Pension. I could see no trace of your famous 'bombardment' and – receiving nothing but smiles and kind looks from the Natives and doffed boaters from the Europeans – was hard put to imagine scenes of fanatical wickedness. But I am yet new to this place and know nothing of it save what can be seen by the most superficial eye.

Mr Barrington says that as I am in Alexandria I must see the sights: Pompei's Pillar, the Mohammedan Cemetery, the Museum and the Catacombs – he is arranging some expeditions to these. He mentioned that Alexandria had boasted two fine Cleopatra's Needles and commented on the oddity of Egypt's rulers giving them away – one to us and the other to the Americans. Then he said that he supposed if they had not given them away they would have been taken in any case, and muttered something about 'Budge and Morgan'? He knows a great deal about the country and cares for it very much, I think. It appears he is an excellent speaker of the native Arabic and I count myself most fortunate in having him for my guide and interpreter.

My thoughts turn often towards you, my dearest friend and parent. How I wish I could have prevailed upon you to undertake this journey with me! I have, however, the comfort of knowing that I am here with your encouragement and blessing – indeed, I would not have gone without – and that the purpose for which we decided I should travel is even now being achieved; for I am better in health and spirits than I have been for a long time. You must tell Mr Winthrop that. Poor man, what a hard time he has had with us these last eighteen months! I will search out the herbs he mentioned when I find my way to the souks of Cairo – although Alexandria must have souks too, for all that it looks so like a European city, but I doubt I shall have the time to find them; besides, I imagine he will want them as fresh as possible.

Dearest Sir Charles, I am rambling, but that is because I miss your company and our conversations. When you are next on the Embankment, pray look at Cleopatra's Needle and remember me in the land of Tuthmosis III. May it please God that you remain well and that I find you so when I return – and that you will be pleased to welcome back your loving daughter . . .

Sir Charles stays in his rooms on Mount Street. The house he had left to his son and his son's bride stands empty. The gardener comes in once a week to keep the flowers in order.

And Anna starts another journal; a handsome, thick volume in dark green with a navy spine:

28 September
My thoughts tonight keep turning to my dear Edward, for four years ago he made this very journey and saw the same shore that I have seen today and disembarked at the very port. The waves breaking against the sea wall beneath my window are not the waves he listened to, but their sound cannot be too dissimilar and I find myself wondering, as I sit here in the shadow of my great bed, whether we would have shared it, had we come here together – whether being thrown together in travel might not have broken down some of that reserve that featured so large in our marriage – and so immovably. Idle thoughts . . .

7

In his first interview with the Governor of St Helena, Napoleon said emphatically: 'Egypt is the most important country in the world.'

Lord Cromer, 1908

I can see her now, my heroine: she sits at the window of her bedroom in the Greek widow's pension, her letters neatly folded, her new journal open on the table towards which she leans to command as wide a view as she can of the Eastern Harbour; two arms of the city stretching out to encircle a portion of the Mediterranean. Did Anna see, as she looked to her left, the lights of the Fort of Sultan Qaytbay? Her edition of *Cook's Tourist Handbook* does not mention the old fort at all. Did James Barrington tell her that this, more than anything, perhaps, is an exemplar of that tired phrase, 'the palimpsest that is Egypt'? For here the Pharos – the great lighthouse of Greek Alexandria – once stood, and from its ruins and with its stones the Mameluke Sultan Qaytbay built his fort in 1480 against the Crusaders coming from the north, and within that fort a mosque was later built, and the minaret of that mosque was destroyed by Admiral Sir Beauchamp Seymour in the bombardment of 1882.

Isabel talks of making a film of Anna's life, the opening credits rolling across a long shot of the old fort. I say, 'It's a military museum now, I don't know if you'd get permission.'

'Sure I would,' she says confidently. 'The guidebook says at dawn its stones look like they're made of butter. It would be a great shot: a fairy-tale cake of a fort, creamy against the blue sea. You could even see it from the sea to begin with, then swing around as the boat docks –'

'It would have docked in the Western Harbour –'

'Then the camera pulls back and back and back until we're with Anna in her window, seeing what she sees.'

'It was night-time,' I say, literally, stubbornly. I want to keep Anna for myself; I don't want her taken over by some actress.

'That's a detail,' says Isabel.

Anna looks out of her window. It is night-time. I insist that it is night-time, and between the lights of the fort and the lights of Silsila the Mediterranean is a black, blank expanse ahead of her. Her hair is brushed and lies soft on her neck and shoulders. She wears a peignoir (is it a peignoir? I like the word; tasting of the nineteenth century, of fashion and a certain type of woman, of Europe and the novel. Anna Karenina might have worn a peignoir as she prepared for bed; certainly several of Colette's heroines did, but my English Anna seems worlds away from Coline and Rézi who are her contemporaries) – a peignoir gathered at her shoulders and falling over her breasts in silken folds. Perhaps it has a trimming of soft fur around the neck and at the end of the long, loose sleeves. It is in a pale, pale grey shading into blue. The card propped up on my dressing table calls this colour 'Drifter'. This colour card has been of no use to me for years, and yet I cannot bring myself to throw it away; it startles me that an object of such beauty should be held in such low esteem – and yet there they were in every B&Q, Sainsbury's HomeBase, etc., not to mention the specialised paint stores and hardware stores: hundreds of cards, stacked, inviting the most casual passer-by to pick one up, glance at it, and throw it into the nearest bin. But look what it does with the seven basic colours; it lobs you gently into the heart of the rainbow, and turns you loose into blue; allows you to wander at will from one end of blue to the other: seas and skies and cornflower eyes, the tiles of Isfahan and the robes of the Madonna and the cold glint of a sapphire in the handle of a Yemeni dagger. Lie on the line between blue and green – where is the line between blue and green? You can say with certainty 'this is blue, and that is green' but these cards show you the fade, the dissolve, the transformation – the impossibility of fixing a finger and proclaiming, 'At this point blue stops and green begins.' Lie, lie in the area of transformation – stretch your arms out to either side. Now: your right hand is in blue, your left hand is in green. And you? You are in between; in the area of transformations. Enough. Enough. And yet, I imagine that Anna would have had these same thoughts about whatever version of the colour card there was in her day, for she was a woman who was arrested by small things, by shades of colour.

Cairo
8 November 1900

Dear Sir Charles,
It is now a week that we have been in Grand Cairo and I have met with the greatest consideration and kindness from everybody here. I have been to dinner at the Residency, where Nina Baring has kept house for her uncle these two years. I am told Lord Cromer is a changed man since his bereavement and that the gentlemen of Chancery were much relieved when Miss Baring came, for she is lively and vivacious and teases her uncle and makes him smile. She has presented him with a complete set of silver brushes inscribed 'Mina', which occasioned a certain amount of perplexity at the Agency until she recounted a family tale according to which the Earl used, as a child, to pick up any object he could carry and cry 'mine-a, mine-a' till that became his childhood name. You can imagine how I thought of you upon hearing this, and I imagined you throw back your head and laugh – as you used to – then say, 'That accounts for his attitude to Egypt, then.'

I find myself seeing many things here through your eyes, imagining that I know what you would think of them. I know you would be interested to learn – if you do not know already – that there is a newspaper, newly started here, that speaks against the Occupation. I learned this when someone mentioned at dinner that the paper, al-Liwa, *is stirring up the people by*

*writing against the Boer War and describing the methods used by
the British army there. My ears pricked up at this – on your
account – but to my questions Lord Cromer merely said it was a
publication of no significance, paid for by the French and read
only by the 'talking classes'. After this the subject was dropped
by tacit agreement and replaced by discussion of a Baron Empain
and a French company that has bought a great tract of land in the
desert North-East of Cairo and is planning to build a city there
along French lines. When I questioned Mr Barrington later
about the paper, though, he said that he believed it was paid for
by subscriptions – although the French may have helped to begin
with – and that it prints ten thousand copies a day. That seems a
great many in a country where most people cannot read. I must
see if I cannot get a copy and send it to you, although of course it
will be in Arabic.*

*I must tell you, dearest Sir Charles, that your views are well
known here, but the respect you command is such that no one has
shown me anything but solicitude and kindness.*

*We are staying, as I told you in my telegram, at Shepheard's
Hotel, which is poised between the old and the new Cairo, and I
have been once to the Bazaar with Emily. It is exactly as I have
pictured it; the merchandise so abundant, the colours so bold, the
smells so distinct – no, I had not pictured the smells – indeed
could not have – but they are so of a piece with the whole scene:
the shelves and shelves of aromatic oils, the sacks of herbs and
spices, their necks rolled down to reveal small hills of smooth red
henna, lumpy ginger stems, shiny black carob sticks, all letting off
their spicy, incensy perfume into the air. It is quite overwhelm-
ing. I had not, however, imagined the streets to be so narrow or
the shops so small – some of them are hardly shops at all but mere
openings in the wall where one man sits cross-legged working at
some exquisite piece of brass or copper. It is difficult, though, to
examine the place at leisure as people are constantly calling out to
you and urging you to buy their wares. I hear you tell me that
those people are there to make their livelihood and indeed I know
it is so, and I would buy, only I do not know the proper price of
things and I have heard that you have to bargain and I have no*

experience in conducting that transaction. No doubt I will learn.
Emily was much relieved to get back to the Hotel for she
constantly feared we would be abducted and dragged into one of
the dark, narrow alleys we sometimes came upon between shop
and shop — and when I asked to what purpose, she said we
should be sold as slaves, for it is well known that Cairo is a great
centre for that trade. My assurances have proved of no avail and
she is determined that neither she nor I will venture again into
Old Cairo except under British guard! So you may be assured
that all will be well with me and that I am most scrupulously
looked after here in Cairo. Your loving . . .

And what of Emily? Anna's references to her sketch out the
portrait we have come to expect of a lady's maid of the period:
Emily 'chides' Anna into going out into the garden; Emily
wishes to be allowed to dress Anna's hair in a more elaborate
style; she distances herself from the spectacle of the parade in
Alexandria; she is fearful in the Bazaar. I try to focus on her as
she waits on the sidelines, guarding the picnic basket, the rugs
and the first-aid box. How old is she? What does she want for
herself? Is she saving up to start a milliner's business? Does she
have an illegitimate child lodged with a foster mother in
Bournemouth? Does she want something for herself? Or is
Anna her whole life and occupation? Can she yet do what
Hesther Stanhope's maid did, who in Palmyra caught the
fancy of a passing sheikh but was denied permission to marry
him? Would she do what Lucy Duff Gordon's Sally did and
melt into the back streets of Alexandria, pregnant with the
child of her mistress's favourite servant, Omar al-Halawani? I
don't know; so far, nothing in Anna's papers gives me any
clue.

Cairo
14 November 1900

Dear Caroline,
I have been in Cairo for close on two weeks now and I have seen
a great many curious sights — the most curious of all perhaps being

*the sky, which is perpetually blue in the daytime and innocent of
any wisp of cloud. How different it is here from November in
England. I would so like it if you were to come out, for I am
certain you would enjoy it. I dined at the Agency last night (the
second time since I have been here) and I fancied myself
exchanging glances with you across the dinner table when the
conversation turned to the Khedive's visit to England last
summer and what a success it had been and how honoured
'the boy' ought to feel (this from Lord Cromer) at the Queen's
giving him the Victorian Order. I remembered you bringing over
the* Illustrated London News *(indeed I have kept the copy)
and how we read it in the garden –*

– and there on the cover is the Toast to His Highness: a long
table loaded with candleholders, flowers, epergnes and fruit
bowls. Ranged behind it – the caption tells me – are the
Prince and Princess of Wales, the Duke of York, the Marquess
of Salisbury, the Lord Mayor of London and the Gaikwar of
Baroda. The company raise their glasses. In the centre, tilting
slightly to his right, towards the upright, tiaraed figure of the
Princess, the Khedive – easily the youngest man there by
thirty years – bows and leans with both hands on the table as
though for support. As a Muslim, he should not drink alcohol.
Looking in from the right of the picture is another fez-
wearing head: the elderly Turkish ambassador, holding his
wineglass uneasily by its stem, looks in a concerned manner at
the young Khedive. Above 'Abbas Hilmi's head hangs a
heavy-looking instrument with a tassel on its end –

*– and Sir Charles came in and looked at the cover and the mace
hanging from the wall of the Guildhall above the Khedive's head
and said, 'That's to pop him on the fez if he steps out of line.' I
believe that was the first time I had laughed since Edward's
death.*
    *I am sure that Sir Charles's opinions are well known here –
indeed they must be, for, far from making a secret of them, he has
published and declared them whenever possible – and I cannot*

imagine they are regarded with any sympathy by this company. No one speaks of this in front of me of course, partly out of natural courtesy, and partly because of the consideration they feel is due to me for Edward's sake. But I hear them mention Mr Blunt, who holds views identical to those of my beau-père, and whom they regard as a crank who chooses to live in the desert, and they use of him the phrase 'gone over' by which I assume they mean he sees matters from a different point of view. I own I am curious to see Mr Blunt but he does not come into Cairo Society and I cannot call on him unless I am invited by Lady Anne. Nothing, it seems to me, could be further from the spirit of the desert than life at the Agency — indeed, while you were there you would not know you were not in Cadogan Square with the Park a stone's throw away instead of almost paddling in the waters of the Nile.

It must be so hard to come to a country so different, a people so different, to take control and insist that everything be done your way. To believe that everything can *only* be done your way. I read Anna's descriptions, and I read the memoirs and the accounts of these long-gone Englishmen, and I think of the officials of the American embassy and agencies today, driving through Cairo in their locked limousines with the smoked-glass windows, opening their doors only when they are safe inside their Marine-guarded compounds.

Lord Cromer himself (or 'el-Lord' as I am told he is commonly known throughout the country — a title, they say here, that denotes both affection and respect) is a large, commanding man with sad, hooded eyes and thinning white hair. I cannot pretend to know him at all well, of course, but I have observed him at the head of the dinner table, where he sits and exudes a quiet strength. He is a man of very decided opinions, to which the conversation in his presence always defers. I suspect you would not be able to work with him for long if you did not subscribe wholeheartedly to his views. He is surrounded by his gentlemen, chief of whom is Mr Harry Boyle, the Oriental Secretary. He is

most interesting as a character (Mr Boyle) and I think makes
something of a point of a certain eccentric untidiness or even
shabbiness of dress and unruliness of moustache, but Mr
Barrington tells me it is said that he has a very sound under-
standing of the native character and he does speak the language –
although Mr Barrington stressed that his knowledge was only of
the vernacular – and it is this understanding that has made him
so useful to Lord Cromer and brought the two men so close that
Mr Boyle has earned the nickname 'Enoch' (for walking with the
Lord!). Lord Cromer himself speaks no Arabic at all – except for
'imshi', which is the first word everybody learns here and means
'go away', and of course 'baksheesh'.

I am hoping to learn a little more of native life here, although I
must say I have no idea how to put that hope into actual form.
But I feel it would be a little odd to come all the way to Egypt
and learn nothing except more about your own compatriots. I
believe if Sir Charles were here he would be able to show me
things I cannot yet see on my own. In any case I am very sensible
that I know very little of the country and must be content to try to
educate myself until such time as I am equipped to form my own
views.

In that same issue of the *Illustrated London News*, there is what
we call today 'an artist's impression' of the Triumphal Entry
into the Transvaal: lots of little people line a wide, dusty road.
Some wave thin sticks fluttering with forked Union Jacks. In
the centre of the road a man in uniform rides ahead of his
troops. But in the foreground, closest to us, the artist has
placed an old bearded man (a Boer?) who turns away from
Lord Roberts and his prancing horse. He faces us, the readers,
with furious eyes, his left fist clenched and raised to his chest.

8

A woman like her
Should bear children
Many children,
So she can afford to have
One or two die.
      Ama Ata Aidoo, 1970

Cairo, May 1997

The loud buzz of the intercom sounds through the corridor. I'd been in my bedroom, working, as is usual with me now, on my Anna project, reading on the period, looking at pictures, trying to imagine. I've always liked working in bedrooms, moving from the desk to the bed to the dressing table and back to the desk. At one stage of my life it had been necessary; now I ignore the empty rooms and spend my days and nights in this one corner of my flat. I think of the table by the window as 'Anna's table' and it is covered with her papers. I've arranged them chronologically as much as I could; the undated sheets I've compared to dated ones and matched the paper. They stand in twelve piles, one for each year – some years are more substantial than others. The journals stand alone. I have tried not to read through them, to read only one year at a time. But then I know how the story ends. I don't think that matters. We always know how the story ends. What we don't know is what happens along the way.

Anna's objects I keep wrapped as I found them, in the trunk which now stands by the wall next to my dressing table.

I was expecting Isabel and I had stopped work and was standing at the window, vaguely watching a woman hang out laundry. She must have done a white wash for she hangs out vests, white vests, one after the other: big ones, medium ones, little ones. She bends down and vanishes for a moment behind the wall of her balcony, then straightens up with a vest in her hand and a clothespeg in her mouth. She shakes out the vest and pegs it by the shoulder next to its brother. When she has finished and picked up the green plastic tub and gone inside, the vests hang in the still air shoulder to shoulder.

And to think that there were times when I grumbled at their washing. But there were also times when I stood still, one wet sock in my hand, struck by a premonition of what it would feel like when there would be no more socks to wash, no more games kits to hang up to dry on Tuesdays and Thursdays, when all my time would be my own to do with as I wished. What do I wish? That I was still with my husband? That my children lived next door? No one lives next door any more. That woman there across the road – who knows where her children will go when they grow up? Canada, Dubai, the moon. Maybe she'll be lucky and one of them will settle here, in Cairo, close enough to give her grandchildren to hold and talk to in her old age.

I looked down at the trees in the garden below. I wondered, if they were washed, if someone just washed them down with a hose, how long would it take for the dust to settle again? I wondered how old the trees were: were they left over from the time when this part of the city was all green, planted fields? Or had they started their lives as town trees? Unlikely, I think. In this city trees are torn up, not planted. The great avenue of giant eucalyptus at the beginning of the Upper Egypt road in Giza, destroyed. Trees that soared up to sixty metres, reached to the sky, planted by Muhammad 'Ali close to two hundred years ago, torn up by the roots to make a wider road for the cars and trucks heading for Upper Egypt.

When the buzzer went I thought it was Isabel come early. I walked to the door and picked up the handset, and Tahiyya's voice rang in my ear: 'Daktora! Ya Daktora!'

'Aywa,' I shouted back, 'yes,' holding the handset away from my ear.

'Can I come up to you for two bits?' she shouts.

'Of course,' I say, 'Itfaddali.'

'Now?'

75

'Yes,' I say. 'Come.'

Tahiyya is the doorman's wife – and my friend. She asks after me and sends her children to see if I need the washing-up done or my clothes taken to the ironing shop. Now she comes in smiling, with her littlest – his leg still encased in plaster – on her hip.

'Please God you weren't asleep?'

'No, no,' I say, crossing the room to close the balcony doors as she puts the child down on the floor. 'But that thing is so loud; it startles me every time.'

'Why don't we get the engineers to turn it down?' she suggests, looking at it.

'We could,' I say, looking at it too.

'Or they might ruin it,' she says.

'Let's not,' I say. It's a new addition, a modernising touch, and she and 'Am Madani are very proud of it.

'We don't mean to wake you,' she says.

'I wasn't asleep,' I say. 'Let's make some tea.'

We go into the kitchen and she says 'You rest', so I sit at the table while she fills the kettle. 'Abd el-Rahman follows us, back to crawling now because of his plastered leg. He settles on the floor in front of my father's tall dresser and opens the lowest drawer. This is where the coloured plastic clothespegs are kept.

'Look at this for me,' she says while we wait for the tea leaves to settle. She puts a large brown envelope in front of me. I open it and pull out an X-ray – no, a scan. I read the tiny English writing and look up at her tired, pretty face; the brown eyes lined with kohl, the eyebrows plucked thin, the blue kerchief tight across her forehead:

'Again?' I say. 'Again, ya Tahiyya?'

'By God, I never wanted to,' she protests. 'We said four and we praised God and closed it on that. It's God's command, what can we do?'

'But hadn't you put the loop? I thought –'

'Yes, I had put it, but I had blood, blood coming down on me and they took it out and said take a rest for a while – and

76

you know what men are like. Then God's command came to pass.'

She tests the tea. It is the colour of burgundy and she pours it into our glasses and spoons in the sugar.

'There are some biscuits,' I say, and she brings the plate to the table and hands a biscuit to her son.

'By the Prophet, I can't keep up with them all,' she says. 'Yesterday the little girl had a temperature and was fretful all day and at night this boy kept me up all night coming and going. The plaster – you'll excuse me – makes his leg itch. All night I'm carrying him and patting him and calming him down until Madani was about to say to me, "May God help you." '

'That's good of him,' I say.

'What can he do, ya Daktora?' she asks. 'All day he's working, and he's got diabetes. His health isn't what it used to be.'

I can hear Isabel: his diabetes didn't stop him getting her pregnant. When his health was what it used to be, did he wake up and soothe the kids at night? But is it Isabel? Or are these my thoughts in Isabel's voice? Of course termination doesn't even come into it. 'Haraam ya Daktora,' Tahiyya would say, 'it's a soul after all.'

'How far gone are you?' I ask.

'I'm not sure.'

I look at the scan. 'Eleven weeks,' I tell her.

'Look at it for me,' she says, 'and read it for me. Tell me everything it says.'

'It says you're eleven weeks pregnant and the baby is normal.'

'Praise God,' she sighs.

'What does 'Am Madani say?'

'What will he say? He says "How will we feed them?" and praises God.'

'God provides,' I say.

'It's known,' she agrees, and gets up to wash the glasses.

'Yakhti, laugh,' I say. 'What do we take from it all?'

77

'Nothing,' she says. 'Man is destined for his God.'

'And they'll be five in the eye of the enemy –'

The buzzer goes again and I get up to answer it.

Isabel comes in as Tahiyya is collecting the clothespegs and wiping the crumbs from the floor. They smile at each other.

'Hallo,' Tahiyya says loudly in English, straightening up and smiling, raising her hand to her head, miming a greeting in case Isabel doesn't understand.

'Hello,' says Isabel. 'Izzay el-sehha?'

Tahiyya's eyes widen as she turns to me: 'She speaks Arabic!'

'See the cleverness,' I say.

'Yakhti brawa 'aleiha. She looks intelligent.' Tahiyya beams her approval. 'Is she married?'

'No,' I say.

'Like the moon and not married? Why? Don't they have men in Amreeka?'

'Maybe she doesn't want an American,' I joke.

'Khalas,' says Tahiyya. 'We marry her here. You find her a good bridegroom among your acquaintance and we'll make her a wedding that shakes the whole country.' She bends to pick up 'Abd el-Rahman. 'Shall I do anything for you before I go?'

'Thank you, Tahiyya, there's nothing.'

'Then I'll excuse myself,' she says. She settles her son on her hip, manoeuvres his plastered leg around the door. 'Salamu 'aleikum.'

'She's always so cheerful,' says Isabel, 'and she works so hard.'

'Yes, she does,' I say.

'She was washing down the stairs the last time I was here. Of the whole building.'

'It must have been Thursday. Do you want – shall I get you a drink?' It's just after seven.

'I thought we might go out,' says Isabel. 'Let me take you out to dinner.'

'I've got some stuff here–'

'Let's go out. Do you never go out?'

I shrug.

'There must be some place you like?'

'Come to New York,' Isabel says. 'Come and stay with me.'

'No,' I say. 'Thank you.'

'You can do your own thing,' says Isabel. 'There's a lot of space. We'll only meet when you want to.'

I shake my head.

'You can see your brother.'

'I'll see him when he comes to Cairo.'

'But he doesn't come often.'

'I know.'

'Have you taken a vow or something?'

'I just decided to come home. I've had enough of travelling.' And would I go to New York without stopping in London? And would I stop in London without seeing my husband?

'You'll come one day. I'm sure of it.'

'Will I?'

'You'll come when they're showing my film.'

'Sure.'

'I'm serious.'

'Isabel. You don't even know the rest of the story yet. You don't know how it'll turn out.'

'It doesn't matter. I can see it. The way you describe it, I can see it.'

I shake my head. I seem to be always shaking my head. But it's brave of me to come even here, just across the river; to this restaurant where we had dined together. Where he had kissed my hands and I had pretended not to notice the stares of the waiters.

'You want to bet?' she asks.

'No.'

'There you are, you see. You won't bet.'

'How are you doing with your work? Your millennium?'

She glances up at me, and we pause as the waiter loads the

79

table with stuffed vine leaves, houmous with a sprinkling of oil, baba ghanoush, cheese and tomato salad, soft bread and toasted bread. 'Did I feel a loaded pronoun there?' she asks gently.

I smile. 'She looks intelligent,' Tahiyya had said.

'Well, it *is* more yours than mine,' I say.

Isabel helps herself to two vine leaves and some houmous. 'You know,' she says, 'I know there's an awful lot I don't know. That's a start, isn't it?'

'Yes,' I say. 'I'm sorry.' And I am, for I – with my banners of 'fair-mindedness', of 'no prejudgement' – have been always, primarily, seeing her as 'the American'.

'How is it going, though, your paper?' I ask.

'I'm not sure. People I've spoken to have been very cautious. They talk mainly of technology and I have this feeling they're not telling me what's really on their minds.'

'It's very difficult.'

'But why? Why is it so difficult?'

'Because you're American.'

'But I can't help that.'

'Of course you can't. But it makes it difficult to talk to you about some things.'

'But it shouldn't. I have an open mind. What kind of things?'

'It'll be OK. Listen, we'll find a way,' I promise.

'Anyway,' Isabel says after a short silence, 'I've gotten interested in so many other things now. I'm not giving up on it – but there are other things I want to do.'

'But, Isabel, may I ask you this? You – you manage? With all this travelling and everything?'

'Oh, my dad left me some money. And I'm selling my parents' apartment. I'm not wealthy, but . . .' She smiles and her perfect teeth sparkle in the light of the glass-covered candle on the table.

A candle-shade of opaque glass. Bell-shaped. Frosted. It was Anna's brush that, dipped in aquamarine ink, traced the

cunning, curving letters: gliding with the stem of an 'alef'
bursting into flower, following the tail of a 'ya' as it erupts into
a spray of fireworks that scatter the text with diacritics. She
knew enough by then to make out the characters, but she
could not yet readily tell where one word ended and another
began.

I lift my head and look at Isabel, beautiful in her dusty pink
velour top across the table. A dead father and a mother as good
– or as bad – as dead. We are both orphans, she and I. A dead
brother and an absent brother – I touch the underside of the
wooden table quickly, secretly: my brother is absent but alive.
A broken marriage – we share that too.

'You know,' I say, sounding casual, trying it out, 'we used
to come here, my husband and I, whenever we came to
Cairo. It was our favourite restaurant. This is the first time I've
been here without him.'

'You're divorced?'

'No. But we've been separated for a long time.'

But I have sons and she hasn't. Though my sons are not
with me and I try not to spend my days waiting for them –
waiting for the phone call: 'Mama, I thought I might come
and see you –' Isabel's hair falls glossy and straight to just
below her jawline, and around the graceful neck lies a thin
silver chain. She is at her beginning and I am close to my end. I
smile at her.

'You know, I'm really glad I got to know you,' she says.

I reach out for a moment and pat the hand lying on the
table between us. 'You amazed Tahiyya with your Arabic,' I
say.

'I've learned the alphabet and they're giving me lists of
words,' she says, 'but . . .'

'But?'

'I haven't got a handle on it. How it works.'

'Listen,' I say, 'you know the alphabet and you've got a
dictionary. Everything stems from a root. And the root is
mostly made up of three consonants – or two. And then the

word takes different forms. Look –' The old teacher in me comes to life as I hunt in my handbag for paper and a biro. 'Take the root q-l-b, qalb. You see, you can read this?'

'Yes.'

'Qalb: the heart, the heart that beats, the heart at the heart of things. Yes?'

She nods, looking intently at the marks on the paper.

'Then there's a set number of forms – a template almost – that any root can take. So in the case of "qalb" you get "qalab": to overturn, overthrow, turn upside down, make into the opposite; hence "maqlab": a dirty trick, a turning of the tables and also a rubbish dump. "Maqloub": upside-down; "mutaqallib": changeable; and "inqilab": a coup . . .'

So at the heart of all things is the germ of their overthrow; the closer you are to the heart, the closer to the reversal. Nowhere to go but down. You reach the core and then you're blown away –

'Is there a book that tells you all this?' Isabel asks.

'I don't know. There must be. I kind of worked it out.'

'That's really useful.'

'I think so. It gives you a handle.'

'So every time you use a word, it brings with it all the other forms that come from the same root.'

Yes, they come swimming along in a cluster, like ovae: the queen in the centre, and all the other eggs, big and little, who will not, this time, be fertilised . . .

'Yes. Vaguely. Yes. Always look for the root: the three consonants. Or two.'

'I'm going to work on this,' she says.

'Tell me what you come up with.'

Isabel folds the paper and puts in her handbag – her 'purse', she would say.

Outside the plate-glass windows night has fallen and along Maspero the cars are fewer and the trees no longer look dusty. The lights of the Bateau Omar Khayyam and el-Basha gleam on the river. The odd small boat drifts quietly along, and by the railings couples linger; the men in short-sleeved shirts, the girls in big headscarves. Single young men walking by turn their heads to stare.

When we leave the restaurant we walk in single file along the narrow pavement to where the car is parked by the Rameses Hilton. I decline Isabel's offer of a drink. I've laid enough ghosts for one day. I want to get back to my flat, to my room.

We do a U-turn in front of the television building, still barricaded with sandbags since '67, and head back towards Qasr el-Nil bridge.

'How's Anna doing?' Isabel asks.

'You're out of touch,' I say.

'I am not. You said she'd gone to Egypt – come to Egypt. I've read the Alexandria bit.'

'Well, she's in Cairo now, and she's very much with the English set. The Agency and all that. The British embassy. She wants to learn Arabic.'

'Who's she going to get to teach her?'

'I don't know yet. James Barrington knows Arabic.'

'Has she found what she's looking for – the Lewis stuff?'

'Only a little bit; in the Bazaar. But not really, no.'

'Will she? Find it?'

'I don't know. I hope so. But she stays a long time, so she must have.'

'So there's a scene in the Bazaar?'

'Yes, complete with donkeys, and little old artisans and street cries and a frightened, disapproving lady's maid and urchins yelling for baksheesh –'

'You're making fun of me.'

'Only a little. And nicely.'

'You know, you're terribly like your brother.'

Ah. I'd wondered when we would get back to him. My brother.

. . . in this story of Turkish, Albanian and British rule in Egypt, it is Egypt that is really counting all the time. It [is like the story] of a public man with a clever wife. While she helps him he flourishes, and as soon as she doesn't he falls, but it is not easy to show how this happened.

George Young, 1927

Dear Sir Charles,

It feels very strange these days not to be in England. I have a sense of momentous happenings – but somehow disembodied, for nothing around me reflects recent events except the lowered flags and general gloom at the Agency – but then I have not known it to be a particularly joyous place. The rest of the country continues, so far as I can see, as usual – the people celebrating the Festival of the end of the Fast of Ramadan, while I know that in England, even for those who have no part in them, the preparations for the Coronation and the Funeral must be stirring both hopes and fears of imminent change. It is most odd to think that the Queen is gone when she has always had such a fixed place in our firmament. I cannot say that I grieve for her; she was too remote – even when one met her – to inspire that emotion; it is more that I am surprised afresh every time the thought comes to me: She is no more.

Are you hopeful of a change for the better? You have always said that the Prince of Wales knows much more of what is going on in the world than his mother, or even Lord Salisbury. Will it be possible to stop the war in South Africa now? I spent the afternoon yesterday at the Sporting Club, and among the party was a gentleman from Finance by the name of Money (truly Charles Dickens himself could not have done better), who said that the South Africa Campaign has now cost us one hundred and fifty million pounds. I told him that at the beginning of the war you had estimated it would cost two hundred million and he said it might yet come to that. Pray do write and tell me what you think of all these events for, of my life in England, it is your conversation that I miss above all else.

Here, in Cairo, the days go on as usual. Today Mrs Butcher (of whom I believe I have written to you before) most kindly allowed me to accompany her on a visit to a wonderful old church, built upon the towers of the Roman Fort of Babylon in the old Christian district to the south of Cairo. It has a most curious wooden ceiling, like an upturned boat, and no domes of any kind. An old man there pointed out to us the image of the Virgin imprinted on a marble column. He spoke earnestly while pointing to it and Mrs Butcher later informed me that the Natives believe Our Lady left her image there as a token when she appeared in the year 969 to the Patriarch Abraham. The Caliph, al-Muizz, taking as his text Matthew 17:20, 'Verily I say unto you. If ye have faith as a grain of mustard seed, ye shall say unto this mountain, Remove hence to yonder place; and it shall remove; and nothing shall be impossible unto you' — the Caliph had asked the Patriarch to move the Muqattam mountain, and the Patriarch had responded by secluding himself in the church to fast and to pray. On the third day, the Virgin appeared to him and a terrible earthquake shook the Muqattam. Al-Muizz was satisfied and ordered the church restored, and rebuilt the Church of Abusifin into the bargain. It is a pretty tale, but the image looks very like the icons of the time, and indeed the face is almost identical to that in another painting, hanging near the entrance to the church, of Our Lady, crowned, the infant Jesus on her knee, crowned also, and St John leaning forward to kiss His foot. Of this latter painting it is said that the Virgin's eyes move to follow you wherever you go, but I put this to a practical test — as much as I felt was proper in a church — and I did not think her eyes followed me. It is a very fine church, though small and dark, and I saw that the inlaid woodwork of the panelling and the pulpit, the tiles on the walls, the oil lamps in their niches and the stone flagging of the floors have much in common with what I have seen in the older mosques. Would you not imagine that this points to some unity of divine impulse and aesthetic principle which has found expression in both?

The Muʿallaqah. Once on a school trip, many, many years ago, I too experimented with the Virgin's eyes. I wanted them to follow me, but I couldn't really say they did. I remember the guide that day telling us that the wooden rafters of the ceiling symbolised Noah's Ark and the eight columns Noah's family. He said that the thirteen marble columns supporting the pulpit were for Christ and the twelve disciples, and the one black column in their midst was Judas Iscariot. I felt then that I understood the building better. Now I am not sure how accurate he was, but it was a starting point. Against the warnings of our teachers we climbed down the uncertain iron staircase to the damp keep below, and we saw how the bottom had filled with stagnant water encrusted with thick green slime. Then a dark creature fluttered past our faces and someone yelled that there were bats down here and we backed off and hurried up the staircase. And what a relief it was to pass through the red velvet curtains and enter the dim comfort of the church and from there emerge once again into the light of day.

We sat under a tree which they say sheltered Our Lady in her flight into Egypt with the infant Jesus, and I own myself touched by the simple faith with which our guide spoke of Settena Maryam and her son Yasu al-Masih and — Mrs Butcher relayed to me — his utter conviction that it was this very tree and no other that had offered them shelter. And, after all, it could have been this tree. And if it was not — since there are other trees under which she is said to have rested — what harm is there in believing that it was your own particular tree that had so hospitably offered its shade? As long as one does not come to blows with one's neighbour over the question. Why should Our Lady not have rested under several trees during her sojourn in this land?

Mrs Butcher is most kind and good-hearted. She and the Dean have lived in Egypt now for many years. She speaks the language and appears to get on well with the Native people and is quite free from any rigidity of mind but holds the most generous opinions. She spoke to me with much interest and sympathy of the religion of the Ancient Egyptians and its similarities – in its most developed stage – with our own Christianity, saying that the Ancient Egyptian, like the modern Christian, knew that he lived in the sight of God, and under the shadow of the Eternal Wings.

Akhen Atun. The young king who rebelled against the powerful priests of Amun. Who took his wife, Nefertiti, most beautiful of the ancient queens, and his household and built a new capital at Tal el-Amarna, and there proclaimed the worship of the One God: Atun. What happened next? We have fragments of a story. Pictures. On the throne itself we see the Queen bending, her hand stretched out to touch with tenderness the royal collar of the seated king, her husband. We have images, unprecedented, of the royal family at play, the King holding one of his daughters on his knee, the Queen kissing another. And then something happened. What made him discard Nefertiti and cast her out? What forces did she then gather against him? What we know is that when he died the priests of Amun-Ra staged their comeback and forbade the burial of his body, so that his sister stole out at night and anointed him and buried him, and for this she was condemned to a dark cell to die of hunger and of thirst.

I see Anna put down her pen. She reads her letter through and folds it. It is eleven o'clock. Emily has gone to bed and Anna is restless. She walks about her room. She opens the shutters of her window and peeps out: it is a January night and there is nothing to be seen except a horse and his syce waiting patiently for their master to end his evening at Shepheard's Hotel and go home.

10 February

I was speaking of learning Arabic and Dean Butcher said, 'Ah! you want to read the Muʿallaqat?' When he saw that, far from wishing to read it, I did not even know what it was, he explained that it was the name given to seven Odes that are the most famous in Arabic poetry from the days before Islam. I was struck by the similarity of the word to the name of what has now become my favourite church in Egypt, and the Dean explained that ''allaqa' means 'to hang' and the Muʿallaqah is named thus because it is hung on the ancient gateway of the Roman fort. The Muʿallaqat are the 'hung' poems, because they were the winning poems in the great poetry competition that took place every year in Mecca and so had the honour of being 'hung' on the door of the House of God (the Kaʿba).

I was loath to give up the idea that the shared name was somehow significant and I asked whether anything else was known by the same epithet. After some thought the Dean said that the only other instance that he could bring to mind was the Hanging Gardens of Babylon on the Euphrates: 'Hadaʾiq Babel al-Muʿallaqah'.

'A, l, q: to become attached, to cling, also to become pregnant, to conceive; and in its emphatic form 'a, ll, q: to hang, to suspend, but also to comment.

I have returned to the Muʿallaqah again and again, and as my familiarity with it grew — as I came to know the figures in the paintings, and their expressions and attitudes became things I recognised rather than discovered, as my ear became attuned to the eastern sound of Coptic chanting or the muffled hush of the empty church broken only by the odd Arabic call from the courtyard without, and my nose ceased to be surprised at the oddly tinny edge of the incense — as my familiarity with the church grew, so my consciousness increased of the effect it was having on my heart and on my soul, an effect that I can only describe as a sense of increased spaciousness within myself, as though the age of the building, the years it had hung as a

hallowed space between its twin Roman towers, were working its
way into my soul and I too, somehow, was becoming a part of
that great tract of time. I cannot express this better, but its effect
on me is of a deep — and I pray enduring — peace.

And now I want to go there again. To read, cut into the stone
gateway, in Arabic: ask and you shall be given, seek and you
shall find, knock and it shall be opened unto you. I lean back
against the side of my bed. Beside me on the floor lies Anna's
open journal; around it lie the letters. I do not want to be
infected with restlessness. I shift and sit cross-legged and
straight-backed, a wrist on each knee. I used to love wandering around in that district: visiting the mosque of 'Amr, then
the churches. Walking through the narrow cobbled streets of
the Coptic quarter and sitting for a while in the cemetery – so
different from our own – where the grand Coptic families are
buried amid evergreen trees and marble statuary. I shall tell
Isabel. I shall tell her she has to go to the Mu'allaqah.

And for Anna, as it happens sometimes, once you start
thinking about something circumstances push you into thinking about it even more: a letter to Caroline Bourke, the first
page missing, but dated, I believe, on or around March 10:

. . . but she was mostly silent except when Mr Barrington asked
her advice concerning a horse he was considering, and on one
other occasion. Among those present was a young man by the
name of Temple Gairdner, a very tall, ungainly young man with
a big mop of hair, who was ordained yesterday in Alexandria
and is shining with his enthusiasm to begin the work of
converting Mohammedans in Cairo. He was rather disconcerted,
I think, when Mrs Butcher questioned him on the wisdom of his
undertaking; he did not expect it from the wife of the Dean. She
did it very gently but there was no doubting her intent as she
pointed out the consequences (to the convert) of his success: the
legal problems of inheritance, the irretrievable loss of family and
friends. For while the native Mohammedan may have a friend-
ship – of sorts – with his Coptic neighbour, she said, to have his

own son or brother repudiate the faith was another matter entirely. Mr Gairdner made a brave defence, declaring that such worldly matters could not be weighed against the suffering of Our Lord and undertaking that he and his Society would be all the family the convert would need. Lady Anne then broke her silence to ask why he deemed it necessary to make a Moslem embrace Christianity since the Moslem is, in any case, a Believer? Was it worth the trouble it would cause to the convert and all who knew him, she asked, that he should worship the same God, but in a different manner? Mr Gairdner thus found himself trapped between two gentle but formidable ladies and I own I felt sorry for his discomfiture for he seems quite without any ill intent; indeed, he is bent on good. It all ended in friendly enough manner, though, for he declined to enter upon a discussion of theology but contented himself with saying that even if we looked at the matter from a wholly historical point of view, the entire edifice of Mohammedan belief is 'in the face of Christianity' and that his wish was to 'reclaim' for Christ souls that were His. The ladies indulged him and let the matter rest and Mr Boyle told a story of a donkey-boy who is famous for falling to his knees in front of lady tourists crying 'Lady, lady, me believe. Gib it plenty Bibble', thus sounding a variation on the usual cry of 'Baksheesh'. But Mrs Butcher said to me privately that she thought Mr Gairdner's kind of activity only led to much mischief here and she doubted whether he would make a single true convert for his troubles.

And now, my dearest Friend, lest you think I am grown too dull and solemn I will tell you that I have attended that apex of the Egyptian Winter Season: the Khedive's Ball. It had been postponed out of respect for our Mourning, but the Coronation having taken place, it was considered proper to hold the Ball – particularly as it is the one Event here at which all the Nations mingle and so has a most particular political and diplomatic standing.

It was a very grand affair, held at 'Abdin Palace, the official Residence of the Khedive (his personal Residence is at the Qubba Palace), and on the night the carriages were nose to back *from the Hotel and progress was very slow indeed. (Made slower by an odd occurrence, for as we came to the southern end of Opera Square we were halted by what I took to be a procession: two hundred or so men, in the official workers' clothes of the Tram Company, together with some young Egyptian men in European dress, all marching, preceded by a brass band! They came from the direction of the Citadel and turned ahead of us so we had to follow them all the way to the Palace. Nobody knew who they were but it was thought they might be celebrating some event.) I went with Lady Wolverton and Sir Hedworth Lambton and we were deemed of enough importance to be presented to His Highness and to be placed well to the front in his train when entering the Ballroom. The Khedive really seems a very pleasant young man, with an intelligent look and a good-humoured smile and perfect manners, and it is a shame he and Lord Cromer cannot get on better with one other. The Lord made an appearance but left early – before supper even – and this was excused on account of his bereavement and his known antipathy to festivities.*

The Ballroom itself is of surpassing magnificence, gilt and crystal and velvet everywhere and on the whole everything you would expect in a Royal Palace and more. At one end it had huge doors which opened later in the evening to reveal a Banqueting-Hall of equal magnificence. At the other end, a kind of narrow gallery ran around the higher portion of the wall and at the back of that was a curious golden grille, behind which I was told the ladies of the household sat and watched the proceedings if they had a mind to. My interest was naturally immediately captured by this and throughout the evening I found myself glancing up at it so that, were I a man, my behaviour would surely have been construed as indelicate. And yet, I think that for all my commonplace curiosity about the world behind that screen, my greater wish was somehow to know how we, in the Ballroom, appeared to the hidden eyes which watched us.

For the dances, they were in every point similar to what we would have at a formal ball in a great house in England – but I have never before seen such a mix of nationalities, for all the

Consuls of the Powers and the Consuls of every other Nation were there together with their Ladies, and naturally there was a very large British Presence. The Native notables were there (and those are the people I was most curious about, not having met any at all though I have been here more than five months) but not one single Moslem lady. No doubt they were all behind the grille! The Natives were in the uniform of the Egyptian Army, or in the robes of the religious orders or, like the Khedive, in Court dress topped by the scarlet fez, and I own I thought some of them looked most gallant. But they kept to themselves. I did not see one of them dancing.

You will want to know what I wore. I chose my violet silk, which Emily did not think was grand enough and I own it probably was not, but as I knew that Moslem notables were to be present I thought it would provide me with adequate covering and would not cause offence. We are, after all, in their country. But I did wear Lady Winterbourne's tiara and my mother's amethyst necklace and I believe I did not disgrace the Empire!

When the doors to supper were opened there was such a rush to enter the room, you would have thought all these people had not had a bite in weeks. Lady Wolverton and I stayed back awhile and I saw that some Native gentlemen did the same and indeed took the opportunity very soon to leave. I had the oddest feeling that I had seen one of them before – I only caught the briefest glimpse of him as he was turning to leave, but something in that moment transported me back to the Costanzi and it seemed to me that I could hear again Darclée's anguished lament rising into the House – with such inconvenient consequences for you, my dearest friend –

But it was the beginning of my healing and I trust you will see from all this that I have made great progress since those sad days which I shall always remember for the angelic kindness you demonstrated towards your devoted,

One of the 'Ulama present that evening, wearing 'the robes of the religious orders', was Sheikh Hassouna al-Nawawi. In a letter to Sheikh Muhammad 'Abdu he writes that of course he knows that foreigners' ways are different, but that of the foreigners' behaviour, the aspect which he found most astonishing was that 'ladies with bare arms and almost bare bosoms danced with other men while their husbands watched with equanimity and apparent approval'.

Cairo
10 March 1901

Dear Sir Charles,
I was delighted to receive your last, so generous in recounting recent events and the conversation of friends that it made me quite long to be in London again. It is melancholy to me to think of the house shut and desolate and cold, but I assure you next winter we shall be our old selves again – or as close to our old selves as possible – and when you come to see me in the evening, I shall have your whisky and water waiting and fires burning in all the grates.

I dined earlier tonight in pleasant company, among whom were your old friend Sir Hedworth Lambton and Lady Chelsea, who both promised to call on you in London next month and give you a good account of me! Lady Anne Blunt was also there (the invitation to visit their house in Heliopolis was not forthcoming – so I have no prospect as yet of meeting Mr Blunt and will have to wait until you can arrange a dinner in London) with her daughter Judith, who is very lively and pretty, and we talked much of England and our common friends and acquaintances.

Yesterday, though, I attended a conversation (I say attended because my part in it was chiefly confined to that of listener) which would have been of interest to you, and in which, unlike me, you would have had a great deal to say. It took place at the foot of the Great Pyramid (which I have eulogised enough already in previous letters), where luncheon was laid out after the expedition by boat and donkey (I have not yet dared to ride a camel!). You can, I am sure, imagine the scene: the rugs spread out, the baskets opened, the food served, the servants employed in shooing away the various turcomans and children offering services, donkeys, camels, escorts to the top of the Pyramid or

95

simply asking for money, and Emily seated on the corner of a rug. I had prevailed upon her to accompany me, saying she could not go back to England without at least seeing the Pyramid. I believe she took this as a sign that we were soon to leave and, wishing to remove any possible obstacle to our departure, came along and sat staring obstinately away from the Pyramid and towards the lush vegetation that precedes Cairo – the closest thing to civilisation that she can hope for at this moment.

I own I cannot as yet believe the evidence of my own eyes in that sudden transition from the sand of the desert to the green of cultivated fields and palm groves. What must it be like for the traveller, after days and nights of crossing the vast and empty expanse of desert, to come suddenly within sight of such green and fruitful abundance? It must seem like a miracle – but I digress.

Our party was made up of Harry Boyle, the Oriental Secretary at the Agency; James Barrington, the Third Secretary; your friend Mr Rodd, the First Secretary, who is soon to leave Egypt; Mrs Butcher (acting also as my chaperone); Mr Douglas Sladen and Mr George Young, both of whom are writing books on Egypt; and Mr William Willcocks, who is responsible for the building of the great dam and reservoir at Assouan – and myself. In the shadow of forty centuries, the talk turned naturally enough to Egypt, to the uninterrupted way of life of the Egyptian fellah and labourer, to Egypt's successive rulers and to our presence there now. Mr Boyle took the line you would expect: that the country had never been run so efficiently and that the Egyptians had never been happier or more prosperous than under Lord Cromer. Opposition came, though, from a most unexpected source: Mr Willcocks (who, I later learned from Mr Barrington, is known to have subscribed Five Pounds to a Nationalist paper, al-Mu'ayyad, and lives under Lord Cromer's consequent displeasure) asked why then were the papers agitating against us? Mr Boyle replied that he was not aware of any such agitation and both al-Muqattam and the Gazette were friendly enough. At this, I fancy a smile passed around the company, and Mr Willcocks said, 'Oh, I do not mean those two. I meant one of the two hundred other papers that come out here: the Native newspapers.' Mr Boyle (with some contempt): 'My dear fellow, those are the "talking classes", the effendis. Professional malcontents.' Oh, how strong the temptation was to whip out my journal and take notes as they spoke! But that would not have done, and so I resorted to subterfuge and took out my sketching-pad and pencils – for the scene was delightful and each person had such a different aspect – and I was able also to jot down the odd note and I have written it all out for you as a little 'scene', which I hope, together with the drawings, will give you some pleasure.

Here is the scene by the Great Pyramid with the gentlemen lolling at their ease, Mrs Butcher sitting very upright on her cushion in a neat dress of grey with navy trimming and a well-restrained bonnet; Emily is in one corner looking away from the party, and I in another with my sketching-pad poised on my knee; the native hurly-burly waits – at a distance of some yards – to erupt. These Egyptians sit (or crouch or squat) quietly for some stretch of time, and you begin to imagine that nothing can move them from their seeming placidity – until suddenly there is a murmur and there are movements and men standing up and arms waving and raised voices and then it all subsides again into quiet, the peace and the restiveness alike being incomprehensible to me. Mr S (whom I confess I do not much like for he has a superior manner which extends to everything except certain old buildings) holds forth on the subject of the 'effendis' whom he terms 'verbose jackanapes' and dislikes intensely for – as far as I can tell – their attempts to emulate us. He derides their golf collars and two-tone boots, their 'undigested' championing of European ideas of liberty and democracy. He is suspicious of their French education.

Mr S, small and thin and sallow, and HB, large and ruddy, seem to agree on all things; each picks up where the other leaves off. HB holds that the people who matter in Egypt are the fellaheen and for them the British have brought nothing but good. You can see him in the drawing with his drooping moustache, his untidy jacket, and his dog Toti, who goes with him everywhere but is so old that he has to be carried. You see the white and blue

97

striped bonnet on Toti's head to protect him from the sun? HB put it on him most solicitously and fed him morsels from the picnic. Meanwhile he describes how the Lord abolished the corvé, the courbash and the bastinado and how the fellah can now stand up to the Pasha and say, 'You cannot whip me for I shall tell the English.' Mr Barrington looks doubtful at this, but he is very gentle and not given to contradicting people – particularly people with strong opinions. You can see, I hope, the gentleness (I would not call it exactly weakness) of his face – and indeed his stance – in my drawing. He wears a suit of fine linen and an elegant cravat in pale lavender. It is he who insists on extracting a portion of food from the picnic and hands it to his manservant Sabir, who he has assured me is utterly devoted and loyal (and indeed they seem to have a regard for each other that I have not seen in other members of the Agency and their servants), to share among the waiting natives. HB concludes that the effendis are not real Egyptians and their opinions can therefore be safely neglected. Mr S, however, will go further: there is no such thing as an Egyptian, he avows: it is only the Copts who can lay claim to being descendants of the Ancients, and they are few and without influence. For all the Mohammedans, they are Arabs and are to be found in Egypt through relatively recent historical circumstance. Mrs Butcher remonstrates: the Ancient Egyptians, she believes, were of so definite, so vivid a character that traces of that character cannot be completely lost to the Egyptians of today. Mrs Butcher's gentleness of manner rather hoodwinks those who do not know her well and Mr S cuts across her with 'Not lost, ma'am, degraded. Completely degraded.' That is a term which I have often heard used to describe the Egyptian character. It is supported by a disquisition (which Mr S now proceeds to set forth) on their subscribing to a system of Baksheesh, their propensity to falsehood, their ability to bend with the wind. Even the Khedive exhibits these traits – and that is why Lord Cromer will not deal with him. Mr Rodd comes to the defence of His Highness, who, he pleads, being educated in Austria and ascending the Throne at eighteen, had princely notions beyond his station and found the heavy hand of the Lord hard to bear.

And yet I wonder whether it is possible for a conquering ruler to truly see into the character of the people whom he rules. How well, in fact, I found myself wondering, do I know Emily? We are both English, we have shared a life for some twenty years, and she is free to give me one month's notice and find another job. Yet I look at her keeping her distance and pinching herself to a little space on the rug, and I imagine her transported into a small cottage somewhere – a cottage that is hers, with an independent livelihood, however small, and perhaps her own children around her, and I fancy I see her bloom and open into more vivid life – but I digress again.

Mr Y, who is an Historian, expressed the view that the Egyptians do indeed have a National Character, but that they are not yet aware of it. He called on the movement of Urabi Pasha (which I have so often heard you discuss) as proof of that incipient character – but that was somewhat too metaphysical for HB, who held forth quite fervently about the economic reforms Lord Cromer's administration has effected: the cotton yield, the sanitation, the trains running on time. But I was distracted by the thought that his clothes seemed to get more and more crumpled – by their own agency, as it were, though he was engaged in nothing more strenuous than eating his lunch. Mrs Butcher – neat as a new pin – suggested that while material progress was, naturally, to be commended, our administration could be reproached for having ignored the spiritual life of the nation we govern. This was a signal for Mr Willcocks, who deplored how little was being done for education and said he did not believe we intended to leave Egypt when we had finished reforming her – or we would be doing more to educate the people that they might be able to govern themselves. He spoke with a clear conscience since as an engineer he is engaged in a task that is of benefit to the country and intends to leave when it is done, but both HB and Mr S held that it would take generations before the Natives were fit to rule themselves as they had neither integrity nor moral fibre, being too long accustomed to foreign rule – and if foreign rule was their lot, then British rule was surely to be preferred to that of the French or the Germans, who would surely

have been here if we were not. On this last, I fancy you would
agree. Mr Y, holding a strip of smoked ham to the nose of Toti,
who showed not the slightest interest in it, said mildly that we
would have to go one day and that if we did not do so of our own
accord, Egypt would do it for us. And Mr Barrington, lying back
and placing his hat over his face and his arms under his head,
said, 'George would have us think that we are a dream only: a
figment of Egypt's imagination.'

Egypt, mother of civilisation, dreaming herself through the
centuries. Dreaming us all, her children: those who stay and
work for her and complain of her, and those who leave and
yearn for her and blame her with bitterness for driving them
away. And I, in my room, home after half my life has gone
by, I read what Anna wrote to her father-in-law a hundred
years ago, and I see the English party, lunching by the
Pyramid, their Egyptian servants keeping their Egyptian
petitioners at bay. I record what she has written, and I
prepare my explanatory notes for Isabel, and I am torn. I
like Mr Young, I imagine him dark-haired and with a hint of
the ironical about his face, and I want to say to him, 'But we
knew very well that we're Egyptians. 'Urabi Basha – at the
bottom of his petition for a representative government, a
petition which so (unwarrantedly) startled your bond-holders
for their money that your Liberal government saw fit to send
in Sir Beauchamp Seymour with his ships and Sir Garnet
Wolseley with his troops to 'suppress a military revolt' –
'Urabi Basha signed himself: "Ahmad 'Urabi, the Egyptian". ' 'Ah,' he would say, 'but he only meant as distinct
from the Turks who were getting all the top jobs in the
army.' 'No,' I say, 'no, he demanded a Constitution. He was
speaking for us all.' And Harry Boyle, big and bluff and
definite, would declare I was talking nonsense. 'Are you
speaking for the fellah,' he would say, 'you with your city
ways and your foreign languages? The fellah doesn't give a
damn about a Constitution. He wants to till his land in peace
and make a living. The man in the street wants a decent place

to live and money to feed his children. Is that what he's getting now?'

Each week brings fresh news of land expropriations, of great national industries and service companies sold off to foreign investors, of Iraqi children dying and Palestinian homes demolished, fresh news of gun battles in Upper Egypt, of the names of more urban intellectuals added to the Jama'at's hit lists, of defiant young men in cages holding open Qur'ans in their hands, of raids and torture and executions. And next door but one, Algeria daily throws up her terrible examples; and when people – people like Isabel – put the question, we say no, that can't happen here, and when they ask why, we can only say: because this is Egypt.

10 March
And now I have a strange confession to make: I used to sit and listen to Sir Charles tell the story of the Bombardment and the Occupation. I used to finger the objects he had brought back with him: the silver filigree coffee-cup holder with its cup of almost transparent white porcelain, the fragment of wooden lattice work, brittle and dulled with age, the soft white velvet shawl ending in a silken fringe – I can see and feel them still. I would read the accounts of travellers; the letters of Lady Duff Gordon lay by my bed for several months. And imperceptibly, a conviction must have grown in my mind that if a creature of such little significance as myself can be said to have a destiny, that destiny bore, somehow, a connection to Egypt. I cannot claim that the thought formed itself in my mind with any clarity, but I know that when the conversation at the dinner table or in the drawing room turned to this country, my interest would quicken and I would listen with more than my usual attention. And when, during the illness of my dear Edward, and ordered by Mr Winthrop to take the air for an hour each day, my feet led me to the South Kensington Museum and I found those wonderful paintings by Frederick Lewis, I had, I believe, some sense of divine ordina-tion. For it seemed as though those paintings had been placed there to cheer me and give me succour. As though they were there

to remind me of Our Lord's bounty and to say to me that the world can yet be a place full of light and life and colour. And when the day came and it was deemed proper that I should travel – with the hope that distance and time and fresh and novel sights would restore me to that healthy appetite without which we are incapable of being sensible to the wonderful gift of life – it seemed the most natural thing in the world that my thoughts would turn to Egypt.

And yet – I sit here in my room at Shepheard's Hotel possessed by the strangest feeling that still I am not in Egypt. I have sat on the Pyramid plateau and my eyes have wandered from the lucid blue of the sky through the blanched yellow of the desert to the dark, promising green of the fields. I have marvelled at the lines between blue and yellow and then again between yellow and green – lines drawn as though by design. I have climbed the Pyramids and danced at the Khedive's Ball. I have visited the Bazaar and the Churches and the Mosques and witnessed the processions of the Religious Orders and played croquet at the Club at Ghezirah. I know a few words of the language and I can mark many streets by the houses of people with whom I am now acquainted, but there is something at the heart of it all which eludes me – something – an intimation of which I felt in the paintings, the conversations in England, and which, now that I am here, seems far, far from my grasp.

10

They said the stolen one was hidden
Inside a fortress grey and strong
They said the nights were monsters. Monsters,
And in every corner danger lurked.

Sabreen, 1997

Cairo, May 1997

And with that the big green journal falls silent. Or, more accurately, the next entry is dated 23 May 1901. With mounting anxiety I search through the papers, through the letters; she cannot vanish like this, disappear from my view for seventy-four days. I go back to the trunk. Is there something I have missed? And yet, why should I expect the story to be complete? Across a century and across two continents, this trunk has found me. I had not known of its existence. I had not known I had a cousin. What had I known? Nothing. The bare facts. That Lady Anna had a daughter who had married a Frenchman named Chirol. That Chirol was not keen on his wife's Egyptian connection and so, when Anna died and when Layla, my grandmother, died, the two branches of our family were severed. I had not even known that Isabel existed. And now here she is, in Cairo. And in love – although she has not said so – with my brother. When we sit and talk on my balcony we are – if I let myself be fanciful – soothing the wounds of our ancestors. But I still want the story. I empty the trunk, carefully, slowly, item by item, and there, among the tissue paper, the fabrics, the glass, is a small blue book. A prayer book, I had thought, and put it to one side. Now I try to draw it out of its leather case but it will not come out. Patience, I tell myself, patience. Under the light of the desk lamp I see the keyhole, cunningly disguised in the embossed gold decoration, and instantly I reach out for the locket lying on my dressing table and press its spring and Anna's mother smiles out at me. I ease the small key from the belly of the locket's concave lid.

12 March at 5.15 p.m.
My thoughts run mainly on my friends at the Agency and how I should prevent any word of this episode ever reaching their ears. As to consciousness of danger, I can truthfully say I have had none, nor do I have any now. Any fear I might feel is conjured up more by the imagined visage of Lord Cromer than by the actual circumstances in which I find myself. I know that he will blame Mr Barrington most severely for encouraging my foolishness, and will probably insist on his dismissing poor Sabir and that will make him most unhappy. Sabir will also be deprived of both his protector and his income. I am determined not to let this happen. For myself, the thought that holds most terror for me now is to become known in London as 'that Lady Anna Winterbourne who was abducted by the Arabs'. Even now I can see a mama bending into her daughter's ear as I pass them on my way to the Park or the Museum, the child ceasing from play and following me with wondering eyes –

I had thought to start this journal in circumstances varying to a degree from those of my ordinary days – to what degree, however, I had no way of knowing, nor could I have foretold –

I set out today, as I have set out before – my plans were more ambitious, it is true, but it was not the scope of their ambition that proved their undoing. For we had not yet ventured into the desert but were barely out of the old religious quarter of Azhar and heading North and East towards the tombs of the Mamelukes when we were set upon, dragged off our horses, bundled into a closed carriage and brought here at a canter.

I write 'here', but I do not know where 'here' is. I know we are roughly twenty minutes' ride from the old Quarter, but I could not say in which direction, for the curtains were drawn close and two young Egyptian men sat facing me.

I do not know if it was they who so man-handled us off our mounts, for there was much commotion and a cloth was thrown over my head and I was only able to remove it when we were secure in the carriage. These youths could not have been far into their twenties, perhaps younger, and were remarkably similar in appearance, both being of slight build and pale complexion, with dark eyes and well-trimmed moustaches. I wondered if they might be brothers. One seemed more agitated than the other and repeatedly pushed aside the curtains by a fraction to peep cautiously outside. Sabir, who from the first has been a most conscientious, though unwilling, companion – and who would not leave my side for a moment even though, I think, the young men offered him his freedom – remonstrated with them constantly, and through his stream of Arabic I made out several times the word 'el-Lord', to which they responded with sardonic smiles.

Their first action, upon our being seated in the carriage, was to draw out clean white handkerchiefs from their breast pockets and mop their faces and their brows. Eventually one, the slightly older and more composed of the two, delivered an address to me in perfect French in which he assured me that they were neither robbers nor brigands, that their actions were prompted by political motives, and that my person, possessions and horses were safe and would be returned to me as soon as their demands were met by the Egyptian Government. I, being anxious both to conceal my true identity – or at least my feminine identity – and to preserve the dignity of the British Gentleman I was pretending to be, sat bolt upright, kept my eyes straight ahead and uttered not a word.

I imagine he thought I could not understand him. It was a pity for I was most curious; it was, after all, the first time I have ever been spoken to by one of the 'effendis' – and I do see Mr Boyle's point: these young men seem quite different from the Arab servants and donkey-boys one is used to dealing with. They are more like the gentlemen I observed at the Khedive's Ball, but younger and not so grand – only I do not know that they should be considered less Egyptian for that; they spoke to Sabir in the native Arabic and they did not seem to have any difficulty understanding one another. It was a great pity that I was not able to converse with them, and find out the nature of their grievance, and how they thought this wild action would bring them closer to redress. Is this event the reason I felt Fate draw me to Egypt? How odd it would be if – through me – the Egyptians got their longed-for Constitution. But I am not important enough, nor will this affair reach that proportion, for I do believe that once they have found out that I am a woman and a mere visitor, they will send me on my way with courtly apologies.

I look at my last sentence and try to fathom what basis I have for this belief. At the Agency certainly they do not believe an Englishwoman should go about unchaperoned. But I have never heard of any harm befalling a lady travelling alone – and I cannot help feeling that the letters of Lady Duff Gordon give a truer glimpse into the Native mind than do all the speeches of the gentlemen of Chancery.

And yet, I had thought it safer to go abroad as a man – I would attract less attention. I had heard of a young lady who had got herself up as a syce and run barefoot before the cavalry drag to a fancy-dress ball at Ghezirah. And how this same lady decided to ride across the desert to Suez, and Lord Cromer, hearing of this, and sending a party of coast-guards on camels to pursue her, had received a report that the only person they had found was a youth on horseback. And though I did not fancy running barefoot in the streets of Cairo, dressing as a man to go on an expedition did not seem so outlandish – it is said that Lady Anne Blunt does it and other ladies besides. And I had prevailed upon James Barrington to give up his trusted Sabir to me for a few days –

For the moment, though, I sit on a wooden bench with my valise at my side and a small spirit-lamp for light. If one could live on grain and seeds alone I believe I could survive in this vaulted room for the best part of a decade.

We alighted from the carriage in a vast walled courtyard. I heard clangings and rattlings, a great door in a wall swung open and I was hurried in, a hand at my arm just above the elbow. I caught a glimpse of a pleasant inner courtyard opening to my left *but I was turned right into a smaller, paved yard and thence into this room, which seemed to be one of many ranged around that yard. It is a middling high room, built of stone, with slit windows high up near the vaulted roof and a stone-flagged floor, and the most part of it is taken up with wheat and grain, tied into hessian sacks and piled to the height of a man.*

I think we must be in some great warehouse by the river.

7.30 p.m.
I have told Sabir, who has been sitting on the floor by the wall utterly dejected, that it would be best if he informed our captors of my true character, for I feel certain that in their eyes this will entitle me to some privileges – at the least to a bathroom and some hot water, and at the best to a more speedy release. I believe he is speaking to them now.

9.30 p.m.
Sabir returned with much shaking of the head and muttering, and from what I could make out, his revelations seem only to have made matters worse and put an end to any possibility of our being released tonight. However, he had gained permission to show me to a small cubicle, where I found a jug of cold water and made myself as clean and comfortable as I could. He then brought me to this new chamber and placed in front of me some bread and milk.

Well, they would not feed me if they intended to do me harm. Oh, how I wish I knew where I was, and how I wish it were light! For this is a room of noble proportions. I have travelled around it with my little lamp and found high windows and recessed divans, rich hangings and a tiled floor leading with dainty steps to a shallow pool, and I feel, rather than see, the presence of colour and pattern. But it is all so dark and Sabir is so unhappy and I am now so sensible of exhaustion that I can do no more than choose one of the divans, lie on it and hope, eventually, to fall into a restoring sleep.

It is, I believe, a stroke of good fortune that, since both Emily and Mr Barrington know that I am intent on an expedition of several days, it will be some time before the alarm is raised. It may be possible, if our release is secured in good time, to prevent this matter ever becoming public knowledge – and to prevent the wrath of the Lord being visited on Mr Barrington and poor Sabir, who has made me come to the door and shown me how he proposes to sleep in the corridor, stretched across the threshold for my protection.

She is so calm. I did not have Anna down as an Intrepid. But there is no note of panic here. I cannot help thinking that when she chose to step off the well-trodden paths of expatriate life, Anna must have secretly wanted something out of the ordinary to happen to her. And now it had. But Sabir had not wanted any of it. I imagine him, plunged in misery. The expedition he had been forced to go on in the first place has gone horribly wrong. The effendis outside refuse to put their minds in their heads and fear God. And his charge, this Englishwoman, kidnapped and locked into a storeroom, what does she do? She sits down and opens a book. At first he had thought she was trying to comfort herself by reading the Bible. But then she started writing. *Writing!* The daughter of the madwoman! Truly they must be made of a different dough –

Anna does indeed fall asleep. Not so the young men, who are thrown into horrified confusion by the discovery that the young British gentleman they have kidnapped is a woman. They must have deliberated, discussed, even argued. They could not let her go, it would be foolishness, she would go straight to the Agency and the repercussions would be terrible. But they dare not simply keep her in their custody for a whole night. Yet what other course is open to them? And in the morning – if the morning should ever come – what will they do? They cannot advertise the kidnapping, send their demands to the Ministry of Justice as they had planned – their hostage is worthless to them now, for they can never say 'we are holding a woman'. At last, they send a messenger (ride quickly but without arousing suspicion) – they send a messenger to a house in the fashionable district of Hilmiyya, and if he should not find the Basha at home, he should go to his sister's house for he might be there. And he is to speak with no one, *no one* except the Basha or the Hanim, his sister, and tell them what has happened.

The messenger rides off into the night. The young men pace the floor. Sabir says his prayers and stretches out on the floor. Anna sleeps.

And now it is time to turn to yet another narrative: the sixty-four pages covered in close ruq'a script in black ink. I have seen some of my grandmother's Arabic writings before: scraps of verse, sections of articles. I have read her words and taken pleasure in the elegance of her hand and her mind. I ease the grey volume open, and place a paperweight at the corner of the page to pin it down – a small, bronze Pharaonic cat that my youngest son used to take such delight in and that we bought together one sunny afternoon at the museum in Tahrir Square. I start to translate my grandmother's words for Isabel:

WHEN I FIRST SAW HER she was still dressed in the clothes of a man. I saw a man lying on the diwan, curled up on himself, his hat placed so that it covered his face and hair. And even though they had told me the whole story and how they had snatched an Englishman, then found out he was a woman – even though I knew that was the essence of the problem – it still felt strange to come upon an Englishman asleep in my mother's haramlek, and I felt so ill at ease that I turned and went back out of the door and nearly banged into the manservant who must have been standing very close behind it and now leaped away looking even more miserable than he had when I first arrived. I pushed the door to and looked at him.

'Are you sure?' I asked.

'Sure of what, ya Sett Hanim?' His eyes on the floor just in front of my feet.

'Sure that what's inside there is a woman?'

'Of course I'm sure, ya Sett Hanim: a woman and an

Englishwoman and an important woman as well. My Ingelisi holds her very dear. He says her father has done him great favours and their house in England is very grand and now we've fallen into this catastrophe and how will we get out of it?'

'May God protect us,' was all I could say. I took him out on the open terrace and sat down and pointed to a spot on the floor. 'Sit down,' I said, 'and tell me everything you know.'

'I swear by God I don't know anything. By the head of our master –'

'Tell me what you know about her.'

'An Englishwoman. Her name is Lady Anna – Sett Anna, it means. She came here two or three months ago and my Ingelisi knows her and knows her people and he said look after her like your eyes – my Ingelisi speaks Arabic and he said look after her like your eyes. I looked after her – but a lady like that, her father is a good man and her people are good people, what's the need to dress in disguise and make problems? He said she wants to know your country and movement is always difficult for a woman –'

'So you've done this before?'

'Twice. Twice only, I swear by our Lord. Once we went up el-Darb el-Ahmar and she went into the old mosques, the antiquities, and once we went on the tram to the pyramids –'

'And no one suspected you?'

'Never. She rides like a man: donkeys, mules, horses, anything – and I tell people an Ingelisi who can't speak –'

'Can't speak?'

'Her voice, you'll pardon me, the voice of a woman, what can we do about that? I tell them he fell on his head and lost the power of speech. They say, may God cure him. Like this also if anyone sees the bandages under the hat –'

'She bandages her hair.'

'There's light upon you.'

'And this time, where were you going?'

'She wanted to go to Deir Sant Katrin.'

'To Sinai?' I could not hide my astonishment.

'But first she wanted to sit in the coffee shops and listen to the storytellers. I said to him – to my Ingelisi – what will she get out of this? Stories and songs in Arabic and she only knows – you'll excuse me – two words. He said, She's put it in her head to go. I said, We get her the storytellers here. She sits like this in the garden like their queen – God have mercy on her soul now – and we get her the storytellers and she can choose what she wants to hear, she can listen to Abuzeid, listen to 'Antar, listen to a mawwal and make of it what she can; he said no, she wants to listen in a coffee shop. And now we've gone and what's happened has happened and what shall we do now, ya Sett Hanim?'

I took off my shoes and habara and sat on the other diwan, across the room from her, with my mind going round and round and not ending except on 'May God protect us all'. The only hope I had was that my brother was due back the next day. What he would do I did not know, but he was my only hope. He had gone to take our mother to Tawasi in Minya to visit her brother and her lands, and he would come back to find, instead of one disaster, two: Husni, my husband, in jail and this English-woman in our father's house.

I contemplated the sleeping figure: in the dark I could make nothing of her except that her build was slight and that she slept very peacefully; she had not moved a hand or a foot. I went to my mother's room and fetched a woollen shawl which I spread over her. I said, The most important thing is when she wakes to make her feel safe and comfortable until my brother arrives to advise us. I sent orders to the young men that they should stay in the shrine with my father. They could not stay in the house, but I did not trust them not to get up to more foolishness if I let them go. I arranged some cushions for myself, covered myself with my habara, loosened my hair, and lay down with prayers in my mind for my husband and for us all.

11

The years like great black oxen tread the world
And God the herdsman goads them on behind,
And I am broken by their passing feet.

W. B. Yeats

Cairo, 29 June 1997

Sleep did not come easily to me last night. I came back from my night on the town with Isabel, kicked off my shoes, undressed, had a cool shower and found I had no wish whatsoever to go to bed. In the living room I switched on the television and the unmistakable voice of Umm Kulthum swelled into the room: there she was in black and white, her head thrown back, her hair swept up in the trademark chignon. I fixed myself a drink with lots of ice and sat out on the dark balcony, listening. 'Nazra – a glance I thought was a greeting/and would quickly pass . . .' I could see into the lit-up living room of my neighbours across the street: father, mother and grown-up children sat in a semicircle, the television hidden from my view catching their outlines in its flickering blue light. 'Nazra.' El-Sett lingers and lingers on the 'n'. Her voice rises and falls and trembles and sways with the one consonant. When she finally completes the word 'nazra', the audience roars. Down below, the young men sit on the cars. An aeroplane drifts lazily through the sky. Something has come back to me. Some sense of – possibility. I look down at my hands: one of them is gently stroking the other.

Whatever it is, it's very tentative and perhaps best left in the dark for a while. Maybe it will grow. A glance I thought was a greeting/And would quickly pass/But in it were promises/and vows/and wounds and pain –

Sucking on my last piece of ice, I switch off the television and go to my bedroom. I look through the last pages I've written and I am tempted to sit down and continue, but my eyes hurt and I know it would be unwise. I get into my bed and lie there, under a cotton sheet, thinking about my grandmother – or, rather, following a chain of thoughts set off by the thought of my grandmother. That March night in 1901, when she snatched up her habara and ran into her carriage and entered the haramlek of the old house and saw Anna for the first time, she would have been in her twenty-seventh year and married to my grandfather, Husni al-Ghamrawi, her maternal cousin: a radical, French-educated young lawyer and a fully paid-up member of Lord Cromer's 'talking classes'. My father would have been one year old. Headed for the Walida school, then the Khediwiyya, then the Military Academy and later the Cavalry Division. He met my mother, Maryam al-Khalidi, during a visit to our cousins in 'Ein al-Mansi in Palestine, and married her in a splendid Jerusalem wedding in 1935. My brother was born in 1942 in the Khalidis' big house in West Jerusalem which I have only ever seen in photographs, although I know it is still standing. When the war ended and the threat to my mother's homeland became clear to everyone, my father resigned from the army and led a volunteer battalion into Palestine. He fought in Birsheeba, al-Khalil and Bethlehem. After the disaster of '48, when families and communities dispersed across the globe, and my mother was among the thirty thousand Arabs who lost their homes to the State of Israel, my father brought her and their son to Egypt, retired from the army and settled on his land in Tawasi. I was born there, in the house on the farm, in the year of Nasser's revolution. There should have been two more of us, whether sisters or brothers I don't know. But my mother had miscarried of them both, one in '45 and the other in '47. I think of them sometimes. I used to think of them more while my mother was alive – on her behalf, really, wondering whether it would have made her lot any

117

better to have more children around her after my father died and she and I were left alone. They had sent my brother to Eisenhower's America in '56. They might have sent him to Russia, for the music there was just as good – maybe better. But he spoke English, and America had just stopped Britain, France and Israel bombing Suez and Port Said, so they sent him to America and he stayed. Not through any particular decision, but step by step: college, the Philharmonic, the almost instantly successful career. He had come to us from time to time to visit, and he had performed in Cairo. When I was thirteen, on his last visit before my father died, he played for us in Hilmiyya, on the old piano that had always stood in the house and that was always kept tuned although no one used it between my brother's visits. I remember my father settling down to listen, his eyes soft with pride, but when I glanced at him later I thought I saw something like regret move across his face. I wondered then how much my father missed him and whether he found it strange that his son's life was firmly anchored there: in New York.

She had wanted to go home, my mother. I only realised that towards the end. She had spoken about it, of course, about Palestine: her school, her friends, her mother's room rich with tapestries, her father's library, the theatre, the park on the Jaffa Road where the municipal band played in the afternoons, the picnics at the olive groves in the harvest season, the house filled with the sweet smell of newly pressed oil, the jars full of the thick, luminous liquid. And I had listened, I suppose, first as children do, storing up the images, then later with adolescent cynicism to those tales of an earthly paradise where everything was always as it should be. But it was only in '67, after the war, when our world was filled with the voice of Fayruz lamenting the fall of Jerusalem 'of the light-filled houses, flower of all cities' and my mother embarrassed me by suddenly breaking out in sobs with a bar of Nabulsi soap pressed to her nose at the grocer's, that I realised she was homesick.

I loved my mother, and I lived with her for twenty-two years, but it seems to me now that I only ever saw her dimly or in part. I wish I had listened more carefully. I wish she had left me something; a letter, perhaps, written on a quiet evening, when I was out and she was alone. A letter that I would read when I was older, and more able to understand.

It was later, much later, when the need to return was upon me and I yearned for the great, cool hall of our house in Tawasi, for the smell of the fields and the black, starry night of the countryside before the High Dam brought electricity to the villages – when I yearned for Cairo, for Abu el-'Ela bridge, for the feel of the dust gritty under my fingers as I trailed my hand along the iron railing, for the smell of salted fish that met you as you drew near to Fasakhani Abu el-'Ela, for the sight of fruit piled high in symmetrical pyramids outside a greengrocer's shop and the twist of the brown paper bag in which you carry the fruit home, when I yearned even for the khamaseen winds that make you cover your face against the dust and with bowed head hurry quickly home – it was only then that I understood how longing for a place can take you over so that you can do nothing except return, as I did, return and pick at the city, scraping together bits of the place you once knew. But what do you do if you can never return?

My mother died. Just as I finished university, she died. And I went abroad.

And then came back to piece together what I could of the Cairo where I had grown up. A flyover squats over Abu el-'Ela bridge and renders it obsolete. They're even thinking of selling it for scrap. The greengrocers still pile the fruit high but mostly they give it to you in a thin blue plastic bag and they don't throw in an extra piece 'on top of the sale'. But the salt-fish shop is still there, and the old banyan tree in Zamalek still stands, although it is so beleaguered by concrete that I cannot see where its coming tendrils can take root. I had sold the house in Hilmiyya many years before and a great concrete car park had risen in its place.

I said to Isabel, 'Come on then, let's see if we can find bits of my Cairo for you.'

In the afternoon we went to the Muʿallaqah. We listened to a guide tell a group of schoolchildren about Noah's Ark and Noah's family. The pillars supporting the pulpit, he said, are for the Disciples. They are in pairs because Christ sent them out to preach the Word in pairs. And the black pillar in the middle is because the Word came to save black and white alike. Judas Iscariot has made way for political correctness. We sat in the quiet pews and walked round the chapels and tried, once again, to get the Virgin's eyes to follow us. At the baptismal font Isabel stopped. 'Look,' she said. I looked where she pointed: a series of wavy lines.

'Water,' I said.

'The hieroglyph for water,' she said. We looked at each other in delight: another layer.

In the early evening we walked the length of Shariʿ al-Muʿizz; we ate sandwiches of clotted cream and honey off the stall by the Mosque of Sultan Qalawun. We sat in the small goldsmith's shop and watched him mend and polish a pair of earrings that had sat in their box on my dressing table for two years. We crossed Shariʿ al-Azhar and plunged into the Ghuriyya and beyond to the Khiyamiyya and bought a small green and blue tapestry and were treated to tea. We walked down Shariʿ Muhammad ʿAli and looked in the shop windows at the lutes and tambourines inlaid with mother-of-pearl, and we followed the sounds of drums and zagharid till we came upon a wedding and we joined in the clapping and the singing and the eating and had our photograph taken and the earrings made a good present for the bride, who even now must be in bed with her new husband.

They say this is the hottest month of the year, but the heat has never bothered me. I lie in my bed with the ceiling fan whirring lazily above my head and when the sheet underneath me gets hot I have the pleasure of stretching out my leg and feeling a new, cool patch under my skin. When the children come – I mean when the boys come, or one of them – we could go to the Red Sea. The days will be hot but the nights will be wonderful. We could even go down to Tawasi for a few days, then drive across from there. I did that once, with their father a long, long time ago. A time so happy that later, in my Spartan years, I came to view it almost with distaste as though its sweetness were excessive.

I did not sleep well and this morning I woke at eleven and wandered out into the living room into a day that felt heavy with indolence. I drew the shutters and sat on the arm of the sofa watching the minuscule flecks of dust suspended in each bar of sunshine that drifted through the wooden slats.

It was early afternoon when I went back to my table and opened my grandmother's and Anna's journals once again, and it was as I settled my son's bronze cat on the corner of the page that the intercom went and Tahiyya's voice warned me that 'Am Abu el-Ma'ati was here and could she bring him up?

And there is the familiar figure in his 'best' galabiyya of dark blue wool and his grey scarf despite the July heat. The white 'imma is wound tightly around the close-fitting brown felt cap and the eyes – a legacy from a Turkish seigneur some-where down the years – are as shocking blue and bright as ever. He stands leaning on his old, thick stick, a little stooped, but still tall and solid. You expect him to open his mouth and utter prophecies. When I shake his hand it is like holding the bark of a tree. Behind him, Tahiyya is bringing the covered baskets out of the lift one by one.

We sit in the living room and Tahiyya goes to make tea, picking her way gracefully through the baskets arranged on the kitchen floor.

'Cairo is filled with light,' I say. And he places his hand on his heart:

'It's lit up by its people, ya Sett Hanim.'

We sit in silence for a while, our eyes fixed on the floor.

'A precious step, 'Am Abu el–Ma'ati,' I say.

'May He make your standing ever more precious, ya Sett Hanim,' he says.

'Am Abu el–Ma'ati is getting old. With every passing year the network of wrinkles on the brown face becomes a more detailed etching of the times he has lived through. I don't know his age, of course, but he's been around for ever. His father was my father's chief man on the farm, and when my mother and I moved to Cairo 'Am Abu el–Ma'ati came up to see us four times a year. He brought news, the accounts and our share of the produce: baskets of chicken, eggs, butter and grapes, mangoes, dates, whatever fruit was in season. And always loaves of freshly baked peasant bread. And when, from time to time, we went to Minya, there he would be at the train station, waiting with the parasol to shade us into the small carriage and drive us to Tawasi.

A month after I came back for good he was on my doorstep, and around him the baskets, looking just as they had twenty years before: each one crammed with food and covered with a large white napkin, its striped blue edges wedged in tight at the sides. When I had asked how he'd known I was back, he had smiled and said, 'It's a small world, ya Sett Hanim.'

Tahiyya brings in the tea and I make her sit with us. Our village is not her village, but it's a village after all and getting news from it makes her happy.

'What news, 'Am Abu el–Ma'ati?' I ask.

'All good, praise be to God.'

'And the family, how are they? All well, please God?'

'Am Abu el–Ma'ati has two daughters and three sons. He had four but one was killed in the war in '67. One of his sons farmed in Iraq but came back after the Gulf War with nothing except his life – and that was precious enough. Another is working in Bahrain, and the oldest is 'in the sea' with a merchant ship. The widow, wives and the youngest of the children all live in our village. His two daughters were married in Minya city itself but one has been widowed and come back to Tawasi. She works in the clinic.

'Praise be to God,' he says. Bit by bit I get the news: the births, the deaths, the arrivals, the departures, the feuds, the weddings.

After he finishes his tea and puts his glass down he says, 'Won't you come to us for a while, ya Sett Hanim?'

'I'd like to,' I begin and then I say, 'Is there something?'

'Not at all,' he says. We pause.

'It's just there are a few little things – if you came it would be good,' he says.

'What sort of things?' I ask.

'Well . . .' He draws out his handkerchief, coughs into it gently, folds it and puts it away. 'There are a few problems.'

'What sort of problems?'

'The school,' he says, 'they've closed it.'

Mustafa Bey al-Ghamrawi, my great-grandfather, was a firm believer in education. In 1906 he had been the first to put up money for the new National University, and, together with his nephew Sharif Basha al-Baroudi, he had set up a small school in a village on the family land and put the revenue of ten faddans in trust for it. His son, my grandfather Husni al-Ghamrawi, had added an adult class to teach the fallaheen to read and write. My father, Ahmad al-Ghamrawi, had in turn added a small, basic clinic, staffed by a nurse and a midwife – and now by 'Am Abu el-Ma'ati's daughter. When Abd el-Nasser built a primary school for the village, our school held literacy classes for the adults. And in '79 extra classes were added for the children to try to make up for the plummeting level of the education they were getting.

'Closed it? Who closed it?' I ask.

The school has been running for ninety years, although it's had rough patches. In '63, with Nasser's land-reform laws, my father, although saddened by the loss of most of his land, saw a historical inevitability in it. My mother raged: 'What more should we lose? Will we be thrown out of this country as well?' 'It's different,' he said, 'it's going to the fallaheen who've lived on it all their lives – not to strangers. And besides,' he added, 'what's left will be enough for our children and grandchildren. What more do we need?' I was a child and did not really understand what was happening. But I understood two things: that we were always to be responsible for keeping the school and clinic going, and that the land that remained to us was held in partnership with the fallaheen who worked it. There was to be no talk of rent. We had a share of the crop that came out of each holding, and we paid our share of the money needed to buy fertilisers or update the watering machines.

'The government,' 'Am Abu el-Ma'ati says.

'But why? Why should we have problems with the government?'

We are not an official school, just two supplementary classes to help the children with their work and one class for literacy used by the women. All the classes are held in the evening, after the day's work is done. And the teachers are volunteers, really, who get paid a small sum for their work.

'There are problems everywhere now, ya Sett Hanim, problems between the people, and between the people and the government. It's been in the papers: battles with weapons, burning down the sugar-cane fields –'

'The sugar cane was burned because the terrorists hid in it.'

'They call them terrorists . . .'

'Well, what are they then?'

'They're our children, ya Sett Hanim. Youth ground down and easy to lead astray.'

'Ya 'Am Abu el-Ma'ati, your daughter was widowed by them –'

'Lives are in the hand of God. It was a battle, ya Sett Hanim, who knows who killed who?'

'In any case. What's this to do with the school?'

'The teachers, the volunteers, they said they were terrorists and ruining the children's minds.'

'And the women's class?'

'That too.'

'And the clinic?'

'Everything.'

'La hawl illah.'

I stand up. I'm not sure what to do so I stand up. I walk over to the balcony and make a business of opening the french windows to let in the afternoon air. It has been some time since anyone presented me with a real-life problem. I walk back and sit down.

'What do you think, 'Am Abu el-Ma'ati? Were they teaching the children wrong things?'

He spreads out his hands. 'They teach them nothing that they're not taught in the government schools in town. You know, ya Sett Hanim, these are just helping classes. The children go after sunset, they do their homework there, and they study.'

'The children can't study at home,' Tahiyya puts in. 'There's noise and there's the little ones —'

'It's just tightening up on people. The government's hand is heavy. And now, of course, there will be more problems.'

'What problems?' I ask.

'Because of the new laws.'

'The land laws?'

'Naturally.'

A new set of laws is to come into force in September. It ends the rent freeze imposed on lands in the Sixties and allows landowners to demand rent according to the real value of the land.

'But what's it to do with us? The people all know I won't move anyone from the land. And rent won't be raised, because we don't take rent. Everything will stay the same.'

'May he put good in your path, pray God,' Tahiyya says.

'They say the teachers have been inciting the children. Telling them the law is evil and the land belongs to those who work it. And talk runs; it doesn't stay in our district. And you know the countryside is boiling —'

'Are they Islamists or communists, these teachers?'

'They speak of justice —'

125

'But people have known about these laws for a while. The government announced them two years ago. They wait till the last minute –'

'Ya Sett Hanim, the fallah tills his land and the government talks in Cairo. If he takes account of every word the government says, he'll go mad. Most of it is talk in the air, it comes to nothing. And even if he believes that there will be a law like this – what will he do? What *can* he do?'

'Will he put his children on his shoulder and leave the land?' Tahiyya asks. 'Where will he go? The land isn't enough for the fallaheen as it is. See how each one is flung out somewhere far: one in Cairo, one in Kuwait, one in Libya –'

'That's why the government tells people to practise family planning,' I say, giving her a look.

'Yakhti ya Daktora –' she tosses her head – 'the ones who plan have as much trouble as the ones who don't. The world doesn't leave anyone alone.'

''Am Abu el–Ma'ati,' I say, 'aside from the school, are there any problems in our village. About the land laws?'

'No, ya Sett Hanim. Everyone knows you are a gracious lady and you preserve the memory of your grandfathers. But it would be good if you came to us for a while.'

'But what can I do about the school?'

'Come and see. Talk to people. Talk with the teachers and judge for yourself. And when you come back you can talk to the government.'

'Me, ya 'Am Abu el–Ma'ati, *I* talk to the government?'

'And why not? Why shouldn't you talk to them? You're here in Cairo and the whole world knows who your father was – a thousand mercies and light upon him. Your father was a Basha – even though they abolished titles, the whole world knew he was a Basha and a man of understanding.'

'Ya 'Am Abu el–Ma'ati, I don't know anyone in the government.' I see myself going to look for 'the government'. I wouldn't know where to begin. There is a big ministry compound in Shari' el–Sheikh Rihan. I see myself going there and I am pulled up short by the memory of Mansur. Mansur was my friend and he was the car-park attendant at Shari' el-Sheikh Rihan between the American University and the ministries. For years I went to the American University to attend concerts, to see films, to use the library, to meet friends. As I crossed the intersection with Shari' el-Qasr el-'Ayni, I'd be scanning the street ahead and he would emerge, short and stocky, stockier as the years went by. There he would be, his arm uplifted, his coloured woven cap on his head. 'Leave it just. Leave it,' he would say. 'Don't worry.'

'How are you, ya Mansur?'

'How are you, ya Sett Hanim?' The keys would change hands. And later, when I came out, there he would be again, with my keys and a few courtly words, pointing out where he had parked the car. Mansur was famous. He acquired two assistants; but he was always the one who had the keys. He was the one who was always there, until one day the bomb the Jama'at meant for el-Alfi, the minister of the Interior they hated, had found Mansur instead. And now all that was left of him was a pale brown stain on the wall of the university. A stain that would not scrub off.

'I don't know anyone in the government,' I say again.

'If you can't speak to the government,' 'Am Abu el-Ma'ati asks, 'who can? Me?'

'You'd be better at it than I would be –'

'Done,' he says. 'My hand in yours. We'll go to them together.' His face breaks into a wide, clear smile and I notice the gaps between the big teeth.

'God give you light,' Tahiyya cries. 'By the Prophet, I'll make Madani go with you. To support you.'

If she lifted her hand to her mouth and trilled out a zaghruda, this would be a scene from *el-Ard*.

When 'Am Abu el-Ma'ati had gone, Tahiyya and I sat on the floor among the baskets distributing the food: some for her family, some for me, some for the men wielding the heavy irons in the steam of the ironing shop across the road, some for the policemen – boys, really – who stand all night leaning on their rifles in the shadow of the bank on the corner –

'Enough, enough, are you going to give it all away?' she protests.

'I wouldn't finish this in a year, ya Tahiyya,' I say. Time was when I cooked for four and often more. Time was when I chafed and grew fretful and said, 'I can't bear this business of having to think of supper every night.' Time was when I dreamed of all the things I could do, all the lives I could lead if I wasn't tied down, beset, beleaguered. And time was – I'm glad to say – when the clasp of small arms around my neck and the feel of a soft face against my own stilled the restlessness and made me grateful and glad for the moment.

'Tomorrow the young Beys will come to visit and fill the house for you again,' Tahiyya says, reading my thoughts.

'Inshallah,' I say.

'You know you should marry them off here,' she says. 'You rejoice in them and they stay near you.'

'Nobody marries anybody off any more,' I say.

'Truly,' she says. 'Each one acts with his own head.'

'Why don't you come with me to Minya?' I say when we've finished. 'Smell the air of the countryside?'

'And the kids, who do I leave them to?'

'Bring them.'

'And we leave Madani alone?'

'Can't he come too?'

'And the building? We leave it without a doorman? They'd fire him.'

'In any case, see. You're very welcome, all of you.'

'May you live long, ya Daktora. Another time.'

Isabel, I thought. She's going away for August. But if I go soon – as I should – she might like to come with me. See the countryside. See what's left of the old house. I imagine opening up the darkened rooms, washing down the pear tree in the near corner of the garden, sleeping in my mother's old bed. I imagine treading the old, familiar path through our orchard, into the open fields and to the village. Would it make problems, taking an American there? No, she's discreet and sensible. And who would I say she is? If I just say she's a friend, people will grow suspicious and clam up. But if she is family – we can say she's my brother's fiancée. That should amuse her. I jump up and go to the phone.

12

May you enter favoured, and leave beloved.
                Ancient Egyptian prayer

Egypt, 6 July 1997

'And so,' I said to Isabel, as we started along the Upper Egypt road, 'there they were; on the twelfth of March 1901, asleep on two diwans, facing each other on opposite sides of the haramlek drawing room of the big house of the Baroudis; these women who were to become our grandmothers.'

'You like telling stories,' Isabel said.

'Yes,' I said, 'I suppose I do. I like piecing things together.'

'Your brother must know you very well,' she said, pulling down the sun screen, peering into its small mirror to adjust her headscarf.

Yes, I suppose he does. My brother likes piecing things together too, in his own way. On the phone from the States he'd said:

'Did you like my gift?'

'It's wonderful,' I said. 'Did you look into it?'

'Only a little bit. Enough. I thought you might be interested.'

'Oh, I'm completely immersed. How much did you look at?'

'Not much.'

'But enough?'

'Enough for what?'

'Enough to know about Isabel.'

'Our long-lost cousin. Yes, I worked that out.'

'But you didn't tell her?'

'What was I supposed to do? Lift my head from the box and announce, "And here are some of *my* grandmother's papers too"? Come on —'

'Listen,' I say, 'did you look at the objects, the things?'

'No, no, I just glanced at the papers —'

'Well, there's a kind of tapestry there, a long strip of woven fabric, and I think it matches the one you've got hanging in your study.'

'What's hanging in my study?'

'A fabric. A tapestry. Pharaonic —'

'Oh, yes, yes. I know the one you mean. No? Really? You mean they're a pair?'

'I think so. I can't be sure, though. Can you bring yours with you next time you come over?'

'But it's a huge thing —'

'Come on. You can roll it up. I need to see them together.'

'But it's framed —'

'Unframe it. You've got that handyman — what's his name —'

'I'd rather pay for you to come to New York.'

'But I can't. I'm taken over by this trunk. I'm practically living inside it. When I read the journals I feel as if I'm there, a hundred years ago. I'm putting together the whole picture and I know everything that happened and wasn't written down —'

'Great. Yalla. Let your imagination run away with you.'

My grandmother had received the message, sensed the danger there was to her husband from the day's events, thrown on her habara, got into her carriage and driven to her mother's house, leaving her baby behind — with a houseful of nannies and maids, I imagine. Her entry is undated, and I believe she wrote down the entire story later, as a record and a testimony. Not so Anna, who wrote in her journal at the end of every day, and sometimes in the middle.

13 March

I woke up from what must have been a deep and peaceful slumber and my first thought on waking was that I had slipped into one of those paintings the contemplation of which had given me such rare moments of serenity during the illness of my dear Edward. There above me was the intricate dark wooden lattice-work and beyond it a most benevolent, clear blue sky. I stretched and found that I was covered with a large woollen shawl in a subtle grey with a thousand small pink rosebuds strewn over it in delicate embroidery. A moment later my circumstances and the fact of my captivity came flooding back into my consciousness and jolted me out of my indolence and I rose to a sitting position with – I believe – the intention of trying the door of the chamber to see whether it was locked. But as I sat up, my altered perspective brought me once again into the world of those beloved paintings, for there, across the room, and on a divan similar to mine, a woman lay sleeping. She had not been there the night before, of that I was certain for I had gone all round the room with my lamp and was assured of my solitude. She must have come in while I slept. I wondered who she was and whether she was the owner of this house I found myself in. She was Egyptian, and a lady – the first I had seen without the black cloak and the veil. She had pulled a cover of black silk up to her waist, her chemise above that was the purest white, and then again, her hair vied with the silken cover for the depth and lustre of its black. Her skin was the colour of gently toasted chestnut, and she lay on cushions of deep emerald and blue, and the whole tableau was framed, yet again, by the lattice of a mashrabiyya. That she was something to do with the young men who had brought me here I felt I could be certain of. But what? What had she to do with my abduction? I had been abducted as a man and in the Oriental tales I have read it has happened that a Houri or a princess has ordered the abduction of a young man to whom she has taken a fancy. She would have him brought to her castle beyond the Mountains of the Moon, and there she would offer him marriage. And if he doffed his disguise and was revealed to be a woman? Why, they would fall laughing into each other's arms and become sworn sisters from then on.

My bandages had become entangled in my hair and I was sure I presented a sorry sight. I worked my hair free and brushed it through with my fingers. I decided that – whoever this Houri was – it must be she who had with such consideration covered me as I slept, and the feeling that I had the night before that I was somehow in safe hands in this house entered my heart again, and this time it did not seem so unreasonable.

I OPENED MY EYES AND found her looking at me. A beautiful European woman, her hair flowing to her shoulders in free golden waves, the bandages it had been tied up in last night fallen in an untidy heap to the floor. Her white shirt was open at the neck, and she sat with her arms crossed in the lap of the brown riding trousers, her feet steady on the floor in their heavy brown boots. I turned on my side to be more comfortable, smiled into her serious face and wished her good morning in Arabic. She repeated my greeting instead of responding to it and when I asked if she spoke Arabic she shook her head with a small apologetic smile. I pointed at myself, said 'English' and shook my head too. We gazed at one another, then I said 'Vous parlez Français?' and her face was lit up by a wide smile of relief.

'Oui, oui,' she said eagerly. 'Et vous aussi, madame?' She tilted her head slightly to one side, waiting for my answer.

'I have lived in Paris for a while with my husband.'

'Ah, this is most fortunate,' she cried, clasping her hands together – and so we started, in this strange situation in which we found ourselves, to pull at the edges of conversation and to weave the beginnings of our friendship.

I explained to her the circumstances of her abduction and apologised for it most fervently. I said that I would wish to set her free upon the instant but that the two young hot-heads pacing outside – her abductors – were completely opposed to this, that I thought their prevailing motive now was fear, and that I had sent word to my brother's house that he should come here as soon as he could. I assured her that upon his arrival this situation would be ended and I promised her that no harm whatsoever would come to her or her servant.

What I find important to record here is that no mark of fear ever showed itself upon her. In fact, I was surprised that it did not seem that her first interest was the regaining of her liberty. She was completely natural in her looks and behaviour and so interested in her own abduction – in the events that had led up to it, in the house in which she found herself, in my opinions with regard to the whole event – that I found myself quite forgetting that she was a stranger. And what a stranger: the British Army of Occupation was in the streets and in the Qasr el-Nil Barracks, and the Lord was breakfasting in Qasr el-Dubara. Because of them my uncle had been banished and my father cloistered in his shrine these eighteen years and now my husband was in jail. And here I sat with one of their women, dressed in the clothes of a man, snatched in the night by my husband's friends and imprisoned in my father's house – and we sat in my mother's reception room and felt our way towards each other as though our ignorance, one of the other, were the one thing in the world that stood between us and friendship.

During this first meeting, it was she who was the more curious and the more full of questions, and it was easy to talk to her; her mind was quick, her sympathy was ready. I told her the stories of our family and she asked about the details and I felt she wove each one into a picture in her head and by the time, just after sunset, when I heard the noise of the carriage wheels and general commotion that signalled my brother's arrival, I had learned too of her mother's early death, her father's saddened life, her mar-

136

riage and the circumstances of her widowhood and her great regard for Sir Charles, the father of her departed husband, may God's mercy be upon him. I had learned of Egypt's attraction for her and formed an idea of the life she had lived since she had come here. She spoke simply and with sincerity and when she turned to the window, her eyes, which seemed oddly dark with all that golden hair, took your breath away with their deep violet light.

I had stumbled – no, I had been abducted into a house I did not know – an event I did not understand. Presently, however, the fair occupier of the opposite divan awoke and, with a smile, bade me good morning in her native tongue. She soon revealed herself, after some dumb-show, to be as reasonably well-versed in French as I and, this being established, she was much at pains to put me at my ease and was clearly relieved that I did not fall to fainting or screaming, but in truth I did not feel I had need of such stratagems – abhorrent to me by nature in any case. For it seemed so odd just to sit there – in one of my beloved paintings, as it were, or one of the Nights of Edward Lane. I took the same pleasure in my gentle jailer that I would have done from those: her appearance, the formal courtesy of her gestures, the melodious intonation of her voice – I had the oddest sense that I had seen her before. And she seemed so utterly unaware of her charm; she gathered her silk robes together with such simplicity and pushed her small foot into a dainty gold-brocaded slipper as though it were the most natural thing in the world. She called for a breakfast of clotted cream and honey and served me with winning gestures; but then the tale she told was not out of the mediaeval East but very much of our times. Her name is Layla al-Baroudi, she has been married for five years to her cousin (the son of her mother's brother), a young lawyer by the name of Husni al-Ghamrawi (it appears that a woman here does not take her husband's name upon marriage. Layla did not seem to see any necessity for this. 'Why would I leave my name?' she asked. 'When it is suitable, I am Madame Ghamrawi, but I am always Layla al-Baroudi') and they have a son, Ahmad, who is one

*year old. Her husband studied law in Paris for a year and she
accompanied him there and made it her business to learn French.
On the circumstances in which we found ourselves, she tried to
explain to me their cause, but I asked so many questions, and she
was a teacher of such wakeful conscience, that we found ourselves
roaming through the entire nineteenth century and into Turkey
and Europe and Japan and Suez, and I understood that even
with what I already know about this country there was much that
I did not know and perhaps might never learn.*

*Of my abductors, I learned that they belonged to a group of
young Radicals who wished to retaliate for the jailing of my
hostess' husband (during a peaceful demonstration) by holding
an Englishman hostage, and that she did not like their methods,
and she was sure both her husband and her brother would take
her view.*

*I believe that the procession that had held up our carriage on
our way to Abdin Palace, and that we had taken for a celebration
of some kind, was in reality that demonstration.*

'THEY'VE GOT ONE OF OURS, we got one of theirs.'

As I hurried down the corridor, I heard Ibrahim's voice,
the younger of the two, pretending he did not care,
pretending to be nonchalant.

'They *arrested* one of ours, we *abducted* one of theirs.'

My brother's voice was precise and clipped. I stood
behind the mashrabiyya, looking down into the entrance
hall: he was in the formal dress of the Council and had not
even taken off his tarbush yet. I knew my brother; he was
angry, but he was trying to be reasonable. Ibrahim spoke
again:

'What difference does it make? At all events we were
only trying to secure –'

'It makes a big difference. They acted within the law
and you acted outside it. You want to secure a fair trial for
Husni Bey? You want to ensure due process of law – by
breaking the law?'

'Ya Basha, the law serves the English.'

'The law serves no one. The law may be bent – or got around – but if we wish the English to respect our law we cannot suddenly put it to one side and say, but this time we will act without reference to it.'

'They occupied our lands through violence and they won't leave except through violence –'

And now my brother no longer hid his anger. He turned full towards the younger man and his voice dropped and a new and menacing note came into it:

'Are you going to make a patriotic speech, ya Ibrahim, here in my house? Have you forgotten who you're speaking to? And what is it you are defending? If even an abduction you were not up to? You want to snatch someone, snatch an officer – or at least a soldier, not a woman who's come to look at the pyramids and go away!'

Ibrahim and the other young man with him, the one I did not know, looked down at the floor. 'We did not realise,' the other young man muttered.

'And how dare you bring her here? You carry out an abduction and bring the person here? To my family's home? Without my knowledge?'

'It was a mistake,' the young man muttered.

'A mistake that you have to put right. Now.'

'We shall put it right, ya Basha.'

'Good. What do you propose to do?'

The two young men looked briefly at each other.

'We are waiting for your opinion, ya Basha,' the younger one said.

'My opinion is that you should go and hand yourselves in – and take her with you. Return her to her Agency and surrender yourselves to the police.'

The two young men glanced at each other again.

'Ya Basha, it would be an honour to die or to be banished in the cause of one's country . . .' Ibrahim hesitated.

'Yes?' prompted my brother.

'But to be jailed for years for an act without consequence – an act that made no difference – what heroism is there in that?'

My brother turned away. He paced the hall, his prayer beads hanging from the hands clasped loosely behind his back. He paced the width of the room two, three, four times. When he stopped and spoke, it was in a gentler voice.

'What I want you to understand,' he said, 'is that abducting – or in any way harming – ordinary people is never an act of heroism. It is wrong. And it has repercussions. This is not the way we want to go. It goes in the balance against everything we have tried to do over the last eighteen years. What the British want is to accuse us of fanaticism. If we give them reason, we lose out.'

'Your history is well known, ya Basha,' Ibrahim and his friend muttered in respectful voices.

'And I don't want it jeopardised. Understood?' my brother said.

I waited, and presently Layla – with what friendly ease that name comes to me already – reappeared. She slipped into the room, closed the door behind her and sat down on the divan opposite me again. 'I think my brother will be coming soon,' she said. And within moments there was a scampering sound as of someone moving hurriedly away from the door. Firm, loud footsteps approached – and paused. A loud cough, and then a knock.

Layla opened the door and said something which ended in the word of welcome that I have come to recognise: 'Itfaddal', and after another pause he came in. He bent to kiss his sister's head and then, as she hung on to his arm, she said, in French, 'Anna, this is my brother Sharif Pasha al-Baroudi. Abeih, I present to you Lady Anna Winterbourne.'

'Madame,' he said, turning to me with a slight bow, 'I beg,' he said in perfect French, 'I beg that you will accept my sincere

140

apologies.' And it was at that moment that I understood my feeling that I had met his sister before; for there was that face that had arrested my attention at the Khedive's ball and that I believe I saw fleetingly at the Costanzi just moments before I was overpowered by the music. As proud as the devil, I thought . . .

'Monsieur, there is no need for apologies,' I replied, 'and certainly not on your part. In your house I have met with nothing but kindness.'

I am glad that I spoke with seeming presence of mind, but in truth, though his eyes rested on me but for a moment, it was enough to bring me to a consciousness of the strangeness of my appearance, my man's riding trousers and shirt – unseemly in themselves, and hardly fresh now, having been slept in and worn for two days – my hair unwound from its bandages but tumbled and unbrushed. The thought came into my head that Emily would be mortified if she witnessed this little tableau, and I kept my eyes on the floor and trusted to that instinct I have observed in Oriental gentlemen that after the first look he would look directly at me no more.

'My sister has told me the story,' he continued. 'She has explained that you have not yet been missed?'

There was a note in his voice – disapproval is too strong a word, but it was clear he considered my escapade pure foolishness – that I had put myself in harm's way, as it were, and somehow not being missed made it worse. I felt as though he would have preferred it if I had been missed. I said nothing.

'I do not know what your wishes are,' he continued, 'with regard to reporting this matter to the authorities. If you choose to do so we will, of course, confirm your account and lend whatever assistance lies in our power. But the first thing to do is to return you immediately to your hotel. And to ensure your safety, I will accompany you there myself. Tomorrow, you may wish to think about the proper course –'

'There is no need for that, monsieur,' I said. I glanced up and caught his look of surprise, and Layla's too. I think he is not used to being interrupted – or contradicted.

'There is no need,' I repeated. 'As to reporting this incident, I

141

do not wish it as I fully understand the circumstances, and as no harm has come to me but on the contrary it has given me the opportunity of making the acquaintance of your charming sister. And now, if you would be kind enough to order our horses to be prepared, Sabir and I can continue our journey and need impose no longer on your kindness.'

Brave words. Why then, even as I uttered them, did a cold finger touch my heart and the journey ahead seem so arduous an undertaking?

'Surely you cannot mean to go riding off into the desert now?' Layla was at my side and gazing earnestly into my face.

'But yes,' I said, 'yes, I do.'

'May I sit down?' he asked, indicating Layla's divan.

'Itfaddal,' I said and was rewarded by a slight twitch at the corner of his mouth and a muffled laugh from Layla.

'But seriously, Anna,' she said, as she and I sat side by side facing him, 'after all this?'

'If I go back now,' I said, 'Emily, my maid, and Mr Barrington at the Agency both knew my intentions. Where would I say I had been — what account can I give of the last two days?'

'The man can be silenced,' he said, 'And you can tell your maid you lost heart and decided to turn back.'

'She thinks I am with a group.'

'What the maid thinks is of no consequence,' he said impatiently. 'What matters is your safety.'

'I would have been safe enough if your young friends had not interfered,' I replied. I surprised myself. I could not recall speaking sharply to anyone before. He leaned back against the cushions and looked full at me. I looked down at my hands.

'And Sabir cannot be silenced,' I added. 'He will be questioned most closely. It would not work.'

'I can guarantee his silence,' he said quietly.

'No. And no one will believe I lost heart. It is not — in my character.'

There was a silence. I looked up. He leaned back on the

142

divan, his eyes on the prayer beads idle between his fingers. Then he raised his head and looked at me.

'*Very well,*' *he said,* '*I understand. You shall go to St Catherine. But not tonight, and not alone.*'

I glanced at Layla, who was looking intently at her brother. Would he propose that she travel with me?

'*Lady Anna has a point,*' *he said to her.* '*And besides, since we are the reason her journey was so unpleasantly interrupted, we have an obligation —*' *He broke off, as though impatient with his own speech.* '*In any case, you will permit me —*' *this to me —* '*you will permit me to escort you into the Sinai and back. I trust you may find it safer and more comfortable travelling with my party than on your own?*'

'*Monsieur,*' *I said,* '*absolutely not. I am completely capable —*'

'*I will not allow you to travel alone.*'

'*Forgive me, but it is not for you to allow what I may do.*'

'*Anna!*' *I heard Layla's whisper and felt her touch on my arm but I sat still and unyielding: how dare he dictate to me?*

'*You forget, madame,*' *he said,* '*you are in my house.*'

'*And that means?*'

'*You will not leave this house alone. You will be escorted from here to your hotel. Whether you go directly or by way of Sinai is up to you.*'

'*And if I refuse?*'

'*Then you can stay here. After all, you will not be missed.*' *And now there was something else in his eyes: a smile.*

'*Monsieur,*' *I said,* '*this is coercion.*'

'*In a good cause,*' *he said.*

I turned to Layla, who seemed to shake herself out of her surprise. '*It is a very good plan,*' *she said.* '*And you will see everything better. I know you are not afraid to go alone, but believe me, once you are in the desert you will feel easier to be in company.*'

I was silent.

'*Good. It is settled then,*' *he said, straightening up.* '*I will need tomorrow to organise matters and to get the Maître out of*

143

custody.' He smiled at his sister. 'We will leave the day after in the morning, and try to make up for your lost time.'

He stood up and Layla stood too. She put on her shoes and her cloak and started fastening her head-dress. He turned and spoke to her in Arabic. After a few exchanges she came to me and took my hands.

'I do not want to leave my child alone a second night. You will not be nervous alone here tonight, will you? I would ask you to come with me but it's best if not too many people know about this. I will come back in the morning and bring Ahmad for you to see.' She smiled and kissed me, first on one cheek and then the other and then again on the first. 'I am very happy to know you,' she said, and when she left, he left with her.

I sat on the divan. How dare he, I thought, how dare he simply put himself in command like this? But underneath that thought I had the strangest feeling of life expanding and opening out. I found myself thinking about Sir Charles, wondering what he would make of this Egyptian Pasha into whose house I had landed in so odd a fashion. And then came the thought that under the same circumstances, Sir Charles himself would probably have acted in the same way. It must be an inconvenience – he had not been planning to make a journey into the desert. And if Lord Cromer should hear of this? It would be worse, in his eyes, than my travelling alone. It dawned on me that Sharif Pasha was putting himself in the way of a great deal of unpleasantness, as well as inconvenience, to give me my expedition.

I heard a knock on the door and called out absently, in English, 'Come in.' But nobody came in, and presently I got up and opened the door. He was in the corridor a few paces away with Sabir hovering behind him.

'Pardon me,' he said, 'I thought you cannot be comfortable. This is the best I can do, for now.' He held something out and I took it, a neatly folded garment with a silken feel. I could not see its colour in the dim light. 'It will be too large, of course, it is mine, but even so –'

'Thank you,' I said stiffly, 'I am sure it will be most comfortable.'

'It is a problem that there is no woman in the house tonight who can look after you, but I have — if you would like to go into the bathroom in fifteen minutes you will find . . . things . . . '
He trailed off with a vague gesture and I found myself hurrying to assure him he was most kind.

'Good night,' he said, and gave me that first grave bow again and turned away.

'A moment, monsieur,' I said, and he paused. 'I have been thinking,' I said, 'I will be putting you to much inconvenience. And —'

He looked weary now. 'I thought it was all agreed?'

'It occurs to me, if word of this should ever reach Lord Cromer . . .'

I felt him stiffen. 'Yes?'

'It would make problems, would it not?'

'You should have thought of that sooner. You are afraid?'

'Not for myself, monsieur.'

'Well, then?'

'I thought it might make an unpleasantness for you.'

'I can manage that,' he said. 'Does anything else trouble you?'

'No,' I said. 'Not at present.'

'Good,' he said. 'Then good night again.' And with that he strode off down the corridor with Sabir behind him.

The 'things' I found in the bathroom were a copper pot full of steaming hot water, a bar of soap smelling of olive oil and roses, and a pile of warm towels.

I sat on the edge of the big marble tub. The flame in the oil lamp hanging from the wall flickered on the tiled walls. I poured water over my head with the blue and white enamel tumbler. Thoughts of Lord Cromer vanished from my head, and I was content.

And when, wrapped in his dressing gown of dark blue silk, with the sleeves turned up several times over, I padded back with my hair wrapped in a towel, I found a large, round brass tray *placed on a folding stand in the centre of the room and on it was a lit candle and yoghurt and cheese and apricots and clementines and olives and warm bread wrapped in a linen napkin and a tall frosted glass of cool water. And I sat on the floor in front of it and ate heartily, my mind a tired blur of contentment.*

And it was only when I lay on my divan, the grey shawl with the pink rosebuds drawn up to my chin, that I fell to wondering whether he too recognised me from our previous encounters, for I am sure our eyes had met . . .

13

But still the heart doth need a language.
S. T. Coleridge

14 March 1901

It is almost the middle of the day. Layla al-Baroudi reclines on linen-covered cushions in the cool shadow of the protruding haramlek terrace. In her hands she holds a small, white garment. She looks down at the needle piercing the fabric, pushes it through with a thimbled middle finger, and as she pulls it away – feeling the thread grow taut against her little finger – she hears Ahmad's laughing shriek and glances up: in the centre of the courtyard the fountain plays on its coloured tiles and Anna holds up her hand and sprinkles drops of shining water on the baby's plump legs. Layla smiles and bends her eyes to the next stitch.

Husni, as her brother had promised, was released on his own assurance first thing this morning. He had walked into the house brisk and cheerful as though he'd been out to breathe the morning air. He kissed her and Ahmad, washed, shaved, put on clean clothes and called for fried eggs. Over breakfast he told her how he had refused to leave prison without his comrades and how eventually they too had been released on his surety. Ready as ever to look on the happy side, he was glad that – like most of his clients – he had undergone the experience of jail; 'Gladder,' he said with a laugh, 'that it has only been for three nights'; and as she poured his tea he looked up and whispered, 'I missed you.'

He was looking forward to his trial; it would give him a chance, he said, to put forward the legitimate grievances of the workers of the country. And now he was back at his office, working, and writing an article for *al-Liwa*. He had been very grateful to his brother–in–law for his intervention and had promised to speak harshly to Ibrahim and the others about their rash action. How harshly, Layla did not know. She had never seen or heard him speak harshly to anyone. He was always the one who said – as he said on this occasion – 'Hasal kheir', it ended well, calm down, everything has a solution. 'But seriously,' she had said, 'you have to speak to them, they're going to take you into a catastrophe – and if not for yourself, then for their colleagues, for themselves even. My brother had half a mind to take them with his own hand to the police –'

'Ya setti hasal kheir,' he said. 'Isn't the lady well, al-hamdu-l-Illah?'

And in fact it was hasal kheir: for no harm had come to anyone, and here was this delightful young woman who was such a charming guest and so taken with everything she saw – Layla glanced up, and Anna, looking up at the same moment, smiled back. She stood up straight and tightened, for the tenth time, the tie belt of the blue dressing gown around her waist. Ahmad was clearly in love, thought Layla, watching the baby sit up and gurgle and babble at the pale feet, the tall white legs, the blue silk and the shining head beyond – a head which bent down, down, down, until the boy was ensnared and raised his hands to wonderingly finger his net of silken gold.

Layla held up the little frock, shook it out, and laid it down on her knee again. Anna had looked so serious when she told her the name of the stitch: 'ish el-naml. 'Why, of course,' she'd said, 'of course,' staring at the intricate folds of cloth, and Layla, examining the name 'ants' nest', for the first time had seen its aptness. Although it would not do to pursue the image too far; she shook the dress out again and considered whether to add some yellow to the blue and white.

It was a pity Anna was going away tomorrow; she could imagine so many things they could do together, so many things she could show her, this woman who had come across

Europe and the Mediterranean Sea to find Egypt, and who had confided yesterday that she felt it had eluded her, that she had touched nothing at all. Layla understood what she meant, for what would *she* have known of France had she not been befriended by Juliette Clemenceau? Still, Anna was going to see Sinai and St Catherine, and she would be travelling safely and in comfort – with her brother. Layla had to admit she had been surprised when Abeih Sharif made his offer yesterday – offer? It had been more like decree, a royal firman: you shall go to St Catherine's, and you shall go with me. And Anna had bristled and answered him in a manner such as Layla had never heard anyone speak to him before. That was always his way: to issue firmans. But it was not his way suddenly to undertake journeys across the desert with strangers – with strange women, foreign women: an *English* woman. And she had wondered, still wondered: could it be that he – that Anna had taken his fancy? Layla had grown, they had all grown, so used to thinking of him as a bachelor, as a man who preferred to live alone, that they had stopped urging him to consider remarriage, had stopped bringing possible brides to his attention, had stopped wondering how he managed. 'Your brother takes everything so seriously,' her mother had said. 'He's read books and taken them seriously, he read your uncle's poetry and it settled in his heart. He philosophises everything and there is no arguing with him.'

Layla had been seven at the time of her brother's marriage and the scandal it had caused when he returned his bride to her family after six months. She had not understood much, but the whole event had had a doomed air, shadowed as it was by the Revolution and then the Occupation, the banishment of her uncle and 'Urabi Basha and their friends. Or was that just how it came to seem later? Later, when married herself and knowing more of the needs of men, she had questioned their mother closely. Zeinab Hanim had been able to unburden her heart and speak to her daughter woman to woman. 'He did the honourable thing,' she had told her in this very courtyard one moonlit Ramadan night. 'He took the blame on himself: he said, "Your daughter is a princess and there is no fault with her. We are just not suited to each other. I cannot make her happy. She will take one who is better than me and God will give her the happiness she deserves." He paid everything they asked for and more, and within a year the girl was married and God has blessed her with three children. The truth is, I think her family were relieved when he left her. Human, my child, after all: when they took him his father was in power, his uncle was head of the government – and then, in a day and a night, the country had been beaten down and the Army of Occupation was in the streets and all our hopes had been destroyed. And he comes and makes a big speech and gives them back their daughter and a handsome gift of money. A good and a blessing. And the girl had not become pregnant by him so they could hide for a while and hope the world would forget they had ever been in-laws of the al-Baroudi family. Anyway, I took him to my side and I said, "Comfort me, my son, and set my heart at ease: men need that thing which God has lawfully ordained for them. I want to know how it is with you." And he bent his head and considered and then he opened his heart to me and said, "Ya Ummi, I cannot live my life with a woman who has no key to my mind and who does not share my concerns. She cannot – will not – read anything. She shrugs off the grave problems of the day and asks if I think her new tablecloth is pretty. We are living in difficult times and it is not enough for a person to be interested in his home and his job – in his own personal life. I need my partner to be someone to whom I can turn, confident of her sympathy, believing her when she tells me I'm in the wrong, strengthened when she tells me I'm in the right. I want to love, and be loved back – but what I see is not love or companionship but a sort of transaction of convenience sanctioned by religion and society and I do not want it." You see the philosophy? I offered to find him a woman, or a girl or two – not slaves, because they had just declared that slavery was against the law, but a couple of good women to live in his hareem and see to his needs, and all I got was another long and wide lecture about the dignity of human beings. He was twenty-one, tall and broad and handsome as the moon. I said, "Very well, but tell me then, frankly, what will you do?" And he laughed and kissed my hand and said, "Leave this one to me, but be comforted – don't they say 'the son of the duck is no mean swimmer'?" and of course he meant your father, and knowing what I knew of *his* merry nights here and there, I was silent.'

Layla considers: she has been so used to thinking of her brother as her brother. The head of the family since '82 when her father went into his retreat and her uncle into exile. Her mother's brother Mustafa Bey, Husni's father, was there but he was in Minya, on the land. Abeih Sharif had always been the man of the family: running the estates, managing the money, looking after the people, conducting his practice as a lawyer, sitting on the Council, pushing for reform. He had maintained a polite but distant relationship with the Palace –

'Mama! Mama!' Ahmad is faltering towards her, upright, arms held high, running before he can walk. Layla throws aside her sewing, rises to her knees, leans forward and catches the small hurtling figure to her breast

'Ismallah ismallah ya habibi,' she cries, passing her hand over the soft, black hair, kissing the damp, shining brow. Berthed and petted, Ahmad struggles to be free; Layla faces him round and plants him down on his feet. A few paces away, Anna sinks to the ground ready to receive the returning child. One step, then another, the face a rictus of concentration, and then that involuntary break into a trot and Anna rises to her knees as Ahmad throws himself full into her arms. When she lifts her face from the warm, fragrant neck, Sharif Basha al-Baroudi is standing at the entrance to the courtyard looking at her and frowning.

He turns to his sister. 'I coughed, I banged – has everyone gone deaf?'

'Welcome, ya Abeih.' Layla has stood up and is approaching him, smiling. 'Good morning.'

'Good morning,' he says. When he looks down at her he

smiles and raises his hand to her cheek. 'Khalas ya Setti? Your husband has returned to you in safety?'

'May God increase the good that comes from you!' She smiles, catching the hand on her cheek, kissing it lightly. 'Itfaddal, have you had breakfast?'

'Al-hamdu-l-Illah,' he says, sitting down in the low wicker chair near her cushions.

And Anna?

'When was it?' Anna asks. 'When did you know? When did you fall in love with me?'

It is that happy stretch of time when the lovers set to chronicling their passion. When no glance, no tone of voice is so fleeting but it shines with significance. When each moment, each perception is brought out with care, unfolded like a precious gem from its layers of the softest tissue paper and laid in front of the beloved – turned this way and that, examined, considered. And so they sit, and touch, and talk, and breathe, and so they string their moments into a glorious chain, and throw it round each other's necks, garland each other with it. Invisible to all others, it shines for them, a beacon across a crowded room, across an ocean, across time.

'When did I know? Well, the first moment – the first moment I saw you was when you sat across the room, in your ridiculous riding costume, your hair tumbling down your back, abducted, imprisoned, unwashed, and said, so coolly, "That will not be necessary, and now if you will kindly saddle my horse –" '

'I did not ask you to saddle my horse! Even then I knew better.'

'You more or less ordered me to saddle your horse. It never even crossed your mind to be afraid.'

'What was there to be afraid of?'

'Me. Weren't you afraid of me? The wicked Pasha who would lock you up in his harem and do terrible things to you?'

'What terrible things?'

'You should know. They're in your English stories. Calling in my black eunuchs to tie you up –'

'Do you have any?'

'You bad, bad woman – but what can one expect from an infidel? You dress in men's clothes, frighten poor Sabir to within an inch of his life, then throw yourself at the neck of the first Arab you meet –'

'You're not an Arab anyway. Not properly.'

' "Native", then.'

'Didn't you remember me from the Khedive's ball?'

'Not really, no.'

'But our eyes met – I'm sure our eyes met. You were standing by a window –'

'You were just one of "them". One of those half-naked women –'

'Stop it! Don't act as if you've never moved out of Cairo –'

'Ah, but this was *in* Cairo, you see. And there you were: laughing, dancing –'

'I did not dance.'

'I know.'

'So you did notice me?' Anna's laugh is triumphant.

'No, I didn't.'

'Yes, you did.'

'Well, maybe a little.'

'And?'

'And?'

'What did you think?'

'I thought you behaved better than some of the others.'

'Thank you. And?'

'And what?'

'And I was beautiful and my dress was simply ravishing and –'

'No.' He shakes his head. 'No. You know, really, the first time I thought you were beautiful?'

'Yes?'

'When I came into the courtyard and you were on your knees on the ground, wrapped in my old dressing gown, holding Ahmad to you. When you lifted your head and looked at me with the sun on your face, I saw your eyes, your amazing violet eyes, and then your face and neck flushed with colour and you looked down and hid yourself in the child and all I could see was your hair. I thought, She is beautiful. Truly beautiful.'

And Anna, who has held on to Ahmad, hidden her face in his neck once more, now allows him to break from her. He calls out to his uncle, and as he starts to toddle forwards she follows him anxiously, stooping, a hand outstretched to catch him, to break the fall if it should come. The other hand holds the dressing gown to her, pulling its folds closer around her neck.

'Bonjour,' she says as she comes close. He is leaning forward, opening his arms wide – 'Lalu! Lalu!' – gathering his nephew into them, placing him on his knee.

'Bonjour. I hope you slept well?' He does not look at her. He is busy with Ahmad, who is now climbing to stand on his knee, leaning against his chest.

'Very well, thank you.' Anna sits in the other wicker chair, to the side of him, slightly behind him. Her eyes are on Ahmad's plump feet trampling across his uncle's light grey lounge suit, the open jacket showing the heavy gold chain of his watch rising in an arch to the pocket of his waistcoat. Layla has once more picked up her sewing, looking up to say 'Bass ya Ahmad' as the child reaches for his uncle's tarbush. Sharif Basha takes off the tarbush and gives it to Ahmad, and holds him steady in the circle of his arm. With his other hand he smooths his own hair back.

'I was thinking,' he says to Layla, speaking in French for Anna's benefit, 'of how our guest should travel.'

Layla glances up at Anna, who says nothing.

'Anna is a good rider,' Layla says. 'Sabir says so and besides, all Englishwomen are good riders, are they not?'

'Where is this Sabir? Why was he not at the door?'

'I gave him leave to go to his family. He will be back immediately. He says he had no chance to tell them he was going away for a few days and he is afraid they will get worried and enquire at the Agency.'

'His family?' Anna asks.

'His wife and children. He says he intended to send word to them but never got a chance. He did seem very anxious.'

'I did not know he had a wife,' Anna says in surprise.

'Neither does your Mr Barrington, I'm sure,' Sharif Basha says coldly.

'But why —' Anna begins, then stops.

For a while there is a silence.

'Let me make you a coffee, ya Abeih,' Layla says. Sharif Basha shakes his head.

'Come and show me the fountain,' he says to Ahmad in Arabic, lifting the child up and standing. He walks to the centre of the courtyard, and with his back to the women puts Ahmad down carefully on his feet and crouches down, keeping his arm around the child. Layla and Anna wait silently for his return.

'Why don't you come with us?' Sharif Basha says to his sister as he sits down again. He sounds casual, but Layla glances up, surprised.

'I can't,' she says, a slight motion of her head indicating the wall of the courtyard. 'Father is not very well, and Mama isn't here.'

'Yes, of course,' he says, 'of course,' shifting the child's feet, lifting him up a little, then putting him down again. He turns slightly to Anna, glances at her for a second, then away.

'You would not consider travelling in a litter, would you?'

'I should much prefer to ride,' Anna says.

'Of course,' he says again, lifting his tarbush slightly off Ahmad's head, adjusting it to show the child's face.

'Then you will have to travel as a man. A young man. A very young man.' He permits himself a wry face as he glances at her again. 'But not an Englishman. You will have to be something else.' He pauses. 'French. You can be the son of an old friend of mine, a Frenchman. We'll get you some clothes, and you can invent a name for yourself —'

156

'Armand,' says Anna, and he smiles.

'Armand, then. Armand Demange. We'll get you some papers and some clothes and I shall tell you about your father as we ride.'

'I knew it was you at the Costanzi, and that you'd seen me —'
'When?'
'When you smiled when I chose the name Armand.'
'But Armand was not in that opera!'
'No, but still. It made you think of opera.'

The three candles in their flickering glasses cannot dim the light of the stars which shine down on the cushions and rugs spread out on the spacious roof of the old house. From time to time Anna catches the scent of orange blossom drifting up from the trees in the garden.

'Anna,' he says, 'do you miss it? That life?'
'No,' she says immediately. 'I am here. I would not be anywhere else for the world.' Her fingers are in the soft, thick hair of the head resting on her knee. With her other hand she traces the line of his mouth, the upper lip hidden under the edge of his moustache.

'Does it trouble you,' she asks, 'that we have to speak in French?'
'I like French.'
'But does it trouble you that you cannot speak to me in Arabic?'
'No. It makes foreigners of us both. It's good that I should have to come some way to meet you.' He catches the hand playing around his mouth and puts the tips of the fingers to his lips.

'It was so sad. Tosca,' Anna says, 'when she sits on the floor, with Baron Scarpia at the table behind her, and asks what she's done to deserve this.'
'Yes. You were in black.'
'I was still in mourning. It had only been ten months.'
'Anna?'
'My darling?'

157

'Where is your wedding ring? Your old wedding ring?'

'It's in a purse. In my dresser, with his ring and my journals of the time.'

'. . .'

'You may read them if you wish. I have no need to keep secrets from you.'

'No.'

'Truly.'

'No, my dear. Not yet. Maybe some day, when we're old . . .'

Cairo

14 March 1901

My dear Sir Charles,

This time I have news of more interest (certainly to me and I hope also to you) to communicate than another musical evening or another day seeing the sights. For I have had, by a curious occasion, the opportunity to meet a young lady of the Egyptian Moslems. I say 'lady' advisedly, for you would consider her such, both in family and demeanour. She is the niece of Mahmoud Sami Pasha al-Baroudi, the Prime Minister in Urabi Pasha's short-lived government and his companion in their ill-starred 'Rebellion' which I have heard you speak about with some sympathy. He (Mahmoud Sami Pasha) was allowed to return home some eighteen months ago, being old and almost blind, and he has no more to do with politics but occupies himself with what they say is a vast collection of poems. Her mother is Zeinab Hanim al-Ghamrawi, from an old and distinguished family in Minya in Upper Egypt, but I have not met her yet.

My new friend's name is Layla and at the time that I met her, her husband, a lawyer, was (briefly) imprisoned for helping to organise a representation by some workers for better conditions. These men laboured on the tram lines and demanded the same terms of employment as foreign workers. Their demands and the refusal of the Government to countenance them had led to their going on strike. The tram companies brought in what we in England call blackleg workers to break the strike, and in the heat

158

of confrontation her husband and a colleague lay down on the lines to prevent the trams running. They, together with some of the more prominent among the men, were then arrested and taken off to jail – from which they were later released through the good offices of my friend's brother, Sharif Pasha al-Baroudi, a lawyer himself and, I understand, a man of influence by reason of his position, his integrity, his patriotic stance and, naturally, his lineage.

You can imagine, I am sure, all the questions I have put to my new friend, and so I know now that what the 'talking classes' are demanding is not only an end to the British Occupation but that the country should be governed – like ours – by means of an elected Parliament and a Constitution.

When I asked what view the Khedive took of this, my friend, with a gentle smile, said that the Khedive expresses to the Nationalists sympathy with their demands and says his father should have granted them when Urabi Pasha first demanded it instead of running to the British. However, there are some who believe that he merely tries to make use of the Nationalists in his conflict with Lord Cromer, but there is no guarantee that left to himself he would grant the wishes of the people and transform himself into a Constitutional Monarch. That is an argument which will have to be resumed at the end of the Occupation.

I know that there are other questions to be asked – regarding the National Debt, for example, of which I have heard so much at the Agency, and what the Sultan in Constantinople would be if Egypt were a Constitutional Monarchy – and I fully intend to ask them when an occasion next presents itself. But for now, I am filled with delight at having made this new acquaintance and at the prospect of getting to know her better and so, possibly, to understand something of this country, which has for so long held such an attraction for me.

It does seem strange to me that I have not met someone like her before, in my now not inconsiderable sojourn here. We tend to meet our own countrymen and the members of the other Consulates – and the only Natives we have to do with are the ones who serve us. I fancy it is somewhat like coming to England

and meeting the servants and the shopkeepers and forming your ideas of English Society upon that. No, it is worse, for in England Society displays itself in public, so the stranger, even with no entrance to it, knows it is there. Here, I have come to see, Society exists behind closed doors – but it is no less Society for that. And then there is the problem of the language. I have conducted my new friendship in French, but I am now resolved to really learn Arabic, and will hope to impress you, soon, by signing myself off in that language as your most dutiful and loving, etc. etc.

An End of a Beginning

One class of tale is typically Egyptian. These tales are distinguished by three characteristics: they are picaresque, feminist and pantheist.

Ya'qub Artin, 1905

And so it is that our three heroines – as is only fitting in a story born of travel, unfolded and shaken out of a trunk – set off upon their different journeys. Anna Winterbourne heads eastwards out of Cairo, bound for Sinai in the company of Sharif al-Baroudi. Amal al-Ghamrawi and Isabel Parkman take the Upper Egypt road which will lead them to Tawasi, in the Governorate of Minya.

'I told you I was going to work on it.' Isabel laughed.

'Well, you certainly have,' Amal said, glancing down at the paper Isabel had given her. As she slows down behind a mule-drawn cart, she smooths the paper out on the steering wheel and examines it. She reads:

> Umm: mother (also the top of the head)
> Ummah: nation, hence ammama: to nationalise
> Amma: to lead the prayers, hence Imam: religious leader
> A blank space, and then
> Abb: father

'And that's it?' Amal says, handing the paper back as she sees her way clear, shifts into second gear and overtakes.

'That's it,' says Isabel, 'unless you can think of something else.'

Amal frowns, concentrating, murmuring, 'Fatherhood, fatherly. No, I can't think of anything.'

'So two incredibly important concepts,' says Isabel, 'nationhood and religious leadership, come from "mother". The word goes into politics, religion, economics and even anatomy. So how can they say Arabic is a patriarchal language?'

'Brilliant!' Amal turns briefly to flash her a large smile. 'On the other hand, you could say that "abb" stands alone because it's unique, because it shouldn't even be in the same realm as any other concept.'

'No,' says Isabel. 'And *you* don't really think that.'

They are so alike, Isabel thinks. Not just the black hair and black eyes. Everybody here has those. It's more the manner: the smile that's both friendly and amused. Their way of throwing you compliments that you couldn't be sure were quite serious. The sudden questions that cut through to the heart. But Amal did not quite have her brother's spark, his vitality. Or rather she seemed to be holding her vitality – her aura – in check.

'Let's stop for a moment,' Amal said.

They had been on the road for an hour and a half. When they got out of the car, the air that hit them might have come out of an oven. They were pacing and stamping their feet when Amal noticed Isabel's long skirt, the loose, long-sleeved top, the scarf tied casually over the hair.

'What is all this? A new image?' she asked.

Isabel shrugged. She had worked it out for herself. She had seen the groups of tourists in the old city, in the Bazaar, their naked flesh lobsterlike in the heat, the locals either staring or averting their eyes as they passed by. And these clothes were much more comfortable anyway.

Amal smiled. 'You still look good,' she said.

They watched a woman coming towards them. Ahead of her a donkey walked, his head drooping patiently. Tied across his back was a big load of long yellow canes and with each step the canes swayed, as though something was in the balance – something that could go either way.

'Salamu 'aleikum.'

' 'Aleikum es-salam.' The woman stopped and she and Amal started chatting: Where are you headed? Who's this moon with you? While the donkey took the opportunity to nose about for a green stalk in the dust.

Isabel had grown used to Amal chatting to people during their rambles in Cairo: the shop owners, the parking attendants, even the traffic police. But as the city had retreated further and further behind them, Isabel had felt herself grow – not uneasy, but somewhat less assured. Here she would not be able to get away. Here there were no service stops, no telephones, nothing but the road running through fields, a small town, then more fields. Occasionally there was a notice spelling out the name of a place she had never heard of before. Sometimes they were trapped behind a cart, sometimes behind a truck. That was the main traffic on the Upper Egypt road: trucks, carts and the dusty Peugeot station wagons that served as taxis in which each person bought a seat. And the road led into the heartland of the terrorists. Or at least that was what it said in the papers. She was putting her trust in her friend, but what if something were to happen to Amal? What if she fainted in the heat or got appendicitis? What would Isabel do? Amal herself seemed to have no fears and was talking happily to the fallaha and selecting one of her canes before the woman went on her way.

Amal stripped back the tough, glossy skin and cut off a segment. Isabel chewed on it, releasing the sweet juice, then spitting the dry white pulp discreetly out into her hand.

'Did she just give you that?' she asked.

'She asked if I would like it.'

'You didn't pay her.'

'She didn't want paying. It's just a stick of sugar cane,' Amal said as they got back into the car.

The first barricade was not too bad. They saw it from a distance: the red and white barrels, the kiosk at the side, the officers waving them to a halt. Amal wound down her window and the young officer leaned into it. Amal el-

Ghamrawi and Isabel Parkman. American. My brother's fiancée. Tawasi in Minya. Our village, our land. A few days . . . Soldiers stood by with guns and the officer stepped back. 'Look after her. We don't want foreign blood spilled here.'

After the second barricade, three hours from Cairo, the car broke down. When it started smoking they decided to press on, but when the smoke got too bad they had to stop. The temperature indicator was on red. They pulled in to the side of the road and opened the bonnet and smoke poured out everywhere. The sun was in the middle of the sky and it was blazing hot.

'What are we going to do?' Isabel asked.

'I don't know,' Amal said. But she did not seem worried. 'Wait, I suppose.'

'Do you have a rescue service here?'

'No,' Amal said. 'Oh, no. Let's just sit in the shade and wait.'

She took a striped rug from the car and laid it on the ground. They sat and ate tangerines; Isabel watched as Amal rubbed the peel into her hands and breathed in the scent. A car pulled up – one of the beaten-up old station wagons, empty apart from the driver, who looked out of the window and said:

'Kheir? Is there something?'

'The car has stopped,' Amal said. 'It got hot and smoked and I was afraid to drive it any more.'

'I'll have a look,' the man said.

He got out of his car. A small, dark man in brown trousers and a patterned shirt and well-worn shoes without socks. He got a cloth from his car and opened the radiator, which hissed at him and belched out more smoke.

'There's no water,' he said.

He went back to his car and brought out a jerkin of water. He poured some into the radiator and they watched it trickle away between the wheels.

'The radiator has a hole in it,' he said.

'So, what next?' Amal asked.

167

The man said something and pointed into the distance, then he got a rope from his car and started to tie their car to his.

'Are you sure this is all right?' Isabel asked in a low voice.

'What do you mean?'

'Is it safe?'

'He says there's a place nearby where they can fix the radiator.'

'But it's OK? Going with him?'

'Yes, of course,' Amal said. 'It's perfectly OK.' Then she turned back to the man. 'My brother's wife,' she said, 'khawagaya. We're going to our village, Tawasi, in Minya.'

'A thousand welcomes,' he said, pulling on the knot, testing it.

He towed them for twenty minutes; twice the rope slipped and he tied it again. Then they turned off into a bumpy side road and came to some ramshackle houses and a small mosque and a marketplace. He stopped in front of a concrete cabin with a couple of car wrecks lying outside. He got out of his car and yelled a few times and a man came out from behind the building. He had black grease all over him and was wiping his hands on a rag. Amal said, 'Stay in the car,' and got out and went towards him. The three of them stood in the glaring sun, talking. Without the air-conditioning the car was like a sauna and Isabel could feel the sweat springing into her scalp. Her head started to ache and the figures in the sunlight rippled in the heat rising from the ground. The mechanic came and vanished under the car. He got up and joined the other two again and they talked some more. Then something was settled, for the man who had towed them raised his hand to his head and went back to his car. Amal followed him and held out a hand, and Isabel watched the now familiar pantomime: the man backing away smiling, shaking his head, his eyes on the ground, his hand on his heart. He backed right into his car, raised his hand again and drove away. Amal went back to Isabel.

'Let's sit inside,' she said. 'It'll be a little cooler.'

Isabel's head was throbbing as she got out of the car. Her dress was sticking to her thighs and she could feel the sweat running through her hair, under her arms, between her breasts, behind her knees . . .

Inside the cabin it was dark but not cool. It smelled of gasoline and it was cluttered with bits of cars, tools, tyres, all thrown in anyhow. Isabel's head was swimming but she could not bring herself to lean against the grimy wall. A small boy appeared, also covered in grime. He brought two chairs and set them down close to the doorway. From the back of the shop he brought an ancient fan, balanced it on a piece of black machinery, connected it up to some wires hanging on the wall, and it started to rotate. He wiped the chairs with the hem of his T-shirt and grinned.

'Itfaddalu.'

Isabel sank down on the chair but jumped up again as the leg buckled.

'Don't be afraid,' the boy laughed. He straightened the leg and wedged it with a bit of cardboard. She sat and the fan whirred at her. It didn't even have a protective grille on the front.

'This place is a deathtrap,' she said.

'Not if you're used to it,' Amal said with a funny smile. 'Are you all right? You've gone pale.'

'I'm fine.'

They sat in silence till the boy reappeared with two bottles of Seven-Up, opened, the dented caps pressed back on to the necks. 'Kattar kheirak,' Amal said. She took one and handed the other to Isabel. They eased off the caps, wiped the mouths of the bottles with their hands and drank. Isabel watched as with bare feet, bare hands, no mask, nothing, the mechanic started using a blowtorch. Blowing, hammering, with no protection of any kind. And when he lay under the car, the boy lay at his side, holding a big electric bulb by its neck to give him light, and all the electricity seemed to come from wires twined into the wires dangling down the wall.

'Isabel,' Amal said, and her voice came from a long way off.

'I'm afraid you may be getting heatstroke. I'll come right back.'

When she came back she had a plastic bucket in her hand. It was bright orange and looking at it made Isabel feel worse.

'Just tilt your head a little.' Amal eased the scarf off Isabel's head and Isabel felt something cool slide slowly into her ear. Then the other ear.

'What is this?' she asked.

'Glycerine,' Amal said. 'It'll take the heat away. Now hold this.' She took a dripping flannel out of the bucket, wrung it out and placed it, cool and wet, in Isabel's hands. She put another flannel on the back of her neck and a third on her forehead and stood holding them both in place. 'You'll feel better now,' she said.

'I'm sorry,' Amal said later, when they were back in the car. 'It was silly of me to bring you. Maybe we should go back –'

'No,' Isabel said. 'No.' And she meant it. She felt she'd been through the worst, and she had come through. She wanted to go on. 'The car isn't likely to break down again now, is it?'

'No. I don't know. Maybe we should go back.'

'But we must be quite close?'

'About another hour.'

'I'm OK now. Really I am. And the car will cool down as we drive. Please don't worry. That trick with the glycerine really worked.'

'That was a memory out of nowhere: my mother used to do that for me. Oh God! Not another barricade –'

Isabel felt that she was further than she'd ever been from everything she knew. That she had delivered herself over into the hands of Amal al-Ghamrawi and it was like being a child again. When had she last been so dependent? She could not remember. It was the language too. She had been working on her Arabic and she could get by in Cairo. She could get the gist of a conversation. But out here it would all be in dialect and how much of that would she get? Everything would be up to Amal. Amal who just over a month ago was reluctant

170

even to go out to dinner and who now seemed to think nothing of driving five hours into the countryside – it wasn't even countryside, really, not as Isabel thought of the countryside. There were no motels, no gas stations. It was fields and then towns that managed to look half-finished and run-down at the same time. And people, always people and animals: donkeys, horses, dogs, water buffalo, goats, camels, all wandering across the road with the trucks honking at them. And the barricades. As they progressed further into the Sa'id, the barricades became less formal; the uniforms gave way to fatigues and sometimes camouflage dress. The officers grew beards and grew their hair longer. One officer even wore a bandana round his head. They had stopped being a police force and had turned into an army in an alien jungle.

'Does she look like she's kidnapped?' Amal had quipped when an officer asked for the third time, 'Why are you taking her with you?'

'We're not playing here,' he said curtly. 'You know what will happen if an American is harmed.'

Another officer hurried up and said, 'Let them go, let them go', and they went, but not before they had seen three young peasants, with blood on their galabiyyas and ropes round their wrists and necks, being pushed into the makeshift kiosk at the side of the road.

It was half past three when, after a series of bumpy dirt tracks, they finally turned into green gates set into a white wall and came to a stop. Isabel's first impression was of a film set from a movie about Mexico: a low-lying white house with vaulted domes and slits for windows. A woman appeared, followed by two young girls, and there was much hugging and kissing and exclaiming and Isabel was introduced: 'Isabel, khatibet akhuya.'

'Ya marhab, Sett Eesa,' the woman said, and that became her name. Returned to its origin, without the Latin 'bella' – just the name of the goddess of this land. Jonathan would have been amused. Once again, Isabel missed her father.

She loved the house. She thought it was air-conditioned when she stepped into the big central hall, but it was the thick walls keeping out the worst of the heat, the vaulted ceiling and the windows to the veranda coaxing in the air, making the most of it. Amal ran around showing her the rooms, showing her how the house worked: the three wings opening on to the veranda enclosing the lush, shaded garden, the mandarah with its separate entrance so the men could receive guests without exposing the women of the house, the big bathrooms with the Victorian tubs resting on their claw feet. Amal had, for the moment, forgotten the three young men on the road and was touched with happiness.

'You know, it feels as if you've come home,' Isabel said.

'Does it?' Amal asked, surprised. 'Well,' she said, 'I suppose – you see, my flat, I only got that when I came back. From England. So I guess this *is* home. I mean, this is what's left of everything I knew as a child. All the furniture and everything.'

And the pictures. Everywhere, the photographs in black and white and the watercolours vivid with light. Isabel walked round examining them.

'It's rather crowded,' Amal said. 'The three houses in Cairo – all the pictures ended up here.'

Isabel guessed immediately about the watercolours. 'Anna's,' she said. 'Are they Anna's?'

'Yes, they are. Look here –' And there, in the corner, was the small, firm signature: Anna.

In one painting a courtyard was bounded by a porticoed gallery. In the centre, a fountain splashed on coloured tiles. A child knelt, looking down into the water. In another you looked through a gap between some flowering bushes into a wide lawn and at a man at the far end, standing with his back to you, pointing, as though indicating a spot where something was to be planted – or buried. In another, darker than the rest, a man lay on a divan; through the mashrabiyya behind him no light came. A woman crouched on the floor by his side.

'She was good,' Isabel said.

'A proper English education.' Amal smiled.

Isabel turned to the photographs. 'Let me guess who everyone is,' she said. 'Oh, this one's very grand –'

'That's el-Ghazi Mukhtar Pasha, the representative of the Ottoman Sultan in Egypt. He was friendly with the big Baroudi, Mahmoud Sami –'

'Look at that beard. And all those medals and decorations. All that brass.'

There was the family group of Husni al-Ghamrawi, his wife and his child. There was a portrait of an elderly man in the traditional white 'imma and dark cloak. He had a white beard and moustache and under the dark eyebrows his eyes were thoughtful, even troubled. 'Sheikh Muhammad 'Abdu,' Amal said, 'the Grand Imam, but look at this one –'

And in that other portrait there was the sheikh, the beard and moustache now jet black, the brow more deeply furrowed, the eyes challenging, angry. And in the room allocated to Isabel, Layla al-Baroudi's room, there was the portrait Isabel had been most keen to see: her own great-grandfather, Sharif Basha al-Baroudi.

'Listen, you'd better lie down and have a rest,' Amal said. She came over and felt her forehead. 'I think you're all right. Do you feel all right?'

'Yes, absolutely. I'm just going to unpack. Can I use the drawers?'

'Use anything you like.' Amal opened the drawers of her grandmother's tall chest one after the other. 'What is this?' Out of the bottom drawer she lifted a soft bundle wrapped in white linen. She laid it down on the bed and unwrapped it. Green fabric; unfolded, it revealed itself to be a large green flag, at its centre a white cross and crescent entwined.

'What is it?' asked Isabel, standing beside her.

Amal stroked out the creases. 'It's the flag of national unity. I'd forgotten I put it here. This dates from 1919.' She looked up at Isabel. 'Sa'd Zaghloul's revolution. The first time in the history of modern Egypt that women went out and demonstrated on the streets. And this was the flag the people carried.

To tell the British that all of Egypt, Christian and Muslim, wanted them out.'

'Just this one flag?'

'Isabel! No. Hundreds. This was the one my grandmother must have used.' She folds it back and tucks it under her arm. 'You really should have a rest. I'm going to.'

Neither of them mentioned what they had seen on the road.

The sun had set simply and without display, a plain red disc descending through a clear, darkening sky into a silver horizon.

As the light faded, the women had started to arrive: small, black tents moving silently up the path. At the door they took off their shoes. In the hall the black wrappings came off and the room was filled with the bright colours of their satin dresses: pinks and purples and greens resplendent against the dark furniture and plain white upholstery. Each had brought something with her: a dish she had made, a batch of fresh-baked pastry, some eggs, a watermelon, Christmassy, when it was broken open, in its red and green. Some had small children with them who wandered round the room, then out of the open door to the larger world outside.

Amal had been hugged and kissed again and again. 'And this is my brother's fiancée,' she said again and again. And then the welcomes, the blessings, the compliments: 'The name of God guard and protect her.' 'He's known how to choose.' 'She's brought light to our village.' 'And she speaks Arabic?'

'Shwayya,' Isabel offered.

'Khalas, stay with us here and we'll teach you.'

'Teach her? You'll teach her our talk, the talk of the fallaheen?'

'What else? Shall we teach her the talk of the television?'

'And what's wrong with the talk of the fallaheen?'

'When she goes to Cairo they'll laugh at her.'

'She can teach us English. What do you say? Will you teach us English, ya Sett Eesa?'

'And what will you do with English, ya habibti?'

'We learn. Put a few words together. It might come in useful –'

'Yakhti, learn Arabic first. Untangle the writing.'

'Neither English nor Arabic. They've closed it down.'

Isabel pieced it together: the words she understood, the women's gestures, Amal's occasional, murmured translations. The tea tray went round. And the little morsels of kunafa and balah el-Sham they had brought with them from Cairo, and glasses of cold water.

'They've closed it down, ya Sett, and we depended on it. Where will the children study?'

'And the Unit. It was useful for us.'

'The one of us had just about convinced her husband about this thing of family planning and now they've closed the Unit. No loops, no condoms –'

'Yakhti, have some shame, you and her! Are your tongues loose or what?'

'Have we said anything? We're women together. Or is the Sett a stranger?'

'No stranger but the Devil. We're all kin –'

'What will you do, ya Sett Amal?'

'I don't know.'

'So who would know? Isn't it yours through your father and your grandfather before him?'

'Yes. But –'

'Talk to the government.'

'And is talking to the government easy?'

'No, but they should have some understanding. The village has done nothing.'

'They've put the soldiers at the doors and no one can come near.'

'They say the teachers were terrorists.'

'There are no terrorists in our village. And the midwife, is she a terrorist too? Here she is in front of you. Ask her.'

Abu el-Ma'ati's widowed daughter, a plump woman with a

smooth face and a blue tattoo on her chin, smiled. 'What can we do? The government has a strong hand.'

'Strong on the weak.'

'They don't want problems.'

'We didn't make problems. Each one of us minds their own business –'

'While we were coming on the road,' Amal said slowly, 'we saw three young men being arrested –'

'No one is bigger than the government. They do what they like. Lock up the people, burn down the sugar cane – they say the terrorists hide in it and they burn it down. The people are weary, ya Sett Amal, weary.'

'I'll go see the school tomorrow,' Amal said.

'God give you light. But the soldiers hold nothing in their hands. Not even the head of police can do anything. It all depends on the government in Cairo.'

'May God smooth the path.'

'And since Sett Eesa is here with us – tell her, ya Sett Amal, tell her to tell her government to lighten its hand on us a little.'

'Everything that happens they say Amreeka wants this: they cancel the peasant cooperatives, Amreeka wants this –'

'And when you go to the bank for the loan to put in your next crop, they tell you you have to pay so much interest –'

'What are they saying?' Isabel had asked and Amal had translated. The women wanted her to translate.

'They cancel the subsidies on sugar and oil: Amreeka wants this –'

'The price of medicines has become like fire –'

'It's not Amreeka.' Amal was part embarrassed, part amused. 'It's the, like, the World Bank and –'

'It's the same thing. Isn't Amreeka the biggest country now and what she says goes?'

'Yes, but the matter –'

'What?'

'It's more complicated than that.'

'Complicated or not complicated, we're here on the land and the one of us works all day till our backs snap and we still

can't live. And the young people – they go and get educated
and then what? They want to get married, they want a house
to shelter them, they want to work and live like humans and
life has become very difficult.'

Isabel had sat and listened, trying to make it all out.

Outside in the garden the children were playing at weddings. A little boy and girl sat on the stairs, green branches and
palm fronds arranged round them to suggest the kosha, the
wedding bower. The little girl had a white cloth on her head
and looked down at the ground shyly as the boy reached out
to hold her hand. Two girls with scarves drawn tight around
what would later become their hips, were dancing in front of
them. The rest of the children sat in a circle at their feet. One
drummed on a sheet of wood and the others clapped and sang:

My father said Oh pretty dark one
Allah Allah
Don't ride no more on your donkey
Allah Allah
I'll up and buy you an aeroplane –
And I want some Pepsi-Cola
For I won't drink tea
Go get me Pepsi-Cola
No I won't drink tea

'Get up, girl, you and her! Get up, you who should be
beaten.'

'Look at the kids in a hurry for themselves.'

'Kids who can be frightened but not shamed.'

My father said No don't go out
Allah Allah
You might get black and never be white
Allah Allah
Just keep your whiteness for your groom –
And I want some Pepsi-Cola
No I won't drink tea

Go get me Pepsi-Cola
For I won't drink tea

Isabel has never known a silence like this before: a silence that is not merely an absence of sound. 'Palpable' — that's what it was: a silence you could imagine touching, pressing into, as you can imagine pressing into clouds. But here there are no clouds. She throws back the linen sheet and sits up in Layla al-Ghamrawi's big brass four-poster. Through the fine gauze of the mosquito netting she can see, on the wall facing her, the portrait of Sharif Basha al-Baroudi. Now she can make it out only dimly, but she has studied it well. From the heavy gilt frame he looks down at her, the fez set squarely above the high forehead, the eyebrows broad and black, almost meeting above the straight nose. The thick moustache covers the upper lip; the lower lip is firm and wide in a strong, square chin. And all the arrogance of the face is perfectly focused in the eyes: proud, aloof and yet, if you look carefully, sad also. A proud man, in control, holding back. And it is in that face, more than in the face of his father out in the hall, that Isabel sees 'Omar el-Ghamrawi. Sees him and longs for him. How many times had they met? She goes over them again. The dinner at Deborah's house, the restaurant on Sixth — that was when she had fallen in love: as she watched him cross the room towards her, his hand briefly raised, the smile dawning in his eyes. Then the meeting at college, pausing every three steps to talk to someone, just like Amal on the streets of Cairo. It was there, after he had stopped to speak to a bearded young Arab student, that she had asked, 'Are you involved with the fundamentalists?'

'What fundamentalists?' he asked.

'I don't know. Hamas, or Hizbollah. Or in Egypt.'

'You should get your fundamentalists sorted —'

'But is it true?'

'Do I look like a fundamentalist? Act like a fundamentalist?'

'No. But that is what they say about you.'

178

'Not so long ago, Hillary Clinton would have been called a communist for her views on public health.'

'So you're not?'

'My dear child, no. Of course I'm not. Look, there's Claudia. What an amazing hat –'

The fourth time had been to see *Scapin* at the Roundabout and dinner afterwards. She couldn't say he had taken her out for she was the one who'd invited him – but he had been happy to be there. She reruns again the moment in the foyer when she had slipped off her coat and turned to him and he had smiled into her eyes.

'You look divine.'

The hand at her elbow guiding her to her seat. And when she had driven him to his door, the slight pause – had he been deciding whether to invite her in?

'Shall I see you before you go?' he had asked.

'Yes,' she'd said, 'I'll call you.' It was better than waiting for him to call. He had leaned towards her, and his quick, dry kiss was over before it had begun.

'Good night.'

And she had called him, and asked him to come and see her find. She'd made some pasta and a salad, and he looked through the trunk. When she told him that Anna, the woman who had written the journal, was her great-grandmother, he must have put it all together straight away, but he said nothing. Later, when they were having coffee, he said, 'You know what you should do? Take it to Cairo and show it to my sister. She lives there. She can help you piece it together.'

'What, the whole thing?'

'Why not? Put it on the plane. Get someone to carry it for you.' And she had agreed because it was his sister. Because he was sending her to his sister and that would be a continuing link between them.

'Do you actually live with her?' she had asked.

'Who? Live with who?'

'Samantha Metcalfe.'

'No, no, my dear. I don't live with anyone. Not any more.'

'How long is it since you've been divorced?' Lightly, making a business of pouring fresh coffee.

'A long time. Ten years. Why?'

'I just wondered.'

'And you? You were married.'

'Yes. Two. Two years.'

'Two years married or two years divorced?'

'Both.' She had smiled. 'Two years married and two divorced.'

'And?' he asked. 'Would you do it again? Marry, I mean.'

'I don't know.' She had looked at him. 'If I find the right man.'

'It's good to have kids,' he said. 'Kids are good. I have two. Well, they're practically grown up now.'

'I know,' she had said.

When he got up to go, when he had his coat on, and his scarf, and was at the door, she had walked into his arms. She had raised her face to his and when he kissed her she put her arms round him and would not let go. She had wanted to stay in the warmth and comfort of him for ever and their kiss had deepened and she felt that wonderful rushing melting in her stomach and her breasts and her arms and then he had put her away.

'Oh, Isabel,' he said, and shook his head. In his voice there was a note almost of regret. But his hand was still tangled in her hair and he pulled her head back so she had to look up at him as he said, 'I'm old enough to be your father.'

'I know,' she'd said. 'It doesn't matter.'

'Yes, it does,' he said. His hand had caressed her cheek for a moment, his thumb had brushed over her lip. He murmured, 'Take care,' and walked out of the door, leaving her with this ache.

This ache that would not go away. Even though she can feel his lips on hers, though in her mind she makes him unfasten her blouse and against the closed lids of her eyes watches his hands move against the white lace of her bra, fingering it, pulling at it, though she lies with him there on the floor of her apartment and feels his weight on top of her and the hard wood of the floor under her back, though she takes herself to the limit – when it's over, she still aches for him.

When she lifts her head again, Isabel sees through the netting, through the wire mesh of the screen on the window, the world outside floodlit by the cold, white moon. She pushes aside the gossamer canopy. She opens the mesh screens, closes them behind her, and on weakened legs steps out on the veranda.

All the cushions have been removed in anticipation of the morning dew and Isabel sits on the bare cane of an armchair, her arms drawn tight around her body, and feels the soft night air on her neck and on her face: a pleasant warmth, broken, from time to time, by a breeze bringing with it the scent of the Indian jasmine spiced with a sharp edge of lemon. Out here, the silence is a backdrop to the chirp of the crickets and occasionally, from further away in the depths of the garden, the throaty croak of a frog.

All around her the house sits, solid and serene in its hundred and twenty years. A house that had grown with the family over four generations. At its heart the spacious hall and the hospitable mandarah, the north wing with the two bedrooms and the guestroom built by Mustafa Bey al-Ghamrawi, the storerooms, bathroom and oven-room. Then the veranda, the bedrooms and bathrooms in the south wing added by Husni al-Ghamrawi. The electricity generator, the plumbing and the new kitchen put in by Ahmad al-Ghamrawi. And the garden, planted and watered and tended over the years. Its trees bearing pears, lemons and oranges. Its bushes heavy with jasmine and roses. And he, what had he done to this house? Nothing. He went to Amreeka.

Isabel looks up: Amal has come out on the veranda. She is in a pale, long nightdress, with a light shawl around her shoulders. 'I had a feeling you were out here,' she says. 'Do you particularly want to be alone?'

'Oh no, not at all,' Isabel says.

Amal leans against the wooden railings looking out at the garden, breathing in deep. 'Isn't it just beautiful?' she says.

'Yes,' says Isabel.

Amal turns to her. 'Did you spray yourself with the mosquito stuff?'

'No,' says Isabel.

'Do it then. Go on.'

'But there aren't any mosquitoes.'

'There might be. Just one would be enough. Go on. Go and get it. Where is it? I'll get it for you.'

'I'll get it,' Isabel says, standing up. She comes back with the canister and they both spray their arms and feet. They spray their hands and wipe the liquid on to their faces.

'Yuk,' says Isabel.

'I know. But in a moment you won't smell it and the mosquitoes will.'

'There's no photograph of you on the walls,' Isabel says.

'No.'

'Well there should be.'

'Why?'

'For continuity. You and your boys.'

'My boys have nothing to do with all this. They've made their choice.' Amal keeps her voice light.

'They're young. You don't know what they might do.'

Amal says nothing.

'In any case,' Isabel continues, 'it would be right. Not a snapshot. A formal portrait, like all the others. We must have one done in Cairo.'

'I'll tell you what,' Amal says, 'let's have one of both of us. We are family, aren't we?'

'Did you give me this room on purpose?' Isabel asks.

'On purpose? Why?'

'Because of his picture.'

'Sharif Basha?'

'He looks exactly like . . . your brother.'

'Does he? I never thought of that,' Amal says.

In the room they stand in front of the photograph.

'See?' says Isabel.

Amal studies the man on the wall. 'Yes,' she says slowly. 'He's more like him than like our father isn't he?'

'It's the eyes and the chin and − it's more than that,' Isabel says, 'it's the whole − it's the energy. And the air of not letting on. Of being more than he's showing.'

'Isabel?'

'Yes,' says Isabel. 'Is it terribly obvious?'

'I don't know about obvious −'

'I can't get him out of my head. I think about him all the time. Whatever I am doing, he is like a current running through my mind −' The relief of talking about it, letting it out. At last.

'And he − has he − have you . . .'

'No. Nothing has actually happened. I don't even know if he shares my feelings. I think he likes being with me. We've been out together and the chemistry is there and it couldn't be there if he didn't feel it too. Maybe he thinks the age difference is a problem. He's fifty-five. It's hard to believe. It sounds so old, but if you didn't know, you'd think he was forty, forty-five, wouldn't you? I mean, he's so *young*.'

The two women sit side by side on the sofa facing the portrait.

'Is it making you unhappy?' Amal asks.

'No, I'm not unhappy,' says Isabel. 'But I just wish he would − God, I just want him so much!'

'He probably likes you a lot. He probably doesn't want you to get hurt.'

'If he was in love with me as I am with him, he wouldn't care about that.'

'Come on −'

'No. He'd think I wouldn't get hurt. It wouldn't *occur* to him that I might get hurt. I *wouldn't* get hurt.'

'But you've been through this before?' Amal asks after a while.

'Are you trying −'

'I just thought –'

'Why? You know I was married.'

'I just thought if you've been through something like this before, you'll know that it doesn't last for ever. I know that sounds –'

'I've not felt like this before – about anyone.'

After a few moments Isabel asks, 'Has he said anything to you?'

'No. No, he hasn't,' Amal says.

'But he must have known, the moment he looked through that trunk. He must have known that we're cousins. That's why he said to bring it to you.'

'Yes. He didn't tell me, though. He left me to find out for myself.'

'And to tell me.'

'He must have liked the thought of us here together, working it out.'

'But it shouldn't make any difference, should it? Our common ancestry. I mean, it shouldn't make him not – care for me? If he does.'

'No. I don't see why it should.'

'Amal. Do you think it was meant? It seems so strange. That I should meet him like that, and then find the trunk and then it turns out we're cousins?'

'But you might not have met. If you hadn't gone to that dinner party or if –'

'Yes, but we *did* meet.'

'Yes.'

'Amal. He's your brother. Tell me what to do.'

'Ya habibti, he's old enough to be your father.'

'Please – just don't say that.'

'It's the obvious thing.'

'But it doesn't *matter*.'

Amal is silent.

'I'm going to do something about him,' Isabel says. 'This time. When I go back.'

⋆　　⋆　　⋆

'Any success?' Isabel asks.

Amal kicks off her shoes at the door and sighs as she puts her bare feet down on the cool tiles. 'No,' she says, 'not really. God, it's hot out there!'

'Come and sit down,' Isabel says. 'Let me get you a cold drink.' It seems so natural to her now, on just the second day here, she is the one playing the hostess, getting the drinks, looking after Amal, staying in the background when people come to talk.

'We couldn't go in,' Amal says, holding the cold glass to her cheek, to her forehead. 'They were perfectly civil. But we couldn't go inside.'

'What would you have gained anyway, by going in?'

'I don't know,' Amal says. 'It just seemed a place to start.' She leans back and tilts her face up to the old wooden ceiling-fan. 'The place looks practically derelict. They won't even let them sweep the courtyard.'

'What are you going to do?'

'I don't know. I thought of going to see the Chief of Police, but I don't think that'd be much use.'

On the wall, Husni al-Ghamrawi stands, pleasant and open-faced, his moustache clipped short, his fez straight on his head. His hand rests lightly on the shoulder of his seated wife. Layla al-Baroudi's black hair is curled and piled on top of her head. Her cloak, fastened by a glittering brooch, falls to the floor about her seat and her dark eyes look straight at the camera. Behind her stands her son, Ahmad al-Ghamrawi. Although he has no moustache yet, he is already as tall as his father. He wears his fez at a slight angle and on his face there is the hopeful confidence of the young.

'What would your father have done?' Isabel asks.

'I don't know. Go see the Governor, I suppose.'

'Then that's what you must do.'

'There's somebody – the son of an old friend of my father's. They own land around here too. I'll go and see him. See what he says.'

For a few minutes the two women sit silently together on

the old Assiuti chairs. The only movement in the room is that of the ceiling-fan revolving above them.

'I'm going to have a shower, then lie down for a bit.' Amal scoops up her long black hair into a makeshift knot and turns to Isabel. 'Are you all right? You're rather cooped up here, aren't you?'

Isabel smiles. 'I'm just fine. I feel so amazingly at home in this house.'

'Good. I'm very glad,' Amal says, but her smile is tired.

'They tell me horrid things,' Amal says after the siesta. 'They say they just round people up in the mornings. Ordinary people going to work. They have their IDs and everything but they round them up anyway. And you can spend five days in the hold till they decide you're not the one they want. And it's not a holiday in there: they beat them and they . . . They say if the police go looking for someone and they don't find him, they take his women: his wife, his sister, his mother, whatever. And they hold them till he gives himself up. And the men won't stand for that and what starts out as one case ends up being a vendetta between the police and the whole village.'

Isabel has nothing to say. Arrest warrants. You have the right to remain silent – nothing of what she knows holds here.

'It's all going wrong,' Amal says. 'Someone robbed a jeweller's shop and the jeweller was a Copt and they say the Islamic militants say it's all right to rob a Copt to fund the Jihad, and so the whole thing turns into a "sectarian" issue. But people – ordinary people – don't believe it's OK to rob a Copt, but then the Americans – I'm sorry –'

'It's OK,' Isabel says. 'Tell me.'

'Well, they're trying to pass some bill through Congress about their duty to protect the Christian minority in Egypt, and of course that's the game the British played a hundred years ago and people know that. It just stirs up bad feeling.'

'Do they feel persecuted, the Copts?'

'Even if they do, they don't want it sorted by some foreign

intervention. Everyone knows what that means. Anba She-nuda has written to Congress saying thanks but no thanks –'

'Who?'

'Anba Shenuda, he's the Patriarch, the head of the Coptic Church, Pope Shenuda the Third. He's really impressive. You know he was exiled by Sadat from '81 to '85–'

There is a sound of footsteps outside and a knock on the door. Isabel opens and stands aside. Abu el-Ma'ati and some other men are outside the door. Abu el-Ma'ati has a gun on his shoulder.

'Kheir ya 'Am Abu el-Ma'ati, itfaddal,' Amal calls, standing up. He comes in but the others stay outside. Amal ushers him to the sofa. 'Kheir? What's happening?'

'There have been clashes,' he says, 'between the people and the police. This new law will tear the place apart. The lands on the other side of the village. They tried to turn the people out but they won't go. The men brought out their weapons and the world caught fire.'

'Ya Satir ya Rabb,' Amal breathes. And then, 'What do you think is going to happen, 'Am Abu el-Ma'ati?'

'Only God knows, ya Sett Hanim. But these are treacherous times and people are got at from all sides. Some of the landowners know God. Yusuf Bey el-Qommos, the head-master of the boys' school, has already said he won't raise his rents. Two others have agreed to meetings with the fallaheen to decide on a gradual raising over a few years. But others have hard heads –'

'But the government has said they'll compensate the fallaheen: give them other lands.'

'Desert lands, ya Sett Hanim. Without water, without money to get them started. Where will they get new farm-land? Is the government – I ask His forgiveness – going to create fields?'

Fields and more fields on either side of the road. From where they are it looks as if the whole world were green. But from higher up, from a hill – if there were a hill in this flat country –

187

or from a pyramid (one of the many that two thousand years ago lined this route from Thebes to Memphis, from the Delta to the Cataract) or from an aeroplane today, you would be able to see how narrow the strip of green was, how closely it clung to the winding river. The river like a lifeline thrown across the desert, the villages and towns hanging on to it, clustering together, glancing over their shoulders at the desert always behind them. Appeasing it, finally, by making it the dwelling of their dead.

Amal and Isabel, three months into their friendship, drive back to Cairo in companionable silence. Since they are heading away from the Sa'id they are waved through the barricades with just a cursory glance inside the car. They drive without stopping. The car behaves impeccably.

Amal is thinking of the village and her promise to 'speak to the government'. But she is also thinking of the table under the window, of Anna's journals. She is impatient to get back to Anna, to go with her into the Sinai.

Isabel is planning her return to New York, her meeting with 'Omar. She is telling him in her head about her plan to make a film of Anna's story. She is wondering if she can get Tawasi into the film. She tries to recognise the town where the car was mended, Beni Mazar, and then the spot where it broke down.

'That man who helped us,' she says, 'he really wouldn't take your money, would he?' Every time she'd seen that pantomime before, money had in fact ended up changing hands.

'No.'

'Why not?'

Amal smiles. 'He said, what would the foreign lady think if he took money for helping women stranded on the road?'

'The foreign lady would think he was smart. He looked like he could use some cash. It's a miracle *his* car didn't break down.'

'Ah, well,' Amal said, 'we have to put our trust in miracles sometimes.'

14

. . . and eased the putting off
These troublesome disguises which we wear.
                                    John Milton

15 March 1901

A fire is lit, and the saddle from one of the horses placed near it for Anna to sit on. A few metres away the men move around settling the animals, putting up a tent, preparing food. When she looks at them, dark figures against the dark night, Anna always knows which one he is.

'Happy now? My lady happy now?'

Anna raises a warning finger to her lips as she looks up at Sabir's smiling face. 'No "lady",' she whispers, shaking her head, reminding him.

He waves his hand dismissively. 'They no English,' he says, then again: 'You happy now?'

'Yes,' says Anna, 'very happy.'

'Sahara,' he says. 'Tent, camels, fire . . .' The sweep of his arm takes in the universe. 'English people, they like tent,' he says. 'Tent very good.'

'Yes,' says Anna. She points up to the sky. 'Stars too.'

'Keteer star,' Sabir says, 'star yama. Not one, two. Much. Too much star.'

I am in the desert: in the desert of Sinai. And no reading of guidebooks or travellers' accounts, not even the stretch of desert I saw at Ghizeh, could have prepared me for this. I will not even attempt at this moment to write down my thoughts and feelings, for they are too confused. It is a vastness which I have never before experienced — the land, the sea and the sky, all stretching unbroken and united. And our little band of men and beasts ambling through it all.

I am writing this in the tent which has been so thoughtfully provided for my comfort — although I am envious of the men sleeping outside under the stars. I asked Sharif Pasha if it would not become too cold later when the fire goes out, and he showed me the cloaks they wrap themselves in at night. These are made of wool, with a lining of brown fleece, and indeed felt wonderfully warm. For myself I am handsomely provided for with a beautiful Persian rug, a large cushion of striped silk on which to sleep and some blankets of the finest wool. I also have a tallow candle in a lantern, and my saddlebags and writing-box were carried into the tent. A copper pot full of water was placed at the back of my tent and I was given to understand by Sabir, who grows more cheerful by the hour, that that portion of desert behind my tent was to be considered my personal domain for the night.

Tonight, as we conversed by the light of the fire, I noticed for the first time how good-looking Sabir is. He is the dark, burnt brown that I understand betokens a Nubian. His features are delicate, his eyes as large and soft as those of a fawn and his whole aspect is one of delicacy and gentleness. He is bedded down across my door and when I looked surprised he said with a broad smile, 'When wolf come, he find me first.' I have been sorely tempted to lift the flap and step over him and go outside, but I have withstood the temptation for I believe it would not be considered correct. I have, however, peeped out and there, far, far away, was a sky of black velvet with stars so plentifully strewn across it that if more had come they would have been hard put to find an empty space. And below, all was blackness, except for the flickering glow cast by the dying fire. I picked out the figures of four men sleeping, with nothing between them and the whole universe but a length of sheepskin.

I hardly trust myself to write about him. I do not know what I should write about him.

I will start from the beginning: in the courtyard of that magical house, with Ahmad on his knee, I understood that I was to meet him at the point where we would begin our journey into Sinai. I

191

*was to travel with one of his men – Mutlaq, a man he trusts
absolutely. And even though we had decided that I was to travel
in Sinai as a Frenchman, there was still the vexed question of the
guise I was to adopt to get to Sinai.*

*'The problem is the train,' Layla explained. 'If you travel as
an Englishman, you will have to travel first class and alone.
There will be attempts to draw you into conversation, and that
will be dangerous. If you travel as an Arab, you will sit in second
class with Mutlaq. But people will be close enough to look at you
and see that you are not an Arab, and they will be curious. So,
on the train you will travel as an Egyptian woman – Mutlaq's
sister. That way you will be completely covered up. You arrive at
Suez, you cross the Canal and on the other side my brother
meets you. You take off your outer dress, put on your kufiyya
and voilà: you are an Arab man. Here, let us try the clothes.'*

'Ça vous va très bien,' Layla says. 'Everything you put on suits
you so well.' She steps back and surveys Anna. 'What shall we
do about your hair?'

'Shall I braid it?'

'Yes; sit down, I'll do it for you.'

Layla brushes Anna's hair and pulls it into a tight braid at the
back of her head.

'Now,' she says, 'this – this is your kufiyya. You can wear it
with or without the 'uqal, this cord, but it does help to keep it
on your head. You wear it loose down your shoulders like
this. Now look.'

Anna gazes into the mirror and a fair, surprised-looking
young Arab gazes back at her.

Layla smiles at her in the mirror. 'All the girls will fall in love
with you.'

'What girls?' Anna smiles back. 'We are going into the
desert.'

'Oh, there are girls in the desert too. Look: you can throw
the ends – one or both – round your neck like this. You can
also wrap the ends round your face and tie them at the back
like this. This is for protection from the wind or the sand if

there's a storm. But if you're just sitting with people you must never cover your face because it looks as if you are trying to hide. Yes?'

'Yes,' says Anna trying the different styles.

'Some men fling it back,' says Layla, 'like that, or fold the sides on top of their heads, like this. But don't do that because, look —'

Anna looks into the mirror. 'I look like a woman.'

'Yes. I think, perhaps, mostly wear it across, hiding your neck and a bit of your chin.'

'Yes.'

'And, you know, I think you should keep your riding boots and socks. Otherwise your feet give you away.'

'I do wish you were coming.'

'Next time,' Layla laughs, 'when Ahmad is bigger.' Suddenly she looks serious. 'You're not worried, are you?'

'Worried?'

'Because Abeih Sharif would never let anything happen to you.'

'You know, Layla, I feel I've disturbed — I mean, he normally would . . .'

'He offered to take you.'

'Yes, but he felt responsible, and —'

'Anna, listen. Do you want to go?'

'Oh, yes!'

'Then go. And enjoy it. It will be wonderful. And remember: constantly put cream on your face and hands. The desert air is very dry.'

And even though she has left her shirts and trousers folded on what she now thought of as her divan, and even though, in one of her canvas saddlebags, Layla has tucked away a small silk parcel: 'in case you get tired of men's dress', Anna hesitates at the door of the haramlek.

'I will see you again?'

'But naturally.' Layla smiles. She holds out her arms and the two women embrace. 'When you return, I shall be here to welcome you.'

A closed carriage at the door and I climbed in wearing the loose white clothing of an Arab, covered by the flowing black outer garment of an Egyptian woman of the city. My head and face were most thoroughly veiled, and my kufiyya and ugal were in the black cloth bag I carried. Sabir came inside the carriage with me for fear that if he sat on the box outside someone should see him and recognise him. He climbed into the carriage with his eyes averted and his head held low, muttering apologies and 'la hawla wala quwwata illa b-Illah'. He sat in the furthest corner from me and muttered all the way to the station. But Layla tells me he would not go ahead with her brother nor yet stay in their house to await my return but was unshakable in that he had vowed to his master that he would not let me out of his sight and would fulfil his vow or perish.

In the station I walked slightly apart from the men as Layla had instructed me, but Mutlaq, like a mother, has eyes in the back of his head, and if I paused he paused and if I walked he walked, so the distance between us remained constant, and that without his once turning round or looking at me directly.

As we walked into the great hall of the station, a train was whistling, getting ready to leave. I glanced at Mutlaq.

'Iskindiriyya,' he said under his breath.

The doors were being slammed shut and people were hurrying along the platform. We walked across the hall and suddenly there was a great bustle and we and many other people were pushed aside as porters hurried by, clearing a path. And as Mutlaq put out a hand to steady me I almost thought I should have died of fright for there, inches from my face, were Lord and Lady Chelsea, Lady Wolverton and Lady St Oswald together with the Honourable Sir Hedworth Lambton – whom I had dined with recently and whom I have met many times across Sir Charles's dinner table. It was a most curious sensation; they passed so close that I could smell Lady St Oswald's cologne and if I had put out my hand I could have plucked at the sleeve of her brown travelling coat. I felt at once the fear of being discovered and the strangeness of their sweeping by me without acknowl-edgement – but the oddest thing of all was that I suddenly saw

194

them as bright, exotic creatures, walking in a kind of magical space, oblivious to all around them; at ease, chattering to each other as though they were out for a stroll in the park, while the people, pushed aside, watched and waited for them to pass.

There was another man with them, and later, when I had leisure to reflect, I surmised it must be Mr Wilfrid Blunt, for his hair, his eyes and his carriage fit well with the descriptions I have heard of him. I had been wishing to meet him these five months and now he walked past me – and I was invisible.

Still, it is a most liberating thing, this veil. While I was wearing it, I could look wherever I wanted and nobody could look back at me. Nobody could find out who I was. I was one of many black-clad harem in the station and on the train and could have traded places with several of them and no one been the wiser.

We arrived at Suez and made immediately for the Canal, which we crossed in a comfortable boat. Mutlaq, as usual, making all the arrangements, myself following meekly and Sabir following not so meekly, and as we stepped out on the far bank and the boatman had turned the nose of his craft back towards Suez, I heard the sound of clattering hooves and looked to see Sharif Pasha cantering towards us on a fine chestnut Arab.

'Dépêchez-vous alors, if you are going to transform yourself,' he said by way of greeting. He swung off his horse and the three men stood forming a screen with their backs to me and I, grasping what was required, peeled off my black woman's garment and veil, unrolled my kufiyya, secured it on my head with the ugal and by the time the curt question came, I was able to answer 'Yes' while rolling up the black garments. And when the three men stood aside, an observer would have seen a fourth man in Arab clothes coming out from among them and bending over the saddlebags on the ground to put away a small, black bundle.

I write 'I looked to see Sharif Pasha cantering . . .' but in reality it was only when he drew near, spoke and dismounted that I believed it was he. He was dressed as I was, in the robe and cloak of the desert Arab – but he also had two carbines strapped to his back. The outfit became him so utterly that it was only with difficulty that I could imagine him back in his European city clothes, and he, seeing the little glances I kept throwing to convince myself that it was truly he, frowned slightly and said nothing.

A shot in the air produced two more men on camel-back leading camels and horses. Four of the camels were made to kneel down in the sand and Sharif Pasha asked me to watch closely the movement of the camel that rose when Mutlaq was mounted. 'Will you be able to do this?' he asked, and on my answer he bade me go to a particular one of the animals, put my foot in the stirrup and mount while he held the reins – and with a loud groan and a great rocking motion the beast rose to its front legs first and then its hind legs, each movement being accomplished in two halves as it unfolded itself first to kneel and then to stand.

When all was organised and we set forth, we were six men on six camels, two more being led with provisions and saddlebags, while the Arabs, a chestnut and a white mare, were led unburdened.

We ambled along, allowing the camels to set their own comfortable pace. Riding a camel is different from riding a horse in that it is more undulating, but when you learn the rhythm it is pleasant and the broad saddle with the stout handle at the front is comfortable. I found that Sabir and I were the only ones to ride with stirrups.

We rode mostly in silence, but he (Sharif Pasha) did inform me that the two men who came with him were members of a tribe with whom he has a connection and they are to stay with us for the whole of the expedition. Tomorrow night when we make camp it will be as the guests of their chief.

We rode through the afternoon and the evening, and it was as though the desert had cast a spell of silence over us all, man and beast. It was as though on this, our first day, only a matter of profound importance should warrant the breaking of this great silence, a silence underlined by the gentle roar of the sea as it washed against the rough shore.

We rode on, and we stopped only twice. Once when we made camp for the night. The other earlier: when the sun set beyond the Gulf of Suez, making clear to me whence came the name the

'Red' Sea; for the setting sun brought out the red and black of the ore in the mountains and the sea reflected it all back. All the reds, and yellow and orange and purple, were in that wonderful landscape, and as it faded and the colours all round us melted more and more into gentleness, I thought there should be some act – some formal recognition of this daily magnificence. Even as the thought formed itself in my mind, we came to a halt as though by agreement. The animals knelt, the men dismounted and turned towards the South-East. One voice was lifted: 'Allahu Akbar', and they prayed silently together. I walked around behind them and observed the sea, and the darkening of the waters that just moments earlier had been so silvery and flecked with light, and I too offered up a prayer – and the prayer that sprang to my silent lips was for peace of mind and peace of heart, for it seemed that more than ever now they were within my reach.

15

The face of all the world is changed, I think
Since first I heard the footsteps of thy soul.
                        Elizabeth Barrett Browning

12 July 1997

I cannot wait to get back into the Sinai, back into Anna's world and away from my own. Cairo is full of talk of the 'Cult of Satan' – which will eventually boil down to a group of young men and women in black T-shirts listening to heavy metal in the spooky halls of the Baron Empain's derelict palace in Heliopolis. The fallaheen riot and the police put them down. The readers' letters in *al-Ahram* are noisy with arguments for and against the new land laws. I have made some telephone calls, reactivated old friendships, found Tareq 'Atiyya, the son of my father's friend, and gone to see him at his office in a tall marble and black glass building in Muhandeseen. A pretty secretary shows me in and for a moment I think the man behind the desk is 'Atiyya Bey, my father's friend. Then he stands to greet me and takes my hands.

'Amal! You haven't changed at all.'

We sit in soft leather armchairs and exchange news: our families, our children, what we have been doing over the past twenty years. We speak as we always have: Arabic, inlaid with French and English phrases. He tells me he imports linings for the huge concrete pipes that carry oil across the desert and owns one hotel in Marsa Matruh and another in Sharm el-Sheikh, in Sinai. He plans to be the first to bring mobile phones into Egypt.

'You have to come to our house,' he says. 'My wife and the

200

girls are in 'Agami over the summer but in September we'll throw a dinner party for you.'

'And you spend the summer here?' I ask. 'In Cairo?'

'I go to them Thursday evening and come back Sunday morning. The road is nothing: two and a half hours.'

'The problem is getting out of Cairo,' I say.

'Next year,' he says, 'the road connecting Muhandeseen to the Desert Road will be finished and it'll be much quicker.'

He has changed. I do not remember him as a particularly good-looking youth, but this is definitely a handsome man. He is tall and broad-shouldered in the beige linen jacket. His dark hair is cut short. His brown eyes are quick. And he is so confident, so easy.

'I need to ask your advice,' I say. I tell him about the school and the health unit.

'It's not a problem,' he says. 'I'll speak to the governor of Minya.'

'Really?'

'Of course. Now, if you like.' He walks to the desk and picks up the phone. He asks his secretary to check whether Muhyi Bey is in Cairo. When she rings back it is to say that he is in Cairo but will not be contactable until after three. Tareq looks at his watch.

'It's one o'clock. Let me take you out to lunch.'

At a corner table of Rive Gauche we order Mediterranean prawns and salads and start to reminisce over those school holidays so long ago when we played together in Tawasi, the university days when we spent time together at the club.

'Then you went abroad and vanished,' he says.

'Yes,' I say, 'I fell in love and got married.'

'Is your husband with you here? Let me take you both out to dinner.'

'No,' I say, 'no, he's not. He's in England.' That is all I say. Then I say, 'Have you been down to Minya recently?'

And he tells me how he had bought out the fallaheen he didn't want long ago, how he had modernised the farm and kept on only the people who could keep pace with what he wanted to do. 'It makes a reasonable profit,' he says. 'Not like business, of course, but it's history and roots. And it can probably be made to give more. I'm going to bring in a good Israeli team to redesign the infrastructure. We'll see what they'll do.'

'A what team?' I say.

'An Israeli team,' he says. 'To revamp the whole place −'

I stop eating. 'But how can you do that? How can you bring Israelis into your land?'

'They've got the technology,' he says, 'and the experience. You look shocked.'

'I *am* shocked. I'm amazed. After all these years, all these wars − and what about the Palestinian cause?'

'The Palestinians are doing business with the Israelis.'

'But Tareq, how can you do it? Don't you know that's what they want? To get into Egypt. To get into the whole area −'

'You know, I think you've been away too long. You sound like you're still in the Seventies. Things have moved on.'

'But they *can't* move on. They *shouldn't* move on. Not while they want power over the whole region.'

'It's up to us not to give them power. If I hire a few Israelis on my land, transfer their technology − how does that give them power? I'm transferring their power to me. You think it would be better to hold on to our old methods and pretend they don't exist? That's hiding our head in the sand. These old ideologies are no good any more. Everything is determined by economics.'

'Everything?'

'Everything.'

'I thought you were a patriot,' I say bitterly. 'We went out on demonstrations −'

'I am a patriot. I do more for my country by strengthening its economy than I would by sitting in a rut and hoping things will take the course I want somehow.'

We fall silent and then I say, 'What you are saying offends me. Hurts me, even . . .'

He smiles at me, with all the warmth of our old friendship. 'You're being emotional. But this isn't an emotional issue. It's a practical one.'

'It's done,' he says, back in the office, putting the phone down. 'The unit will be reopened next week. The school can open if the teachers are approved. You'll need a list of their names, and once they're vetted, the school will open.'

Isabel, of course, can't see why the fallaheen should mind giving a list of names to the authorities. 'They won't be doing anything wrong,' she says. 'They're volunteering to man the school.'

I try to explain: centuries of lists being used to tax people, to take their sons away to dig canals or till the Khedive's land or be killed in wars; centuries of distrust, broken only briefly by what the fallaheen now call 'the good time': the time of 'Abd el-Nasser. She looks quizzical and I try to steer our conversation to where it's safer, where I feel more comfortable: to the past. It's not difficult.

'I want to see Sharif Basha's house,' she says. 'The one in the story – I mean the one in the journals. Is it still there?'

'Yes. It's a museum now,' I say. 'You can go whenever you like.'

'I'd like to visit it with you,' she says.

And so we go. Along the river, then eastwards into lanes broad enough for a carriage to roll through, but strangled now by the cars parked on either side. A lane opens on to a clearing and the house stands before us: three storeys of mellow cream stone broken here and there by the dark brown of the mashrabiyyas. To the western side is the extension with the small green dome. A group of women in black galabiyyas sit outside it with their children.

We pass through the massive doorway of the old house. Out of the bustle and noise and heat of the city, we enter into the cool, hushed, ordered space and once again the feel and smell of the past wraps itself round me – even though the house is stripped to a shell and the guide who insists on taking us round tells us proudly that it has been used as a film set for an Agatha Christie movie. But we see the storeroom where Anna spent her first hours, the haramlek drawing room with the two divans where she and Layla slept and woke to a new friendship, the courtyard where she played with the one-year-old child who was to be my father. We see too the room hidden under the floorboards of the main bedroom where Sharif Basha's father must have taken refuge after the failure of the revolution. When things calmed down he found he could not live under the Occupation, but he could not fight against it, and he would not go abroad. He moved into the shrine of Sheikh Haroun attached to the house and there he spent the last thirty years of his life. We found the door to the shrine chained and padlocked. When I asked if we could go through, the guide laughed.

'No, no, ya Sett Hanim, it's become a proper mosque now and you can't get to it from the house. The door is outside, on the street.' He said that when the house was turned into a museum, a waqf had come into place for the upkeep of the mosque and the support of one sheikh to live there.

As we leave, Isabel asks if she can go back with a camera. 'Ahlan wa sahlan,' he says. 'But there's a charge of five pounds.'

The house has cast its spell on us and we walk around the district, reluctant to leave. The women have gone and the door to the small mosque is closed. Behind it rises the great old mosque in whose shadow the house was built back in the seventeenth century. To the left, where the gardens would have been, small houses, shops and lanes have grown over the last thirty years. But in a clearing with a small kiosk we find a group of trees, dusty now and uncared-for. We stand under them. We touch and name them. There is a jacaranda with a few loose blue pyramids of flower, a sarw and a handsome poinciana, a magnolia with no flowers, a zanzalacht and a sifsafa. We sit on two upturned crates by the kiosk, sipping

Pepsi–Cola, and Isabel tells me she's going back to the States in August.

'I need to see him. And I want to see my mother. You know, there's so much I want to ask her and now it's probably too late. Even the biggest things in our lives we never really talked about –'

'Did she ever talk about her grandmother, about Anna?' I ask.

'Yes.' Isabel plays with a twig, tracing triangles in the dust. 'She used to say Anna had set a pattern for the women of our family: they would all marry foreign men and live far from home.' She glances up at me. 'My mother married an American. Her mother, Nur, married a Frenchman. I married someone from my country, from the States – but then I left him. And do you know, my mother was not even surprised.'

When Isabel decided to leave Irving for no reason other than that the days had grown grey and the nights greyer, she arranged to meet Jasmine to break the news to her. They met in the Metropolitan, for her mother liked the museum and Isabel wanted the setting, at least, to be on her side. Over steaming corn chowder, in response to the unsuspecting 'And how is Irving?', Isabel said 'We're getting divorced', and was taken aback when her mother merely nodded. Jasmine patted her mouth with her napkin and said, 'You'll both get over it, I guess.'

'But you don't even seem surprised,' Isabel said.

'Well, you've neither of you been happy for a while now, have you?' her mother said.

'I thought you'd . . .'

'Make a fuss?'

'More than this, anyway.'

'If you're not happy, you're not happy. You don't have kids. There's really no reason for you to stay together.'

'I thought you liked him?'

'I do. He's a lovely boy. But that doesn't mean you have to stay married to him.'

'Well, that's settled then,' said Isabel. She was relieved, but she was disappointed too. What was it she had wanted? To make her case? To overcome her mother's objections? To surprise her? Why was it so easy? Because her mother knew her? Or because she didn't care? All the questions that Isabel continues to ask.

As they walked towards the exit, Jasmine lingered by the Pompeii mosaics. 'Just think,' she said, 'there they were, having lunch or whatever, and suddenly the volcano erupts and it's over. Just like that. It's so easy.'

This was dangerous territory. 'Let's go,' said Isabel, and steered her mother out of the museum.

'Maybe she'll have a remission,' I say, and then I think, how foolish! People don't have remission from Alzheimer's. But Isabel says 'Maybe', and we linger under the old trees as the daylight starts to fade.

And now it is evening. Nothing more can be asked of me. Cool in my loose dressing gown, with a tall glass of mango sherbet in my hand, I can sit down at the table in my room, free once more to join Anna Winterbourne and Sharif al-Baroudi as, dressed in the flowing white of the Bedouin, they ride together into the Sinai Desert.

16 March 1901
I have just come back into my tent from an evening of revelry and fantasia and I am so tired, yet my pulse is so quickened that I have been pacing the confines of my tent, unable to settle either to sleep or to my journal.

What a pity it is that I can write neither to Sir Charles nor to Caroline, for I should so delight in describing to them all the events of this day — there are so many aspects of it that I am sure each one would enjoy. But that pleasure will have to wait until I am back in England, I think, and can persuade them by my presence that my adventure was not foolish or rash. Although I confess that earlier today it was difficult to persuade myself of the same thing.

We had travelled the day mostly in silence — and I was grown somewhat uneasy. The plain we traversed was of unbroken gravel, the landscape desolate. I knew from my guidebook that the magnificent scenery was yet to come, but I was almost overcome by a sense of my own foolishness; for the trek to St Catherine and back will take some fourteen days and I could not rid myself of an unease of conscience that I had so precipitately removed Sharif Pasha and his men — not to mention Sabir — from their daily concerns and occupations. As to my host himself, I could gauge nothing of his thoughts, for the kufiyya, hanging down on either side of the face, protects its wearer against the casual or surreptitious glance, and on the few occasions when he turned to speak to me his expression was impassive, his manner distantly polite. His French would pass for that of a Frenchman. I cannot believe he has no knowledge of English, but he seems a man who would not do a thing at all in preference to doing it less than perfectly — and perhaps his English is not perfect. French suffices for what little conversation we have, however. He has informed me that my name is Armand Demange, and my father is none other than Maître Demange who defended Captain Dreyfus in that infamous trial three years ago. It appears that the Maître is a friend of Sharif Pasha and I have been given information on my mother, our estates and my schooling — none of which I expect to need as we are hardly likely to come upon an enquiring passer-by in this desert. When he was satisfied that I could ride as well as any of them and that I suffered no undue weariness, we rode without break except for prayers and a little food and drink at mid-day, mid-afternoon and sunset, and I came to feel that there is something about the desert that discourages idle chatter. And besides, of the men with us only Sabir and Mutlaq knew the truth about me, and perhaps he feared that I should raise my voice and so betray myself. His manner towards me is courteous but most reserved and distant. I am happy that it should be so, for, after all, any true friendship between us cannot — in the nature of things — be possible, and there is no form here that needs to be preserved through polite conversation.

I was surprised that we did not make camp at sunset. As dusk fell, we saw a group of men on horseback come cantering towards us. I glanced towards him in some alarm but he said 'Friends' and, raising his arm in greeting, rode forwards to meet them. They were the men of the 'Alawi tribe, for we had entered their territory, and they rode out to welcome us and escort us back to their settlement, where we are camped tonight as guests of their Chief, Sheikh Salim ibn Husayn.

Their encampment is in a most pleasant spot, in the Wadi Gharandal, through which runs a clear stream of sweet water, sweeter still for being the first we have come across in this desert, and there are many acacia trees about which are sparse and thorny, the better to survive the harsh climate. The 'Alawis' homes are black tents woven out of goats' hair; the people subsist through grazing their flocks of sheep and goats and trading in thoroughbred horses, of which I have seen several fine examples in the fantasia that was held tonight in our honour.

And indeed, they did honour us with sheep roasting on a spit, large dishes of aromatic rice and a light, bitter coffee poured out of elongated jugs, any one of which could be fittingly displayed in the South Kensington Museum.

The old Chief is a small man with a hand as hard as a desert stone (indeed they are all small men and, I think, have to be so — like the acacia — to live in the desert). He was most gracious to me and sat me down on his right — Sharif Pasha being on his left — and pressed morsels of lamb upon me and apologised for not speaking to me in my 'native' French, and he seemed much pleased at my delight with their fantasia which truly is a most wonderful affair, the men performing feats of horsemanship, bareback, to the accompaniment of wild cries and whoops and drumming, and the whole scene lit by flares. In that company Sharif Pasha seemed to shed his reserve and leaned back on his cushion, talking and laughing with the old Chief. For a moment I even had a suspicion that he had apprised the Chief of my true nature; I cannot tell whence that suspicion came except that they seemed on such frank and easy terms with each other and that the

Chief's smile was of a conspicuous broadness as he bade me good night.

My only regret tonight is that I could not spend any time in the company of the women but perforce saw them only as a man would: slight figures in long, embroidered gowns, flitting about as they handed the food to the men who served us, their movements light, their sequined veils glittering in the firelight, their black eyes above them darting at me with curious looks which added piquancy to my situation. And although they took no part in the feats of the fantasia, they joined in the drumming and clapping and their voices rose so that I thrilled to that ululating joy-cry which I had read about but never heard.

If I am to believe my guidebook, tomorrow we should traverse the terrains which have given this desert its fame for magnificence. So far I have found that the book, like my friends at the Agency, has a fairer view of the land than of its inhabitants.

And in Anna's Thomas Cook I read:

The people who live in the desert have always been a favourite subject of romance, but a very short experience is sufficient to dispel such youthful delusions. The Bedouins, at least such of them as are found between Egypt and Palestine, are of a very prosaic character; rude, ignorant, lazy and greedy, they offer no points of attraction . . . the ordinary Arabs are destitute alike of grace and strength; their clothing is ragged, their feet are never furnished with shoes, and only occasionally with very rude sandals, and their hands and faces show very plainly that water is scarce . . . [They] are ignorant and careless of the advantages of civilised life; they constantly carry arms if they can obtain them; a man whose best garment is an untanned sheepskin, will wear a sword, or shoulder a gun, or both . . . Yet they are apparently a cheerful, contented race, very much like the American Negroes in their simplicity, thoughtlessness and good humour . . . None of them fails to understand the word baksheesh; it is the first word the young child learns, the last the old man utters.

19 March 1901
Oh how I wish it were possible to go without sleep entirely, or that the hours of each day would be doubled, that I might have time to see and to feel all there is to see and feel, and then still have time to reflect on it, to let the impressions wind their way through my mind, settling here and there in small, shining pools, or merging with other thoughts and progressing towards some great conclusion! And then again I would have time to write it all down, to record it all, for in that act, I have found my thoughts clarify themselves and what starts as an hysterical burbling of impressions resolves into a view, an image as lucid and present as a painting.

I have never cared for the paintings of the Sinai that I have seen, preferring to them the intricate interiors, the detailed portrayals of domestic life. The paintings with grander ambitions never seemed to come to life for me and now I understand why. I have found myself thinking of the wonderful Turners hanging in Petworth, for surely no lesser genius than his could do justice in watercolours to the magnificence of these landscapes. And in oils, of all the painters I can think of, perhaps Corot comes closest to the possibility of rendering these mountains – and yet a painting would do justice only to that spot it depicted, and the viewer would be mistaken in thinking that now he had an idea of the whole of the Sinai. For each day brings us to a different aspect of this amazing land, this conjunction of the two mighty continents of the Ancient World. One day it is a bare gravel plain stretching as far as the eye can see, and then you are surprised by a small stream and thorny acacias digging deep into the sand for the little water that will help them sustain the small life that is their lot; the next day you find yourself amid stupendous ranges of solid rock, some black, some purple, some red, and you are treading the same land in which the Ancient Egyptian laboured to extract copper and turquoise – indeed, you can see the remains of his excavations still. You then come out on an open plain by the Red

Sea and there you are joined by huge flocks of birds, pausing, resting for the night on the shore where you are camped, and as the sun rises, while the men perform their morning prayers, the birds too rise. They soar and wheel and call out to each other and set off in a great swooping cloud across the sea and towards their summer homes in the North. And then, opening out among cliffs more than a thousand feet in height, a wadi lies before you and life is plentiful again, with gardens of tamarisk and apple trees and fields of wheat and barley. What one painting could even suggest all this?

Tonight we are camped a single day's ride from the Monastery of St Catherine and in full view of the mountains of Sinai. We rode, Sharif Pasha and I, through the most spectacular pass, called the Nugb Hawa, so precipitous and narrow that camels cannot go through it but have to be sent the wider and more level route through Darb el-Sheikh. Sharif Pasha put the question to me: would I prefer the spectacular route or the easier one? And naturally I chose the first. He said, 'It can only be done on horseback. And since we have only two horses, we would have to go alone.'

I said, 'You will have to convince Sabir,' and he smiled.

For the first time Sabir consented to leave my side, and Sharif Pasha and I broke off from our companions and rode off into the narrow pass of Nugb Hawa. The granite cliffs on either side of us rose to fifteen hundred feet or more and at times, by leaning slightly to one side or the other, I could have touched both walls of the pass with my hands. Sometimes it seemed that we were riding towards a solid rock face, but as we drew near, an opening would miraculously appear and we would turn into it. The incline meanwhile was for stretches so steep that only the most sure-footed and even-tempered of horses would have climbed it without harm to his rider. Our mounts were willing and agile, however, and we rode on, mostly in single file with me at the front, but sometimes my companion drew abreast and with the briefest of looks satisfied himself that all was well with me.

It was on one of those occasions, and sensible that this was the first time we had had a possibility of private conversation, that I

211

started to tell him how grateful I was for all he had done for me and assured him that I was well aware of the great inconvenience this must have caused. But he cut me short with 'C'est rien. You would have made the journey anyway.'

'I would have tried,' I said, 'but I think I would have met with a tour in Suez and travelled with them, and that would not have been the same thing at all.'

'Why not?' he asked, seeming surprised. 'You would have travelled in comfort and without the necessity of disguise.'

'I would have . . .' I did not quite know how to put this. 'I would have remained within the world I knew. I would have seen things through my companions' eyes, and my mind would have been too occupied in resisting their impressions to establish its own –'

'Have you always been like this?' he asked.

'Like what?' I said, surprised in my turn.

'So insistent on making up your own mind.'

'You make me appear wilful.'

'And are you not?'

'I have not given free rein to my will before,' I said. And with that the pass narrowed and he pulled in his horse and fell behind. He had not said it was no trouble, nor assured me that he did not find my company irksome, but I was not displeased with our exchange – and I was glad that I had thanked him.

Nugb Hawa ended as abruptly as it had begun and suddenly we emerged from the dark cool of the pass and into a bright open plain with the majestic mountains of Sinai in full view before us. We were rejoined by the men on camel-back and Sabir greeted me with smiles and with no evidence of any anxiety. I believe he now trusts that I am in safe hands. Indeed, as the days pass and we go deeper and deeper into Sinai, I am quite frightened (although I would not for the world admit this other than to my journal) to think that I tried to do this with only Sabir for company. I had not spoken falsely when I said to Sharif Pasha that I had thought I would meet with a company of Cook's travellers in Suez and perhaps travel with them, but there was a strong part of me that did not wish to be in the company of my own kind here. As though I had an instinct that their conversation, their presence itself, would preclude my truly entering into the Sinai. And I know now that it would indeed have been so. The encompassing silence and the ease (or indifference) of my companions have left my soul free to contemplate, to drink in the wonder of this place. How fitting it is that it should have been here that Moses heard the word of God! For here, where Man — if he is to live — lives perforce so close to Nature and by her Grace, I feel so much closer to the entire mystery of Creation that it would not surprise me at all were I to be vouchsafed a vision or a revelation; indeed it would seem in the very order of things that such an epiphany would happen. I have found myself, every time the men stopped for prayer, offering up prayers of my own; simple offerings in praise of Him who fashioned all this and who sent me here that I might see it. I have also prayed for His mercy to be visited on the soul of my poor Edward, for I have fallen, from time to time, to thinking that if he had come here as a pilgrim instead of going to the Soudan as a soldier, he might have been alive today and at peace.

21 March
It is afternoon and the monks have retired to prayer and we to our siesta.

We have been to the summit of Jebel Moussa and have watched the dawn break to the accompaniment of the melodious chant of the Muezzin calling for prayer.

The air is dry and light and its effect on the mind is similar to that of a glass of Champagne before dinner.

I have not written anything of this Monastery where we are lodged. The Father is very kind and — as the men are encamped outside the walls — Sharif Pasha has told him who I am on the grounds of it being wrong to accept hospitality under false pretences.

The building is rather like a mediaeval Castle and was established in the Sixth Century and soon afterwards, as the Moslem armies advanced Westwards from the Arabian Peninsula, somebody had the prescience to build a small Mosque in its courtyard to guard against it being burned or demolished. At the time of the Crusades it was the turn of the Monastery to protect the Mosque, and so it has been down the ages, each House of God extending its shelter to the other as opposing armies came and went.

Last night it was early when we all retired, and I thought to try on Layla's gift. It is a lovely, loose gown of deep-green silk, and even though there is, naturally, no mirror in my cell, I was happy to be wearing it.

I went out into the dark garden. I knew we would rise early, but the night was not much advanced and I thought there could be no harm in slipping out for a breath of air.

I saw him come out of the Chapel. He too had doffed his desert attire and was in plain trousers and a woollen jersey with his head uncovered to the night air.

I fancied he started when he saw me. He came towards me and I thought he would be angry that I had ventured out, and that in my woman's dress with the kufiyya draped loosely about my shoulders. And indeed his first words were 'Que faites vous ici?' I said I needed air as my room was close and he said, 'You should go in.' But presently, when I did not move, he gestured towards the seat and upon my giving him leave he sat himself down beside me. That he was troubled I could tell without even looking into his face. We sat in silence but there was that about his posture, his air, that betokened a restlessness, a disquiet, and eventually I ventured:

'Could you not sleep?'

'I have not tried.'

'You were in the Chapel,' I said. And he heard the question in my voice.

'I was looking at the monks. The old ones. The bones,' he said, and his voice was harsh and bitter. He sat stooped forward, his elbows on his knees, gazing into the darkness.

I could think of nothing to say. Indeed, all I was conscious of was a desire to put out my hand and touch that arm that was so close to mine, to put my hand upon that troubled head – a desire that grew in intensity so that I folded my arms about myself. He turned.

'You are cold?'

'No,' I said.

'But you are shivering.'

'No, not really.'

He studied me for a moment, then turned away. 'What brought you to Egypt, Lady Anna?' he said into the night air.

It was the first time he had said my name.

'The paintings,' I said. And when he turned to me I told him about the paintings in the South Kensington Museum, about their world of light and colour. I told him about my visits there when Edward was sick. When he was dying.

'You have been very unhappy,' he said.

'Yes,' I said. 'He did not need to die like that.'

'Like what?'

'Troubled. Not at peace.'

'But he did what he believed in, surely? He believed he should fight for his Empire.'

'It was an unjust war.'

'But he did not know that.'

'I think – I believe he knew. But he knew too late. And it killed him.'

There was a silence. It was the first time I had said this to anyone. Perhaps it was the first time I had put the thought so clearly to myself. I was shivering in earnest now and had he put his arms around me I believe I would have allowed myself – but he stood up and said, 'You must go in.'

'No,' I whispered, shaking my head, and with an impatient sound he strode off. I thought he was going away but he strode about the garden, then he came back to a stop in front of me and said:

'So. Tell me. What do you think? Which is better? To take action and perhaps make a fatal mistake – or to take no action and die slowly anyway?'

I considered. I tried to consider, but it was hard with the trembling upon me and he standing tall in front of me, blocking my view of anything but himself. At last I said, 'I believe you have to know yourself first – above all.'

215

'So. She is wise, as well as beautiful and headstrong.'

I shook my head and kept my eyes on the ground. There was a mocking tone to his voice. But – 'aussi que belle' – he had called me 'belle'.

'What if you know yourself too well? What if you do not like what you know?'

I was silent.

Within moments he had collected himself: 'Forgive me. It is all those skulls and bones in there. The dead monks. So –' He sat down again. 'You came to look for that world you saw in your museum. And you have found it?'

'In your house, monsieur,' I said.

'Ah, there are other houses like mine,' he said dismissively. 'We must arrange for you to see them.'

I did not know whether to be pleased or disappointed. He was sending me somewhere – but he was sending me away.

'What is the matter?'

'Nothing.'

'I did not mean to frighten you earlier. Forgive me.'

'I am not frightened.'

'Then why are you shaking?'

'It is grown – rather cold.'

'Then you must go inside. Now.' He stood. 'Will you go or shall I have to carry you?'

'You are a bully, monsieur,' I said. But I stood up.

'Yes,' he said, 'I have been told.'

At my door I held out my hand and he took it in both of his. 'Will you be warm enough?' he asked.

'Yes,' I said.

'Then sleep well. Sleep well, Lady Anna who is never afraid,' he said. He raised my hand and for a fleeting moment I felt on it the pressure of his lips. And even though I was warm, I cannot say that I slept well.

16

Our frailties are invincible, our virtues barren; the battle goes sore against us to the going down of the sun.

Robert Louis Stevenson

Cairo, 13 July 1997

An old story and plus ça change and all that. I too did not sleep well last night for I was in a magic garden of my own, in a London square one cool summer night, at the moment when a man I had met a few hours before took me in his arms and changed the course of my life. How could I at that moment have foreseen the desolate spaces we would later inhabit? And then the question I had for so long put aside: will there ever be another? Will there be time – will there be heart for another? Having lunch with Tareq 'Atiyya was the closest I had come in years to a man I could imagine fancying. But he was married – and thinking of doing business with the Israelis. I do not believe I am living in a time-warp, but I confess I find the events of a hundred years ago easier to deal with than the circumstances we are in today.

So when I let my mind wander, it wanders back to Anna. I see her in her shimmering silk gown, her golden hair loose on the kufiyya draped around her shoulders. She stands for a moment, half leaning against the door she has just closed behind her, her hand still glowing with the imprint of his kiss. She lies on her bed and lives again the scene that has just taken place. And she sees again another country where a man had sat helpless and dumb with misery. A man who could not be comforted. But tonight Sharif Pasha al-Baroudi had shaken himself free of his thoughts, walked about the garden, and come back to her. She thinks of his words, his tone, his aspect, how he has made her feel. What woman will at that moment think about signs and significations? Wonder 'do we – by the same words – mean the same things?' I think of Isabel and her confident cry: 'If he cared for me as I care for him, I should not be hurt.' And Isabel is determined to share my brother's world. She shares the American one already – and now she wants this one. She wants to surprise him when she goes back by her grasp of things Egyptian. And I have arranged to take her to the Atelier. I have told people – yet again – that she is engaged to my brother, and also that she is doing a graduate project on how people here view the millennium. I've lied a bit and said she has been on a march to end the suffering of the women and children of Iraq.

15 July

In the Atelier 'am Ghazali, the waiter, spoons coarse sugar into the glasses of tea that he hands out. In a corner of the long, low room, its whitewashed walls coloured with the smoke of thousands of cigarettes, my old professor, Ramzi Yusuf, is once again conquering Mahgoub al-Tilmisani's white army on the old chessboard. Deena al-'Ulama sits with them, correcting the proofs of a set of papers for the Nasr Abu-Zeid case. They stand up to greet us and Mahgoub says:

'Khalas ya Doctor?'

'Mafish khalas,' Ramzi Yusuf says. 'You play to the end.'

'But the guests?'

'They will wait.' He gestures round the room. 'Sit and look. Experience the ambience. I will beat him in a minute,' he says to Isabel. 'You do not mind to wait, do you?'

When we sit, Deena stuffs her papers into a large bag and calls out to Ghazali to take our order.

'So, is this your first visit to Egypt?' Deena asks Isabel. Deena teaches mathematics at Cairo University and does a lot of volunteer work for the Teachers' Union, the human-rights organisation, the Legal Aid Bureau and the Committee for the Support of the Palestinian people. She is in sandals, jeans and a loose, dark blue top. She looks tired. There is a general hubbub and people continually leaving or coming in or passing through looking for someone. A telephone rings incessantly. Two exhibitions of painting are showing: one in the gallery upstairs and one in the smaller room next door. One of the artists has just been placed under Administrative Detention for signing a statement against the land laws. The other from time to time joins the main group in the room.

'Sallim silahak ya 'Urabi,' Dr Ramzi says in a low singsong.

'Lessa, ya Bey, lessa,' Mahgoub demurs, moving his wazir to protect the king.

'Mafish lessa,' Dr Ramzi says triumphantly, moving his horse. 'Kesh malik!'

'Lek yom ya Doctor!' Mahgoub says cheerfully, collecting up the pieces, pouring them into their wooden box. He shakes out his cigarettes and offers one to Isabel, who smiles and refuses. 'Egyptian cigarettes,' he says. 'Look!' He holds the white pack up, showing her the image of the queen. 'Cleopatra. No?' He puts the pack down on the table.

'We have not seen you for a long time, Amal.' Dr Ramzi smiles. 'You must wait for an American to come with her?'

'You know how it is, ya Doctor,' I say lamely, 'circumstances.'

'You are from New York?' he says to Isabel.

Ramzi Yusuf is around seventy. The thick, smooth hair and dark, gentle eyes that made his philosophy lectures so popular when I was a student are still there. But the eyes, although they seem brighter, are smaller and more deeply set. And the hair is completely white. He has always been fond of women and now he looks at Isabel with unconcealed admiration.

'Ah, if I was twenty years younger – only twenty years – I would show you an Egypt . . .' He shakes his head ruefully.

'And twenty years from now?' Isabel asks.

'Twenty years?' He bursts into loud laughter and then a slight fit of coughing. 'I can show you my other home, in the Imam. Or paradise, maybe.'

'Isabel wants to know how we see the next millennium, ya Doctor,' I say. 'She's doing a project –'

'I know, I know.' He waves his hand impatiently. 'I am the wrong person to ask such a question. I am old –' he shrugs – 'for me it is all the same.'

'Youth is the youth of the heart, ya Doctor,' Mahgoub says. He works for an airline but he has been suspended for spitting into the drink of a passenger in first class who touched up a stewardess and made her cry.

'Even the heart too, it grows old,' Dr Ramzi says. He is silent, gazing into the middle distance. I cannot tell what he sees. 'But you are young and you will not believe me. For the millennium – everything, it is always the same,' he says. 'It will be the same.'

'How can it be the same, ya Doctor?' Mahgoub objects.

'Haram 'aleik, ya Doctor,' Deena adds. 'Ya'ni everything we're doing will come down on nothing?'

'Eh!' Dr Ramzi shrugs. 'What you are doing, this is because you are young. Young people, they must struggle. If they don't struggle they think life has no meaning. They feel lost. You see –' to Isabel – 'in countries where there is no need to struggle – in Norway, in Sweden – the young people kill themselves.'

'So we're killed either way,' Mahgoub says. 'Thank you.'

'Surely that's too simple,' Isabel says. 'Things change. You have great changes happening here –'

'Toshki,' Mahgoub laughs. 'Toshki will solve everything –'

'Toshki walla ma Toshki,' says Dr Ramzi. 'It is all –' he spirals a hand gently into space – 'it is all talk in the air.'

A woman hesitates in the doorway, then takes a few steps into the room. People glance up. Deena stands.

'Arwa!' she cries and goes to greet her.

'Who is that?' Isabel asks.

Arwa Salih, one of the leaders of the student movement of the early Seventies. I remember her from the night of the Great Stone Cake in '72, when our comrades were arrested in the university and we staged a sit-in in Tahrir Square and all of Cairo came to join us. That too ended in nothing. We were defeated – or diffused – and she opted out. She chose to work at a press agency, translating the financial news. In the evenings she helps out at a small art gallery in Zamalek. She has married three times and never had kids.

'She's stunning,' Isabel says as Deena brings her over.

'I don't want to interrupt –' Arwa begins, and then she sees me and we go into a big hug. It's been more than twenty years. Mahgoub brings over a chair.

'Look, ya Setti,' he says and starts to tell her what Isabel wants. 'And Dr Ramzi is saying that everything will stay the same,' he ends.

'It won't,' Arwa says, sitting down, hanging her handbag on the back of her chair, crossing her legs. 'It will get worse. We're headed for an age of Israeli supremacy in the whole area. An Israeli empire.'

'Bravo!' Mahgoub cries. 'Arwa goes to the bottom line.'

'Do you really think so?' Isabel seems astonished, but then we have never talked about this; I judged our friendship too fragile.

'Yes. That's what they're working for – and they have America behind them. A pax Americana, and within it an Israeli dominance over the area that they like to call the Middle East.'

Arwa has always surprised people: she speaks more directly than you expect of a woman – a beautiful woman with a shy, hesitant air.

'Surely that's extreme?' Isabel says.

'They're already talking of Israeli brains and Arab hands,' Deena says. Deena, with her jeans, her spectacles, her cigarettes, was always expected to be militant, and she is – militant but tired. That is the first thing you notice, I think, when you look at these three women: Arwa and Deena, with faint circles under their eyes, a slight droop of the shoulders, a certain dullness of skin, look worn. While Isabel, shining with health and a kind of innocent optimism, looks brand new.

'And look at the whole region,' Mahgoub says. 'Look at Algeria. Look what happened to Lebanon. Look at the Palestinians. The Sudan. Libya. Look at Iraq. The next millennium? The future being planned for us is a terrible one—'

'What's terrible,' says Deena, 'is how we've taken on the role of the victim, the Done-To. We sit here and say "they're planning for us, they're doing to us" and wait to see what "they" will do next.'

'And what's in our hands to do?'

'It is history,' Dr Ramzi says. 'The conjunction of certain conditions. After a hundred years the historians will say what happened was inevitable. If we look now at Egypt a hundred years ago we see that what happened was inevitable.'

'What happened?' Isabel says.

'We were a part of a dying Ottoman Empire. Our Khedive Ismail loved modernism and Europe and — le spectacle. He likes the Suez Canal project and so he borrows money. He is not careful where he borrows. He borrows from Europe — from Britain and the Rothschilds and France. At the same time — you see, here is the conjunction.' The index fingers of his two hands come together. 'Europe is strong and moving outwards —' a huge expansive gesture with the arms — 'colonialism is the spirit of the age. Their old enemy the Ottoman Empire is dying. So they use the Khedive's debts to expand into our part of it. Into Egypt. The rest is history.'

'And what about the national movement, ya Doctor?'

'The national movement did not matter. The British pretended they thought it threatened their money. They made it the reason for the Occupation. But they will have come anyway. They will find a way.'

'I don't think that's fair.' Deena pushes her spectacles up with a characteristic gesture. 'The British came in at a crucial point in our history. They froze our development: our move towards democracy, towards education, industrialisation, towards modernity —'

'Tayyib ya Setti, we have now fifty years — fifty-six years of our own — of national government, and what have we done?'

'Compare us,' Arwa says, 'to our cousins across the border.

223

You think if the British hadn't helped them, if there had been no Balfour Declaration, there would be no Israel today? There would have been. They wouldn't have sat back and said, "Oh, but the British won't help us, the Sultan won't sell us Palestine, the Arabs won't go away —"

'But they were part of the whole colonial movement. They had the spirit of the age behind them.'

Mustafa al-Sharqawi has been standing silently by us, listening. Now Mahgoub turns to him. 'Why are you so quiet, ya Mustafa? It's not like you. Tell us what you think.'

Mustafa is a small intense man, with old-fashioned horn-rimmed spectacles. If he had worn a beret he could have been at the Deux Magots in the Fifties.

'What do I think? I think we're a nation of cowards,' he says bitterly. 'I hate to say it, especially in front of a — guest. But we live by slogans. We take comfort in them: "The Great Egyptian People." "The peaceful, patient Nation, that when it is aroused shatters the World." Shatters the world? Tell me, when in all of history did the Egyptian people rebel? When? When 'Urabi spoke up for them, they sold him out. They ran away and let the British in. You'll say 1919, but 1919 wasn't a revolution. It was a few demonstrations and it changed nothing —'

'Slowly, slowly, ya Mustafa. 1919 —'

'Fifty-two? That was not a rebellion of the people. It was an army movement which rode the people and told the people that it spoke with their voice. The people have no voice.'

'What are *we* then?'

'We're a bunch of intellectuals who sit in the Atelier or the Grillon and talk to each other. And when we write, we write for each other. We have absolutely no connection with the people. The people don't know we exist.'

'The people know more than you think,' I say. 'They watch television. Out in the villages they have satellite dishes.'

'Good. And what do they watch on television? They watch

censored news. They watch soaps – emasculated because television needs to sell them to our masters in the Gulf. They don't watch you–'

'What about the fundamentalists?' Isabel asks. 'Where do they come into all this? Would you say that *they* spoke with the voice of the people?'

'The fundamentalists are nothing,' Dr Ramzi says. 'They just need some food and a place to live –'

'They are the ones on the ground,' Mahgoub says. 'Can anyone explain how they've managed to occupy the amount of space they have?'

'All the other parties have been hit,' says Deena. 'We've had fifty years of an absence of democracy –'

'They've been hit as much as any other party,' Mustafa al-Sharqawi says. 'They've been forced underground and they've come back. Their leaders were killed and they got new ones. Their economic projects turned out to be a fraud and their credibility survived. Their young men are killed every day and they recruit new ones. They will not go away. They've even taken the political platform – the idiom – of the left: they talk of social justice –'

'They have an Idea,' Arwa says, 'and their Idea appeals to the people because it reinforces who they are. It says hey, you don't *have* to become the dumping ground of the West. You're worth something. It appeals to those thousands of young men and women who go through school, through university, and then find the road blocked in their faces –'

'Have you heard the one about the lamp?' Mahgoub says. 'This young man is engaged and he can't find a flat to get married in. His girl is threatening to leave him and marry a rich Arab. As he's walking around one day hanging his head, he sees 'Ala ed-Din's lamp lying in the gutter. He can't believe himself; he picks it up and rubs it and the jinni comes out: "Shobbeik lobbeik, Khaddamak bein eidek, what do you desire?" "A flat, ya'ni, just a little flat: a bedroom and a hall and a little bathroom and kitchen." The jinni looks at him in disgust. "And if there was such a flat," he says, "would I be living in this damn lamp?" '

Everybody bursts out laughing and I – with misgiving – translate the joke for Isabel, who nods and laughs.

Ghazali comes in with coffee for Dr Ramzi. 'Anybody ya bahawat wants sandwiches?'

'Yes. What do you have?' Dr Ramzi says.

'Ya'ni what would he have, ya Doctor?' Deena laughs. 'Cheese and roast beef. For thirty years he's had cheese and roast beef.'

'Am Ghazali smiles. 'Today we have chicken as well.'

'Tayyib, I'll have chicken. Mind it's not rotten.'

We give our orders and Mustafa al-Sharqawi says: ''Am Ghazali, where will we be in the year two thousand?'

'We'll be under the protection of God by His grace.'

'There you are. See,' he says when Ghazali has gone: 'a cliché. It stops him having to think.'

'It stops him having to answer you,' Dr Ramzi says.

'That's the ground the Jama'at are using. The ready-made pieties,' Mustafa says.

'Ya akhi, no,' says Mahgoub. 'No. The pieties speak *against* killing and bombing. It all comes back to economics.'

'And government policy,' Deena says. 'They have been allowed space. Encouraged even. When Sadat wanted to destroy the leftist movements, he encouraged them –'

'And not just Sadat,' Arwa adds, although she hated him. 'Who gave them the big push they needed in the Eighties? Who funded them and armed them in Afghanistan?'

'Would they come to power in free elections?' Isabel ventures.

There is a silence. A long silence. A man who's been shouting into the phone looks around in surprise and drops his voice. Then Deena says, 'Probably yes. They're organised. And funded. And they have a ready-made publicity machine in every mosque.'

'And then what?'

'And then they'd string us all up.'

'Would they really?'

'They'd be in a mess. They have no political programme beyond "Islam is the solution". Ask them any detailed question and they don't have an answer —'

'Do you realise,' Dr Ramzi says, smiling broadly, 'when you speak of a political programme, that your programme now is the same that Mahmoud Sami al-Baroudi's government tried to establish more than a hundred years ago?'

'Is that right?' Isabel says.

'Yes. Yes, for sure,' Dr Ramzi says. 'Listen: the ending of foreign influence, the payment of the Egyptian debt —' he counts them off on his fingers — 'an elected parliament, a national industry, equality of all men before the law, reform of education, and allowing a free press to reflect all shades of opinion. Those were the seven points of their programme. These young people —' the wave of his hand takes in the group — 'they still ask for this.' He shrugs. Ghazali balances his tray on one hand and starts unloading it with the other.

'Do the fundamentalists want this too?'

'Possibly,' Mahgoub says. 'But they won't want the free press. And they'll put their own conditions on who can stand for parliament —'

'We went up to Minya a few days ago,' I say.

'Who went? You didn't take your guest with you, did you?'

'Yes. We went to our village. The number of barricades on the road was incredible. And on one of them we saw three young men, ordinary fallaheen, being arrested. They were tied with ropes. On their arms and necks.'

'It's become a war. Especially in the Sa'id.'

'But I don't think those young men were terrorists, or even Islamists particularly —'

'When you set the police loose on people, khalas, they do anything.'

'The thing is, it's now getting mixed up with the land

227

laws,' Deena says. 'If someone is close to the authorities and he wants people off his land, he can use the "terrorist" issue and get rid of them. We are documenting cases but it's difficult to convince a fallah to start a legal action. But some are doing it.'

'They closed down our school,' I say. 'And I got someone to speak to the Governor and he said we could open it if we gave him a list of the people who'd be teaching there. It's only a couple of classes where the kids come to study in the evenings –'

'You can't give lists of names to the Governor,' Deena says, 'and nobody'll give you such a list anyway.'

'Centuries of mistrust,' Dr Yusuf says. 'You cannot get out of your history.'

'I know,' I say.

'Ya Doctor, history can be changed,' Deena says, 'it's people who make history. The problem is that we are allowing other people to make our history –'

'But it's people with power who make history,' Arwa says, 'and we have no power. At least when there were two superpowers in the world, we could negotiate a path in the space between them. Now there is no space.'

'We do have power,' Deena says. 'We're being told we haven't – but we have. But to use it we have to have the will. And we can't afford to be rich against poor, Copt against Muslim –'

'I believe the Islamists could be defused if we had a true democracy,' Mahgoub says. 'If everybody, and they too, were allowed to speak publicly. To debate the issues in front of the people. Put them on television, in a proper free debate with Muslim intellectuals, with the Sheikh of al-Azhar –'

'People will switch off,' Mustafa says. 'Salamu 'aleikum. None of this will come to anything. I have to go.'

'What's the rush?' Mahgoub says. 'Stay with us.'

'No, I'm going. I'll leave you to put the universe right.' And raising his arm in a general salute, he leaves.

'The government won't do that anyway,' Deena says. 'It

opts for the security solution and it tries to outbid the Islamists in the religious stakes: we're more Muslim than you. And so it plays their game.'

'What popularity they have is because the people need an Idea. In Nasser's time — for all its drawbacks, all the mistakes — there was an Idea. A national project. Now what do we have? The Idea of the Consumer? Trying to hang on to America's hem —'

'Where will you get a national project now?' Dr Ramzi asks. 'You think you can sit here and design a national project? And what is the end of Nasser's project anyway? What is the outcome?'

'Ya Doctor, a national project comes about as an embodiment of the will of the people,' Arwa says. 'Nasser's project finally did not work because for the people to have a will it has to have a certain amount of space and freedom, freedom to question everything: religion, politics, sex —'

'So the sans-culottes had freedom and space?'

'No, and your revolution here will be an Islamist radical one. Because every other ideology is bankrupt. And capitalism isn't an ideology, it isn't something that people can live by — and in our case it just makes people discontented. Look at the advertisements on television. Advertisements for things people can't have if they saved up for ten lifetimes —'

'They're for the ones with palaces in 'Agami,' Mahgoub says. People, I think, like Tareq 'Atiyya.

'You know,' Isabel says, 'we have that problem in the States: the widening gap between rich and poor. Some people see it as a threat already. I read an article that compared life in America now to the last years of the Roman Empire.'

'Capitalism,' Arwa smiles. 'In a word.'

'It seems to me,' says Isabel, after a moment, 'that people are completely caught up in trying to analyse the situation. But no one says, "*This* is what we should do." '

'I don't think anyone knows what we should do,' I say.

'I know some things we should do,' Deena says. 'We

should speak out against the sanctions on Iraq. We should put a time limit on this so-called peace process. What's the use of sitting around talking peace when the Israelis are constantly changing the landscape – putting things on the ground that will be impossible to dismantle?'

'And when the time came, you'd go to war?' Isabel asks.

'If we had to. And I would stop this charade of "normalisation". What normalisation is possible with a neighbour who continues to build settlements and drive people off the land? Who has an arsenal of nuclear weapons and screams wolf when someone else is suspected of having a few missiles? And it *is* our business – because what's happening to the Iraqis or the Palestinians today will happen to us tomorrow.'

'And when America cuts off your aid?' Mahgoub says, with a mischievous glance at Isabel.

'What aid? Do you know that 70 per cent of what they give us feeds directly back into the American economy? *Directly*, mind you. You think they give us aid because they want to help us? Personally, I'd close the door anyway. I'd mobilise the people to get our economy straight –'

'They can't do that. Too many powerful people have links to the West now. Money links. Big business.'

'There you have it!' Deena sits back. 'The interests of the governing class are different – are practically opposed to the interests of the majority of the people.'

'Ya Deena ya 'Ulama!' A man stands by the phone, waving the receiver at Deena. She jumps up. 'It's my son,' she says. 'I told him he could call me here.'

'Khalas ya Mahgoub,' Arwa says. 'It's either Israeli domination – backed by America – or the Islamist radicals. Take your pick.'

'Neither this nor that. We'll keep both out,' Mahgoub says. He turns to Isabel. 'You know, your government,' he says; 'all the Americans I meet are good people, but your government's foreign policy is so bad. It's not good, you know, for a country to be hated by so many people.'

'Well,' Isabel says, 'as I said, some people think we are already in decline. Moral decline.'

'History,' Dr Ramzi says. 'This is all –' he waves his hand – 'nothing. Egypt has been here so long. It has seen many things. In the next millennium – it will still be Egypt.'

17

But we, like sentries, are obliged to stand
In starless nights and wait the 'pointed hour.
John Dryden

It can't be that bad. Surely it can't be that bad. There must be a way, only we can't see it yet. A way of making a space for ourselves where we can make the best of ourselves – we just can't quite see it yet. But things move on and by the time you've plotted your position the world around you has changed and you're running – panting – to catch up. How can you think clearly when you're running? That is the beauty of the past; there it lies on the table: journals, pictures, a candle-glass, a few books of history. You leave it and come back to it and it waits for you – unchanged. You can turn back the pages, look again at the beginning. You can leaf forward and know the end. And you tell the story that they, the people who lived it, could only tell in part.

3 April 1901
No message. No note. Nothing. We have been back three days.

James Barrington knows something – enough. I deemed it best to remain as faithful as possible to the truth. Indeed, now that I have made the journey I do not see how an account depicting myself and Sabir travelling alone into the Sinai would be in the least believable. I did, however, omit the first section of our adventures and had us meet Sharif Pasha's party in the Eastern Desert where, learning of our destination and being bound that way themselves, they took us under their protection.

I relayed this amended version to Sabir, who grasped it with agility, and we rode together to James's house better friends – I fancy — than when we started out. James was touchingly relieved to see us, although how much of that relief was due to his fear of having to face the Lord's music had some ill befallen us, I cannot tell. However, he forgot himself so far as to put his arm round Sabir's shoulder and punch him playfully a few times. And having changed back into my usual costume (how strange that seemed with all the lacing and fastening and fuss) and sent word to Emily of my return, I sat down — without a chaperone — and told him of our adventures. And perhaps my account showed something more than I intended for as I came to leave he took hold of my hands and said, 'You won't let it go to your head now, Anna, will you?' And I laughed and asked, 'Let what go to my head?' 'All that desert and stars business,' he said. 'You know it won't do.'

As for our earlier return to the old Baroudi house, it was so like a homecoming that tears of joy were in my eyes. It happened that our return coincided with the first day of the Festival marking the end of the Pilgrimage, and under what different circumstances we rattled up to the great door this time. As I slipped inside and threw off my veils, Layla came running to greet me. We embraced as sisters and she held me at arm's length and surveyed my appearance. 'What a handsome young man you have become — and so brown! You will have to put on lots of powder for your next English party.' She laughed. And little Ahmad called out my name and would not be content but I had to carry him and sit him on my knee while I drank my cold sherbet and told his mother about the journey. But when I was dressed again in my Englishman's clothes with my hat clamped firmly down on my head, Layla became uneasy.

'It's still me,' I cried.

'Oh, I know,' she said. 'But all the same . . .'

So I did a pantomime, clicked my heels and kissed the tips of her fingers, and she promised to send me a note; and indeed she has, and I am due to go with her on a visit tomorrow to some ladies of her acquaintance.

Tomorrow I may hear some news of him.

My dear Sir Charles,
*I have now been back in Shepheard's Hotel for almost a week
and while it is pleasant enough to have a bathroom, a feather bed
and a wardrobe full of clothes, I still miss the simplicity and the
grandeur of life in the desert. I am conscious that I have not yet
given you a full account of that life I enjoyed for some two weeks
– but it was so different from anything that has come within my
experience, the scope of it so vast and grand, that I fear my letters
will not do it justice.*

*Now that I am returned to Cairo I find it harder than ever to
sit back and listen to the complacencies uttered so uncaringly at
the Agency – I fear I am becoming more prickly than is found
becoming in a woman.*

*But on a happier subject: my new friends only improve with
further acquaintance. Yesterday I went out with Layla al-
Baroudi to call on a lady named Nur al-Huda Hanim. I have
heard the ladies at the Agency speak of the boredom of the visits
they have to pay on occasion to the High Harem, and how after
the greetings all the ladies sit silent in a circle and sip coffee until it
is time to leave. Well, nothing could be more different from the
gathering I was admitted into yesterday in a small jewel-like
palace by the Nile. Nur al-Huda Hanim (being barely twenty-
two) is younger than both myself and Layla, but she is very
serious and formidably well educated. I found nothing in her,
though, of that lightness of spirit that I treasure so much in
Layla. In fact, she seemed rather sad. I learned later that she had
recently consented to return to her husband after a seven-year
estrangement and that this was an unwilling return undertaken
only because her brother (who is older than she and whom she
adores) had taken a vow not to marry until he saw her 'safe in her
husband's house'.*

*In her company we found two ladies from France: one a
Madame Richard, who is the widow of a French engineer who
worked on the irrigation projects. She had elected to remain in
Egypt after his death and has apparently been a companion and a*

kind of tutor to Nur al-Huda Hanim since then. The other is a most interesting lady by the name of Eugénie le Brun who is married to an Egyptian Pasha (well, a Turkish Pasha really) by the name of Hussein Rushdi. They make a distinction here between the Notables descended from Turkish lineage and those of Egyptian origin. She has made her home here in Cairo and, I understand, become a Moslem. The occasion of this gathering was a visit from a certain Zeinab Fawwaz who normally resides in Alexandria. She is originally Syrian and is very well thought of and has published several articles on the 'woman question' – I see you grow restless immediately but I do assure you, dear Sir Charles, that you would find these ladies congenial. They uphold the idea that a woman's first duty is to her family, merely arguing that she can peform this duty better if she is better educated. They also write articles arguing against the enforced seclusion of women and point out that women of the fellah class have always worked side by side with their menfolk and no harm has come to society as a result. Madame Fawwaz has published a book which is a collection of short biographies of ladies of note – apparently our own Queens Elizabeth and Victoria are among them!

All in all, I do confess, I found the company and conversation most pleasing and quite contrary to the prevailing view of the life of the harem being one of indolence and torpor.

I shall stop now for I feel I am running on and you will start to think I am now become a 'feminist' while I am in truth, as ever, your loving daughter,

I find a changed and invigorated Anna now. Each morning she expects something new and good from the day. The 'something at the heart of it' which had eluded her now beckons her in. As a friend of Layla Hanim al-Baroudi and Madame Hussein Rushdi she is welcomed into the homes and gatherings of the ladies of Cairo. Emily notices the change and is glad to have a happier mistress but concerned that there seems to be no prospect of going home. And indeed, there is no prospect of going home – yet. For, while her mind is busy with all the new perceptions crowding into it, Anna's heart is waiting for something more.

4 April
Today, in the carriage, I took the occasion to ask Layla whether Sharif Pasha had returned well from the Sinai and to hope that his work had not suffered too much as a result of his absence. She replied that he was indeed back and that she was sure he could manage his work — in any case he did not seem troubled by it. 'He said you rode extremely well and showed no sign of weariness,' she reported. And that was all. But later I understood that he travels tomorrow to Upper Egypt to accompany his mother on her journey home. So now I know there is no possibility of hearing from him for the coming four or five days.

Cairo
8 April 1901

Dear Sir Charles,
I have received yours of 23 March and am glad that you are well and in good spirits and so hopeful of Irish Affairs — at their best, you say, since Parnell died. I hope that makes it up for you — a little — for the events in South Africa. I own when I hear the news from there my immediate concern is for the effect I know it must have on you.
We have had a sand-storm here yesterday and today and it is worse, to my mind, than our London fog. For at least with that you can take refuge in your home and forget its existence. Here, the sand has found its way everywhere, through the most firmly shuttered windows and into the papers and garments in every one of my cabinets. Emily was tutting as she brushed it out of my hair. I find myself thinking longingly of England. For now it is April and everything will be in bloom. I can see the smooth green of the lawns, shimmering with moisture, and I can smell the freshness of the first mowing. I find myself thinking particularly of the magnolia — for its blossoming is so short that I have now missed it for a whole year.
On our last drive I noticed a beautiful tall tree with almost

238

horizontal branches. It had no leaves but the branches were covered with large, solitary red flowers. I asked Layla its name, to my surprise she did not know but said that presently the red flowers would be surrounded by leaves. Mr S, on the other hand, told me immediately that the tree is a Bombax malabricum, also known as a Red Silk-Cotton Tree, and has been imported from tropical Asia. He did not know its name in Arabic. What I find most strange is that he – and others – seem to love this country as much as they dislike its inhabitants. They have a very clear separation in their minds between the two.

I had a somewhat unfriendly exchange two days ago with Mr S. We were walking along the rue Qasr el-Nil and we chanced to pass a coffee-shop where a group of Native gentlemen were engaged in a discussion of something in a newspaper: I saw one of them hand the paper to another, folded as though at a specific article. They paused as we drew near and glanced up at us, resuming their conversation when we had passed. Mr S took this as an occasion to inveigh against 'the older type of Nationalist' to be seen sitting at cafés, indulging in 'seditious talk' and 'embarrassing every passing European gentlewoman' with his 'bold and libidinous stare'. I said, quite gently, that I had not been aware of anything untoward in the gentlemen's looks and he told me – more or less – that I had not the ability to judge the 'Native character' and that it was my good fortune that I could not understand what they were saying about me even then and that he had it on good authority that they were all rascals who desired nothing more fervently than to dishonour a European gentlewoman – particularly, I suppose, if she be English. I did not point out that he knows even less Arabic than I, but I asked if he knew any Egyptians personally and he said most decidedly not of 'this type' but he was acquainted with Mr Faris Nimr, the Editor of al-Muqattam, who is 'a true gentleman and an anglophile', and he has based his views on his conversations with Mr Nimr. I confess that as I have not met Mr Nimr, I do not know what to make of this.

On Thursday I shall go to the Opera with Madame Rushdi to see Sarah Bernhardt in La Dame aux camélias. I shall be in *a harem box and I am looking forward to it enormously and you may be sure I shall report on the evening at length. Till then, I remain,*

10 April

Still nothing. But word from Layla that her Mama is back and would be happy to receive me. So I shall call on them tomorrow.

We had a musical evening at James Barrington's yesterday and Temple Gairdner was in fine form. He has a true feeling for music and plays the piano like one inspired. Mrs Butcher remarked to me privately that he does indeed have soul, she only wished it were occupied in something more to the general good than trying to convert Moslems.

I had a curious conversation with James. Among all the people here, he is the one I feel closest to, in part because he knows of my 'adventures' (although I have promised not to indulge in any more. It was hardly a difficult undertaking, as I have not any longer the need, for – since knowing Layla – I have so many more opportunities to learn about Egypt than wandering round dressed as a man could ever have afforded me) but mostly, I think, because he has a sympathy with people and is not so ready with his judgements and pronouncements. He said that I should be more careful and that I was becoming quite outspoken in defence of the Egyptians and that it would be noticed. 'For example,' he said, 'you were quite nasty to Mr S the other day, and you stopped only because I pinched your arm.' I said I had been sorely tempted to tell Mr S that I had spent sixteen nights under the protection of one of those 'rascals' of whom he spoke and only wished I could expect the same chivalry in an English country house as that I had received from him. 'It won't do, Anna,' he said again, shaking his head. 'You know it won't do. I thought you were sensible.'

And I do believe I am sensible – only I am sensible too of the wrong being done here and that there is a living world which people are refusing to see or even hear about. I know that this sensibility is born of my affection for my new friends but it is none the less trustworthy for that.

My dear Caroline,

*You have been much in my mind tonight for I have spent the
evening at the Cairo Opera House watching the Divine
Bernhardt — a memorable experience and one you would truly
have enjoyed. I went as the guest of Madame Hussein Rushdi, a
French lady married to an Egyptian Pasha, and we were both
guests of a 'Princess Ingie' (although the Princess herself was not
there) and so we sat in one of the boxes set aside for the Royal
Harem, all red plush and red velvet with the softest wall-light
and at the front a delicate wrought-iron screen decorated with
gilded flowers to hide us from all eyes while not impeding our
view of the House and the Stage. To watch the play and the
people while so exquisitely cocooned was — I cannot quite find the
words but it was delightful. I did so wish you could have been
with me.*

*We had supper à deux at Madame Rushdi's afterwards. She
is very clever and speaks both Arabic and Turkish and I mean to
learn a great deal from her. As we were having coffee a servant
appeared and whispered to Madame, whereupon she told me that
her husband had arrived and was asking whether he could be
received. Is that not charming? Upon my giving my assent, the
servant disappeared and the Pasha came in shortly afterwards.
He is quite elderly, but most charming and courteous and quite
approving of my plans to learn Arabic and know all I could of
Egypt. He said I could not have chosen a better teacher than
Layla Hanim al-Baroudi. I laughed and said I could not claim
the wisdom of the choice for it was Fate that had chosen for me,
and he replied, 'Ah! What better guide than Fate?' So there we
are.*

*I have been to Layla's home twice now. It is very beautifully
furnished in the French style — but, to my mind, the old house in
the Arab style is both more beautiful and more naturally suited to
the climate here. I went there a few days ago and was introduced
to Layla's mother, Zeinab Hanim al-Ghamrawi, a good-
looking, dignified lady of perhaps sixty. She was very kind*

and welcoming, but we did not have much conversation, as she does not speak French and my Arabic is as yet limited to greetings and expressions of politesse. But it was charming to watch her with her grandson. Layla complains that she spoils him terribly but I cannot see that the child is any the worse for it. He takes being with adults as completely natural and comes and goes as he pleases while his nanny sits in a corner and calls him to her from time to time to wipe his face or straighten his shirt or – more often – merely to give him a kiss. I observed her blowing in his ear and when I asked Layla she said, 'Oh, she thinks that will blow away any evil spirits!'

You will gather that I am having a most pleasant time. I still see my friends at the Agency but these new experiences of being 'in' Egyptian life, as it were, are – for the moment – of more interest to me. Perhaps merely because of their novelty. I wonder whether, if one of my new friends were to visit us in England, they would find us as interesting or as pleasant.

I have not received any letters from you for a long time. Pray do write and tell me all your news for I fear you may be forgetting your loving friend,

20 April

Today is the first day of the Moslem year 1319. There is still no word. I know he is in Cairo for this much I managed to learn from his sister. What can I – what must I believe? I go over our conversations. I reread my own journal. A friendship grew – of that I am in no doubt. And certainly after our conversation in the garden of the monastery I no longer felt my presence burdensome to him. He did not seek me out, it is true, but he cared for my welfare – but then he would have cared for the welfare of any stranger thrown into his care. We did not have another conversation like it – but then circumstances can hardly be said to have permitted such an occurrence.

I go over our farewell at the edge of the desert as – clad once more in my black veils – I waited for the boat that was to take me back to Suez. He merely waited silently at my side. He spoke to Sabir and to Mutlaq, instructing them, I imagine, on the

242

continued need for caution until we should arrive at his house in Cairo. And then, as the boat drew near, I heard him say, 'It has been a pleasure travelling with you, Lady Anna.' He did not wait for my reply but turned and mounted and rode – at a gallop – back into the desert.

I did not question but that I would see him again. I thought that he would call. I waited for a note. Layla and Zeinab Hanim are most welcoming and friendly but they do not speak of him except naturally, in passing.

MY BROTHER TOOK ANNA INTO the Sinai. She saw the desert and lived its life and visited the Monastery of St Catherine and climbed Jabal Moussa and her thirst for adventure was watered and she returned safely to my father's house here in Cairo. How happy I was to see her – and how happy she was to see me! She told me about her journey and I felt then in her mentioning of his name and her praise of him that my brother had left a good impression on her spirit – and I would almost say more.

When I met Abeih Sharif after his return I asked about the journey and all he said was, 'It ended safely, al-hamdu-l-Illah.' I tried to lead him on a little and asked, 'And was Lady Anna a good rider?' 'Very good,' he said. 'Was she any trouble?' 'No, not at all.' I told him she had recounted to me the story of the trip and that she had praised him for the care with which he had looked after her – and he said nothing. But I noticed, as the days went by, that he seemed more abstracted and restless than usual. And when my mother came back from Minya she noticed it too.

And it happened that I was sitting with him and I mentioned that I had taken Anna to visit Nur al-Huda Hanim and that Madame Hussein Rushdi was there and what a pleasant time we had all had together and how happy Hussein Basha's marriage seemed to be, and he looked at me sharply and said, 'Madame Hussein Rushdi is a Frenchwoman. There's a difference.'

So I asked innocently, 'A difference between what?'

'A Frenchwoman and Englishwoman – in our circumstances,' he said.

'Ah, but you always said we should judge people as individuals,' I said, 'not as examples of a culture or a race.'

'So one should go with one's own feet looking for trouble?' he asked.

'I think in this case,' I laughed, 'trouble has come looking for you.'

'Thank you, my sister,' was all he said.

Cairo
21 April, 1901

Dear Caroline,
I received with joy yours of the 7th. I had heard from Sir Charles about poor Bron Herbert losing his leg in the Boer War and now yours with news of Miss Herbert joining the Theosophists and going off to live in California – how odd that two such things should happen in such a short space of time in one family! Do you think, perhaps, that one might have led to the other? I wish you were here and we could sit and converse with one another for I have so many new impressions now, but so vague that they seem to resist being rendered solid on paper. But I suppose it is too late in the year for it to be practicable for you to come to Egypt – even if you were willing.

The weather is starting to heat up now, although it is not yet anything like the heat I have heard described. I am making a study of the trees and plants – I saw a hoopoe flitting around on the polo ground at the Club at Ghezirah the other day. I am enclosing a drawing I did of him for you.

Cairo
24 April 1901

Dear Caroline,
I am just returned from the strangest party and wanted immediately to tell you about it. It is a kind of Salon, literary and political, held by a Princess Nazli Fadhil at her palace from time

244

to time. *She is the niece (I think) of Muhammad Ali himself, and indeed is (again I think) quite old – in age but not at all in spirit.*

Normally women are not admitted to her Salon, but I expressed such curiosity when I heard of it that Eugénie (Madame Rushdi) persuaded her husband to ask the Princess's permission for me to attend. Permission duly granted, I accompanied Hussein Pasha there tonight.

There were maybe ten gentlemen there, Hussein Pasha and a Mr Amin being the only Egyptians. Our own Mr Young was there (he recounted a most amusing story that Mabel Caitland had told him. It appears that while shopping for some necessities at Harrods on her last visit to London she had fallen into conversation with an American lady tourist. After a while the lady, understanding that her new acquaintance did not live permanently in London, asked where she was from. 'From Egypt,' said Miss Caitland. 'Why, isn't that wonderful,' the American lady said, 'and you not black at all!') and also Mr Barrington, two French, two Italians, a German and a Russian. I see you frown, but since the Princess was there it was not improper, surely? She is an extraordinary lady: she wore a skirt and blouse in European fashion, her hair was coloured exceeding black, she smoked incessantly and spoke in a husky drawl in French, English, Turkish and Italian (using Arabic only to speak to the maids). She was amused by me, I think, and insisted on referring to me as 'la petite veuve' and 'la veuvette'. The talk flew wildly from Feminism to the Cinématographe (of which apparently there are regular performances in Cairo and Alexandria) to the naiveté of Americans to the Boxer Rebellion to the interpretation of dreams to Karl Marx to the most recent discovery of Egyptian mummies – and heaven knows what else. And all the while the champagne corks were popping. Suddenly she calls in one of her maids (they are all dressed in the most sumptuous silk robes) and gives an order and without further ado a small ensemble is gathered of musicians with various instruments, of which the only one at all familiar to me was the lute – but the most important one of all was a kind of drum, held under the arm and played with the fingers and palms of both hands. Another order and one of the maids – an exceedingly beautiful girl – moves to the middle of the room and starts performing an Oriental Dance. I will spare you the description but I found it a most fascinating mixture. The Egyptian gentlemen looked faintly bored, the British faintly embarrassed, but the others were very animated and the Russian and the German, not content with clapping, must needs get up and join the girl. It was a wonderful sight to see the two big bearlike men try to imitate the sinuous twists and turns of the sequined dancer.

The dance over, more champagne is called for, and cups of Turkish coffee and Italian liqueurs, and everybody goes quiet for a while when suddenly the Princess cries, 'Look at the little veuvette, how happy she looks! Won't one of you Englishmen of the red blood snap her up before she falls for one of our handsome young Egyptian Nationalists with the dark eyes and the mustachios?' And beneath the laughter I felt a certain discomfort in the room. I am sure she knew what she was doing for she looked most wickedly amused.

I doubt I shall be going back there, for Madame Rushdi can only ask it of her husband once and I doubt I shall find another sponsor. And besides, I do not think I could be friends with the Princess – or rather I do not think she could be friends with me – I am a little too ordinary for her, I fear. Now you, my dear Caroline, would be another matter entirely –

Cairo
25 April 1901

Dear Sir Charles,
I am so glad to receive yours of the 18th and to learn that our friends spoke well of me to you. Although I do think Sir Hedworth Lambton's comments were more flattering than I deserve.

I am amazed that you say you had a long conversation with him about Urabi and that he had seen him three years ago in Ceylon. When we dined here he made no mention whatsoever of that – which is not strange in itself, but you would not have thought he knew him or had any Nationalist sympathies at all.

Perhaps it is not so strange. I certainly find it most difficult to speak of my Egyptian friends to my English ones here. When I mentioned having been to the Opera with Madame Rushdi, Lord Cromer went quite stiff with disapproval and Harry Boyle took me aside afterwards and said to me 'You know she has turned Mohammedan?' as though that placed her outside the boundaries of polite society.

I have tried – since what they know they seem to know from hearsay only – to tell them about my experience. And they appear to listen but then resume their conversation as though I had not spoken. I tried – when two ladies were commiserating on the dreariness of having to go to yet another of their Harem visits – to tell them of the ladies I have met and they simply seemed annoyed, as though the women here were tiresome enough being in the Harem and would only be doubly tiresome by seeking to get out of it!

My dear Sir Charles, I understand so much more now of what I used to hear you say. I have started to believe that what we are doing is denying that Egyptians have a 'consciousness of themselves' – indeed that was what Mr Young said in that scene by the Pyramids I transcribed for you many months ago – and that by doing so we settle any qualms of conscience as to our right to be here. So long as we believe that they are like pets or small children, we can remain here to 'guide them' and help them 'develop'. But if we see that they are as fully conscious of themselves and their place in the world as we are, why then the honourable thing is to pack up and go – retaining perhaps an advisory role in economic matters – which I think the Egyptians themselves would wish.

It is all quite confusing – and, if not confusing, terrible. I wish you could be here and I could share my thoughts and experiences with you in a more immediate manner. I know it would benefit me greatly and I am sure would provide you with some interest. For the moment, though, I have to be content to be your faraway daughter,

30 April

I am grown less and less comfortable with my British friends. Mr M and Mr W both hold sympathetic opinions, indeed the former said only yesterday that we were 'emasculating' the Egyptian upper classes to ensure they would be unfit to rule. He then begged my pardon – he had not meant to use such strong words. Mrs Butcher continues to be my friend but I cannot speak even to her of what I feel. For Lord Cromer, I tried to interest him in what my Egyptian friends desire for the education of women and he said that if I knew Egypt better I would know that the religious leaders would never agree to women being encouraged out of their lowly status, and he would not hear another word.

At the mention of Cromer's name Layla's face grew hard and when I pressed her she said, 'Lord Cromer is a patriot and he serves his country well. We understand that. Only he should not pretend that he is serving Egypt.'

2 May

The days pass, and the happiness I felt in the Sinai has shrunk and compacted itself into a knot of misery lodged underneath my heart. Every morning I wake to its heaviness weighing me down and then the thought: he has not written. He has not called. I believe I know now that he will not.

5 May

They say the heat of the summer is soon to be upon us and I am thinking of returning to England. I have grown to love Layla dearly and little Ahmad also. I am also fond of the other ladies I have met through her. But English society is no longer so pleasant to me – apart from that of James, who continues to be my good friend and urged me just the other day to 'Buck up, old girl'. But I cannot seem to shake off this restless unhappiness. I have told myself that I imagined a feeling that did not exist. That for him I was nothing more that an eccentric Englishwoman to whom he was obliged to be courteous while she was in his care. That he does not give a thought for me.

Yet I cannot stop looking for him every time I am in the street, *or hoping to see him every time I visit his sister, or expecting to find a note every time I come back to the Hotel. Perhaps the only way to make an end of all this is to place myself far away in England. To go home.*

A knock on the door. A letter is delivered. Anna breaks open the seal:

Cairo
5 May

Madame,

I understand from my sister that your present intention is to travel; to return to England.

I have decided, after long consideration, to write to you. We have travelled together, and I hope we have become friends sufficiently to – my dear Lady Anna, let me dispense with attempts to be clever or discreet. I am in love with you. There. It is said. For many, many years I have believed it was my fate never to say these words. A long time ago I had hoped, as all young men hope – no, I had more than hoped, I had confidently *expected* to be overtaken by those feelings I had read so much about. It never happened. And now it has.

I have tried to convince myself it is an illusion. I do not really know you – perhaps can never really know you. I have told myself it is the foolishness of a man seeing his old age draw near, and afraid, afraid to have missed that which poets would have us believe is the most transforming of experiences – is the essence of life itself. But I do not believe that this is merely my fear or my fantasy fastening itself on you; it is you. You yourself, Anna, with your violet eyes, your slender wrists, your way of sitting absolutely still and listening and watching with your head held high, your frank look, your fearless questioning, the notes of your voice, the grace of your movements – but I forget myself.

I have – you may have noticed – since we came back from our journey, avoided seeing you. I will not tell you

with what difficulty and at what cost. There has not been a
moment when my heart has not whispered of your
whereabouts: she is visiting your sister, go to her; ride
past Shepheard's Hotel, she may be sitting on the terrace; it
is Sunday, ride past the Mu'allaqah. I have resisted and
would have resisted still, but that my sister came to see me.
And she has led me to believe that perhaps a word from me
– a letter, such as this one – would not be unwelcome.

My dearest Anna, for this you are whether you will or
no, I am most sensible – I am sure you know this – of all
the circumstances, all the considerations that are at work
against us. I say 'us' before I even get your response! This
will bear out whatever you may have heard of my
supposed arrogance. But believe me, dear, sweet Anna,
you would not find me arrogant or proud or impatient if
I could truly call myself yours

Sharif al-Baroudi

PS I will ask the bearer of this letter not to wait for a
reply. This is to give you time to consider your answer. I
will be waiting.

And there is the hushed moment, not quite understanding,
not quite believing, the hurried glance through the paper
once again, the wave of joy so powerful it shakes the heart like
grief, the rush to the window, the turning back:

'Emily, Emily, run and see if that messenger is still there.'

But he is not there. True to his orders, he has gone, and
now there is nothing but to pace the floor and wait for the
morning, to fold the letter, then open it and read it once again,
and again, and again.

'Why, madam, whatever is the matter? You'll make me
pull your hair like this.'

'It's enough, Emily, you've brushed it enough –' shaking
her head impatiently – 'I'll just braid it now, and you go to
bed. Oh and Emily, don't pack any more. Let's wait a while.
Oh, and is my blue silk not packed?'

'Not yet, madam.'

'Good. I shall want it in the morning. Thank you, Emily. Good night.'

He loves her. Circumstances and considerations – what are those? The whole world recedes and there is room for only one thought: he loves her. She had not misunderstood him. She is not an eccentric and a burden. He has been thinking of her as she has of him. Above her bed the broad fins whirl gently; the night will pass and morning will come and he loves her.

18

Wandering between two worlds . . . one dead
The other powerless to be born.

Matthew Arnold

I sit here, holding my great-uncle's letter in my hand. I imagine him sitting at his desk to write it. He has been standing at the window of his study in his house at Hilmiyya – the house that had stood next to ours. What is he wearing? I can only imagine him in European dress, for that is how both Anna and his sister describe him, and that is what he wears in the portrait hanging in Tawasi. Besides, I have never seen my father or my brother in the old costume of an Egyptian gentleman. I lay his letter out on the table and wonder once again at the things that survive us. He was my age when he wrote it: a man, tall and vigorous and alive, a man who filled a room when he entered, who thought and spoke and suffered and loved and – all that is gone and this piece of paper remains. The paper that he smoothed out and wrote on, fast and deliberately, with a broad-nibbed pen. The ink is brown now but you can see the strength and control in the hand: the letters upright, the strokes sharp, the words each within its definite space. I am half in love with him, I believe – with my own great-uncle.

I have heard his story from my father, who more or less worshipped him as a child, and from my mother, who never met him but heard of him from our cousins in 'Ein el-Mansi. His history is there in al-Raf'i and Hussein Amin and other chronicles of the times and his own writings are in *al-Ahram*, *al-Liwa* and, later, *al-Garidah*. In Layla's account of him I see my own brother, and in Anna's I find the dark, enigmatic hero of Romance. And now it falls to me to weave all these strands together and write Sharif Basha al-Baroudi as the man I imagine he must have been.

My great-uncle Sharif Basha al-Baroudi made his move, as this letter in front of me testifies, but he did not make it without misgiving. For five weeks – no, seven (for the two weeks in the Sinai should be counted as well) – he pulled away from the impulse that drew him towards Anna. He had distrusted impulse for so long now – oh, he had thrown it the odd, appeasing crumb: a purchase here, a trip abroad there, but on the main road of his life, as it were, he had held himself in check. His friend Sheikh Muhammad 'Abdu had done the same and had grown into a staid, measured man whose pronouncements showed wisdom not uncoloured by diplomacy. What was left of that fiery, black-eyed young Azhari who had been prepared to consider assassinating Tewfiq for the cause of Egypt's freedom? Time was when it had seemed that courage was all you needed: the belief that what you wanted was yours by right – and the courage to take it. They had been taught that that was not true. They had seen lives ended on the scaffold, cut down on the battlefield, destroyed by exile and by retreat. Caution and calculation became a habit.

But in the Sinai, in the garden of the monastery of St Catherine, Anna – and his feelings – had taken him by surprise. And even though next day he withdrew into formal politeness, away from the desert, when she was no longer at his side, she took root in his mind and would not be shaken.

Tawasi, 7 April 1901

Sharif Basha crumbles the rich black soil thoughtfully in his hand. He sits back on his haunches and looks around at his fields. The cries of the children playing by the canal reach him from a distance. When he was last here, in the month of Toubah, the sugar cane had just been harvested and the land set ablaze to burn away the stubble. Bare and charred and desolate it was then. And yet now, less than three months later, in Baramhat, the old roots, vigorous in the earth, are pushing the new crop through. Sharif Basha stands up, stamps his feet, stretches. Here he is away, away from thoughts of her. He wipes his hands on his cotton trousers. Beyond the sugar cane, the last rays of the setting sun catch the fields of kittan and burnish them into a sea of purple, blue and gold. Two, three, four thousand years ago, men stood as he is standing now and looked at this same scene, these same colours, felt this same light gust of breeze that brushes the heads of the flowers and sends a slow wave rippling from end to end of the shining field. To his mind, the magic of this scene equals that of the desert. Perhaps surpasses it. Would she be moved by it as he is? She has land in her own country, he knows. But is it farms or forests or meadows? He does not know. In the middle distance a young girl untethers an ox from the water wheel, removes the blindfold from its eyes, and child and beast start ambling slowly towards home. He walks over to the water wheel, takes off his shoes and socks and starts to wash.

In the village mosque, the men make room for him in the front row and when the sunset prayers are over he walks with the 'Umdah through the darkening lanes. They sit in the 'Umdah's mandarah with the door open to the road. Men come and men go, the tea tray goes round and round again, and always, in the distance, there are the sounds of children playing. Landlord and 'Umdah talk of the new school Sharif Basha and his uncle Ghamrawi Bey are putting up in the village. The children will still have to go to the kuttab of course, the sheikh need not worry about that. But in the new school they will learn to add and subtract. They will learn the geography of the whole world and the history of their country. The fallaheen will be persuaded to spare their children (boys *and* girls, Sharif Basha repeats) from the fields for two hours every day that they might learn. Not that they should become afandiyyah, but that they should be educated citizens more able to look after their own interests.

'You are right, ya Basha.' The 'Umdah sighs. 'Nobody knows what the days will bring.'

256

'All good, insha' Allah, ya 'Umdah. But we should do what we can.'

'Every day there's something new. First it was the wine shop and we put our hands on our hearts and said may God protect us, but people were wise and it was only the bad lot who went there anyway. Now it's the moneylenders and it's not enough for them that they set up shop in the town, they have to come to the villages and try to hook people —'

'We've talked about this and you said our people here are comfortable?'

'Comfortable, yes, ya Basha, al-hamdu-l-Illah, but a man gets cornered, he wants to get his daughter married, he has sudden circumstances — and they charge a lot for their money. Greeks, all Greek —'

'Tell them to come to me. To come to Hasib Efendi, my agent. I'll speak to him. We'll forward the money, in an emergency, with one per cent interest and the crop as surety.'

'May God give you light, ya Basha. The village will rejoice.'

'Tell them.'

'I'll tell them on Friday. Will you pray with us?'

'If I'm still here.'

They should set up a cooperative, Sharif Basha thinks. If each man puts by a little money, after the harvest, they can draw on it when they need to. Other villages have started to do that. Hasib Efendi can look after it. Bank it for them. He'll speak to him — and promise him a pay rise to make up for the extra work. Sharif Basha walks from the village to his house, exchanging easy greetings with the men he meets on the way. It's simple living on the land. The Ibrahimiyyah gives them water all the year round and he has persuaded the fallaheen not to shift wholesale into cotton as Cromer would have them do and put themselves at the mercy of a market over which they have no control. Some cotton, yes, but they still plant their beans and their peas, their wheat and barley. Their watermelons, each now lying like a queen in her bed of yellow flowers. The worst that can happen is misguided

British officers following a fox. Here on his land the problems are problems he can solve.

He washes and changes, then rides out to the house of his uncle Mustafa Bey al-Ghamrawi for dinner. Here, a man could forget about Cairo, about the Occupation, about the world. And yet, for him, it had never been an option. He loves the land, but he loves the city too: the lights, the noise, the speed and action of it. Living on the land is too much like retiring – giving up.

Sharif Basha sees a horseman cantering towards him from the direction of his uncle's house. As he draws near, the greeting rings out in a familiar voice: 'Ya misa' al-khairat!'

Shukri al-'Asali, the nephew of his uncle's wife, and his childhood friend. The two men leap from their horses and embrace. Back in the Sixties and the Seventies there had been long visits between their two households. The children spent the winter months together here on the land in Tawasi and the summer months there on the land in 'Ein el-Mansi between al-Nasirah and Jenin. They still write to each other, and when they visit from time to time they find their old friendship still strong in their hearts.

'When did you arrive?' Sharif Basha asks.

'Just now, an hour ago. And they told me you were here and they were expecting you for dinner. We had better go. They are all waiting for you.'

'How's everything with you?' Sharif Basha asks, as the two men mount and set off together at an easy pace.

'Well, well, all well. Apart from the usual problems. You should come and visit us. It's been a long time.'

'It is the same problem everywhere.' Shukri Bey al-'Asali is fairer-skinned than his Egyptian cousins. His hair is a lighter brown and he wears it in a slightly longer style. But like Sharif Basha, like Mustafa Bey, he has the air of confidence and gallantry that comes from being assured since birth of the love of his womenfolk. Some years later – in 1915 – the Turks will hang him for his part in the Arab Revolution. But now, in

April 1901, he sits at the dinner table of his aunt's house in Tawasi and says, 'The Turks are weak and cannot protect us against Europe. But they are our rulers and we are only allowed to protect ourselves through them. Here, they could not protect Egypt against the British. With us, they cannot protect us against the Zionists.'

'But 'Abd el-Hamid has stood up to them so far?' Mustafa Bey al-Ghamrawi says, taking the plate that Jalila Hanim, his wife, has handed to him.

'So far. But they tempt his court with money. Huge sums. They want to imitate Cecil Rhodes. When he was given the charter to colonise the Zambesi, they asked the Kaiser to give them a German charter to colonise Palestine.' Shukri Bey reaches for the jug of water. He fills the glass of his aunt sitting next to him, then his own.

'But what about the people?' Jalila Hanim asks. 'The people on the land. What happens to them?'

'Exactly.' Shukri Bey looks at his aunt. 'And they have been told, the Zionists. Abraham Shlomo Bey travelled to their congress and told them, in case they had not noticed, that 650,000 Arabs – Muslims, Christians and Jews – have lived for centuries on the land they propose to colonise. So they sent a special commission to investigate. And the commission went back and said the same thing, so they put the report in a drawer and forgot about it.'

'But you have restrictions in place, have you not? They can only come in on pilgrimage for three months, hand in their passports and all that?' Sharif Basha says.

'Yes. For twenty years we've had restrictions. But they get around them. Governors who enforce them – like Tevfik Bey – don't last long. And the Powers, and the United States, are constantly sending their ambassadors to object to this "discrimination" –'

'But the settlers are not from the Powers or the United States?'

'No. They're coming from Russia, Rumania, some from Germany –'

259

'So what's the interest of the United States in this?'

Shukri Bey shrugs. 'My guess is as good as yours. Pressure from influential people. Dislike of Turkey –'

'Turkey has to be got rid of. For all of us,' Sharif Basha says. 'It has had its day.'

Zeinab Hanim looks at her son anxiously. Her brother smiles at her. 'Don't worry, sister. 'Abd el-Hamid has no spies here.'

'I'm going to talk to people,' Shukri Bey says, 'in Cairo and Alexandria. I shall meet Rafiq Bey el-'Azm and others with family ties in Palestine. Whip up some public opinion. And I shall speak to the newspapers –'

'*Al-Ahram* has already printed several letters,' Mustafa Bey says, 'describing how the settlers plough the common grazing land and confiscate livestock they find there –'

'They have a variety of ways,' Shukri Bey says, 'all aiming to possess the land and make life uncomfortable for the fallaheen. I might try to meet Cromer – I know you hate him, but Britain is the most powerful of the Powers. If they get her backing, the matter will be practically finished.'

'Enough. Enough politics,' Zeinab Hanim says, before her son can speak. 'Our whole life is politics. Tell us about our people. Your children – may God preserve them for you – and their mother. How are they all?'

Cairo, 12 April 1901

Sharif Basha puts aside his papers.

'Have the 'Isha prayers been called?' he asks Mirghani, and when the man says yes he asks him to prepare his horses; he will be going out after he has prayed.

He drives through Darb el-Gamamiz and out into the open space of Midan 'Abdin. A glance at the palace – but Efendeena must be home in Qubba by now. He resists the impulse to veer into Shari' 'Abdin, which would lead him eventually to Shepheard's Hotel. Instead, he drives up Shari' al-Bustan.

The Club Muhammad 'Ali is ablaze with lights. The

doorman steps forward to greet him: 'You've absented your-self from us, ya Basha.'

'I was away. Who's here tonight?'

'Everybody, ya Basha: Mustafa Fahmi Basha, Boutros Basha, and Hussein Basha Rushdi. Milton Bey and Prince Gamil Tusun are in the dining room. Prince Ahmad Fuad and Prince Yusuf Kamal are in the billiard room. And –' dropping his voice – 'Mr Boyle arrived ten minutes ago.'

Sharif Basha looks in on the main lounge, he greets Mustafa Fahmi, Boutros Ghali and Hussein Rushdi but does not sit down. He notes Harry Boyle sitting nearby with a newspaper. Boyle makes a habit of dropping in for half an hour every few days.

In the billiard room, Prince Ahmad Fuad is winning. This does not prevent him looking dour. It was in this same room that Prince Ahmad Sayf-el-Din shot him a couple of years ago and, had it not been for Milton Bey, he would have been dead. As it was, he was ill for a long time and that did not improve his habitual moroseness. Yusuf Kamal is completely the opposite: quick and nervous, perpetually worried, but a man of vision and enthusiasm.

Sharif Basha lights a cigarette and settles down to wait. He wants to talk to Prince Yusuf about the new art school. Work on the museum is going more or less to schedule. The university is a slow business – mainly because of Cromer's opposition. The art-school project is still in its beginnings. Well, these are good things to be working on. But it all takes so much time. Raising the money is not easy. All of it private. Not one piastre of state money will they get as long as Cromer is in power. 'The budget does not permit . . .' the British Agent repeats and repeats. But the budget permitted more than one and a half million pounds of Egypt's money to be spent on the Sudan Expedition and another quarter of a million every year to make up the Sudan deficits, and what was the benefit to Egypt in this? The budget permits the employment of British officials in Egypt at triple the salaries of the equivalent Egyptians. But it does not permit an extra piastre for any project to do with culture or education. Technical education Cromer is coming round to; schools to produce clerks and workers. British brains and Arab hands is Cromer's recipe for Egypt. Sharif Basha stands up, stubs out his cigarette and walks over to the window. Over there lies Qasr el-Dubara, where even now 'el-Lord' is making his plans for the country. 'Come, come, man. He's probably eating his dinner.' A brief smile touches the corner of Sharif Basha's mouth as he imagines what his friend Ya'qub Artin would say if he could hear his thoughts. 'Even Cromer has to stop scheming sometimes. You'll find he has guests there now and they're not thinking of Egypt at all. They're talking about the latest news from London –' Anna. She might be there. Sitting at the table. Dressed in her own clothes. Speaking her own language. Her eyes raised to some young officer – Sharif Basha reaches in his pocket for his prayer beads. He stands at the window, his hands clasped behind him, the beads going round and round between the fingers of his right hand. How can he permit himself to think that an understanding might be possible between them? It cannot be. In any case she would have forgotten him by now. Or, if not forgotten, he would have receded into an exotic part – a remote part – of her Egyptian journey. A better kind of 'Native' she had travelled with in the desert and spoken with one night in a moonlit garden. And now she is back where she belongs: at the Club in Ghezira, the donkey races and paper chases, the fancy-dress balls and Agency dinners with her own people. There are men out there, younger than he, who would shoot Cromer and hang for it and consider their lives well spent. And what would be the use? The Qasr el-Nil Barracks are right there: five minutes' walk away. The British will not go. They will never go of their own free will. The only force that will make them go will be the force of arms – or interest. And they know that. Hence the disbanding of Egypt's elite forces; the scattering of the army, the British officers at the head of every regiment. And meanwhile the British Army of Occupation costs one million pounds every year. A million pounds that could go towards paying the country's debt and setting her free of her foreign masters. And the people will not fight. Cannot fight. Oh, he held back the hot-heads and talked about due process of law. That was one point on which he was in agreement with Cromer: 'due process of law'. Cromer also wanted an end to the Capitulations by which every foreigner in Egypt was tried by his own consul, not by the Egyptian courts. But Cromer had shown bad faith by bringing in the Special Laws to deal with 'Natives' confronting British personnel. He had brought them in after the Gelgel case that he, Sharif Basha, had defended. Ending the Capitulations would only deliver Egypt more completely into Cromer's hands. They should hold on to them, even though they placed every foreign national above the law. To barricade your soul against the thousand indignities you suffered as a man ruled by outsiders – And meanwhile time was being lost. The generations that should have been educated, the industries that should have been introduced, the laws that should have been reformed, and worse, the ascendance of those who curried favour with the British, how would you dislodge those when the occupier had gone? The distrust sown between Muslim and Copt – A hand on his shoulder and he turns –

Prince Yusuf Kamal is a slight man with a sensitive, intelligent face. He has a passion for art and intends personally to fund the school if no other money can be found. 'Where has it all gone?' he is fond of saying. 'Look at the statues, look at the temples our grandfathers built. Look at the mosques of the Fatimids, the book-bindings and the glass of the Mamelukes – and now? The Ottomans have a lot to answer for.' But at this moment it would appear another opposition is gathering force.

'Would you believe,' the Prince says sadly, 'they are accusing me of encouraging kufr?'

'Kufr, your Highness?'

'Drawing! Sculpture! Here —' He takes out an envelope from his pocket, draws out a letter and shakes it open. 'Read this.'

Sharif Basha reads:

. . . and doubt does not enter into our hearts regarding the elevated nature of your Highness's intentions and the nobility of your aims, but we find it our duty to remind you, with all the respect that is due to . . . of the clear injunction against the activities that you propose to foster in the establishment Your Highness intends to set up. This injunction is expressed in the sound Hadith of the Messenger of God — the prayers and peace of God be upon him: 'Those who will be most severely tormented on the Day of Judgement are the image-makers.' Therefore, we now request that you reconsider . . . money can be better used to promote and strengthen our Faith which is being daily eroded by the presence in our land of the unjust and infidel Occupier . . .

Sharif Basha hands back the letter. 'Your Highness can hardly give weight —'

'I have to take them seriously,' Prince Yusuf says. 'They could incite the people. Ya Basha, all they would have to say is that I am in collusion with the British to import evil European arts into the country, to train our young men into them . . .'

Harry Boyle strolls into the room and Sharif Basha places a hand on his friend's arm. 'Shall we go and get something to eat?' he suggests.

In the dining room the two men pause to greet Milton Bey and Prince Gamil Tusun. They take a corner table and order grilled pigeon and salad. A pitcher of lemonade sits in its silver castor between them.

'What do you propose to do?' Sharif Basha asks.

'I don't know. Give me your opinion.'

'Set up a public debate. You can wipe the floor with them.'

'What's the use —'

'Accuse *them* of conspiring with the British to hold us back.'
Sharif Basha laughs at his own idea, but Prince Yusuf is
troubled.

'You cannot convince these people with logic. You have to
speak to them in their own language.'

The waiters appear with the food and the two men shake
out their napkins. Prince Yusuf pours olive oil and vinegar on
the salad.

'If you speak to them in their own language, you have
already agreed to fight on their ground,' Sharif Basha says,
picking up his fork. 'Our position should be that faith is one
thing and colleges – civil institutions – are another.'

'They will never accept that,' Prince Yusuf Kamal objects.

'But we shall have this problem with the university, with
the education of women, with banking – with everything.
This is the question that has to be decided once and for all: to
what extent should these people interfere in the practical
development of the country? And notice that their interven-
tions are always in a negative direction – everything in their
book is haraam –'

'Ya Sharif Basha, this is a debate we cannot enter into now.
With the British here, people will not say of us, "These men
are patriots who think differently from us." They will say,
"These men are in the pay of the British", and they will
conspire even more with the Sublime Porte to tie us closer to
Turkey. For the moment, we keep our eye on our target, our
limited target: the School of Fine Art.'

'Let me speak to Sheikh Muhammad 'Abdu,' Sharif Basha
says impatiently, taking his napkin off his knee, crumpling it
on the table by his plate. 'He supports the school. He can give
us arguments for it – arguments that they would find convincing.'

'If he would declare his support,' Prince Yusuf says hope-
fully, 'that would be the end of it. After all, he *is* the Mufti and
the highest religious authority.'

'I shall speak to him,' Sharif Basha says. Then, after a
moment: 'As soon as he gets back from Istanbul. And if he's

for it, and willing to declare himself, you reply to this letter by asking *them* to put the question to the Mufti. Say you will abide by his decision.' He pushes back his chair. 'But these are piecemeal solutions in the end.'

No question that needs settling can be settled now. There is always a reason to avoid confrontation. Sharif Basha orders his driver to go slowly over Ismail Bridge and back before returning home. He wants to look at the Nile. He would have liked to walk home: a long, brisk walk in the crisp air. But now, at one o'clock in the morning, it would be asking for trouble. He was bound to come across some British soldiers and if challenged in any way he could not trust himself to keep his temper. Sharif Basha leans back in his carriage as the horses turn and wheel to recross the bridge. On the right he can see the low-lying form and the lights of the Agency. Even if she has been to dinner there, she will be back in her room at Shepheard's by now. And something tells him she is not happy. He imagines her walking into her room, dressed in European clothes. She pauses by a mirror and raises her arms to take the pins out of her hat. Sharif Basha sees his own image in the mirror behind her. He stands so close that he can feel the warmth of her body, can smell the scent rising from her liberated hair . . .

Sharif Basha has neglected his heart for so long that it had fallen silent. And now it speaks. It lies in wait for him and chooses its moment: as he enters his house where the servants are all asleep. As he walks into his library Anna lets the curtain fall, turns from the window and smiles at him. 'Tu es en retard. Je commençais à m'inquiéter.' 'Tu!' He grimaces; he already has her calling him 'tu'. He checks his desk to see if any messages have arrived while he was out. There is a copy of *al-Mu'ayyad* with a note from Sheikh Ali Yusuf pinned to it. There is also a large embossed card, an invitation to attend the opening of Mustafa Kamel's new school in Breem on the 15th. He turns off the lamp and walks from the room and up the stairs. Mustafa Kamel is a patriot, absolutely. He is rousing people against the Occupation. He is establishing schools.

Why then is Sharif Basha not comfortable with him? As he dries his face he frowns into the bathroom mirror. Is he jealous? Because Mustafa Kamel is young and fiery and a good rhetorician? No. He detects something in the younger man, something on the make, something too fond of itself. And he is too close to the Sultan. He does not wish for the end of Turkish rule in Egypt. And he invests too much trust in the French. He thinks that because they are the traditional enemies of Britain, they will stand by Egypt. He did not live through the Joint Note, the ultimatums. He goes to Paris and they fête him and spoil him and call him Caramel Pasha behind his back and he believes whatever Madame Juliette Adams chooses to tell him. But traditional enmity is not enough. Britain and France are both European countries in any case and sooner or later they will do a deal. They will unite as they had done for the Crusades and the Caisse de la Dette and the Joint Note. An alliance between Britain and France is more natural, after all, than an alliance between Egypt and France. But at least Mustafa Kamel has started a newspaper and what has he, Sharif al-Baroudi, done? Now in its forty-fifth year, what did his life amount to?

In the bedroom he lights a cigarette, pushes aside the curtains and stands out on the balcony. The moon is in its last quarter. A few more days and when you look at the sky you will see no moon at all, only darkness. But now, if he looks hard enough, Sharif Basha can make out the shape of the whole moon, the dark bulk made visible by the shining crescent. If his mother were here now perhaps he would speak with her. Ask her what she thought. She has met her, he knows that. And Layla has told her the whole story, what she knows of it – possibly what she guesses as well. The sycamore closest to the house rustles with sudden movement. He wonders if the gardener has cut the figs – a delicate incision to allow the fruit to breathe and grow. He will remind him tomorrow. Perhaps he should speak with his mother anyway. She knows him well enough to judge.

On the train back from Minya he had been mostly silent.

Because he felt bad about her — as he always does — but particularly when he has to take her home after she has spent time in the country. The bustle of her brother's house. Her nieces' children coming and going. And this time Shukri's visit. God has blessed Shukri with acceptance. He lights up any room he enters and he is comfortable instantly with whatever new person he meets. Sharif Basha has promised to introduce him to Muhammad 'Abdu and the owners of the major newspapers and anybody else he wishes to meet. Cromer he will have to do for himself and get from him what help he can. He had not even commented on Shukri's wish to see Cromer, although he could see his mother expected him to make some unpleasant remark and she had hurried to change the subject. Walking with her in the garden later he had said, 'I have no problem with Shukri seeing Cromer. It would be good if he could get his help.'

She had glanced up anxiously. 'I don't want you falling out with your cousin. Who do we have except each other?'

'Why are you so worried? Who have I fallen out with?'

'Your father.'

'My father is not even there to fall out with.'

To be locked up in a house with a husband who has turned into a magzub. Sharif Basha throws the cigarette butt on the floor and grinds it with the heel of his slipper. When his father went into hiding in the shrine they thought it would be a few weeks, at most a month or two, and then he would come out. But the months went by. Mahmoud Sami, 'Urabi and the other six had been exiled. Sulayman Basha Sami had been hanged and his father — probably in shame at having hidden in the first place, although he never said so — held fast to his shrine. There was no shame in it, they had told him; 'Abdallah al-Nadim had gone to ground and he was no coward. But he would not even talk about it — 'When God permits' was all he would say. Eventually Tewfiq had summoned him, Sharif, to an audience and said, in front of Riyadh and Malet, 'We know about your father. Tell him he can come out of hiding. As long as he stays silent, no harm will befall him. And as for you, your youth and the bad example set by your uncle intercede for you. But we shall be watching you – so take care.' And all he had been able to do was to draw himself up and say, 'I am proud to call Mahmoud Sami Basha my uncle. And I would be happier following him into exile than living in my country under foreign rule.' And the Khedive had merely dismissed him with a wave of his hand and a repeated 'We shall be watching you'. He still smarts at the memory of that interview – now, when Tewfiq is dead and almost twenty years have passed. He had reported this to his mother, with tears of anger and shame burning in his eyes, and she had said, 'Well, since they know where he is, there is no harm now in us moving to the old house until we can persuade him to come back.' But he had refused to go. Despite her tears and her entreaties, he had refused to go. He had wished, oh, how he had wished then that he had not been the son of that father! And she had left next day, taking Layla with her and leaving him with that poor young woman who was meant to be his wife and who was forever visiting her mother and returning to sit silently in the house with clear traces of weeping on her face and starting in fright every time he entered a room so that in the end he could not come near her at all. Well, he had set her free and she had been happy to go and what was he doing now thinking of starting again after the best of his life had gone by? Ah, but *she* would not be like that. If it had been her he was married to he would lay odds she would have stayed by his side, perhaps more so because it was her country that – supposing he had been married to a Sudanese woman, say, and a battalion of Egyptian soldiers had attacked her village and burned it down. Would that not have made him hold her even closer to his heart?

Sharif Basha paces to the end of his balcony and back. Did she have to be English, this woman who has made him think once again of love? She steals up on him at unguarded moments, looking up, her candid face ready to break into a smile across the breakfast table. What would it be like to leave her, knowing she would be there when he returned, at home in his home and happy? What would it be like if she was standing close beside him now, if they looked out at the dark garden together while he told her about Yusuf Kamal's school of art? She would throw herself into that – she who had come to Egypt because of a painting. And how would he explain today's events? Tell her about the letter? How much explaining would that take? That you should need a religious fatwa to open a school of fine art? It would sound medieval. Could he trust her to understand?

Sharif Basha feels in his pocket, then goes back into the bedroom for his cigarettes. And there is the high, carved, curtained edifice of his bed. The bed he has shared with no one for twenty years. He has his arrangements – abroad. But here, in his own house, to make love to her with no corner of his heart knowing he is doing wrong, to watch her eyes cloud with desire, to hope for a child, to be tender with her as she grows big – he turns away. How much of this is simple lust? If he had met her in Italy, in France, would they have had an affair and thought no more of it? He thinks not. There is a seriousness and a depth to her. See how she spoke of her dead husband, her fool of a husband who had everything a man could desire – who had her and lived a free life in a free and powerful country, governed by a parliament he had elected, who rode through streets policed by his own people – who could have done anything he wished, and who chose to go and fight half a world away so that Kitchener might have the Sudan and grow cotton there to make the Manchester manufacturers wealthier than they were already. Had he even asked himself why Britain should conquer the Sudan? Had he asked himself, what of his old father? What of his young wife? To be fair, he probably had not planned on letting it kill him – just thought he would go and see some action and teach the heathens a lesson and come back to cut a fine figure and tell tales of his exploits at his London club. In any case, he, Sharif al-Baroudi, ought to be glad Captain Winterbourne was dead. Will it trouble him that she had been married to another man? He would wipe him out – burn him out of her body and her mind. No, it will not trouble him. He will not allow it to trouble him. What does he have left? Ten, fifteen years maybe – just enough time to make something of a life if he keeps it in focus, keeps it simple. And yet, how can it be simple? An Englishwoman. Sharif Basha turns abruptly from the garden. There will be no sleep for him tonight.

20 April 1901

'Enfin, what is the problem if you are inventing her? We all invent each other to an extent.' Ya'qub Artin Basha bends forward offering a cigar. His plump, compact body is wrapped in a silk robe de chambre with a brown, red and green paisley design. A deep green silk cravat is at his neck. Under the black trousers his Moroccan slippers are of green chamois. Sharif Basha selects a cigar and sits back, rolling it between his fingers before he reaches for the cutter.

'Our poet here will tell you that.' Ya'qub Artin gestures towards Isma'il Sabri. The three friends are sitting in deep easy chairs in Ya'qub Artin's library. A low marble-topped table between them carries tomatoes, cucumbers, olives, cheeses, cold meats and bread. The french windows are open to the terrace.

'I have some good, excellent whisky. Here –' Ya'qub Artin gets up again. He goes to a sideboard in the far corner of the room. 'And since our friend will not drink, there is more for the two of us.' He upends the bottle over the two glasses. 'It is almost a crime to put water in it, mais alors –' He carries a glass over to his friend. 'Let us drink to your dawning happiness!'

Isma'il Sabri toasts his friend in lemonade. 'You need children,' he says. 'We all need children.'

'I could see that she was inventing me. Piecing me together as we travelled.' Sharif Basha places a match to the tip of his cigar and takes several short, strong puffs.

'Ah! The Hero of the Romance! The Corsair! And why not, my friend? You have the looks –'

The desert and the stars and an ancient monastery with a mosque nestling within its walls. Those were his settings.

Those and the old house out of the paintings that had brought her to Egypt in the first place. And what would she make of his doubt, his despair? Of how he sometimes hated himself for piecing a life together under a rule not of his choosing? 'A citizen life, ruled by an alien lord.' Could she ever know him? Could he ever know her? Or would they always hold fast to what they imagined of each other so that life together would for each be more lonely than life alone?

'We cannot speak each other's language. We have to use French.'

'Well,' Isma'il Sabri reflects, 'perhaps that is better. You make more effort, you make sure you understand – and are understood. Sometimes I think, because we use the same words, we assume we mean the same things –'

'Ah! The poet!' Ya'qub Artin cries. 'You see! That is true. That is very true.' He lifts his glass.

'I have been meaning to ask you,' Sharif Basha says. 'Is it not time we had a collected edition? One has to keep pieces of paper in a file –'

'He refuses,' Ya'qub Artin says. 'It is too much work.'

'If you print it I shall buy fifty copies for the school in Tawasi.'

'I think he is afraid if people see what he is doing he will be attacked –'

'I'm not afraid!' Isma'il Sabri laughs. 'I simply haven't got all my poems –'

'They will say he is destroying poetry.' Ya'qub Artin leans forward to offer the plates of food to his friends.

'They are saying that already,' Sharif Basha says, picking up a small piece of flat bread, twisting it into a miniature shovel and dipping it in the beaten white cheese.

'Nonsense! If anything, I am preserving poetry. No one has time to read those huge long rambling epics any more. If poetry is to have a place in modern life, the poem has to be short and intense –'

'Comme l'amour,' Ya'qub Artin says thoughtfully, taking an olive stone out of his mouth with delicacy.

Sharif Basha laughs: 'he never stops, the old Don Juan.'

Ya'qub Artin shrugs. 'Eh! What do we have to live for? He is lucky –' gesturing towards Isma'il Sabri. 'He is a poet. He will live for ever. But you and I, mon ami, we live today and are gone tomorrow. Like this –' he puffs an imaginary fleck from his palm – 'just a breath and we are gone. You have your practice, the cases you defend. What will they bring you? Joy? Eternal life? Go. Go marry your petite Anglaise. Carpe diem.'

Isma'il Sabri hands Sharif Basha a piece of paper on which he has written a few words. Sharif Basha reads out loud:

'Take your fill of the Moons before they set;
The days of parting are dark and long.
Will you be strong, my Heart, tomorrow?
Or will you follow where her steps are bent?

Did you just write that now?' he asks his friend in admiration.

Isma'il Sabri shrugs. Ya'qub Artin says:

'Promise you will write him a song for his wedding.'

'I still love that old tune of yours,' Sharif Basha says.

'Leave off your coyness and nay-saying
and water the fire of my love
A moment of closeness to you
Is more precious than my whole life –'

The voices of the three men rise gently as they sing together until the last verse:

'For you sleep has deserted me
For you I've lost all my friends
And for the sake of your love
I befriend other than my people.'

There is a silence and then Sharif Basha yawns, throwing his head back. 'I have to go.' He rises from his chair. 'Do I have your support for the school of fine art?'

'You Muslims will have to fight it out among yourselves.' Ya'qub Artin chuckles. 'I am only a poor Christian, what do I know? But if you go ahead, yes, you have my support – and some of my money.'

Sharif Basha looks at Isma'il Sabri, who nods.

'And your decision?' Ya'qub Artin asks.

Sharif Basha picks up his tarbush.

'You are not afraid of displeasing the Lord, are you?' Artin Basha asks with a mischievous smile.

Sharif Basha places the tarbush carefully on his head. 'As you see,' he says, 'I tremble.'

27 April 1901

This is where he had first seen her properly. He had left a defiant, dishevelled creature in a man's riding clothes and returned to find a sunny, golden woman, wrapped in his dressing gown, playing with his nephew by the fountain. As they travelled through the Sinai, he had laughed at himself – at the end of his time he would desire a man. A fair young amrad, who rode with grace and skill, who raced him neck to neck – there were times when he would forget that his companion was a woman, she blended so well with the taciturn men, with the silence of the desert. And then he would look at her and remember and the image of her wrapped in blue silk, her feet white and bare on the stone of the courtyard, would spring into his mind.

Sharif Basha strides through the courtyard. He enters the small vestibule at the foot of the back stairs and opens the door that leads to the shrine. Another courtyard and another door. He pauses. In the dark interior, an old man lifts his head slowly. Sharif Basha crosses the room.

'As-salamu 'alaykum.'

' 'Alaykumu's-salam wa rahmatu Allahi wa barakatuh.'

Sharif Basha sits on the wooden bench by his father's chair. The old man bows his head, his eyes on the prayer beads moving slowly between his fingers. His robes and turban are spotless. His prayer beads shiver slightly with the tremor of his hands.

'How is your health, father?'

'Al-hamdu-l-Illah. Al-hamdu-l-Illah.' The old man nods but does not look up.

What can he talk to him about? What is he thinking about? Is he thinking at all? His father is sixty-six. Only sixty-six. Muhammad Sharif Basha was seventy when he died and look what he was like – look at Tolstoy. The long, stone-flagged room is dim and cool. The only light comes from the small windows set high up in the stone walls and the few candles by the tomb of Sheikh Haroun which stands at the far end of the room covered by a dark cloth. For eighteen years his father has never left this place. At night he sleeps in the small adjoining cell. During the day he sits in this room. Sometimes, in winter, he is persuaded to sit in the courtyard, in the sunshine just outside the door.

'Your brother, Mahmoud Sami Basha, sends his salaam. He enquires after your health.'

'Al-hamdu-l-Illah. Al-hamdu-l-Illah.'

Does he even remember his brother? Or 'Urabi? Does he know who he is? He might as well be – Sharif Basha stands up and paces the length of the room. His father does not move. In St Catherine, in the room of skulls, he had been lost to bitter thoughts. What had become of his life? What would he leave behind? His uncle had rebelled, had made his mark. He would leave a name to be honoured by Egyptians throughout history, he would leave descendants, and poetry. What had he, Sharif al-Baroudi, done that would be remembered? He had led as honourable a life as was possible, had done what good he could – but was that enough? His thoughts had drifted, as they mostly did, into what life would have been like without the Occupation. If the Revolution had been left to run its course. If Tewfiq had been forced to give in to their demands. If they had been free to build their country as they had dreamed they might, to develop its institutions, to reform education, the law, to establish industries – instead their lives

275

had been taken up in this inch-by-inch struggle against the British, the battles to set up a legislative council, to fight each unjust tax the British tried to put in place, to vote more money for education – and always caught between the Sultan, the Khedive and the British. And what had he done about it all? Now it would not be long before he would become even as those ancient monks: a heap of bones and a skull, and it would be as if he had never lived. He might as well have been like his father, content to slide into senility in the shelter of a mad sheikh's shrine. There was still time, he had thought, there was still time. But time for what?

And thinking these thoughts he had walked out of the chamber of skulls and into the garden – and had come upon her, sitting on a wooden bench. God, or the devil, had presented him with an answer to his question. Time for this. Take her. This beautiful, brave woman who had strayed into his life and who sat looking up at the stars, womanly again in some loose silken thing that shimmered in the moonlight. His impulse then had been to sweep her into his arms. To dispense with all the stuff of language and hold her and forget himself in that fair body that called out to him from under the silk. Then her story and the way she told it had touched his heart. That she should have tried so hard to understand – to offer help – and been turned away so often. Oh, he would not turn her away, he would take what she had to give and count himself rich for it. His father sits silently, the prayer beads trembling in his hand. How many times must his mother have wept in front of him? How many times must she have tried to draw him gently back – to no avail? And had he no thought for him, for the son that he had left to take up his responsibilities? The son who had no longer been able to allow himself his youth but had to calculate his every move with his mother and his sister firmly in mind?

'Father.'

His father does not look up and Sharif Basha speaks louder:

'Father.' When he has his attention he continues, 'I am thinking of getting married.'

A pleasant smile crosses the old man's face but he says nothing.

'Father. What do you say?'

' "Marriage is half of religion",' his father quotes.

'To an Englishwoman,' Sharif Basha says.

The smile vanishes from his father's face and he looks down again.

'I am thinking of getting married to an Englishwoman. What do you say?'

The old man, still looking at his prayer beads, quotes, almost in a whisper, ' "And we have created you of nations and of tribes that ye may get to know one another. The most honoured among you in the eyes of God are those who fear Him most." '

Sharif Basha regards his father sadly. Eventually he speaks: 'Then I shall consider that I have your blessing.'

He finds his mother in the kitchen with two maids. She is selecting the fruit to go into the bowls which stand ready at her side.

'Ahlan ya habibi!' She holds out her arms. She hugs him and he bends to kiss her forehead.

'Have you had breakfast?'

'Al-hamdu-l-Illah.'

'Then I shall peel you an orange. Smell.' She holds out a smooth, shining orange. 'The last of the season. From Yafa. A present from Shukri Bey.' She takes his arm to lead him out of the kitchen. 'Shall we sit here? It's not too hot yet,' she says, leading him to the covered loggia where he sat that first morning with Anna and Layla.

'Kheir ya habibi,' she says, when they have sat down. 'You look tired and the world is still morning?'

'I've just been to see my father. He seems in good health.'

'Al-hamdu-l-Illah,' she sighs.

After a pause, Sharif Basha says, 'What does he think about all day?'

'Who knows? He recites the Qur'an.'

277

'Does he know you?'

'I think so. He smiles when I go in.'

Sharif Basha makes an impatient movement and his mother continues:

'You have to clear your heart towards him. He is your father. And if he has been unjust to anyone, he has been unjust to himself more.'

'Every time I think of what he has done to you –'

'He has done nothing to me. He was kind and good to me for twenty-six years and then this catastrophe came to us –'

'He could have handled it differently.'

His mother shakes her head. 'What could have happened? We could have been exiled. He could have been (may evil stay far) killed. He could have been in prison for years. You with all your philosophy – can you not see that? Once the revolution was defeated, all of life had to change.'

'My heart does not forgive him.'

'Because you feel he shamed you. My son, "God asks of no one except what he can give". God forgives, and you cannot? Your uncle has brought us honour enough. And you, you have lived an upright life. I know it has been hard on you, but you have borne it and you have made a name and a reputation – even in these difficult times. Don't carry bad feelings in your heart towards your father.'

Yes, he had made a name and a reputation. But he had always felt that he held himself in abeyance, as though he were negotiating a narrow mountain pass and the day would come when a road, previously unseen, would open before him. He looked at his mother, good-looking still at sixty, her skin smooth and her eyes deep and clear. She had been forty-two when his father had gone into his cloister.

'It cannot have been easy for you,' he attempts. 'You were young –'

A smile of sudden mischief lights up Zeinab Hanim's eyes. 'What are you trying to say? That I could have married? When I had a son who was a tall, broad man with mustachios? Oh, what shame!' She laughs. 'Ya Sidi, I had Layla and I had

278

you and my family. I had what was ordained for me of this world and more. And as for you who are so anxious about me – look at yourself! You are happy with yourself like this? No son to call you father, no daughter to sit on your knee? Who is going –'

'Mother –'

'I know, I know.' She holds up her hands. 'A subject we are forbidden to open. But if you are concerned for me, it is more fitting that you should be concerned for yourself. Who is going to look for you when you grow old? All your friends are married –'

'This is what I wanted to talk to you about.'

'What?' Zeinab Hanim's eyes open wide and she leans forward and puts her hand on her son's knee. 'By the Prophet? You have come to talk to me about marriage? What should I do? Ring out a zaghruda? I have even forgotten what the sound is like. Who, ya habibi? Who do you want and I shall go right now and ask for her –'

'Listen to me, Mother.' As his mother's happiness burst forth, Sharif Basha looked more and more troubled. 'Listen to me well. I need your opinion and your advice. My thoughts have gone to someone – but the matter is full of problems.'

'Problems? What problems? Every problem has a solution.' Zeinab Hanim sits back, her eyes still wide and fixed on her son.

'She – you know her. I am thinking of Lady Anna.'

'Lady Anna? The Englishwoman?'

He nods, watching her.

She lowers her eyes and lets out a long breath. When she lifts them to his they are full of concern. 'You don't have enough problems already?'

'I told you.'

'She is English.'

'I know.'

'And she is the one you want?'

'It would seem so.' He smiles.

'You have the pick of the girls of Egypt. Any one of them would wish for you.'

'Yes, but I don't know them.'

'You get to know them during the betrothal and –'

'I am too old for that. And besides, we have had this conversation a hundred times, a thousand times –'

'Yes, ya habibi, I know, I know. But an Englishwoman . . .'

Sharif Basha stands up and paces the small distance to the wall and back. 'I go round and round in the same circle. I wish she were Egyptian, French – anything but English. Then I think of her and I end up thinking, very well, so she is English, there we are, does this mean it is impossible, it cannot work? I don't know. What I know is that she has entered my heart and she refuses to leave.'

'Have you spoken to her?'

'No.' He shakes his head, sits down and leans back in his chair. But she would probably accept him. And maybe for the wrong reasons. She saw distance and pride in his demeanour and she would imagine what she wished underneath. And she was brave enough and lonely enough to fly in the face of her Establishment. Perhaps even to take pleasure in defying it –

'Ya habibi. You look so tired.'

'It is nothing.'

'Well, there is the "love" you have been waiting for. But you had to go and love an Englishwoman.'

'Mother, have mercy. Where would I have met an Egyptian woman to love her? Yes, I see them at family occasions, but to sit with one and talk to her – can this happen? Layla was lucky that Husni is her cousin. I have not been so fortunate.'

'Khalas, khalas. Don't upset yourself. You love her and you want her. May God do what brings good.'

'Shall I speak to her?'

'Do you know who her people are? Her father, her mother –'

'Yes. Her parents are dead.'

'She was married before.'

'Yes. She is a widow.'

'And you accept that?'

'Yes.'

'Then speak to her with God's blessing.'

'She might refuse me, of course, and then all the problems will be solved.'

Refuse her son, the Basha? Zeinab Hanim knows that the monkey, in his mother's eyes, is a gazelle, but this is not a mother's fondness; the whole world would agree that her son is a fine man, a true man who fills his clothes. But then, an Englishwoman to marry an Egyptian – even a Basha like him? And it is true, if she will not have him there will be no problems. And now that his thoughts have turned towards marriage, maybe –

'Wait. Don't go yet.' Zeinab Hanim puts a restraining hand on his arm as he moves to stand up. 'Let's drink a cup of coffee together while I think a little.' She calls out and orders the coffee and they sit in silence till it comes.

'Listen, my son,' she says, after the first sip. 'As you know, I have met the lady. Of course we could not speak together, but Layla also has spoken to me of her. She is beautiful, and she seems good and straight. But the problems for her will be even more than the problems for you.'

'Is that what you see?'

'Yes.' Zeinab Hanim nods. 'For her, her whole life will change. Her people will be angry with her. And the British here will shun her. And even if they soften, it will be difficult for her, as your wife, to visit them or receive visits from them. She will be torn off from her own people. Even her language she will not be able to use –'

Sharif Basha pushes back his chair but his mother holds on to his hand.

'If she feels for you as you feel for her, she will throw away the world and come to you. But if you take her –' Zeinab Hanim holds her son's hand firmly in both her own – 'you will be everything to her. If you make her unhappy, who will she go to? No mother, no sister, no friend. Nobody. It means if she angers you, you forgive her. If she crosses you, you make

281

it up with her. And whatever the English do, you will never burden her with the guilt of her country. She will be not only your wife and the mother of your children – insha' Allah – but she will be your guest and a stranger under your protection and if you are unjust to her God will never forgive you.'

Sharif Basha's eyes are moist as he presses his mother's hand to his lips. When he releases her she picks up his coffee cup and turns it upside down on its saucer, tilting it slightly to allow the excess liquid to trickle away.

'Back to the old superstitions?' Sharif Basha says, but he smiles at his mother.

'Mabrouka!' Zeinab Hanim calls, and when her old Ethiopian maid appears she motions her to sit. 'Come and read the cup for the Basha!'

Mabrouka settles cross-legged on the floor. She tilts the cup and peeps into it, then closes it down again. 'Not yet,' she says and smiles up. 'It's been a long time, ya Sharif Basha.'

'I shall let you do it this once only for my mother's sake.' He smiles back. Mabrouka had been a gift to al-Ghamrawi Bey and he had given her to his daughter. She had been with Zeinab Hanim since they were both girls. She had been married twice but had never had children and when the anti-slavery laws came in she had shrugged them off and stayed just the same. She wore all her savings in gold on her arms and her neck and when he was small she had always matched his mother piastre for piastre in his tips for the Eid. Now she righted the cup and held it thoughtfully in her hand.

'Kheir ya Mabrouka,' Zeinab Hanim says.

'I see a path. A narrow path. It goes up and it goes down. A difficult path. I see a figure – it's a man, with a slight, slender body, and he is wearing a hat. Not a tarbush or a 'imma; a hat. But his intentions are sound. And he is waiting for you, ya Basha. You have got something he wants –' Zeinab Hanim smiles at her son and he raises his eyebrows. 'I see the path ending in a clear space. A clear space with a lot of light. Allah! A lot of light and joy. And I see a small – a child, it is a child coming towards you. Look!' She holds out the cup to Sharif

Basha who glances at it and starts straightening his jacket and reaching for his tarbush.

'Do you see the child?' Mabrouka insists.

'The truth is I do not,' he says.

'There!' She turns the cup towards Zeinab Hanim. 'There! A child running towards the Basha.'

'And then?' Zeinab Hanim says.

'I don't know,' Mabrouka says. 'I can't see after that. It is all white. You didn't swirl the cup properly, ya Setti, before you upturned it.'

1 May, 1901

'Ya Abeih, I will always be your little sister, but now I am asking your permission to speak to you frankly.' Layla stands in his study. She has thrown off her cloak and is dressed in a beautiful costume of dark pink and blue.

'Good, you may speak. But do you have to remain standing in the middle of the room like this?' Sharif Basha motions towards the sofa.

'No.' Layla shakes her head. 'I prefer to stand. I want to talk to you about Lady Anna.'

'What about Lady Anna?' Lady Anna with whom he had talked in the moonlight as he had never talked before with a woman other than his mother and Layla. And with them he had to be careful, for they loved him too dearly to be allowed to think of him as other than strong and if not happy then at least contented – or resigned. He keeps his voice light:

'Has she been kidnapped again?'

Layla looks at him with reproach: 'She is leaving.'

'Leaving?'

'She is going home. To England.'

He turns away. Walks to the window. What had he expected? That she should stay for ever? Of course she would go back to her country. It was natural. He turns back to Layla.

'So? And then?'

'Abeih. She has been waiting for five weeks. Waiting for a word from you.'

'Ah. And how do you know that?'

'Because I am a woman.' Layla moves forward and puts her hand on his arm. 'I *know*. From the way she mentions you, as though in passing, I know that her mind is occupied with you. I would have said it is better that she goes home, except that I know that you too are thinking of her —'

'And how do you know that?'

'I know it for myself — and Mama told me that you had spoken with her.'

'You women! A bean does not have time to get wet in your mouths.' Sharif Basha moves away from his sister. 'And did my mother tell you her objections? Did she tell you of the picture she painted of the lady's life if she — if she lived here?'

'Yes. She did. And of course it will not be easy for her, and if it had been anyone else I would say she would not be able to do it. But Anna is different. She has a big mind. And her life has not been happy. And . . . you want her. Abeih, put your trust in her and let her decide for herself. She is not a child.'

'Layla.' Sharif Basha looks into his sister's eyes. 'Do you think I can make her happy? Do you think I could make up for what she will lose? Not for the space of a month or two but for all that is left of life?'

'Yes, ya Abeih.' Layla's eyes are shining with unshed tears. 'Yes. I know that you will make her happy. And she too will bring you happiness and blessing.'

THAT WAS WHAT I SAID to him that day. I was sure of what I said, sure that I was doing the right thing, otherwise I would never have been able to gather my courage to go and speak to him like that. I know that I looked at the matter from the perspective of my own happy marriage. I know also that I did not wish to lose this new friend who had made the ordinary things of my life new to me by sharing them. But my true and overriding motive was my love for him, and my conviction that were he to allow Lady Anna to leave the country, he would remain alone for the rest of his life, his solitude adding to his bitterness day by day. And I spoke truly when I said that I believed he would make her happy. How could he not, this brother in whose love and kindness I had spent all the years of my life?

'I had thought – in the garden of St Catherine's – that you liked me.'

'It took every atom of strength that I had not to pull you into my arms.'

'Was that why you kept your hands behind your back all the time?'

'I had to. If I had let them they would have just reached out for you – like this.'

In the circle of his arms, Anna places three kisses on the line of his jaw.

'Look what I have found,' he says, 'a button. And here's another. And here's treasure –' His fingers brushing her skin, he opens the locket at her throat.

'My mama.'

'It could be you. If you crimp your hair and let it loose – so pretty . . .'

Anna raises her arms. She reaches behind her neck and unfastens the locket. She holds out her hand: 'Take it.'

'What? Why?'

'Because you admired it. It says in all the guidebooks if someone admires something you have to give it to them.'

'No, it does not. It says if *you* admire something *they* will give it to *you* –'

'Then it works the other way round too.'

'No.' He looks at her, catching the laughter in the violet eyes. 'Anna, you are teasing.'

'Please take it. I should like you to have it. Then I can be with you all the time: at work, and when you are having your manly gatherings –'

'I cannot wear it, dearest. And it shall get lost if I just carry it.'

'Why can you not wear it?'

'Because it is gold, and look at this tiny chain —'

'Then I shall change it so you *can* wear it —'

'Anna, Anna, I do not need it. I have *you*. Look: this is what I want. And this —'

But Anna catches hold of his hand, will not let go. 'So why did you not let yourself reach out for me? You must have known I wanted you to.'

'Not that you wanted me to. I just thought you would probably let me.'

'So why didn't you?'

'Because I thought it would not be fair. There's an English answer for you.'

'Why would it not be fair?' Still holding on to the hand.

'The desert . . . the stars . . .'

'You think they turned my head?'

'Well, listen. This is what I thought — do you want a cigarette? No?' He puts her out of his arms. He reaches for his cigarettes, gets one out and lights it. 'If we had met on a boat, say, crossing the Mediterranean —'

'Why particularly on a boat?'

'I am trying to think of a situation where we would have naturally spent time in each other's company. It is not easy.'

'Very well. On a boat then.'

'Or somewhere in Europe, somewhere that was ordinary to you, familiar, Paris, say, would you have stood in front of me like that, willing for me to touch you?'

'Yes. If I had got to know you the way I did here.'

'You could not have.'

'I know. So you see, it had to be here, mon amour. And the desert and the stars are all part of it.'

'Merci le desert, merci les étoiles. Anna, stand up. There. I want to look at you. Now, undo those buttons. Slowly.'

Later, resting her back against his chest, feeling his breath in her hair, Anna asks:

'Do you think it was meant?'

'Our meeting?' he asks softly, holding her close, marvelling that life could be so altered by nothing more than the presence of this one woman here, in his arms.

'Yes. Do you think Fate has been trying to throw us together? At the Costanzi, at 'Abdin Palace —'

'And then Fate grew desperate and had you kidnapped —'

'And delivered me to your house, so you *had* to pay attention.'

'Mabrouka saw you in my coffee cup.' Anna can hear the smile in his voice.

'That settles it,' she says as she snuggles into him contentedly. 'Mabrouka knows all about Fate.'

A Beginning of an End

But from these create he can
Forms more real than living man.
P. B. Shelley

Is it Fate? Or the pull of the past? Is the empty, unchanging house easier on the mind than the voices, the points of view, the hope and the despair? Or is it merely a conscientious application to a project?

A bend in the dark stairway. A thin strip of light betraying a door not fully closed.

Two days after her evening at the Atelier, Isabel paid her extra five-pound charge for the camera and slipped through the old doorway and into the cool, echoing courtyard. She shook off her guide with a small gift of money and wandered about the empty house, trying to imagine it as it must have been a hundred years ago with evidence of daily life strewn about the rooms: a ruffled newspaper by the window, a book lying open, a glass of water half drunk, a set of keys on a table, on the floor a pair of slippers left empty when their owner had settled on the divan, tucking her feet comfortably underneath her. Isabel wandered round the house. With her mind she put curtains up on the bare windows and watched them move gently with the breeze. She crumbled incense into the hanging burners and it filled the air with its sweet smell. She turned on the fountains and heard the soft patter of water on the tiles. And above it came the sounds of children playing and women's voices calling out to them when their play got too rough. From the kitchen below the smell of frying spices and freshly baked bread came wafting into the room. She sat behind the mashrabiyya and watched Sharif Pasha once again stride the great entrance hall, his hands locked behind his back, Anna's dejected young abductors waiting silently for him to speak. Time and time again she framed a scene in her viewer, adjusted her focus on the empty halls and clicked. She would surprise him with these photographs. She would surprise him with how much she knew.

And now she makes her way down the dark back staircase with its steep steps and as she arrives at the bottom she sees the streak of light. Isabel pushes the door. It opens and she steps out into blinding sunlight. Shading her eyes, screwing them against the glare, she sees that she is in yet another courtyard. Two plain walls enclose it on the right and the left. Straight ahead, it is bounded by a low building crowned with a dusty green dome. A door opens and a woman comes forward. There is something vaguely familiar about the welcoming face, about the loose blue and white garments, about the woman's posture as she stretches out her arms.

'Marhab,' she calls out in a sweet, low-pitched voice. 'Welcome! We have been waiting for you.'

She stands to one side to let Isabel through the door. A cool room bathed in shadows. To the right, and separated from the room by a wrought-iron screen, stands a high tomb surrounded by lit candles; some have been burning for so long that they are reduced to flickers in pools of wax, others are tall and straight with ripples of varying length hardening down their sides. The flames illuminate the rich greens and reds and golds which pattern the cloth covering the tomb and falling on three sides to the marble floor. Near the tomb, a door stands ajar, seeming to lead out to the street. To the left, a large space opens out until it is curtained off by an arrangement of straw mats, while more straw mats cover portions of the stone-flagged floor. There are two cushioned settles and a wooden coffee table. The only light comes from the small windows set high up in the stone walls and the distant flames of the candles. Under one of the windows stands a tall wooden loom, a length of shiny fabric rolled up beneath it. Near the loom Isabel sees an old man sitting on a straight-backed chair. He wears the gibba, the quftan and the white turban of a sheikh. His head is bent and he seems lost in thought. The noises from the street are faint and far away. Isabel turns, but the woman in blue is no longer by the door.

Isabel takes two steps forward. The sheikh does not stir.

'As-salamu 'alaykum,' she says in a hesitant voice.

'Wa 'alaykum as-salam,' comes the response, 'and the mercy of God and His blessings.' The sheikh lifts his head and turns towards her. The weakened beams of light coming through the door behind her fall upon an open, youthful face.

'Come closer,' the sheikh says.

Isabel moves forward to what she considers a seemly distance and stops. The sheikh looks up and into her face. He speaks, and it seems to Isabel that she hears the wistful eagerness in his voice before she hears the words:

'Have you come to marry me?' he asks.

'I . . .' Isabel falters.

'Salamu 'aleikum,' a voice rings out in the courtyard and a woman hurries in through the door. She wears the usual loose black smock of the working-class woman, over the usual plump figure, topped by a cheery, round face wrapped loosely in a black tarha.

'Salamu 'aleikum ya Sheikh 'Isa,' she cries again as she hurries up to Isabel. 'Marhab ya Sett, welcome!' Isabel scents a whiff of orange blossom as she is folded against the woman's warm, substantial breast. 'Welcome and a hundred times welcome,' she cries again. 'Sit down, my darling, sit down, lady of them all, why are you standing like this? Shouldn't you ask your guest to sit down, ya Sheikh 'Isa? Never mind, my darling, don't hold it against him. We don't get many visitors. Apart from those who come to visit Sidi Haroun –' waving at the tomb – 'they come in nations. Of course they don't come in here, but they bring light for us too as you see. But you have brought us light and honour. Welcome, welcome! Shall I make you some tea, or what would you like? Will you drink tea, ya Sheikh 'Isa?'

'No,' Sheikh 'Isa says, 'I want something cold. I want Seven-Up.'

'Very well, my love. I'll get you a bottle of Seven-Up. And the lady? We've not been honoured with your name?'

'Isabel,' says Isabel.

'May the name live long. Your servant Ummu Aya. Well, Sett Isabel – that's right, sit down, sister, sit down and be comfortable. You see this cloth –' smoothing out the cover on the settle cushion – 'it's full of barakah. Sheikh 'Isa himself made it. Will you drink hot or cold, my darling?'

'Whatever you've got,' Isabel murmurs as she sits down, placing the holdall with her camera, open, on the bench beside her.

'Everything we've got,' cries Umm Aya, unwinding her tarha from round her head to reveal the white kerchief beneath. She folds the tarha into an untidy bundle and tucks it under her arm. 'Hot and cold, in a second they'll be with you. I'll tell you what: I'll bring you something cold first, and the tea in a little while. Welcome, welcome. Talk to your guest, Sheikh 'Isa. Don't let her sit and be bored.'

She hurries out and the room is once more silent. The sheikh stares at Isabel.

'Are you a foreigner?' he says.

'Yes,' she answers.

'Your hair is yellow,' he says.

'My father's hair was this colour.'

'And your mother?'

'My mother's hair is – was – dark, almost black.'

'Do you love your mother?' he asks.

'Yes,' says Isabel. 'Yes, I love my mother.'

'Paradise,' the sheikh says, 'is at the feet of mothers. Remember that.'

Isabel fingers the fabric she is sitting on. In this light she cannot quite make out the colours, but she sees strips of varying dark and, at irregular intervals, a gleaming strip of gold.

'So, you made this?' she asks.

'Yes.'

'What else did you make?'

'Oh. Many things,' he says, and his voice is sad. 'I can only work when my hands are well,' he says.

'What is the matter with your hands?' Isabel asks.

'Sometimes they hurt,' he says, 'sometimes they are wounded.'

He spreads his hands out and looks at them. In the dim light Isabel can just make out a faint mark in the centre of each hand before they are covered by the long, white hands of the woman in the blue robe. She kneels at his feet and in the face looking up at the sheikh Isabel sees a look of melting tenderness.

'Are they hurting?' the woman asks.

'No,' he answers. 'No.'

The woman bends her head and places one kiss in the palm of each hand. Then she folds them together and places them in his lap.

Umm Aya hurries in carrying two green bottles on a small brass tray. 'Salamu 'aleikum, Our Lady,' she says. She puts the tray down on the table and, as the woman rises to her feet, Umm Aya catches her hand and kisses it.

'Don't you find him well, the name of God protect him?' she asks anxiously.

'Praise be to God,' the other answers.

'And now, Sett . . .' She turns to Isabel.

'Isabel,' says Isabel.

'Sett Isabel has come –'

'I – Perhaps I shouldn't have –' Isabel begins uncomfortably but Umm Aya interrupts:

'Why shouldn't? "And enter the houses by their doors" ', she quotes; 'you entered by the door and we gave you welcome.'

'But still, maybe . . .' She makes to stand but the woman in the blue robes turns towards her with a smile of great sweetness.

296

'You bring us good company,' she says. 'Stay in comfort. The house is your house.'

'Do us the honour,' Umm Aya says, wiping the mouth of a bottle with her sleeve and offering it to Isabel. Isabel takes it and Umm Aya gives the other bottle to Sheikh'Isa. 'Drink, my darling, in happiness and health,' she says.

The woman in blue is by the door. 'I leave you in good health,' she says and vanishes into the sunlit courtyard.

Umm Aya sits on the other settle. 'So, tell us now, my darling,' she says, 'where did you learn Arabic?'

And Amal has made up her mind. When Anna's story is finished she will close down her flat and move to Tawasi. Not for ever, but for a while. If she has any responsibility now, it is to her land and to the people on it. There is so much there that she can do, so much she can give, so much she can learn. If only she can sort out the business with the list; she cannot ask the fallaheen for a list of names – and she cannot reopen the school without it. As she approaches the end of University Bridge the statue of Nahdet Masr rises before her: the statue at whose feet they had gathered in the days of the demonstrations. When, after the war of '67, their whole generation had seemed to sense what that defeat would do to them, how it would stretch its ill shadow over all the years of their lives, and they had spilled into the streets to try to ward it off. In '68 when it had seemed that the young would conquer the world and they, the students of Egypt, would be among the conquerors. They had taken Nahdet Masr as their symbol: a fallaha, one hand on the head of a sphinx, rousing him from sleep, the other putting aside her veil; a statue at once ancient and modern, made of the pink granite of Aswan. Designed by Mahmoud Mukhtar, the first graduate of the School of Fine Art, and funded by a great collection to which government and people had contributed. Well, it still stands and the renaissance must surely come. If she can open up the school she'll whitewash the walls and put bright posters up on them. She'll record the children's songs and learn to make bread.

297

She'll find some old man who still has an Aragoz and a Sanduq el-Dunya − and a storyteller. There must still be storytellers around −

As she waits at the traffic lights she becomes aware of somebody looking at her and glances up. From the high window of the police van next to her, a young man stares intently. His beard is thick and black, his dark eyes are intense, his hands grip the iron bars of the window. Amal averts her eyes and then looks straight ahead. But she feels ashamed. Ashamed that she should be free, here in her car, free to drive wherever she wishes, while this young man is caged like an animal. Whose country is it? That is what it amounts to now. The light turns green and she accelerates forward. She had cried when she told 'Omar over the phone about the men she had seen, tied together and huddled in the roadside kiosk, when she had told him the stories the fallaheen had told her.

'It's an ugly world,' he'd said, 'on the whole.'

'But it doesn't have to be like this,' she'd said. And that is what she will hold on to. What's twenty years, fifty years, in the life of Egypt? As long as some of us hold on and do what we can. And what she can do is go and live on the land. She cannot do anything about the sale of the national industries, about the deals and the corruption and the hopelessness and brutality that drive young men to grow their beards and try to shoot and bomb their way into a long-gone past. But she has a piece of land and people who depend on it. She can hold that together. She can learn the land and tell its stories. And perhaps her sons will visit her. It's been such a long time since they've been to Minya. Perhaps one of them will pick up the phone and say, 'Mama, I'm coming to stay with you for a while.' Then she can show him the school and the clinic. Introduce him to the people; 'Masha' Allah!' they will say, 'How he's grown, may God preserve him for you.' She can sit with him on the veranda and listen to his stories. And if he stays long enough, she can show him Anna's story. And as they sit together in the dusk they will feel the presence of Anna and Sharif al-Baroudi and Layla and Zeinab Hanim and all their ancestors and perhaps sense – however dimly – the pattern of the weave that places them at this moment of history on this spot of land.

'Look at this,' Umm Aya says, 'and this.' Bringing out folds of cloth, unfurling them and throwing them over Isabel's knees.

'They are beautiful,' Isabel murmurs, holding them up to what little light there is and wondering if Umm Aya wants her to buy something. 'Is there enough light in here for his work?'

'My hands need no light,' Sheikh 'Isa says.

'His heart gives him enough light, the name of God bless him,' Umm Aya says. 'Tell us, Sett Isabel, are you staying in Egypt long?'

'I'm leaving tomorrow,' Isabel says, putting the fabric down.

'But you will come back.'

Isabel is not sure if that was a question. 'Yes,' she says. 'But I have to go home and see my mother. She's not well.'

'May God set your heart at ease and you come back comforted, insha'Allah. And you're not married?'

'No. I was married but we divorced. Without children,' Isabel adds, knowing enough now to anticipate the question.

'God will compensate your patience, ya habibti.'

'Insha'Allah,' Isabel says, and she must have blushed for Umm Aya smiles and says:

'But your mind is occupied with someone.'

And Isabel, before she can think, says, 'Yes.' And then to her own surprise she says, 'But I don't know his feelings.'

'His feelings?' Umm Aya draws in a breath 'What can his feelings be? Can someone be desired by the moon and say no?'

Isabel smiles, shrugs.

'It's certain that he wants you,' Umm Aya says, 'if he is a man. It could be that he wants you and there's a reason making him not speak.'

'I intend to speak to him,' Isabel says. 'This time.'

'Speaking is no good, ya habibti. Ask one with experience and don't ask the physician. Talk goes forward and backward and each understands it as he desires.'

'What then?'

'You adorn yourself and scent yourself and sit with him in a comfortable way – and you are a woman and you know the rest –'

'El-'Asr,' Sheikh 'Isa says as the call to prayers floats into the room.

'I have to go.' Isabel moves towards the sheikh. He holds out his hands and she places hers in them.

'Go, my daughter,' he says, holding her hands between his own, 'go. May God light your path, and give you that which you hold in your heart and compensate your patience with all good.'

Isabel turns to see Umm Aya zipping up the holdall.

'Don't forget your things,' Umm Aya says, 'and let your heart guide you.'

And once again Isabel is enveloped in the smell of orange blossom.

19

Only believe and thou shalt see.

J. S. B. Monsell, 1865

6 May 1901
I am to be married.

I look at the words and I can hardly believe them — and yet it is true. I am to be married in just over two weeks. And if Sharif Basha were to have his way we should be married tomorrow, but he wishes the ceremony to be performed by his friend Sheikh Muhammad 'Abdu, who is at present in Istanbul, so we shall wait for his return.

Anna puts down her pen. She looks out of her window, but the men sipping their sundowners on the terrace of Shepheard's Hotel, the Egyptian boys and the passers-by on the street beyond reflect nothing of what is going on in her heart and mind. She crosses the room and examines her own face in the mirror. Something *must* show there, and indeed there is a flush on her cheeks and her eyes seem to shine with a deeper colour. She puts her hand to her face . . .

I went, as he requested, to his mother's house, and upon being admitted made my way to the great entrance hall. He was there, in the formal city dress I had first seen him in, his back to me, his hands joined behind it, his prayer beads working between the fingers of his right hand. As I came through the door he turned, and every aspect of him — the eyebrows almost joined above the dark, now troubled eyes, the thick, black hair invaded by white at his temples, the straight set of his shoulders, the way he held his head – every detail I had painted in my heart over the last five weeks held true, and my heart grew so agitated that I stopped and stood still in the doorway. For a moment, when he turned and saw me, he appeared taken aback, but it was just for a moment and he instantly collected himself and strode forward.

'Lady Anna,' he said and took my hands. 'Forgive me,' he said, 'it is just these –' The movement of his head indicated my dress. And of course, from the time I had been abducted into his house, he had only ever seen me in men's clothes, or in his old dressing gown, or in the loose silken shift his sister had given me; never in the normal dress of a European woman. He stood and looked at me, my hands still in his grasp, as though he needed to ascertain that I was indeed the same person he remembered, the person to whom he had written his letter. I suppose I must have looked uncomfortable, for presently he said again, 'Forgive me. I am overcome with . . .' He did not complete his sentence but then said, 'Come. Shall we sit down?'

I sat down on a divan and he sat next to me but immediately stood up again and positioned himself in front of me. When I glanced up he was looking at me intently, and a smile came into his eyes.

'You are as beautiful as I remember you,' he said.

'But a little different,' I replied.

He made a slight assenting movement. 'But it is still you, yes?'

'It is indeed,' I said, and after a pause, 'My desert clothes can still be found –'

'That will not be necessary.' He laughed. 'I must get used to these. Oh, Anna –' with a gesture of impatience, turning away – 'I want to have done with words.' He pushed his hands deep into his pockets. 'But. There are the arrangements we have to make –'

'Arrangements?' I asked.

'For the marriage.'

My heart made one sudden bound, and then all was stillness. His face darkened.

'You —' He looked at me intently. 'Have I misunderstood? My letter, I thought was clear. And this morning I received your note —'

'Yes,' I said, 'yes.' And now my heart beat so hard and my blood rushed about so that I thought I would surely faint.

'You have gone pale.'

His voice was quiet — I would say curt. And I felt he was somehow retreating, moving away, although he yet stood in front of me. And I knew that I wanted him, I wanted him back with me. And I knew that it was paramount that he should not misunderstand me now.

'Monsieur,' I said, above the beating of my heart, 'you do me honour and I am indeed happy to accept your offer.'

There was a silence and I made myself speak again:

'If I seem strange it is just that I thought it would take a little more time — a few days perhaps — before we came to the point . . .'

I looked up: he still glowered. I held out my hand. 'Sharif Basha,' I said gently.

He took my hand and I drew him to sit down close to me.

'Yes,' I said, looking down at our hands. 'Yes. I should very much like to marry you.'

'You have to be sure,' he said, my hand gripped tight in his. 'You have to be completely, absolutely sure. You will be giving up so much —'

'I am sure,' I said. And I was.

I heard him breathe out and then with his other hand he touched my face, feeling its contours as though to learn it. He fingered what loose curls he could find of my hair and I — I was lost to everything except his nearness and his touch. But when I thought he must surely kiss me, he moved away. On my new-released hand the rings I was wearing had made dents in the sides of my fingers. I studied these as he paced the floor.

'If Muhammad 'Abdu were here we could be married tomorrow,' he said impatiently.

'It has to be him?' I asked and felt myself blush for I had not intended my words to sound so forward, and indeed I saw his face

– so dark and impatient a moment before – light up with a wicked smile: 'So, so? A few days my lady wanted to come to the point? But yes. No one else would dare do it. And it would not be right to ask. He has the authority –'

At that moment, with cries of 'Lalu! Lalu!' little Ahmad came bursting into the room and his uncle turned to scoop him up into his arms. 'Et alors,' he said when Ahmad had finished hugging him, and then he said something in Arabic in which I caught the sound of my name and Ahmad, released on to the floor, came running up to kiss me and as I held him Layla ran in beaming, so that soon I was being embraced by both mother and child.

'Mabrouk ya Anna, alf mabrouk,' she cried and went to hug her brother. 'Mabrouk ya Abeih!' I saw the tears of joy in her eyes. 'When?' she cried. 'When will it be?'

'We were just saying –' Sharif Basha said.

Layla seemed to understand immediately and her joy was replaced by a worried look. 'You must be careful, both of you,' she said. 'Very careful. No one must know until it is done.'

I believe it was only then that I saw the true import of the step I was taking. It did not make me think again, no, not for one second. But alongside my new happiness an unease too was in that moment born, for I saw that I could not perhaps expect my friends to share in my joy. Sir Charles and Caroline, James Barrington and Mrs Butcher – I cannot believe I will be estranged from them for ever, yet at the best something different will colour our relations. I thought of the scandal it had caused three weeks ago when a German lady had dined at Shepheard's with a gentleman who looked Egyptian and how the waiter – a Greek – had presented the gentleman (who turned out to be a cousin of the Khedive) with a fez full of salad with the compliments of the management. And then I thought of Lord Cromer and the Agency and a cold sliver of fear entered my heart – although not for myself.

'Anna,' he said, 'we will follow every proper procedure. But I think we should contract an Egyptian marriage first, and then have it ratified at the Agency.'

'An Egyptian marriage is enough for me,' I said.

'Lady Anna,' he said and smiled, 'Lady Anna who is never afraid. No, we will do it correctly. But meanwhile –' a bitter note came into his voice – 'meanwhile I am sorry that I cannot take you out and court you properly. There is nowhere for us to go.'

'You will have to court me later, monsieur,' I said. 'Meanwhile, I shall wait.'

We went upstairs, where Zeinab Hanim kissed me most tenderly – indeed she kissed us both, with tears on her cheeks, and Mabrouka, her Ethiopian maid, clapped her hands so that her heavy bracelets jangled, but Sharif Basha stopped her in mid-zaghruda with a stern 'Not now. When it is all done.' But then he patted her shoulder and dropped a kindly kiss upon her head, for I understand she has been like a second mother to him all his life.

'As for my father,' he said, 'you can see him when we are married.'

Looking up from Anna's journal I am, for a moment, surprised to find myself in my own bedroom, her trunk standing neatly by the wall, my bed, the top sheet folded back, waiting for me to ease myself in. I had been so utterly in that scene, in the hall of the old house, in my great-grandmother's haramlek. My heart had beaten in time with Anna's, my lips had wanted her lover's kiss. I shake myself free and get up to walk in the flat, to stand on the balcony, to look down at the street and bring myself back to the present. Who else has read this journal? And when they read it, did they too feel that it spoke to them? For the sense of Anna speaking to me – writing it down for me – is so powerful that I find myself speaking to her in my head. At night, in my dreams, I sit with her and we speak as friends and sisters.

In the kitchen I pour myself a cold glass of water from the fridge and pick up a cucumber which I bite into as I go back to the bedroom. Isabel is gone. All her things, the clothes she would not need, the big holdall with her camera and all her lenses, the books and tapes she has acquired, they are all here,

306

stored in the boys' room. And she is somewhere over the Atlantic headed back for Jasmine and my brother. I have to speak to him. I have to talk to him straight. About her. I do not know what to make of her story of the shrine in the old house. Isabel is a practical, sensible woman. She is also romantic and full of feeling, but she is not mad. Not UFOs and alien abductions. Yet she was certain that she had pushed open a door and entered the shrine. She had sat there drinking Seven-Up and, by her account, conversing with a strange sheikh, a cheery serving-woman and a woman dressed like a Madonna in a painting.

We had gone back to the house next day and of course the door to the shrine was locked. Locked and padlocked and covered in cobwebs as it had been before. We went round to the front of the mosque. The tomb was covered by the usual green cloth and, yes, there were candles, but there are candles in many shrines. Beyond the iron screen the rest of the place was too dark for us to make out anything. I called the caretaker and told him we wanted to see the sheikh.

'Here's the sheikh,' he said, pointing at the tomb.

'No, the other sheikh,' I said. 'The one who lives inside.'

'Ah! El-sheikh el-mestakhabbi? There isn't one right now,' he said. 'The old one died and they haven't brought a new one in his place yet.'

'When did the old one die?' I asked.

'About a year ago,' he said. 'He was a youth, almost. But he was a pious man and the veil was lifted from him. And his father was here before him. They've been here a long time. For a hundred years. From before the house was taken by the government and turned into a museum.'

'So for a year now there hasn't been a sheikh inside?'

'It's known, ya Sett. The thing is, a sheikh who lives here has to be – as you know – a man of God. It means he wants nothing of this world. This is the condition of the waqf. And you won't find a man like that every day.'

As we turned to go I thought of one more question: 'And Umm Aya, does she still live around here?'

307

'I don't know, ya Sett,' the man said. 'I haven't heard of her.'

Isabel is upset. She wants to argue with the man but I pull at her arm. In the car she says 'I do not understand this. They *were* there. I saw them. I *talked* to them.'

'Isabel,' I say, 'sometimes I think of people, or places, and the image is so strong that I'm quite shocked when I realise it was only in my head.'

'They were there,' she says, 'just as you and I are here.'

Tomorrow, I think, as I smooth on my night cream in the mirror, tomorrow I'll place a call to her. And one to 'Omar. I haven't got an international line. I would have been constantly tempted to call the boys.

Cairo
12 May 1901

Dear Sir Charles,
I have just received yours of the 8th, in which you write that the Duke of Cornwall has promised to intercede for Urabi Pasha with the Sultan and the Khedive. This is welcome news indeed and will go — I hope — some way to redressing the wrong done these many years ago. I believe I have mentioned that Mahmoud Sami Pasha al-Baroudi lost his eyesight in Ceylon — so little did the climate agree with him — and now employs his daughters and grandchildren to read to him, for he is engaged on a work of compiling the best of Arabic poetry in one edition, with his notes. A formidable task for a blind gentleman. The others, of course, are now all dead. So I pray that the pardon of Urabi may heal some of those wounds which are still felt here today.

Life here is much the same. There was a Grand Ball in fancy dress at Shepheard's last week. The Moorish Hall is very grand and well suited to such occasions. Four officers who wished to attend but — arriving late in Cairo — had no costumes, availed themselves of some ladies' gowns which are kept hung in closets in the corridors outside the rooms. They were a great success at the Ball but, by neglecting to return the dresses before they retired, caused a great deal of upset to the management next morning. The ladies were eventually pacified and peace reigned again. Such is the tenor of our amusements here.

James Barrington has confided to me that he thinks of returning to England. His mother has been recently left a widow and as an only child he is sensible of his responsibility towards her. He thinks he would not be unhappy – and could be of some use – on the staff of a London newspaper. I have promised to write and ask if you know of an opening? He is a very able young man and I believe you would find him sympathetic.

You ask when I think of returning. I have not made any plans. I do not yet find the heat too burdensome and I am making good progress with my Arabic –

Anna breaks off. She feels too false writing glibly to her beloved Sir Charles about the progress she is making with her Arabic. She sets this page aside and starts again. She must have copied out the first four paragraphs for the letter continues on a different sheet:

. . . and I believe you would find him sympathetic. I think he will be in England before me, so I shall enlist his services in carrying to Mr Winthrop those herbs he asked me for last autumn. If there is anything at all that I can send you from here . . .

And yet, the truth is that for the last two months, as her life in Cairo became more and more real to her, it has seemed to me that Sir Charles and Caroline and her home in London have receded in her mind. She worries about Sir Charles, but she knows that she is powerless to lift from him the greatest grief of his heart. Did she also fear that if she were in England she would be for ever ensnared in that grief?

17 May
Today I removed Edward's ring from my finger and put it – together with the ring I gave him – into the felt purse Emily

made for me many years ago. Perhaps it is as well that I have had this time alone to prepare for the great change which is about to overtake my life. To bid farewell to the past, in as much as that can be done, and lay it to rest.

I should have thought that I would feel some concern towards Edward at this time. But I believe that were he alive, he would be indifferent to my marrying again — perhaps even happy for me and relieved for himself. Except — except that I think he would only feel that if I were marrying someone acceptable to him. As for this marriage —

I try to imagine Edward and Sharif Basha (I still cannot use his name without the title!). I try to imagine them meeting but even in my mind I cannot get them to shake each other's hand. Piece by piece it is coming to me: the distance I am placing between myself and those I have known and cared for all my life. I can imagine Caroline meeting Sharif Basha, and perhaps flirting with him a little. But of the men — even dear Sir Charles — I can only imagine my father. He, I think, could have been his friend. Not here in Egypt, nor yet in England, but had they met in some other country I can quite imagine them conversing with quiet amicableness — even though it would have had to be in French. As for my mother, I am sure they would have become great friends upon the instant.

I have not seen him these eleven days. Nor will I — if all goes according to plan — until the 23rd. But Layla — my dear friend and soon to be my sister — has relayed his messages and tells me with smiles how he chafes and frets at each passing day that I am not with him. 'Dear Anna,' she cries, 'I am so happy! I thought it would never happen. And now you must hurry and give us a bride for Ahmad!' Sometimes she looks at me thoughtfully, though. And once she said, 'You know Abeih will let you go home and visit whenever you want.'

'I am sure he will,' I said.

'Only —' She looked troubled. 'You must not expect him to go with you.'

'Yes,' I said, 'I had realised that.'

'He could wait for you in France.'

'Layla,' I said, 'all is well with me. It is too soon to start worrying about my homesickness.' And indeed, I would not wish him to come to London and be stared at – or worse. One day, perhaps. When Egypt has her independence, we can take our children and open up Horsham for the summer months and I can show him – but that is a long time away.

Layla has told me of the arrangements. The contract on one day. The ratification at the Agency on the next – for the contract being in place, Lord Cromer can do nothing to stop the marriage. And the wedding itself will take place on the third day. We have discussed the details and I have said I should like as much as possible of the events to take place as though I were an Egyptian, for I feel sure that will bring much pleasure to Zeinab Hanim, who has been waiting these many years to rejoice in her son's marriage. I think also it will make him happy. And, for me, since it will not be the old church at Horsham, then it may as well be entirely different. So I have told Layla that I leave myself in her hands and she is to arrange all things as she would for her sister. She is well pleased and has started by ordering me an evening gown of gold lamé from a French seamstress on the rue Qasr el-Nil which I am to wear as a wedding gown. And whenever I go to the old house, I find her and Zeinab Hanim and the maids all stitching and embroidering various garments which they hold up against me and pin and adjust until I beg for mercy. It is a shame for Emily's sake that she cannot be made a part of all this for she would well love to – except, I do not know how she will take this marriage.

18 May
Today I asked Layla to ask Sharif Basha if we could live with his mother. I have not seen his house, but I understand it is in the European style as all new houses are – and I have grown to love the old house more with every hour I have spent there.

'Could we not live here?' I asked. 'If only for a while. It will be very hard for me to learn to keep house in the way he likes, and I would far rather learn from your mother than from the servants.' I know also that Zeinab Hanim would dearly love to

311

have her son once more under her roof, although she will not suggest it. And I should like, if one day pray God there is a child, to sit with Layla in the loggia at the edge of the courtyard, embroidering frocks, and watching our children play by the fountain, while I listen for the clatter of hooves and the bustle at the door that tell me my husband is come home.

20

And lend me leave to come unto my love.
                    Edmund Spenser

22 May 1901

Sheikh Muhammad 'Abdu shakes his head. The level brows, still black, are knitted over the lowered eyes as he reads the letter addressed to Prince Yusuf Kamal. In the large, austere room, its diwans and cushions covered in plain white fabric, its bookcases rising to the ceiling, the men sit in silence. When he has finished he hands the letter to Sheikh Muhammad Rashid Rida sitting at his side.

'Those people —' he says sadly. 'We will never move forward as long as people think in this way.'

'Those people have to be educated,' Shukri Bey al-'Asali says, 'and Fadilatukum is in a position to educate them.'

'A word from you would silence them,' Sharif Basha says.

'Let me think about this,' Muhammad 'Abdu says. Sharif Basha feels for his old friend. It is his first day back from Istanbul and the stream of well-wishers and petitioners has not stopped for a moment. Muhammad 'Abdu looks tired.

'Shukri Bey has been delaying in Cairo to see you,' he says. 'But if you are tired now we can come back another time.'

'No, no,' Muhammad 'Abdu says, 'I am at his service.'

'We were hoping you would stop by Jerusalem, ya Sayyid-na?' Shukri Bey says.

'Next time, insha' Allah. My hope is to pray one more time in the Aqsa if God permits.'

'And how was your visit to the Sublime Porte?'

'The same as every time.' Muhammad 'Abdu's smile is

weary. 'Plots and conspiracies. I was shadowed by the Sultan's spies everywhere I went –'

'He trusts nobody.'

'He has reason,' Sharif Basha says. 'He knows many people want to get rid of him.'

'Ya Sayyidna,' Shukri Bey says, 'I hear the Sultan has just met with Dr Herzl and David Wolffsohn. Is there anything new?'

'I understand they made the same representations,' Muhammad 'Abdu says. 'They told him that the Zionists are loyal to the Ottoman throne. That they do not form secret societies like the Armenians or the Bulgar, nor, like them, appeal for help to foreign powers –'

'That is a weave of lies!' Shukri Bey rises to his feet in exasperation. 'They refuse to take Ottoman nationality precisely so that – as foreign nationals – they may constantly appeal to the Powers. So that in any dispute with an Arab they have to be tried by their own consuls. How much did they offer him?' Shukri Bey is abrupt in his exasperation. But Muhammad 'Abdu answers him mildly:

'No specific sums were named. They merely said they know his treasury needs money and their friends control one third of the money in the world. If he gives them Palestine, lets them govern themselves there, as they do on Samos –'

'Samos was returned to its people. Its *own inhabitants* were allowed to govern themselves –'

'That was the model they used,' Muhammad 'Abdu says. 'They would in return pay a specified sum to the palace and a yearly tribute.'

'And?' Shukri Bey waits, his eyes narrowed, concentrated on Muhammad 'Abdu's face.

''Abd el-Hamid listened, but it came to nothing. 'Izzat Basha al-'Abid was there and he frightened the Sultan by telling him the whole province would revolt if he sold the land out from under them.'

'Why does he agree to meet them?' Shukri Bey asks. 'He

turned down their offer to buy Palestine in '96. He knows that is still what they are after.'

' 'Abd el-Hamid is very cunning, ya Shukri Bey. I think he is a match for Dr Herzl and more. He is being pressed to consolidate Turkey's debts – and my belief is he agreed to a meeting with Herzl to throw off the bigger threats.'

'Herzl *is* a threat,' Shukri Bey says. 'His Jewish Colonial Trust has just bought some prime land in Tabariyyah and the fallaheen are up in arms about it.'

'Herzl told the Sultan that he has been in correspondence with Sheikh Yusuf al-Khalidi –'

'He is not "in correspondence," ' Shukri Bey cuts in contemptuously: 'Al-Khalidi wrote to a friend of his in Paris, Rabbi Zadok Kahn, begging him to use his influence to deflect Zionist interest from Palestine. Kahn showed the letter to Herzl, who took it upon himself to answer.'

'So you know all about it?' Muhammad 'Abdu says.

'Did you see the correspondence?' Sharif Basha asks.

'Yes. Al-Khalidi wrote an emotional letter, invoking History and God and ending: "Au nom de Dieu, laisse tranquille la Palestine." Herzl wrote a sly one, full of financial temptation and veiled threats –'

'The Jews have always lived in Palestine,' Rashid Rida says, 'but now –'

'They lived as other people lived,' Shukri Bey says. 'But now they are coming in thousands. They are supported by the Colonial Trust – look.' He takes a newspaper cutting out of his pocket, *al-Ahram*, 24 April. The paper quotes an item from the American *Morning Post* reporting that the Zionists had held a big meeting in Milwaukee and started a worldwide campaign to collect contributions from Jews in all countries to buy Palestine from the Sultan.

'They offer a lot of money for land,' Shukri Bey says, 'and some landlords – the big landlords, the ones who live in the cities – they sell. And the fallah, instead of working the land and giving a share of the crop to the owner, finds himself turned into a hired labourer – or turned off the land. They wish to have nothing to do with the Arabs. Their children don't attend our schools and they don't allow our children into theirs. They speak their own languages, run their own affairs, hold on to their nationalities. What are they doing in the midst of us?'

In the silence that follows, Shukri Bey walks over to the window and stands there for a moment. When he returns, Sheikh Muhammad 'Abdu looks up from his beads.

'I understand your concern,' he says. 'Personally, I think their dream is impossible. Their Zion is a heavenly place and Heaven cannot be created on earth. But I shall speak to Cattaoui Basha and see what he advises. He would not wish fresh divisions to come among us.'

'Indeed we are divided enough already,' Sheikh Rashid Rida says.

'It is our destiny,' Shukri Bey says, 'our luck that we were born in these times.'

'Things looked very different in the Sixties and Seventies,' Sharif Basha says.

'Perhaps because we were young,' Muhammad 'Abdu says.

'Perhaps it is only when you are young that you can achieve things, make great changes —'

'We are all making changes,' Muhammad 'Abdu says. 'Not great changes — not the French Revolution — but small ones that will add up in the end. And the cost will be less.'

Sharif Basha smiles. Twenty years ago Muhammad 'Abdu saw nothing wrong with the French Revolution.

Shukri Bey al-'Asali comes forward to take the sheikh's hand. 'I thank Fadilatukum and I will take my leave and impose on you no longer. But I beg you to remember, al-Khalidi and I are not the only ones who feel uneasy about what is happening in Palestine.'

Rashid Rida leaves with Shukri Bey, and Sharif Basha and Sheikh Muhammad 'Abdu are left alone. The sheikh sighs and draws his hands over his tired face.

'What do you see in all this?' he asks his friend.

'I think it is a matter of concern. And so is the letter I gave you. And the tax on spun thread that Cromer is trying to push through.' Sharif Basha shrugs, then leans forward, his elbows resting on his knees. 'But there is something else I want to talk to you about. A big favour I need from you.'

'Kheir?' Muhammad 'Abdu's eyes are instantly alert. 'Command me.'

'Tomorrow,' Sharif Basha says, 'you contract me in marriage —' and as his friend's face lights up in joy, he adds, 'to an English lady: Lady Anna Winterbourne.'

Muhammad 'Abdu studies his friend's face and asks quietly, 'And why tomorrow?'

Sharif Basha leans back in his chair. 'Because if it gets known that we intend to do this, you can imagine what will happen. Because I cannot see her until she is safely my wife. Because I have been waiting for you for seventeen days already and I am growing old and have no more time to lose. Do you want more?'

Muhammad 'Abdu's eyes have not left his friend's face. And now a smile spreads over the sheikh's face until it takes complete possession and he leans forward to embrace his friend.

'Mabrouk ya Sharif Basha. May God complete it for you in all good.' He holds him away, claps his shoulder and embraces him once again.

And as I put my signature to the contract Mabrouka's joy-cry trilled out loud and true and nobody thought to stop her. Sharif Basha's friend Sheikh Muhammad 'Abdu married us, and if any human has the power to bring down a blessing, then truly it is that holy man. The Contracts were in both Arabic and French —

and indeed, both are in Anna's trunk, contracting 'the Lady Anna Winterbourne (Christian) daughter of Sir Edmund DeVere (deceased) and Lady Aurora DeVere (deceased) and widow (of the late Captain Edward Winterbourne of the 21st Lancers in her Britannic Majesty's army) of sound mind and of legal age, in marriage to Sharif Basha al-Baroudi (Muslim), Landowner and Notable and Member of the Consultative Legislative Council and by profession a Lawyer.' The contract notes that Sharif Basha's sidaq to Lady Anna is the sum of five thousand pounds Egyptian. I do some calculations and decide that this money would have bought 120 faddans of prime land. Sharif Basha pledges a further twenty thousand pounds should he divorce Lady Anna against her wishes and he moreover bestows upon her an equal authority to effect a divorce. A clause is also added stating that in the event of Sharif Basha availing himself of his legal right to take another wife, the divorce would take effect and the balance of the sidaq be payable from that moment. The contracts are witnessed by Husni Bey al-Ghamrawi and Shukri Bey al-'Asali and officially registered on the same day: 23 May 1901. The day that Anna closes the secret blue book and returns once again to the big, handsome green volume.

– and though I demurred on some points – for the Contracts made it appear as though I had not enough confidence in his good faith – Sharif Basha said 'It is better so' and so it was done. My Bride-Price he gave me in gold coins in a heavy bag which I begged him to keep for me but he is determined it shall be sent to my Bankers in London.

My head is in such a muddle of feelings and impressions. Shukri Bey and Husni Bey were very gallant and Layla and Zeinab Hanim were so happy that I was glad – alongside my own happiness – to be the instrument of their joy. Mabrouka kept repeating 'Did I not see it in the cup?' and I had not the faintest idea what she meant when she asked it of me but I said yes.

And my husband? He slipped a broad gold band upon my finger and kissed my hand. 'Two more days,' he said, 'and we shall be together.' And my heart thrilled as though it would leap out and lodge within his breast.

This is to be my last night in this room which has been my home for more than half a year. I have asked Emily to pack all my things, telling her that I am leaving in the morning and will send for her shortly. She is surprised, but I believe she fancies I am going to Alexandria and that after a short stay there we shall be leaving for England.

Tonight I must also write to Sir Charles.

24 May

This is the last night that I shall sleep alone. A sweet note was delivered to me a half hour ago from my husband: 'Sleep well, Lady Anna. Tomorrow you and I have serious business to attend to.' And indeed I shall sleep — or attempt to. But I must record the events of this extraordinary day.

I left the hotel and found my husband's carriage waiting, as we had arranged, at the corner of rue al-Maghrabi and rue Imad el-Din. We drove to the Agency, him holding my hand the while. He had already sent a note to Lord Cromer 'to save a certain amount of explanation', he said. Upon our arrival we were met by a young gentleman from my husband's office who was to act as translator. I understood it was the first time Sharif Basha had entered the Agency, and the place, once so familiar to me, grew strange as I saw the consternation on the faces of the staff and how they avoided meeting my eye as we were ushered through and into the Lord's office.

Lord Cromer stood to greet us and bowed to my husband but did not offer to shake his hand, and as we sat across the desk from him he came immediately to the point:

'I understand you wish to get married?' He addressed himself to me and he spoke with such obvious distaste that I was stung and replied in French so that my husband could understand:

'We are already married, Lord Cromer. We wish to register the marriage so that it may be recognised in Britain.'

I saw his colour rise but he mastered his anger and asked when the ceremony had taken place. Our young translator rendered this into Arabic and my husband replied — and throughout the interview Lord Cromer spoke in English, I in French, and Sharif Basha in Arabic. No tea or coffee was offered, no pleasantries exchanged. My husband motioned to his assistant, who brought out a copy of the French marriage contract and placed it in front of Lord Cromer. He studied it briefly and turned to me:

'Lady Anna,' he said, 'do you realise what you are doing?'

If he had been sad or puzzled, I should have warmed to him, but he showed only distaste and anger.

'Does Sir Charles Winterbourne know of this?' he asked.

'I have written to him,' I said, 'and to my other friends.'

'This is nonsense,' Lord Cromer said. 'And Muhammad 'Abdu should have had more sense than to lend himself to it.'

My husband uttered a few curt words.

'The Basha says,' said our translator, 'that our interest is to register the marriage, not to learn Lord Cromer's opinion of it.'

'Lady Anna,' Cromer said, 'I think it would be best if we conversed alone.'

I placed my hand briefly on Sharif Basha's arm and said I did not believe I had anything to say that my husband could not hear.

'My dear, you are making a mistake,' the Lord said, and his voice was sorrowful now, and anxious. 'My staff will tell you of the young women we find wandering about, having contracted such marriages. They will tell you of their condition —'

When the translator had stopped murmuring I replied that I had heard those stories already and had felt that there was a certain relish in the telling of them. I did not think they were pertinent to me.

'Lord Cromer —' my husband spoke slowly, the translator keeping pace with him as he went — 'I think I understand something of what you feel. It would not have filled me with joy if my sister had wished to marry an Englishman. In fact I would probably have done everything I could to stop her. Whatever mistaken ideas you have, you seem to have a true regard for my wife and you believe that you are acting in her *best interest. My assurances – and hers – will mean nothing to you now. But –'*

'Sharif Pasha.' Lord Cromer finally turned to him, his voice gruff but his manner conciliatory. 'Sharif Pasha, we have not met before, but I have heard of you –'

My husband bowed.

'Despite everything,' Cromer continued, 'I know you are a man of integrity and a man of the world, and I am sure you are aware – to put it bluntly – of all that Lady Anna stands to lose through entering into this . . . contract. She is a woman of rank and position. As a man of honour surely –'

'Lord Cromer,' I interrupted, for I felt a sudden fear that his words might find their mark – and now it was my husband's turn to lay his hand briefly on my arm. When he finished speaking, the translator said:

'The Basha says he is aware of the great honour the lady does him. If she loses position in your society because of this marriage, that will be your society's fault – and its loss. The Basha is certain that the circles she will be moving in will give her all the consideration due both to her rank and to her position as his wife.'

'What circles?' Lord Cromer now erupted. 'I will not countenance this –'

'Milord,' I said, 'we are already married. If the marriage cannot be registered, we shall have to do without.'

At this Lord Cromer left the room. I fancy he must have consulted one of his gentlemen, for he was absent for a few moments. Upon his return he took up his position once more behind his desk. But he did not sit down. He stood and, glaring down at Sharif Basha, he said:

'I want you to sign an undertaking that you will not take another wife while you remain married to Lady Anna.'

His tone would have not been inappropriate used to a tradesman whom he suspected of shabby dealing. I felt myself go hot with anger. I was angry on behalf of my husband, but I was also angry on behalf of England – that Sharif Basha would think we all did not know how to behave.

'Lord Cromer, this is insulting —' I began.

'Lady Anna, I must insist. It is clear that you have no idea —'

'It is already in the contract,' my husband said quietly, rising. 'And other clauses too that you should look at. I would be grateful if you could order the finished documents sent round to my office. I believe we have taken enough of your time.' He turned to me: 'Madame?'

We left. I am sure Lord Cromer read the Contract. But I am also sure that the reading of it will not for an instant have shaken his belief that he has the measure of my husband — for he is not a man given to self-doubt. In the carriage I started to apologise, but my husband put his finger on my lip. 'Hush,' he said. 'We are the ones who are happy.'

I had a similarly dreadful interview with Emily, whom I sent for as soon as I was installed in the house. She was cross with me, I know, although she did not betray it except by a slight tightening of the lips and a 'So madam won't be needing my services any more, then?' I said indeed I wanted her, in the first place to make sure these two letters — putting them into her hand — would be delivered to Mrs Butcher and James Barrington immediately, and for the rest I would need her as long as she cared to stay, but our circumstances would be so changed that I was not sure whether she would be happy. I have given her three days at Shepheard's to think about it and then I shall send for her again.

And it is just as well that she has not been here today, for today was my 'Henna Day' and even though I have not actually had henna applied to my hands and feet, as Layla tells me it is démodé at the moment, I have had such a scrubbing and a plucking and a pummelling and polishing that I feel as though my bare limbs alone would light up a room. There have been maids rushing around all day — apart from the women who have been attending to me, and Zeinab Hanim busy with more women in the kitchen as they prepare for tomorrow's feast, and Ahmad in the middle of it all, and other children I do not know who were all stealing bits of fruit and raisins, climbing over sacks *of provisions left in the courtyard, blowing jets of water at anyone who passed near the fountains, for they knew that today they might do as they pleased and go unpunished. And all the while the singing and the zaghrudas and from time to time Layla would bring something to show me — a gold ornament, a set of crystal goblets or a silver tea service — and say 'a gift from so-and-so' and whisk it off again; and the flowers: baskets and baskets of flowers arriving all day.*

Layla told me with some anxiety that I would find our apartments rather bare, as her brother thought I should enjoy furnishing them myself, and I assured her he was right. I had not thought of it before but now I look forward with great pleasure to the choosing and fashioning of the furnishings — and I can draw on my beloved Frederick Lewis for inspiration.

For tonight I am in a small guestroom, close to Zeinab Hanim's apartments. She has already looked in on me several times to ensure I was not lonely or unhappy in my strange surroundings.

I am happy. With a big, soaring happiness that needs to burst into a great song and fill the whole world around me. And indeed I am not lonely — but that I would have wished to share my present joy with one of my old friends, Caroline perhaps . . .

Sharif Basha sleeps in his own house tonight.

And all his doubts and questionings have disappeared. She is no longer 'Lady Anna, the Englishwoman'. She is Lady Anna, his wife. 'Anna Hanim, Haram Sharif Basha al-Baroudi.' He smiles to himself as he soaks in the bath, as wrapped in a loose white towelling robe he walks around the house he will leave tomorrow, after so many years. It is strange to feel so happy, so calmly happy. Even in that wretched meeting with Cromer he had not found it in his heart to hate the man. Ah, but how Cromer had hated him! And hated having to sit there with the marriage contract in front of him. Sharif Basha grins. And she had been magnificent — not one word of English, not one concession. At every turn she had delighted him. Her wish that had made it possible for him to no longer worry over his

324

mother's loneliness. Her surprise at the extra clauses he had put in the contract. Her hand on his arm in front of Cromer. In his bedroom he opens once again the black velvet case on the dressing table. Tomorrow night, when he sees her, these sapphires will be shining in her ears and at her throat, and it will be his hands which – later – will unclasp them.

21

In the act of love there is decreed for every part a portion of pleasure: so the eyes are for the pleasures of looking, and the nostrils are to smell sweet perfume. The pleasure of the lips lies in kissing, and of the tongue in sipping and sucking and licking. The teeth find their pleasure in biting, and the penis in penetration. The hands love to feel and explore. The lower half of the body is for touching and caressing and the upper half is for holding and embracing – and as for the ears, their pleasure is in listening to the words and sounds of love.

al-Imam Jalal al-Din al-Sayuti, Cairo, 1495 AD

5 August 1997

She is determined that my brother should make love to her.

'I cannot take her on,' he said. 'I am too old. Too used to living the way I live. It's a hell of a juggling act already. I just cannot go through all that again –'

The operator came on the line: 'Say goodbye.'

'Your time's up,' 'Omar said. 'I'll call you back.'

'Goodbye?' said the operator.

'And what's with you anyway?' my brother said when he came back on. 'Can't you get an international line?'

'I don't want to.'

'So you'd actually rather go and queue in one of those centrale dumps to book a phone call? They are the most depressing –'

'I don't queue. There's hardly anyone there. Most people *have* international lines.'

'So why don't *you* get one?'

'I don't want to.'

'I see. It's an informed position. Well, OK, what was I saying? Your friend –'

'*My* friend? You sent her here.'

'I took her out last night. She called me. She is very . . . I can't deny that I'm attracted to her.'

'I didn't phone to ask you to – take her on.'

'No, but you intimated –'

'I just thought you ought to know she's pretty hard hit.'

328

'Yes, well. I know that.'

'What modesty, ya 'Omar!'

'No. Look, come on. What am I supposed to do? I'm fifty-seven. I've had all that. I cannot bear . . .'

'Cannot bear what?'

'Explaining everything all over again – a whole new sadness.'

'Does it have to be sad?'

'It always is.'

'Good. Khalas. You're free.'

'Free?' He laughed.

I did not tell him about her vision, epiphany, whatever, in the old house. 'Omar has never had patience with old wives' tales. I can imagine him cutting in before I've even finished: 'And you want me to take her out? No, ya habibti, no. Cousin walla ma cousin, I'm out of this.' 'Omar has remained good friends with every woman he's been involved with. His children adore him. If he is attracted to Isabel, why doesn't he 'take her on'? And then I think maybe there isn't enough time for it to turn sad. A sad thought.

'Tell me,' he says, 'what about that trunk I sent you? How are you getting on with your story?'

'Very well. They're almost married. I'm thinking of taking the whole lot and going up to Tawasi.'

'Why?'

'I thought I'd stay there for a while. On the land, you know.'

'In August? You must be mad. Listen, I might be coming over in the second half of the month. We can have a couple of days together.'

'That would be wonderful,' I say. 'Will you let me know?'

I did not ask why he would be coming or via where. I knew it was possible – even likely – that his phone was tapped. For thirty years New York had played up his Egyptian ancestry, loved him and congratulated itself on its own broadminded-ness. It had winked at stories of his being in the fighting in Amman in '70, at his membership of the Palestine National

Council. And then, with the world celebrating another diplomatic triumph, another reluctant handshake on the White House lawn, he broke with the PNC. He was the spectre at the party telling anyone who would listen that Oslo would not work, could not work.

THAT NIGHT, THE NIGHT OF the 6th of Safar, 1319, she looked like a queen. She glittered and shone as she moved among the ladies and God had touched her with His blessing so that her every word and movement found its true place in the hearts of those around her.

It was our custom that the bride should sit in her bridal bower where the ladies would salute her as they arrived and then take their seats or walk about conversing with each other. But Anna could not do that for long and soon she rose and began to move among the ladies, conversing with those who could speak French and exchanging smiles with those who could not. And after their first surprise the ladies warmed to this and considered it a mark of her lack of affectation and her desire to find favour in their eyes and they liked her well for it.

For a wedding gown she wore the long, golden sheath that Madame Marthe had made for her, the low neck showing off her delicate bosom and shoulders. On her arms were the heavy golden clasps that were my mother's wedding gift to her. Around her neck and in her ears were the sapphires and diamonds my brother had sent that morning. She had gasped when she opened the box and looked up at me; the sunshine caught her face and I said, 'They are exactly the colour of your eyes.' We dressed and pinned her hair into a loose, golden crown in which her tiara was embedded. She wore no veil.

Mabrouka had lit the best amber incense and carried it round the bridal apartments muttering spells and incantations all day and when Anna was dressed, the old woman circled her with the burner and made her step over it seven times and recited every spell and aya she

330

knew to protect her from the evil eye and from misfortune, and Anna submitted to it all with good grace and rewarded Mabrouka with gold made even sweeter by an embrace.

All day the trays of sherbet were carried around our quarter and that night the flares were lit in the courtyard and at the entrance of the house, the gifts were laid out for inspection, the baskets of flowers with the cards from my brother's well-wishers filled the rooms and the carriages rolled up to the door, the men staying in the courtyard and the great reception rooms below, while the women came up to the haramlek drawing rooms and terrace and the children moved perpetually between the two floors.

From behind the lattice I kept an eye on what was going on downstairs: my brother, in full court dress and flanked by my husband and Shukri Bey, greeting his guests, receiving congratulations. All the Cabinet was in our house that night and the Azhar and Prince Muhammad 'Ali on behalf of Efendeena and Mukhtar Basha on behalf of the Sublime Porte. My uncle Mahmoud Sami Basha was helped to a seat and made a poets' corner with Ahmad Shawqi, Hafiz Ibrahim, Isma'il Sabri and Ibrahim al-Yaziji. Mustafa Bey al-Ghamrawi was staying in our house with his family. Mustafa Bey Kamel was there and Qasim Bey Amin, but they avoided each other. Cattaouie Basha and his son Henri. Anba Kyrollos and Muhammad Bey Farid, Sheikh Muhammad 'Abdu, Sheikh 'Ali Yusuf and Sheikh Rashid Rida and many, many others. In short, all of Cairo celebrated in our house that night. And an English gentleman arrived and I went to Anna and drew her to the lattice and she said, 'That is James Barrington, so he *has* come.' And Mrs Butcher also came and took Anna's hands in hers and kissed her kindly and wished her happiness.

Sheikh Yusuf al-Manyalawi had sent word that he would sing for us and the takht was set up and he sang two beautiful turns, and just as he had finished 'b'iftikarak eih yefidak' we heard a noise and a stirring and voices raised and I looked and saw that 'Abdu Efendi al-Hamuli had arrived, and Sheikh Yusuf was insisting that he would sing no more but give up his place to 'Abdu Efendi and sing behind him with the chorus. And soon that wonderful voice rose up to the haramlek and to the sky and all talk and movement ceased and I remember that I looked around the room and I saw the young women transported with tarab, and I saw them become grandmothers and I heard them say to their grandchildren, many years from now, 'That was the night I heard Si 'Abdu Efendi: at the wedding of Sharif Basha al-Baroudi and his English bride.'

How do I translate 'tarab'? How do I, without sounding weird or exotic, describe to Isabel that particular emotional, spiritual, even physical condition into which one enters when the soul is penetrated by good Oriental music? A condition so specific that it has a root all to itself: t/r/b. Anyone can be a singer – a 'mughanni' – but to be a 'mutrib' takes an extra quality. 'Abdu Efendi al-Hamuli's recognised title was 'the Mutrib of Kings and Princes', and that night, in the old house in Touloun, his gift kindled joy and sorrow in the hearts of his audience. What did Anna make of this strange music? My guess is that she opened her heart to it as she did to everything in her new, strange life.

IT WAS AFTER MIDNIGHT WHEN we heard the relay of zagharid and the beat of the drums that told us my brother was coming up to claim his bride. There was a general movement as the ladies found their seats, some drawing their silk veils across their faces and fastening them with golden pins. Anna returned to her throne in the bridal bower. The drumming and zagharid grew louder and louder until they were at the door, then all was silent as my brother stood alone in the doorway.

In my whole life I never saw him look more handsome than he did at that moment. His eyes found Anna and they lit up with a smile that found its answer shining in hers. Slowly he crossed the room while she sat waiting for him, still and straight.

He took his seat at her side in their bower and the drumming started up again, joined now by the women musicians and singers in the songs of the zaffa and after a while my mother, whose happiness was overflowing and who had long sworn that the day her son married she would dance at his wedding, stood up and danced for them the slow, stately dance of the hanim. Presently she was joined by Jalila Hanim, Husni's mother, with the waving handkerchief and the rhythmic, dignified steps of the Palestinian dance. Abeih had covered Anna's hand with his and Anna had tears in her eyes as she noted the great honour these two elderly ladies were doing her.

My mother never danced her Palestinian dance at any of our weddings. 'Omar's first marriage was the only one that took place in her lifetime, in '66 – the year after my father died – and it was such a hurried affair that we did not even have time to go to New York for it. 'God have mercy on your father,' my mother said. 'If he was still with us, this could not have happened: your brother is sitting in Amreeka getting betrothed and marrying with his own head as if he has no kin.' And when the marriage ended with the war in '67, my mother was even more bewildered that such momentous events should take place with such seeming casualness. I remember her sitting in the drawing room of our old house in Hilmiyya, saying, 'It's good I did not meet the girl's people; where would I have hidden my face from them now?' And I remember looking at her helplessly, for how could I begin to tell her how out of touch she was? When 'Omar came to visit after the war she reproached him as if his American bride had been a friend's daughter:

'How will she be regarded now? What will people think of her?'

'It was a joint decision, ya Ummi,' he said. 'It's better for both of us like this.'

'But what could have happened so soon?' she asked. 'In a year?'

'The war,' he said.

'The war? A war makes a husband divorce his wife?'

'We both discovered I was an Arab,' he said lightly.

I THINK OF THAT TIME and of how that night our happiness was complete. For my father, we had grown accustomed to his state and those closest to us among our guests had visited him and saluted him and he was not unhappy. I believe, in a way, I was happier that night than on the night of my own wedding. For although I loved Husni as my cousin, on that night six years before, I knew that by marrying him and going with him to France, I was entering into an unknown world. And leaving my mother alone in the old house weighed heavily also on my mind. But now, my happiness with my husband and my delight in Ahmad were secure, my brother was at last marrying, and marrying a woman he loved, and my mother's happiness was twofold, for her son was getting married and he was coming back to fill her house once again with life.

My brother stood up. In front of the assembled guests he kissed our mother's hands and her head and held out his hand to Anna. And with her on his arm he made their way slowly through the zagharid and the drumbeats and the singing and the shower of wafer-thin golden sequins thrown upon him and his bride by us all. And I would swear by all that I hold dear that there was not a heart in that room that did not wish them well that night.

Sharif Basha took his bride to her new quarters and the closed door behind them did not quite shut out the sounds of the house and the street humming with the noise of their wedding party and their guests.

26 May
My husband has taken his leave, for urgent business calls him to his office. I do not know its precise nature but I know it is to do with the news he received last night of the Khedive's pardoning Urabi Basha. When he told me this, I informed him that I had heard that the Duke of Cornwall had visited Urabi Basha in Ceylon some two weeks ago, and I thought he looked at me somewhat oddly. Then he said, 'Come. We have better things to do than to talk about politics.'

And indeed we did. For I have had – as the late Queen said so famously half a century ago – a most bewildering and gratifying night. And now, today, I feel as if – I hardly know how to describe it, but it is as if my body had been absent and now it is present. As though I am for the first time present in my own body.

Before he left, I went with my husband to meet my new beau-père. He is a very gentle man and appears far older than his sixty-six years. My husband kissed his hand and I followed suit and old Baroudi Bey smiled and nodded.

The house is very quiet today and – apart from a visit from Zeinab Hanim and Mabrouka, who came to wish us a 'happy bridal morning' as we were seated at breakfast – I have been left quite alone. I imagine Zeinab Hanim and the servants are in need of a rest after their labours of the last few days. And Layla is naturally occupied with her house guests. And I am content. I am content just to be. To perform my toilette slowly and lie on the divan under the mashrabiyya watching diamonds of sunshine change form on my hands and my clothing. To sleep and wake and wait for his return.

10 August 1997
Isabel calls me and says, 'I'm missing you.'

'I'm missing you too,' I say. 'How are you getting on?'

'My mother is – I think she's going. She's very, very thin, and she hardly speaks.'

'I'm sorry.'

'She's quite calm. She's not unhappy. But she's not there.'

'What do the doctors say?'

'Nothing much. I keep looking at her and wishing I knew more about her life. Not as I saw it. As *she* saw it.'

'It's all this stuff we've been doing with Anna.'

'Yes. Why didn't I speak to her – ask her, when I still could?'

'One tends not to,' I said.

'God, you sound so British!' She laughs. 'One tends not to,' she mimics, putting on her version of a posh English accent.

'Well,' I say, 'you're the American. Ask her to share her feelings with you – or better: to share *your* feelings with you –'

'I've seen 'Omar a couple of times.'

'And?'

'He's very – sweet to me. He's terribly busy and always in a rush. We went to an exhibition of photographs of China at the ICP and he just whizzes past the photos – just takes them in as he passes. He stopped a couple of times and said – for my sake – 'Shall we linger?' But when he's waiting like I'm taking a really long time to work things out, I can't even think about the photograph because I'm thinking about him waiting. I just followed him round at high speed. But he bought me a wonderful dinner afterwards.'

'Isabel. Are you all right? You sound a bit hyper.'

'Yeah, sure. No. No, I'm not. I just want him to be in love with me.'

'Oh, Isabel!'

'I do. I can't help it. Honestly. I've tried. It's like I know it could be wonderful. It's almost as if –' she pauses, searching for her words – 'It's almost as if it's already there and already wonderful, only he won't look. I know that sounds crazy.'

'Isabel –'

'That is what it feels like. I can't believe he doesn't feel it.'

'He's older. He's been through a lot.'

'And Amal –'

'What?'

'I'll tell you something crazier.'

'What?' I said again.

'You know that thing with the Hidden Sheikh and how we agreed it couldn't have happened? Or you said it couldn't have happened?'

'Yes?' My heart sinks. Her mother is dying. She has built this thing up round my brother. I have drawn her into an obsession with Anna and our history –

'Well, listen. I opened my laundry bag today, just now, for the first time after I'd been in there. In the house. That's where I put the clothes I was wearing that day. And you know what I found?'

'What?'

'They smell of orange blossom.'

'Isabel!'

'It's true. I swear to you. Where would I get a scent of orange blossom?'

I can think of nothing to say.

'Amal?'

'Yes.'

'What do you think?'

'Listen, Isabel, you know you shouldn't talk about this to 'Omar?'

'He'll think I'm nuts.'

'Yes, he will. And he'll run. That'll be it.'

'I know. I know I shouldn't. He has to go away anyway. In a week.'

For a moment I almost say I'll go over. But if 'Omar is coming – 'Are you going to be all right?' I ask.

'Yes, of course I am.'

'You sound a bit fraught.'

'No, it's just – I'll be fine.'

'How about your work?'

'I saw my programme director yesterday. She's quite happy.'

'Look. Concentrate on your mother. And your work. The rest will come.'

'I know.'

'And call me soon.'

'Of course I will.'

I sit on the edge of my bed. I do not believe in the sudden and miraculous opening of sealed doors, but I have always tried to keep an open mind. After a moment I carry on dressing. I look at myself in the mirror with more interest than I have done for a long time. I look like one of my school-friends' mothers. Passable, I decide. Nothing like what I used to be, but passable. When the buzzer rings and Tahiyya calls out, 'Tareq Bey says he's waiting for you in the car', I dim the lights, pick up my handbag and go.

Over our drinks in the sky-high bar of the Rameses Hilton we look down at the necklaces of lights twined about the banks of the Nile, the bridges, the squares of Khedive Ismail's Cairo. There is Qasr el-Nil Bridge, and beyond it the gracious lines of the British embassy and beyond that the fortress of the American embassy in the heart of Garden City.

'You know, I was wrong that day,' Tareq says. 'You *have* changed.'

'Hardly surprising.' I smile.

'You have grown even more beautiful.'

When I make a face, he says:

'No, seriously. You were always beautiful. But now there's something more. Something very special about you.'

'Yes,' I say. 'The past.'

'We should have got married,' he says.

'Sure,' I say. 'Then you would have been saying these pretty things to someone else right now.'

'Since when are you so cynical?'

'Me? You're the one who's thinking of doing business with the Israelis.'

'Forget about the Israelis,' he says, 'I'm talking personal.'

'The personal is the political,' I quote.

'OK then,' he says. 'Tell me. What are *you* doing about all those things you say you care so much about?'

'What's in my hands I'll do,' I say. 'I shall go live in Tawasi and look after the land myself –'

'You believe that will help Egypt?' He looks incredulous. 'Looking after a bit of land and keeping a few fallaheen happy?'

'I'll activate the health unit –'

'Now you'll say you'll teach them to do their own weaving –'

'And I'll get the school going.'

'Have you found teachers?'

'No.'

'Why not?'

'Because nobody will give lists of names to the government. And your friend Muhyi Bey knew that very well.'

'So what will you do?'

'I don't know. Man the school myself.'

'You'll go sit there every evening?'

'If I have to.'

'Nonsense! You can't do that. I'll send you a couple of young men from my farm.'

'What?'

'I'll send you a couple of men. I'll guarantee them to the Governor.'

'Would you really do that?'

'I've just said I will.'

'Egyptians?'

'Come on, ya Amal –'

'I'm sorry. It's just – why? Why would you do that?'

'Because I don't want you sitting there. Because you want the school opened. Because it's right that it should be opened.'

'We can't pay them proper salaries.'

'It's all right. I'll look after that.'

Is he taking over my life? It is so long since anyone has told me what I can or cannot do. So long since anyone has intervened in my life. But he is considering doing business with Israel. And he is married. But he is also my friend, isn't he?

'Tareq,' I say, 'you said ideologies are dead. Is there any idea that you believe in?'

'Justice,' he says, without a moment's hesitation. 'I believe in justice.'

I cannot quarrel with that. I do not say, What about justice for the Palestinians? I'll save that for another time. I think of telling him about Isabel and her orange blossom. I think of telling him about my marriage and its end. I look out at the river and the lights below us and I say:

'Isn't it just heartbreakingly beautiful?'

'There's nothing like it in the world,' he says.

'You'd think it deserved a better deal,' I say.

He tips the car-park attendant five pounds.

'That's just to make you happy,' he says and grins at me.

In the low-slung Mercedes, looking straight ahead, he asks, 'Shall I kidnap you?'

'No, please,' I say, 'I'm expecting my brother.'

18 August 1997

Tahiyya and I are working in the guestroom. We have removed the dustsheets from the furniture. I am taking the books out of the bookcase and dusting them while she polishes the mirror above the dressing table with old news-paper and water. We have the radio on and the news is coming through of the Southern Lebanon Army Militias turning their artillery on Saida. The count so far is six killed and thirty wounded. All of them civilians. Tahiyya is tutting 'Ya Sattar ya Rabb' and asking, is this destruction never going to stop? I am thinking of a time back in '63 when my father was still alive and we had gone to Lebanon for a week, and visited cousins and visited also Saida and Tyre and climbed into the ruins of the old Crusader castles and looked out at the sea, shimmering away into the distance, leading to Africa on the left, to Europe on the right, and straight ahead into the broad blue of the Atlantic.

It was around six when the telephone rang – eleven in the morning in New York.

'I've just seen your brother off at the airport,' Isabel said. And then she told me about yesterday.

Jasmine had been lucid, coherent, but in another time and another language: she would only speak French.

'Mama is so sad,' Jasmine says. 'And Papa keeps reminding her England is her home after all and telling her it is only for a while, but she will not go without him –' It's 1940. Paris is about to fall to the Nazis and Nur is desperate for Jean-Marie to leave. She fears that once she and the sixteen-year-old Jasmine are safely in England, her husband might stay and take his chances. She will not let that happen.

'Then she started going on about getting her out safely,' Isabel said. 'And it was really spooky when I realised she was talking about me –'

'I've been ill, very ill,' Jasmine says. 'That's why I've been in here so long. I don't know how Jonathan is managing. I truly don't. He can't do a thing for himself. Such a sweet man! And he dotes on the baby already. I have to make sure I get her out safely –'

'How do you know it's a girl?' Isabel asks.

'What? Of course it's a girl. Isabel. Jonathan adores her already. Only there's too much pressure. You understand? Too much.'

'Yes.' Isabel nods at her mother's bedside. 'I understand.'

Outside the sun was burning down on the Manhattan streets, but in the room, the curtains were drawn and the air-conditioning hummed gently.

'If I can get her out she'll be safe. She'll be a bit early. But she'll be safe. They've got good doctors here. The best doctors in the world are right here in London. Isn't that right, Nurse? Yes, I know I mustn't talk so much. Bad. Bad for the baby.'

Isabel looks up at the nurse, who has come in quietly and now lifts Jasmine's arm, holding the frail wrist gently while she looks at her stopwatch. Isabel wonders whether the nurse speaks French.

'It's OK, Mrs Cabot,' the nurse says in English. 'You're doing great.'

Does she speak French? Or does it not matter any more what her mother says?

'I can't feel her kicking any more, Nurse. She's gone very quiet.'

'You'll be fine, Mrs Cabot, just fine. Try to relax now.'

'She was kicking and moving about all the time. And now she's gone quiet. Perhaps she's sleeping; getting ready for her journey.'

Jasmine closes her eyes. When she opens them again it is 1944 and she has just met Jonathan Cabot, the bright young diplomat attached to Eisenhower in London.

'I am not blaming you or criticising you,' she protests to Nur. 'I am saying simply that I like his frankness. It is all simple with him. He says what he means. He knows what he wants. He is full of hope and energy. I love Papa dearly but I would not choose to marry him −'

The nurse asks if Isabel wants to talk to the doctor about sedating Jasmine.

'He has one room, one big room in an attic with large windows tilted to the sky. And he has a gramophone. And the floor is bare and good for dancing. Our apartment, it is so heavy: the big drapes, the chandeliers forever being dusted and polished, the huge, gloomy paintings. Nothing is less than a hundred years old. Perhaps I love him for the bareness of his loft −'

Isabel says to let Jasmine be. The once black, glossy hair is a spiky halo of white, the movement − now redundant − of the trembling hand to push it back from the temple reminds

Isabel of an elderly ballerina showing how things should be done.

'I never stopped loving him. No, not for a day. Even when I was in his arms I did not stop loving Jonathan. It was different. Something drew me to him. His youth. His hair and eyes were dark, like mine. Layers of trouble I sensed behind those eyes – but I had to let him go. I knew it would not do. I had to let him go, though it was like tearing out part of my heart all over again –'

'Are you sure now?' The nurse asks again.

'Valentine,' Jasmine sobs, 'Val, Valentine –' She curls over on her side, holding her pillow close, ducking her head to wipe her streaming eyes, her mouth, her nose against it.

When it was over, Isabel called my brother:

'Can I see you?'

'You know I'm leaving tomorrow,' he said. 'I still have a lot of things to do.'

'How long will you be away?'

'A week, maybe ten days.'

'I – my mother died.'

'Oh, Isabel. Isabel, I'm so sorry. I'll come right over.'

'No. I don't want to go to the apartment.'

'Where are you?'

'I'm – I'm in a public –'

'OK. Stop a cab and come over. OK? Now.'

So she went over and when he saw her at his door he took her in his arms: a beautiful, forlorn, parentless child. He poured her a drink. He rubbed her cold hands and breathed on them. He took her in his arms again. I imagine she held on to him and wept and he kissed her tear-drenched face and then her mouth and she held on to him as though for life itself.

My brother took Isabel into his bed and made love to her and when, later, she fell asleep, he drew the covers over her. And when he had finished his packing he went and lay by her side and she awakened and turned to him again. And it was as the sun was rising that she started to talk to him about her mother.

20 August 1997

Now I know where my brother is and why. He must be in Ramallah where – the radio tells me – the Palestinian Authority are holding a 'Conference of National Unity'.

'And about time too' I can hear him say.

I am not easy. My brother hates seeing the Resistance turn into the Authority.

'The first thing they do,' he said, 'the *first* thing is set up the security services. *Eleven* security services. So what are they doing? They're going to do the Israelis' dirty work for them?'

My brother speaks his mind, and he speaks it where it will be heard – and dangerous.

I arrange a cloud of pink sweet peas in a shallow bowl in his room and promise myself he will be here while they still bloom. I blow on their petals and make sure each one has room to breathe while I listen to the radio report Washington's criticism of the conference for giving a platform to the Islamists, and a tune repeats itself insistently in my head:

Weinha Ramallah? Weinha Ramallah?
Tell me, oh traveller, where is Ramallah?

In the newspaper, today's batch of photographs from the Territories are pretty much the same as every day: young men lined up against shuttered shops in a cobbled street, old men standing by, watching, as their olive groves are torn up, women wailing as bulldozers smash through their houses – any one of these women could have been my mother. A particular photograph arrests my attention: a child of three or so rides high on men's shoulders at his father's funeral. He carries a machine gun and wears a headband inscribed 'We shall return'. His expression is tranquil. Is it right that a child's path should be so firmly set so early? I have tried not to weigh

down my sons with our history. Now I try to be glad that they
are free.

Weinha Ramallah? Weinha Ramallah?

We used to sing this when I was a student. We were in
1968 and Ramallah had just been lost to us.

22

That handkerchief
Did an Egyptian to my mother give.
William Shakespeare

22 August 1997

I wait for my brother. I wait for my sons. I wait for Isabel. I wait for news from Minya. I wait. The ceiling fans work all day and I open my blinds only at night. The Nasr Abu Zaid appeal has been refused and now there is nothing for it but he and his wife must stay in Europe, for our state cannot ensure their safety. I think of this most Egyptian of men: a round, jolly, loquacious, balding, bearded man. I think of him huddled in his overcoat, finding his way in the clean, cold streets of the north, making a new life away from home.

> *27 May 1901*
>
> *Emily has informed me of her decision to return to England. I have furnished her with everything necessary and my husband is making the required arrangements.*

A terse entry. I ponder over Anna's feelings. Is she disappointed? Angry, even, that Emily, after all the years in her service, has decided not to stay? Or is she perhaps relieved that now she can set off into her new world without a constant monitor from the one she has left behind? And what about Emily? I do not wish to do her an injustice, but – try as I might – I can see nothing but pursed lips and a shaking head as she tells, back in London, of how she left her ladyship.

29 May

Zeinab Hanim has detailed a young woman by the name of Hasna as my personal maid. She has a delicate blue tattoo on her chin and is of a sweet disposition and has already shown her skill in dressing my hair and laundering some small items. Shall I one day converse with her with the same ease that I observe between Zeinab Hanim and Mabrouka?

3 June

We have decided to dispense with a honeymoon for the moment and to go to Italy later in the year. Indeed I have no need of change for here is change enough for me.

My husband showed me an article by Mustafa Bey Kamel in l'Etendard attacking the idea of Urabi Pasha's return and saying it would be more fitting for him to die in exile as most of his comrades had done. My husband is saddened by this as an expression of division among the nationalists and because Urabi is old and so should merit more courteous treatment. He does not see much good coming of his return, however.

7 June

Visit from the dressmaker as I had expressed a wish to have some costumes made in the Egyptian fashion. I chose some deep blues and aquamarines, set off with scarlet and old pink. Colours which would have looked most overblown in European dress but suit the style of clothes here wonderfully well.

My days have fallen into a happy pattern. We wake and take breakfast together. My husband goes to work and I spend the morning with Zeinab Hanim. I accompany her into the kitchen and the storerooms and the linen room and watch what she does and she invites me, with a motion of her head and hand, to show her how I would have things done. The responsibility of arranging the flowers has now by consent become mine and I have already learned to make a dish of lamb soaked in the juice of the Tamarind flower. We have coffee in the loggia at eleven. A most gentle friendship is growing between us, based not on conversation but on shared tasks and these mornings spent together, and each day I am sensible of the happiness our arrangement has brought her. How wonderful it is that a circumstance that has brought me such joy should also be the cause of contentment for others!

When my husband comes home we have lunch en famille, generally at around two o'clock, after which we repair to our apartment for a 'siesta'. In the afternoon, when he has returned to work or to Hilmiyya (for he has not yet moved his study to this house), it is the time for visiting or being visited by other ladies. I am always accompanied on these occasions by Layla, who guides my steps with great delicacy. For now I am not simply myself, but Haram Sharif Basha al-Baroudi, and everything I do reflects on him. If there are no visits I may go to the shops (always in a closed carriage and always accompanied by Hasna and a manservant) to choose materials and furnishings for our apartments. I fashion our rooms with patterned cushions and bright silk curtains and tables inlaid with mother-of-pearl.

I feel happiness – I could laugh aloud as I write the words – as surely as I would feel the warmth of a fire upon coming to it from a cold, damp night. And the oddest thing is that I am grown fond of my own limbs. The hands and feet that have served me these thirty years, the hair I have brushed unthinkingly each night – I feel a tenderness for them now as though they were cherished creatures in their own right –

But one week later, in a hurried, distraught hand:

15 June
I have been alone in my room for two hours. I cannot believe that the man I have chosen above all others – the man for whom I have left everything I ever held dear – can I have been so mistaken? I go over our argument and I am at a loss to understand it in any way that might bring me comfort.

When he came in to lunch I noticed that his face was changed and he ate in silence. Zeinab Hanim and I exchanged glances and when I was alone with him I asked whether he had received news not to his liking, to which he responded by asking me where

I had been the day before. I listed the shops I had gone to and he asked where else I had been. I searched my memory and then said that I had also been to the bank.

'Why did you go to the bank?' he asked.

'Why, because I needed some money,' I replied, surprised.

'Do you not realise you are married?' This in a cold tone that I had not heard from him before. I was at a loss and said yes, I realised I was married but I did not see what that had to do with visiting the bank.

'You are my wife,' he said, 'and you go to the bank and withdraw money – and without telling me?' He spoke so angrily that I was stung and retorted that surely as it was my money I could withdraw it if I pleased and that I was disappointed that he employed his servants to spy upon my actions.

'It seems, madame, my servants have more sense than you of what is fitting.' And with that he left the room. I could hear him moving next door but I would not go to him and presently I heard him leave.

I do not know what to think. He has been so generous with his gifts and with the terms of the marriage – have I been blind?

Surely Madame Rushdi would have warned me? But we kept the impending marriage secret. I have since felt no reservation in her happiness for me. Oh, how little I really know him! Could my heart have been so mistaken?

Can it be that all I am to him is a foolish, wealthy English widow? Oh, hurtful, hurtful thought –

All certainty is dissolved. The rooms she has so lovingly arranged, the wordless companionship with his mother, the bond she had thought so secure with his sister; what is Anna to make of those now? Images from the hours she has spent with him, in his arms, in this very room, bring a hot blush of shame and anger to her face and her tears spill out yet again.

I DO NOT ALLEGE THAT all was always well between them. How could that be when they had fallen in love across countries and seas?

And I recall that once I entered upon Anna during the first month of their marriage, and I had heard from my mother that there was a problem between them, the nature of which she did not know. My mother was worried, for my brother's face was dark and thunderous as he left, and as for Anna, she kept to her room but Hasna, her maid, said she had been weeping. Anna would not sit but I begged her to tell me what had happened, for are we not sisters? I asked. At that she looked at me strangely but eventually I understood that she had been to her bankers to withdraw money and that my brother had found out and questioned her and she had taken this amiss. I told her she must expect him to be angry if he is insulted, as he surely would be – for if she needed money, why did she not ask him? I explained that with us, if a woman is married, her money is her own and her husband, if he is able, is obliged to furnish her with all the money she needs for her personal expenses as well as any household expenses she might incur.

'If you use your own money, Anna, you are accusing him of negligence, or of being miserly. Or you lay yourself open to the charge of having some secret expense which you cannot divulge to him.'

'And why does he have me spied on?' Anna holds on to her anger a little longer.

'That is more difficult,' Layla says. 'But look into your heart: what were you thinking of him before I came in? You know so little of each other. He is a public man and, as well as his heart, he has placed his reputation in your hands. Think of the bank clerks whispering why Sharif Basha al-Baroudi's wife should come in person to withdraw money from her account. That news will already be with the Agency.'

Anna's face has been changing as Layla speaks. Now she rushes to her dresser.

'I must send it back immediately,' she says.

AND IT WAS WITH DIFFICULTY that I persuaded her that that could make matters worse. For she had that impulsive generosity of spirit that made it a necessity to her to right a wrong upon the instant.

Oh, wicked, wicked, wicked! How could I have doubted him so? I am ashamed of my thoughts and happy beyond measure to be in the wrong.

I have prepared a note to Mrs Butcher saying that as an act of grace for my present happiness, I wish to make a donation to her charity for orphaned children. I placed it in a purse with the money and waited.

28 June
Last night my husband came back early and walked into my room and stood before me with his hand outstretched, looking pale and tired. 'I could not work,' he said. 'Come, Anna. Let us not quarrel. I cannot believe you meant to wound me.'

'Would you send the money to Mrs Butcher tomorrow?' I asked. 'For one of her charities?' And he took me in his arms.

Late in the night, he held my face between his hands and said, 'Our ways are so different. Let us be patient with one another.'

5 July
It is grown hot and Ahmad and I are not allowed into the courtyard during the day without our bonnets. Hasna is constantly appearing at my side with glasses of cool water scented with rose-water. I am aware at times that my husband is regarding me with some anxiety, for it seems he cannot feel certain that I am happy and content. He persists in thinking that I find my life too confined, but in truth, it is not so dissimilar to life in London — except in that we cannot do things together outside the house, for Egyptian Society is segregated, and there is no place for him among the Europeans. But where we cannot walk in the park, we walk in our garden, and he has procured for me some bushes of an English rose which we have planted in a

shady spot. I have warned him that he is to draw no conclusions if they do not thrive, 'for I am no rose', I said.

'So, what are you?'

'I do not know. But I know that I have everything I need.'

'Tell me, then,' he said, drawing me close. 'Tell me what you need now.'

Can love grow infinitely? Each day I feel my love for him push its roots deeper into my soul. I rest in his arms, so close that I can feel his heartbeat as though it were my own, and I wonder that just four short months ago I did not even know him.

12 July

It has come about quite naturally that I am learning Arabic of my husband's father for I had taken to visiting him for a few moments each day, and as I saw that he welcomed me but we did not converse together, I took my book with me and he, seeing my attempts, read for me and I repeated after him and so we began our lessons. He is a very gentle man, made frail and uncertain by his long seclusion and by the great sadness he has carried for so long. My husband is unfailingly courteous to him but I sense he is impatient of him, not because of his present infirmity but because of the path he chose some twenty years ago. They are so different to each other that it is hard to think of them as father and son. But I used to think that of Edward and Sir Charles.

Sir Charles writes to me, but not so often. And after the first letter in which he wished me happiness − 'although, my dear, I cannot say I confidently expect it' − he writes without mention of my new condition, so that I feel constrained not to mention any particulars of my life to him and restrict myself to reports on my Arabic and the garden and such political news as I hear from my husband. Caroline writes from time to time with news of our friends and she expresses curiosity about my life but I find in myself a strange unwillingness to provide a detailed picture of 'life in the Harem'. If she were to visit, however, I would be glad to have her as my guest for it is only then, I think, that she would gain a true picture of my life here. Mrs Butcher is the only one of my English acquaintances here who continues to see me and she brings me news of James Barrington, who is soon to leave for London. I have given her a parcel to give to him with the request that he deliver it to Sir Charles that he may in turn give it to Mr Winthrop. It contains the camphor and the oil of Habbet el-Barakah he asked me for many months ago, and will serve as an introduction between Mr Barrington and Sir Charles. Mrs Butcher has promised to write some pieces for the ladies' magazine that we are planning. The magazine is the idea of Madame Zeinab Fawwaz and a young woman by the name of Malak Hifni Nasif. They plan Arabic and French editions and wish to attract writers from as many communities as possible and – while the idea is to compare the condition and the aspirations of women in different societies – it is not to confine itself to the 'Question of Women' but to enter into matters of more general concern and so demonstrate that women are ready to enter a wider arena than that to which they have hitherto been confined.

My husband speaks of a School of Fine Art that is being planned and has said that he wishes me to have a part in the planning. Nothing is to be done until November, though, for all of Cairo is now gone either to Europe or to Alexandria for the summer months and, if we can prevail upon my beau-père to travel, we shall go to Alexandria as well and I shall be most curious to see – in such different circumstances – that city which was my first port of entry to this my new world.

25 August 1997

My brother is incapable of walking slowly. He takes long strides along the sea's edge and I find myself playing my old game of secretly trying to match his footsteps. I manage to stay in rhythm for seven long steps, then I have to do a speedy little cha–cha shuffle forward. My earliest memories of him are on this beach – no, my earliest memory is of him leaving: there I am, in focus, in a red sun frock with ribbons for straps, seated on my father's shoulder waving goodbye. My mother stands next to us and in the distance, across from the men rushing about on the quay, across from the expanse of brownish water dotted with small boats with more men in them, my brother stands at the rails of his ship, a pale, slim figure, his black hair shining in the sunshine. After that my memories of him are here on this beach at 'Agami, where our father built his own modest beach house for us after he sold the big villa that my grandfather and Sharif Basha had built on the other side of Alexandria so that their wives might play and swim with their children in privacy. My brother came back in the long vacations and amused himself as best he could with a sister twelve years his junior. We built sandcastles and he taught me to swim and to play racquet ball and we went for walks like this one: he marching by the edge of the sea, kicking up the spray with his feet, while I ran along at his side.

I catch his arm and hold on, slowing him down.

'But it must be good,' I say, 'in principle, anyway, to get everybody together to talk?'

'It's just containment,' he says. 'What 'Arafat is interested in is containment and maintaining his credibility. But what's he doing? He's got eleven security services. Eleven!'

My brother speaks with vehemence. I've hardly ever heard him speak except with vehemence – each word underlined. To look at him you would think he was a dandy, a dilettante, with his good looks, his fine clothes, his fastidious attention to detail; then he moves into action and you are caught up in a whirlwind. A whirlwind with method.

'He has his own prisons and he uses torture and bone-breaking just as much as the Israelis. At least with them there's some kind of process by which people can question what goes on in their jails. But with him there's nothing. Nothing at all. The only ones with anything to offer now are Hamas. They're the ones with credibility on the streets. And they've earned it. They're the ones who're putting up resistance – and suffering losses.'

'So?'

He's shaken free of my arm and once again I am breaking into the occasional trot to catch up. The sea is turning iron grey and people are rolling up their straw mats and shaking out their towels.

'So it's very sad. They turned up to my talk and they asked good questions. They're intelligent. They're committed. They certainly have a case. But one cannot approve of fundamentalists – of whatever persuasion.'

'And the conference?'

'Nothing. Empty talk. He wants Hamas to stop operations. But they said, quite rightly, that without them the Israelis have no incentive to give up anything.'

'And you? How did you leave it with him?'

He kicks the water, bends down and picks up something, wipes it on his trousers and holds it out to me: a smooth shiny black stone, a perfect egg-shaped oval, polished by sea water and sand and sun over who knows how many hundreds of years.

'Keep it,' he says. 'I told him this was the first meeting – the first official meeting I'd attended since I resigned from the PNC, and it would be the last. It's a good job I have an American passport. But I'm going back. I am going to Jerusalem. I want to see our mother's house.'

'You want to be careful,' I said. Hate mail is a normal part of my brother's life and his house in New York has been letter-bombed twice.

'So tell me about her, about Isabel,' I say at last. Outside the glass panes of Zephyrion the night and the sea are all one blackness. We are in Abu Qir, where my grandfather's house used to be; a large, many-roomed villa with an enclosed sand-garden where the fig trees grew. It was pulled down years ago and everywhere now there are small cement shacks which families that used to be middle class but are now poor rent for their summer holidays. But it is mercifully dark and we cannot see them. We can hear the gentle roar of the waves. The old British soldier who had stayed behind after the war and beat his unending tattoo on this beach is no longer there. We used to sit in this restaurant and the strains of 'Scotland the Brave' from his bagpipes would float in as he approached, and recede into a ghostly echo as he retreated. Perhaps he is dead, I think.

Lay down and died on this beach and people found him in the morning and picked him up and gave him a shroud and a grave as they had given him food and shelter when he was alive.

'I don't want to talk about it,' he says. 'It's too terrible.'

'Why terrible?' I ask, surprised.

'I spent my last night in New York with her.'

'Yes. She told me.'

'Her mother had just died. I mean literally: just.'

'That's all right, isn't it? I mean, fighting death with life and all that?'

'No, but the thing is, I'd been in love with her.'

'Who? Isabel?'

'No, no. Not Isabel, her mother.' He picks up his glass of Gianaklis, takes a sip and grimaces as he puts the glass down. 'This stuff gets worse every year. Why can't they produce decent wine in this country?' he asks.

I am trying to take in this new twist.

'When were you in love with Isabel's mother?' I ask. 'Before she died?'

He gives me a look. 'Yes, my dear. Many years before she died. In '62 to be exact.'

'But –' I am trying to imagine this. 'She must have been a lot older than you.'

'She was. It didn't seem like it. I mean, I didn't think of that. I was just a kid.'

'But then – how did you know, I mean, when did you know –?'

'Just that last night in New York. She woke up at dawn practically – Isabel, that is – and I hadn't slept well and we made coffee and she started to talk about her mother and I suddenly realised – it's just too awful. Really.' He lays his knife and fork diagonally beside his half-eaten fish, pushes the plate a little way from him and wipes his mouth roughly with his napkin.

'But had you not stayed in touch? I mean, how come you didn't know –?'

'No, no. It was a very brief thing. Very dramatic. I was pretty hard hit.' He grins. 'Literally. I was hit on the head. I was in some demonstration. A youthful folly. And it turned nasty and I got hit on the head and the next thing I knew I was in a bed somewhere and this beautiful woman was bending over me.'

'And then?' I prompt.

'Nothing. I fell in love with her. I stayed in her house for a couple of days. And we met twice after that. And then she dropped me. I guess she just decided it wouldn't work. And it wouldn't have, of course. But of course I didn't think so then.'

'And that was it?'

'I wrote to her a few times. Many times, I think. Imploring and arguing, you know the kind of thing. She wrote one letter. A short letter. Her decision was final and all that. I went around with an interestingly broken heart for a while. And then – khalas. Can you get me some cold water?' he says to the waiter. 'And can you clear all this? And –' to me – 'would you like some dessert? I'm having coffee.'

I ask for coffee too, and water.

'When Isabel started to talk about her mother it fell into place. I'd thought there was something about her from the beginning. Something familiar but I couldn't place it. But the name, the dead kid – her brother – the American embassy in London. It all fitted. She'd reminded me of her mother.'

'Have you told her?' I ask.

'No, no. Of course not.'

I am not sure what I think. I can't quite make out what I think. But what I say, after a while, is 'It's not so terrible. Of course it's a shock and it brings back all sorts of things and it's a bit weird but it's not – like, it's not a disaster, surely?'

'It could be. She was born at the end of '62 and my affair with Jasmine was in March.'

'You don't think – you can't think –?'

'It's a distinct possibility, as they say.'

The waiter brings the coffee and my brother downs a tall glass of water in one go and wipes his mouth again with his napkin. We sit in silence. Family, yes, but this is too close. Did Isabel fall in love with him because he is her father? I pick up my glass.

'I don't think so, you know,' I say after a few sips. 'I would have felt something familiar about her. And I didn't. I still don't. There's nothing about her that's like you.'

'Let's hope you're right,' he says. And then he says, 'That's why I forgot your tapestry. I had it unframed and I was going to roll it up and put it in my bag at the last minute, but with all that stuff coming at me, I just completely forgot.'

We have a long drive back into Alexandria and out of it again and all the way to our beach house.

Thirty stars shine
On the valley of cypresses
Thirty stars fall
On the valley of cypresses . . .

We listen in silence to the tape of Sabreen he has brought back from Ramallah.

When we get to the house I make tea and serve it in the living room. We settle into our cane chairs and my brother looks at me.

'You grow more beautiful each time I see you,' he says.

Surprised, I run my hand through my hair tangled with the salt sea air.

'It's true,' he says. 'Is there someone around?'

I shake my head. I consider telling him about Tareq 'Attiyah.

'There should be,' he says.

'No thank you,' I say, 'I'm done with all that.'

'Come on,' he says. 'That's ridiculous. A woman like you?'

'I'm through.' I smile. 'Unless, of course, I find someone like you.'

'Nonsense,' he says. 'You don't want anything to do with someone like me.'

'At least we know for sure you're not *my* father.'

'For God's sake, Amal! This isn't a joking matter –'

'You are not her father.'

'How do you know?'

'I know.'

'*How* do you know?'

'There are too many coincidences in this thing already. She finds this trunk, you meet her and it turns out you're cousins. That's enough, surely?'

'What? Bad art? Is that what you're saying?'

'Look. Tell her and do a DNA.'

He groans. 'I told you I didn't want this,' he says. 'I told you it was going to be trouble.'

12 September 1901

I should not have thought I would mind so much. I met today two ladies with whom I had a slight acquaintance – I say 'met' but that is hardly accurate: I went into the jeweller's on rue Qasr el-Nil and they were there and, naturally – I did not stop to think – I bade them a good afternoon, whereupon they looked away and made a great business of gathering their purses and parasols and left the shop immediately, all the while being careful to preserve a studiedly blank expression on their faces. Six months ago they would have been flattered that I recognised them.

I continued with my business, made my purchase and left – the shopkeeper pretending that he had noticed nothing. But my hands were frozen the while and for a few moments I could hardly see the trinkets laid out before me. I will tell no one of this – least of all my husband, for I can imagine his hurt and anger on my behalf – but any hope I had of one day resuming a normal relationship with my compatriots here must now be set aside. If Mrs Butcher seemed extraordinary to me before, she seems doubly so today and I shall make sure I value her friendship accordingly. I do not truly set store by the good opinion of these ladies – and yet I am wounded.

This incident will, I am sure, be a source of satisfaction at many dinner tables –

23

How do I love thee? Let me count the ways.
Elizabeth Barrett Browning

17 December 1901

Painting is a kind of visual poetry as poetry is a kind of verbal painting. If you ask me about the Prophetic Tradition 'Those who will be most severely tormented on the Day of Judgement are the image-makers', I would say that this Tradition comes from the days of idolatry, when images were made as empty entertainment or with the purpose of setting them up in shrines to worship and implore. If both these motives are absent and painting or sculpture is attended by a seriousness of purpose, then the representation of the human or the animal form is of the same standing as the representations of flowers and other plants which we find decorating the margins of the Qur'an itself since ancient times. On the whole I would regard serious art as a means to elevate the emotions and educate the spirit –

'It is preposterous,' Sharif Basha explodes, the letter from Muhammad 'Abdu in his hand, 'preposterous that we should need this – this *testimonial* before we dare set up a school. What are we? A nation of infants?'

'Ya Sidi, calm yourself! At least we have an enlightened friend in the Mufti. I should have thought you would be glad to get his endorsement?' Isma'il Basha Sabri raises a quizzical eyebrow as he regards his friend.

'It is I myself who asked for it.' Sharif Basha strides the room impatiently. 'But it galls me that every basic thing should have to be spelled out again and again. Art elevates the spirit. Don't we know this? After five thousand years? Do we have to keep going back to the beginning?'

Isma'il Sabri spreads out his hands in a gesture of momentary helplessness. 'These are difficult times,' he says.

Sharif Basha frowns. 'Let us go,' he says abruptly, folding the letter and putting it into his pocket. 'Let us go and get this over with.'

The two men pause to adjust their cravats in the great mirror in the hall of Isma'il Sabri's house. They settle their tarbushes on their heads and get into the waiting carriage.

'But you have seen 'Urabi already, since his return?' Isma'il Sabri asks.

'I called on him. But we were alone, and it was before these recent . . . developments.'

'Perhaps he won't be there,' Isma'il Sabri suggests, as the carriage rattles through the dark streets and they lean back in their opposite corners.

'Let us hope so,' Sharif Basha says. 'But I believe he is not even aware of the effect he is having. That the day should come,' he says, 'when I find myself siding with Mustafa Kamel against 'Urabi!'

'Whatever possessed him to give such an interview?' Isma'il Sabri wonders. 'To say he is happy to see the British in Egypt? After all these years?'

'He has gone senile. Turned into another foolish old man. He should have sensed a trap the moment al-Muqattam approached him.'

'He was never very clever,' Isma'il Sabri says. 'He was patriotic and brave, and he had presence. But he was not clever.'

'He should have remained silent. Come home if he wished, but remained silent.'

And there indeed is Ahmad 'Urabi. Sharif Basha spots him the moment he enters Wisa Basha Wasif's salamlek. The room is crowded with men come to celebrate the return of Wisa Basha's son from Europe. Smoke and the buzz of conversation and the clink of glasses and beyond it all 'Urabi stands alone. The head that towers over most men in the room is grizzled now, the beard completely white. 'Our own Garibaldi', Sharif Basha thinks bitterly, even as he feels again that surge of affection he had felt when he had called on his father's old commander upon his return from exile at the end of September. A historic affection now, and suffused with sadness. It angers him that 'Urabi should now, at the end, have betrayed the Revolution – but it pains him to see the old man stand so markedly alone. He seeks out Wisa Basha and says a few words of congratulation, then makes for 'Urabi's corner. He is aware of heads turning as he greets the old man and yet, beyond enquiring after his health and that of his family, he finds himself with nothing to say and is relieved when Mustafa Basha Fahmi eventually strolls over. Well, both men are avowed friends of the British and can converse with each other freely. After a moment he leaves them together – the prime minister and the failed revolutionary – and turns away. Anna is upstairs with the women. He wonders if she is near the lattice, if she is even now watching him. But he does not, of course, raise his eyes to the haramlek.

'Sharif Pasha al-Baroudi?'

He turns. Milton Bey stands before him. Sharif Basha takes the extended hand briefly and steps back.

'I believe we have never been properly introduced,' Milton Bey says.

'I regret, Milton Bey, I speak no English,' Sharif Basha says in French.

'Ah! Quel dommage!' The physician gives him a shrewd look. 'My French is very poor. We have need of an interpreter.'

Sharif Basha bows slightly and when Milton Bey is accosted by Ibrahim Bey al-Hilbawi, he excuses himself and turns away. He has nothing against Milton Bey: a doctor who came to Egypt and opened a hospital and is doing good work by all accounts. He is even training some young Egyptians. But the man has never spoken to him before; why come up so publicly to greet him? Is it being said now, of him, that he is a friend of the British? Sharif Basha is frowning when Qasim Amin puts a hand on his shoulder.

'We are at a wedding, ya Basha,' he says.

Sharif Basha smiles. 'May we dance at yours,' he teases his friend.

'You know my opinions,' Qasim Amin says. 'But if I were lucky like some –'

'I shall pray for you.'

'I have been meaning to congratulate you.' Prince Muhammad Ibrahim joins them. 'You did a good job in the Council stopping that new tax. I was just talking to Mustafa Kamel about it.'

'The Council does what it can.' Sharif Basha shrugs. 'But our opinion, as you know, is not binding.'

'It was a nasty move, though,' Qasim Amin says.

'They will try again –'

'I wonder Cromer has the face to do it,' Prince Muhammad Ibrahim says. 'To try to tax local textile manufacture. Even thread! To beat down our industry to give an advantage to theirs?'

'Shameless,' Qasim Amin says.

'We stopped it in the Council, but let us hope the General Assembly does not pass it next year.'

'We shall have to talk to each one of them,' Prince Muhammad Ibrahim says. 'And Mustafa Kamel will keep the case alive in *al-Liwa*.'

'A carriage,' Sharif Basha says to the doorman.

'Your carriage is here, ya Basha. I'll get the driver –'

'No. I'm leaving that for the ladies. Just get me a carriage for hire.'

He has had enough. He cannot shake off his restlessness tonight. The letter from Muhammad 'Abdu giving him what he wanted, 'Urabi among the guests – If he were in Tawasi, or in the desert, he would gallop it off. If he were in Alexandria or by the Red Sea, he would go into the water. He is possessed by a sudden desire – almost a need – to go swimming. He imagines diving into the cold water, swimming, swimming against a strong current that would blank out his mind and leave him empty. But he is in Cairo, so he climbs into the waiting carriage.

'Touloun,' he says to the driver. There is no point in going to the Club; everybody is at the reception. He takes his watch out of his pocket: it will be at least another hour before Anna gets back. They drive past his sister's house in Hilmiyya and then his own shuttered house, the old horse trotting doggedly, his head held low. He gives the driver the name of the street.

'Near Beit el-Ingeliziyya?' the man asks. He is a rough, uncouth fellow, slouching on his box, flicking his whip by his horse's ears for no reason.

'What did you say?'

'Near the house of the Englishwoman?' the driver repeats.

'It is called the House of Baroudi, ya hayawan,' Sharif Basha says, 'not the House of the Englishwoman.'

'But there is an Englishwoman living there,' the man insists. 'It's well known: she fell in love with the Basha and married him. It's a known story.'

'And is something the matter with that?' Sharif Basha growls.

'Not at all. They say she is a good woman and does not go out except veiled even though the Basha did not make her become Muslim. But they say she's like the moon: what whiteness, what –'

'Let me off here!'

'And then it must be good for the Basha. They rule us in any case –'

And what good would it have done to whip him? Sharif Basha leaves his tarbush in the hall and wrenches off his cravat as he walks through the silent house. The man was only saying what everybody must be saying. First Milton Bey greets him like a friend, then a 'arbagi calls his house 'beit el-ingeliziyya' . . .

Hasna gets to her feet as he arrives at his apartment.

'Go to bed,' he says.

'But Setti —'

'I shall tell her. Go.'

She is a curiosity, he tells himself. If he had bought a giraffe, people would have called his house 'Beit el-Zarafa'. It has nothing to do with her being English.

In Anna's room her atmosphere washes over him, laps at his jagged edges. The large wardrobe he persuaded her to have built fits discreetly into one wall, the frames of its mirrored doors echoing the woodwork of the mashrabiyya. The flowers on the low inlaid table pick out the colours of the cushions heaped on the diwan. The mirror above the dressing table reflects the graceful loop of the mosquito net above the bed. Her silk dressing gown, a soft white with a hint of bluish grey, the colour of doves, is draped over the back of a chair. He has only to come in here, even in her absence, and her tranquil spirit gently breathes its way into his own. Her journal lies on her table. She had looked up from her writing when he came into the room and said, 'You can read English, can you not?' And he had to admit he could — 'a little,' he said. 'This has no lock,' she said, her hand on the big green book, 'I have no secrets from you.' 'No,' he said, 'no. I am content with what you tell me.'

He throws his jacket and waistcoat on a chair and goes back downstairs and into the library. Sometimes it seems to him it could vanish in a breath, this world she has made for him, right here alongside his own — but different. She had looked splendid tonight when she came down to say goodbye, shimmering in violet silk, her hair like a cluster of golden flowers on top of her head.

'All the ladies wear European dress to parties,' she had murmured, half apologising, as he looked at her.

'You look beautiful,' he had said, and bent to kiss the top of

369

her arm where the skin glowed between the violet of her dress and the soft black of her long glove.

Now he stands at his desk and surveys the papers spread out before him. The draft for the manifesto of the art school, the draft project for an Egyptian university, the draft for the bylaws of a workers' union, the text of the speech delivered by the Khedive to Wingate in Khartoum: '. . . it is a source of the greatest joy to me to see you here in this wide land . . . the British and the Egyptian flags fluttering side by side . . . ' A disgraceful speech, almost certainly written for him by the Agency. And who knows how 'Abbas Hilmi might have turned out in different circumstances? He had been willing to do good. They might have made a constitutional monarch of him. As it was, he had ascended the throne and each time he made a move Cromer threatened him with his guns. Now all his intelligence had curdled into cunning and all his energy was gone into plotting and making money, and the British could despise him as much as they wished and be right to do so.

Sharif Basha lights a cigarette and moves away from his desk. He sits down in an armchair, leans back and closes his eyes. He wonders what his father would make of 'Urabi's interview in *al-Muqattam*. It is just as well that he will not read it.

When he opens his eyes they meet the heavy wine-red curtains veiling the wooden doors that in spring will stand open once again to lead into the courtyard of his childhood. It has taken weeks to move all his things out of Hilmiyya. Now his books are arranged in the bookcases that line three walls of the library. His desk sits at an angle in the far corner. He had hesitated over moving into what used to be his father's favourite room, but his mother and his sister had both urged it and the old man had smiled and nodded and looked kindly when he went to ask his permission. The house in Hilmiyya is closed down and no one remains there but the gardener.

Anna had looked doubtful when the cushioned armchairs and the big rosewood desk had been carried in. 'I'm sorry,' he had said to her, 'I have lost the knack.' And she had blushed as he read her thoughts, then rallied and said, 'I suppose you can still be an authentic Egyptian and sit at a desk.' And when he thought about it he realised that even in Sheikha 'Aisha's kuttab in Tawasi he had never learned to sit comfortably cross-legged and work at a wooden floor-desk. But she had had the cushions covered in the plain, coarse kittan from his fields, and the new furniture had merged comfortably with the old room, where he sits and reflects on what it means to have inherited from his father like this while the old man is still alive.

He stubs out his cigarette and leaves the room. He goes out into the cold courtyard and crosses into the smaller one next to it. He pushes open the door of the shrine and Mirghani, who lies sleeping on a wooden pallet inside, sits up.

'There's nothing,' Sharif Basha says. 'Go to sleep.'

The big room is dark except for the candles that light up the simple tomb. Sharif Basha picks up a candle and, shading it with his free hand, he enters the inner room and stands looking down at his father. The old man lies on his back under some blankets, snoring gently, one thin foot uncovered and almost falling off the edge of the low, narrow bed. His mouth is slightly open and his head is bare. How long has it been since Sharif Basha has seen him without a turban? His pale scalp shows through the thin white hair. He is old. The day is not far off when it will fall to his son to close those eyes, to stop that mouth with cotton wool and wash the thin body and wrap it and carry it down into the family tomb. And how he had loved him! Sharif Basha squats down and holds the candle close to his father's face, trying to find again the laughing, handsome face he had adored as a child, as a young boy. When he brought home his reports, when he graduated from law school, each step he made, his first thought had been to make his father proud of him. And how proud *he* had been of his father in his army uniform. And prouder yet when he joined 'Urabi's movement with his older brother, Mahmoud Sami. Looking into the sleeping face, Sharif Basha al-Baroudi re-imagines once again the scene twenty years ago with his father and the other officers behind 'Urabi at 'Abdin, Auckland Colvin at the Khedive's side urging him to shoot, 'Urabi putting up his sword and Tewfiq hesitant but summoning up a weak-chinned anger:

'You are nothing but the slaves of our charity.'

And 'Urabi's reply, taken up by the whole country: 'We are owned by no one and shall not be enslaved beyond this day.'

He goes through the demands they had drawn up and the nation had learned by heart – had they been too much for men to ask? Could 'Urabi have known that demanding reform of the Khedive would bring the whole weight of the British Empire down on the country? Sharif Basha stands up. None of them were clever enough. A collection of army officers, poets and lawyers – even 'Urabi would sooner hold forth on Byron than discuss strategy. Patriots but not politicians. And they had paid a heavy price. He lays his hand gently on his father's balding head.

I wanted nothing more than to go home to him. But Layla and Zeinab Hanim thought it proper to stay until the suhur was served, and it would have been discourteous to leave without them. I had sensed the darkness of his mood when I went to bid him goodbye before I left the house, and when I looked down from the haramlek and saw him standing silent at the side of 'Urabi Basha my heart went out to him, for I know how that old gentleman troubles him.

I CAN SAY IN ALL truth that my brother and Anna found happiness and joy in their marriage. And Anna lived among us in gentleness and mercy. She brought companionship to my mother and love to my son and even some joy to the heart of my poor father. And for me, she became my close friend, for she had none of the arrogance or the coldness we were used to imagining in her countrymen, so that we almost forgot that she was English except that she would wonder at things and admire things that we were so accustomed to that we no longer saw them or thought about them, and the result of this was to make us look afresh at the things surrounding us and, seeing them through her eyes, find them fascinating once again.

It was enough to see her face light up when we heard the sounds that told us my brother was come home, or to catch the sudden tenderness that came into his eyes when he looked at her, to realise the depth of the love that had grown between those two strange hearts. And I remember once my brother came upon us while we were making music together: she at the piano he had bought her and I with the 'oud I had learned from Husni's mother. We were playing a piece by Debussy that we had modified to allow room for the 'oud and we did not hear him come in or realise he was there till we heard the sound of applause and when I turned I was almost sure I saw tears in his eyes, and the blood rose to Anna's face as it always did when she was taken by surprise and she went to him and he took her in his arms in front of me and said, 'By God, in my whole life I have not heard music sweeter than this.'

But she was not able to bring him peace of mind. It was as though he was angry that his happy private life should exist within public circumstances that he hated. Or as though he longed that his personal happiness should extend to encompass all of Egypt. We all felt his impatience and his desire for change grow more acute, and he worked constantly to bring about this change in all the spheres in which he was involved. And Anna started to help him, to translate for him from the British newspapers, and to use her connections in England to bring him what news she could that had a bearing on life here.

21 December 1901
Yesterday my husband invited a number of the most noted leaders of Egyptian public opinion to a Ramadan Iftar.

*Among the guests were Sheikh Muhammad 'Abdu, Mustafa
Bey Kamel, Qasim Bey Amin, Tal 'at Basha Harb, Ahmad
Lutfi al-Sayyid, Anton al-Jmayyil and a few others. His idea
— his hope — was that they might be able, through amicable
and private discussion, to agree upon positions that they could
publicly hold in common upon certain questions. On some
matters they were all agreed, and the first among these was the
ending of the Occupation and the payment of the foreign debt.
Beyond that they were agreed in general upon the need to
modernise Egypt. Surely they could agree on other, more
detailed questions?*

'You know what they are discussing?' Layla says, nodding
towards the curtains.

Anna shakes her head, glancing up for a moment from her
paper, the pencil still in her hand.

'They are discussing us,' Layla says, a small smile forming on
her lips as she bends her head again to her sewing.

'How? Discussing us?' Anna asks, intrigued.

'Here —' Layla leans over, riffles through the newspapers
and magazines lying untidily on the low table by the diwan
and comes up with a small book in a plain cover. She holds it
up. Anna puts down her sketch pad and rises from her
cushions to take it. She spells out the title as she sits down
next to Layla:

'*Al-Mar'ah al-Jadidah*, "The New Woman"?'

'Well done!' cries Layla, clapping her hands. 'See how well
she is learning, Mama?'

'She's quick, the name of the Prophet guard her.' Mabrouka has come in with the coffee tray. She puts it down on
the floor and sits cross-legged in front of it, her bracelets
jangling as she settles, adjusts, makes herself comfortable.
Zeinab Hanim smiles, her eyes on the ledger of household
accounts open in front of her.

'May God always open the paths for her.'

'So,' says Layla, branching off into a pedagogic side stream;
'what if, instead of having this —' changing two diacritics on

374

the cover of the book − 'we had this instead? What would it be?'

Anna gazes at the word. 'Mir' aah'?' she hazards.

'Right,' says Layla, 'and what does that mean?'

Anna shakes her head. Layla points at the large mirror on the left wall.

'Mirror?'

'Yes,' Layla nods.

'But why are the two words so close?' Anna asks. ' "Woman" and "mirror"?'

'Well, "mirror" must be from "ra'a": to see. But I don't know where "woman" comes in − oh, wait − mar' is "person" so mar'ah is the feminine. Can it be that mar' has to do with being visible?' She turns to her mother. 'What do you think, Mama? Mar' from being visible?'

'Is it just people who are visible, child? Animals and trees and all the created world is visible.'

'Perhaps it is only people who see themselves −'

'Some see with their eyes, some see with their hearts. The name of the Prophet preserve you and guard you.' Mabrouka presents a cup of coffee to Zeinab Hanim.

'We'll have to look it up,' says Layla. 'Or ask Abeih.'

'Do you think "mirror" came from "mir'ah"?' Anna says.

'I don't know,' Layla says. 'Who had mirrors first?'

'If it comes from a root in Arabic,' says Anna, 'it must have originated in the language.'

'*You*'ll have to look that one up,' says Layla.

'But what about this book?' Anna says. 'And why did you say they were talking about us?'

'The author −' Layla points at his name on the book − 'is down there, with Abeih. This is his second book. When the first came out there was such a fuss he was even banned from the Palace. He says women shouldn't have to wear the veil and girls should be educated just like boys − Isn't that so, Mama?' She says it again in Arabic.

'Not wear the veil? We live and we see!' Mabrouka exclaims.

'The veil is a Turkish thing, ya Mabrouka, not Arab or Egyptian. The women in the countryside, the fallaheen, do they go veiled?'

'They have their ways and we have ours. No respectable woman would go out of her house without the veil.'

'Anyway, he's not saying to abolish it. He's saying they shouldn't *have* to. They can choose —'

'And what does he do with his hareem? He lets them choose?'

'Sheikh Muhammad 'Abdu agrees with him.'

'The Mufti?'

'Yes. So will you know better than the Mufti?'

'By God, if they give me the wealth of Qaroon, I wouldn't go out with my face uncovered.'

'And who do you think is going to look at you?' Layla laughs.

'Even so. A woman is a woman. Isn't that so, ya Sett Zeinab?'

'Ya Mabrouka, has anyone asked you to unveil?'

'Even so. Are women going to walk in the street with their faces showing?'

'Ya Setti, it's their time. For you and me it's over, we can't change. Let the young people decide what they want.'

'All your life you've been too good —'

'Anyway —' Layla turns back to Anna — 'everybody's been talking about this, and the press is full of it. *Al-Liwa* is against the book: Mustafa Kamel is for education, but wants to keep the veil. Tal'at Harb wants everything to stay as it is. They're both down there now, and the author and Sheikh Muhammad 'Abdu. So of course they're talking about this.'

'Sheikh Muhammad 'Abdu is a great man,' Zeinab Hanim murmurs, her eyes on her ledger. 'May God preserve him for his country.'

Mabrouka murmurs 'Ameen' as she does for all her mistress's prayers large and small.

'What do women think?' Anna asks.

'They're divided too,' Layla says, 'as you see,' tilting her head at Mabrouka with a smile. 'Shall we go and listen?'

'We shouldn't, should we?' asks Anna.

'Of course we should. Mama, come with us, let's go and listen.'

'Leave the men alone, ya Sett Layla,' Mabrouka warns.

'Don't be afraid, I'll only look at my husband. Mama, come with us.'

Layla goes over and takes the pen from her mother's hand, lays it on the ledger and pulls her up. She turns to Mabrouka mischievously: 'Are you coming?'

'No, ya Setti, I'll stay here with Si Ahmad. He's man enough for me.'

'Get something and cover him,' Zeinab Hanim says, 'the boy will catch cold. I don't know why you won't just let him go to bed and you can have him in the morning,' she says to Layla, who is already holding aside the heavy partition curtains to let them pass.

And now they are in what feels to Anna like a box in the opera. Behind them, the dark curtains have fallen silently closed. In front of them the mashrabiyya that looks down into the salamlek. Layla puts a finger to her lips in warning, rests her knee on the narrow wooden bench that runs below the latticework, and carefully pulls open the thick glass panes. Immediately the sound of coffee cups rattling in their saucers comes to their ears. In the dark Anna and Zeinab Hanim move quietly forward to join Layla. The three women kneel on the cushioned bench, their faces pressed against the wooden screen.

The effect of being in one of these enclosures is most haunting. When I first went in it reminded me of nothing as much as the box in the opera I sat in with Madame Hussein Rushdi: the heavy velvet curtains closing behind us, the screen in front, the darkness, the anticipation of the action to take place there, beyond the screen, framed, on the lighted stage. But then the

*effect of kneeling on the banquette — its cushion harder than any I
have encountered here in Egypt — brought a certain awe into my
heart and I realised it was like being in church. And when I saw
Layla's face pressed against the wooden grille, illuminated in
patches by the light from the room below, why, my head was
filled with the notion that here was the perfect painting of a
beautiful woman at the confessional in some Italian church. In
the real confessional there would be no light, but the light in the
painting would be the light of His all-encompassing Forgiveness
and Grace.*

Sharif Basha has given his traditional place to his older friend
Sheikh Muhammad 'Abdu. The Grand Imam of Egypt sits
on the central diwan, his fierce eyes and brow rendered
mellow by the thick, carefully trimmed beard and moustache, now almost completely white except for a graceful V
under his lower lip. His gibba is of white striped silk and his
quftan of dark brown. On his head the white wound
turban. The other men are ranged on diwans and easy
chairs. Sheikh Rashid Rida is also in gibba and quftan; the
other men are all in suits.

'It is quite clear that Arabs form a natural unity,' Sheikh
Rashid Rida says. 'Here am I, a Syrian, and Anton Bey from
Lebanon, and we live and work here. Our ideas are the same.
Our aims are the same —'

'And we belong within the Ottoman Empire,' Mustafa
Kamel says. 'Without the Empire we are divided and weak.'

'The Empire itself is weak,' Qasim Amin says. 'It is dying.
Every time Europe makes a move, the Sultan backs off. If he
were strong, how is it that Britain is in Egypt?'

'And we should note the troubles in Palestine,' Anton al-
Jmayyil says. 'The Sultan is unable to stop the Zionist immigration.'

'These are a few people. Persecuted, oppressed —' Tal'at
Harb's steady, deep voice rises through the room — 'and the
Empire, since the fall of al-Andalus, has a tradition of wel-
coming the Jews.'

'I believe Anton Bey is right,' Sheikh Muhammad 'Abdu says gently.

Anna watches this man she has held in her affections since the day of her wedding.

'There is more trouble to come from this quarter,' he says. 'You see the news from their Fifth Congress? They request donations from the Jewish community all over the world.'

'This money will be used to buy land in Palestine,' Anton al-Jmayyil says.

The women, kneeling in the dark, remember Shukri al-'Asali: his impassioned talk, the letters he carried with him –

'We should learn from them,' Rashid Rida says. 'Even though we do not like what they are doing, we should learn from them. They have determination and they work together.'

'They too are divided.' Her husband speaks and Anna moves slightly to get a better view of him. 'Some of the younger ones have broken off and formed a new group, the Democratic Zionist Faction. And then there are the rabbis who are against Judaism becoming political and the wise men who say, "But there are Arabs living on the land" –'

'The rabbis and the wise men are a minority,' Anton al-Jmayyil says.

'And what is new in that?' Muhammad 'Abdu smiles.

'In any case,' Mustafa Kamel says impatiently, 'the Zionists are one of our concerns. There are others that are more immediate. The Capitulations, for example, and the special laws –'

Silently Mirghani clears the empty plates from in front of the men, replacing them with full ones. Silently he circles with the tray of hibiscus, tamarind and apple juice.

'Cromer himself is anxious to get rid of the Capitulations,' Husni Bey says. 'They undermine his authority –'

'I think we should leave the Capitulations to him,' Sharif Basha says. 'They detract from our sovereignty – but that is a theoretical matter. Without them his grip on the country is even tighter. The special laws are another matter –'

379

'You will never get rid of those, ya Basha,' Tal'at Harb says. 'As long as the British are in occupation, they will have special laws to protect themselves –'

'So much for Cromer's "equality of all men before the law",' Sharif Basha says.

'Industrialisation,' Tal'at Harb says, 'that should be our first concern now. That is the real battle against Cromer. Al-Minshawi Basha and others have started to put money into textile manufacture. The new taxation Cromer proposes will bankrupt them within a year.'

'We opposed it in the Council,' Sharif Basha says. 'Now we have to make sure the Assembly opposes it too.'

'This is all a waste of time,' Mustafa Kamel says impatiently. 'The Occupation itself is our problem. At every turn we come up against it. All our efforts should be concentrated on ending it. We should stand close to the Sublime Porte, anything that strengthens him strengthens us. We should appeal to France, and we should appeal to the United States; they have no interest in seeing Britain in Egypt and the principles of liberty and democracy are clearly set out in their constitutions.'

'We can do all these things,' Muhammad 'Abdu says. 'But meanwhile, we cannot allow our internal affairs to remain stagnant.'

Qasim Amin speaks: 'Take the Question of Women, for example,' he says.

Layla nudges Anna.

'The Question of Women, with all respect –' Tal'at Harb bows towards Qasim Amin – 'is a fabricated question. There is no Question of Women in our country.'

'With Tal'at Basha's permission,' Qasim Amin says, 'I believe there is a question and that we expose ourselves to grave danger in ignoring it.' And now Anna remembers: the Egyptian gentleman in the Salon of Princess Nazli. She wonders whether he has told her husband that he had met her. She thinks not; Sharif Basha has never mentioned it. 'We cannot claim to desire a Renaissance for Egypt,' Qasim Amin continues, 'while half her population live in the Middle Ages.

To take the simplest matters, how can children be brought up with the right outlook by ignorant mothers? How can a man find support and companionship with an ignorant wife?'

'I have nothing against girls being educated,' Mustafa Kamel says. 'But we should leave the veil alone.'

'I believe we can leave the veil alone,' Sharif Basha says and his sister makes a face. 'Women will decide for themselves about the veil. But if we can agree that girls should be educated –'

'Ya Sidi, educate the boys first. Are all boys getting an education?'

'No.' Ahmad Lufi al-Sayyid speaks for the first time. 'But if we are to have a general drive for education, if we are to have a law that makes education up to a certain age compulsory, then that should apply to girls as well as to boys. We must start in the right way.'

'And where will you end?' Tal'at Harb asks. 'By allowing them to work? Giving them the right to divorce? Changing the laws of inheritance?'

Anna sees her husband stand up and sees Muhammad 'Abdu lay a hand on his arm: 'Ya Sidi, no one is talking about changing the law. We are talking about teaching girls to read and write –'

They did not agree. Later that night my husband said to me, 'Yes, the laws should be changed. And if I had my way they would be changed tomorrow.'

He is happiest up in Tawasi, on his land. There, if he makes a decision it becomes a fact. And if he cannot do something, it is because Nature herself will not permit it. He finds it intolerable to submit to the will of other men. He is happy in Tawasi, and he was happy in Rome. It was as though there he was free, free to be himself, to be only himself. We were two anonymous travellers avoiding the places where the English congregate, going where the Italians go. We walked in the streets, went into the churches, ate in out-of-the-way restaurants. The smallest things delighted us. The novelty of arranging to meet in a hidden piazza, of my taking his arm as we walked along the street, of sitting side by side in the theatre – these were all new adventures for us and he was light and playful and happy. But I believe that even without the consideration of his family he would find it impossible to live abroad. He would be a man without a purpose; for his purpose, his vocation, is Egypt.

Cairo
30 December 1901

Dear Sir Charles,
I have received yours of the 1st in which you tell me of Mr Barrington's appointment on the Tribune. I am most glad of that for he has a thorough knowledge of affairs here and he combines sympathy with a quick mind and an ability with words and his appointment can only lead to good. I am sure he is most sensible of your kindness and will prove worthy of it. I trust it may contribute to your good opinion if I inform you that he was most anxious to secure good positions for his servants before he left and has placed them with British residents – for Egyptian households will not readily take a servant who has been employed by foreigners.

I fear this year has not brought about any changes to your liking in the way the world is run and I do not have much hope that the coming year will do better. Mrs Butcher tells me that Mr Blunt, on hearing that Rosebery has offered himself for Prime Minister, said, 'Salisbury is bad enough, but Rosebery would merely mean Government by the Stock Exchange.' A sentiment with which I imagine you would heartily concur.

Mr Blunt has been much in the news here these past months. Some officers gave chase to a fox over his land and his men gave chase to the officers. These last would not leave and a fight ensued; the Egyptians were arrested, tried by the Special Court and given jail sentences for assaulting British officers. Mr Blunt, it would appear, intends to use this event to bring about a change in the law, a change that would be much favoured here, as this business of hunting across cultivated land – for every inch of land that is not desert here is cultivated — does much damage and is a cause of constant grievance to both fellaheen and landowners.

You ask if I have seen the new Lady Cromer and the answer is I have not, for I have no longer any commerce with the Agency; indeed, of all the residents I only see Mrs Butcher, who has been kindness itself and continues to call on me and I on her.

I have, I confess, been missing our English Christmas. Perhaps more so this year than last. Although Sharif Basha surprised me with a handsome gift, an Ethiopian cross set with rubies, yet it seemed odd to me that the twenty-fourth and twenty-fifth of December should on the whole be passed like any other day — and especially so this year as Christmas falls in the month of Ramadan. Of course the Coptic Christmas here is celebrated on the sixth of January. But even that will not have the music I am used to and love so much. I played some carols on the piano my husband bought for me lately, but it was not quite the same thing — indeed, I think it made me miss the carols at St Martin's a little more. Last year we had some quite outstanding music, largely due to Mr Temple Gairdner. But I hear now that he has started his work of conversion in earnest and is preaching to the Nile boatmen in Bulaq, and I fear much mischief will come of this.

I have begun to have some understanding of the complexity of things here and of the difficulty of my husband's situation — the difficulties for all those who think as he does and the delicate balance they must be constantly at pains to maintain.

The British presence here has had the sad effect of dividing the national movement, which was united, under 'Urabi Pasha in 1881, in its desire to embark on the path of democracy and modernisation. The reasons for our intervention at that time I have heard you speak of often, and always with distaste. Had we not intervened, the conflict between the people and the Khedive would have been resolved in some manner private to them. Egypt's ties to Turkey had been considerably loosened over the previous hundred years and it is likely that the Khedive alone would not have been able to stand in the face of the will of the people.

Now, although all are united in their desire to get rid of the British, some believe it can be done now, while others believe it can only be done gradually through a strengthening of the national institutions.

And there are other divisions: people who would have tolerated the establishment of secular education, or the gradual disappearance of the veil, now fight these developments because they feel a need to hold on to their traditional values in the face of the Occupation. While the people who continue to support these changes have constantly to fight the suspicion that they are somehow in league with the British.

And the relationship of Egypt to Turkey is another point. There are those who believe that to counteract British influence, Egypt should ally herself ever more closely to the Moslem Sultan in Istanbul. Others argue that the Turkish Empire is in decline. They point to the Sultan's apparent inability to protect his territories from European incursion and argue that a young and vigorous Arab Caliphate should be established in Hijaz, and Egypt should ally herself with that. And there are others yet who feel that Egypt should stand by her history and stand alone, a secular state, embracing its Moslem and Christian citizens alike. And so the very thing that should make Egypt strong — the richness and diversity of her culture — serves to divide her and make her weak. My husband believes that had it not been for the British, the Sultan in Istanbul would have gradually become an irrelevance and Egypt would have found her feet alone, while the natural bonds of history and language linked her closely to the other Arab nations.

And so our presence — at best hampering, at worst oppressive — makes itself felt at every turn and renders the accusation 'Traitor!' ever ready to be thrown at someone who does not think as you do on the smallest question . . .

Cairo
30 December 1901

Dear James,
I have just heard the good news from Sir Charles that you have been appointed to the Tribune. I am very glad for you and I hope

384

you will be happy in London. It is odd to think that we can continue to be friends now better than we could have, were you still living in Cairo.

I shall ask my husband where best you may write to me and I will let you know.

I can hardly give you any news, for of our friends I only see Mrs Butcher, as she is kind enough to continue to call on me from time to time. Apart from her and Madame Hussein Rushdi, my friends now are all from among the Egyptians. I am quite taken up with my family and am happier in my marriage than I would have thought possible. Sharif Basha is loving and considerate and Layla is the sweetest of sisters. Ahmad, her son, is the most adorable child. I am grown great friends with my belle-mère and we demonstrate our recipes to each other in the kitchen. And I am grown fond too of old Baroudi Bey, who sits silently in his shrine all day long but will look up and help me with an Arabic word when I am in need.

I still paint and sketch but my new passion is weaving. My husband has bought a middling-size loom for me and — after I had asked him whether he meant to absent himself for twenty years — I have quite taken to it. I find that when I work at it I am still a part of everything that surrounds me. It is not like reading or writing, when you are necessarily cut off from everything so that you may not hear when you are spoken to — indeed you may look up and be surprised to find yourself where you are, so transported were you by what is on the page. When I work at the loom I am still part of things and it seems as if the sounds and the smells and the people coming and going all somehow get into the weave. I can see you thinking 'Ah! Anna is getting metaphysical', but I am really most practical, for when I work at it I can still join in with Ahmad's chatter. When I paint I am always afraid of smudges and one has to get to a certain point or the light will change or the colours go dry. And then there is the pleasure of using the object you make — oh, I forget myself and preach. Preach weaving, now that's a comical notion. But truly, I believe that my sitting at the loom in his courtyard has brought some pleasure to old Baroudi Bey —

17 December 1901

Sharif Basha straightens the covers over his father. He gently moves the old man's foot in from the edge of the bed and covers it with the blanket. Then he leaves the room.

It was here, outside the shrine, that he had first come upon his father and Anna at their lessons: the fair head and the turbaned one bent over the book, his father's finger, trembling slightly, pointing to something on the page, Anna looking up, her violet eyes smiling into the old man's face. Anna. He walks back to the house. Her contentment delights him. If she is content. He watches out for signs of restlessness. It would not surprise him – God knows he would be restless in her position. He keeps her supplied with paints and paper, with every sheet of music he can find. When she exclaimed over a tapestry, he had a loom sent round and a woman to teach her how to use it. She set up the loom in the courtyard by his father's door and there she would sit, working slowly as she learned this new art while the old man watched the balls of brilliant silk twitch and roll in the sunshine. 'God has compensated you well for your patience,' his mother said, and his heart was warm as he watched this strange wife of his busy herself around the old house as though this was where she had always wanted to spend her days. And his heart was full when she came to him in his bed as though this was how she had always wanted to spend her nights.

'I told Hasna to go to bed. You have no need of her tonight.' He fumbles as he unclasps, unhooks, unties. He loses patience before it is all done and, crushing the silk, the lace, the yielding body beneath him, he groans into her neck, 'Oh, Anna, Anna! You have no idea how much I love you.'

1 January 1902
'Hubb' is love, "'ishq' is love that entwines two people together, 'shaghaf' is love that nests in the chambers of the heart, 'hayam' is love that wanders the earth, 'teeh' is love in which you lose yourself, 'walah' is love that carries sorrow within it, 'sababah' is

love that exudes from your pores, 'hawa' is love that shares its name with 'air' and with 'falling', 'gharam' is love that is willing to pay the price.

I have learned so much this past year, I could not list all the things I have learned.

24

That moment when we dreamed we could change the face of our world was a luxury which later generations were denied. But for that short, dazzling moment we paid a heavy price.

Arwa Salih, 1997

15 September 1997

Three Palestinian suicide bombers killed seven people in West Jerusalem. An Israeli army unit tried to land in Ansariyyeh in southern Lebanon and was fought off by the people and an Amal unit killing eleven Israeli troops. 'Arafat and Hussein arrived in Cairo for a summit meeting with Mubarak. An Israeli soldier shot randomly at thirty Palestinians in a bus in Hebron. One hundred and seventy Palestinians were arrested on the West Bank. The Palestinian Authority also arrested thirty-five members of Hamas and Israel arrested sixty-seven other Palestinians. In Algeria forty-nine were killed and sixty wounded in the Beni Sous district in the capital, sixty-four were killed in Beni Musa and one hundred and thirty-seven alleged terrorists were killed in Jibal al-Shari'ah. One hundred and thirty Algerians who had fled their country were killed when their ship collided with another off the coast of Nigeria. The United Nations had to borrow from its peacekeeping budget to pay its staff and Princess Diana died and five million joined her funeral. Mother Teresa died. Mobutu died. Austria agreed to compensate victims of the Nazis for their stolen gold. These were some of the things that happened during the two weeks that my brother stayed with me. I know because he could not last for two hours without reading a paper or switching on some radio or TV news channel.

He got restless with the beach and we went back to Cairo, where each morning he took seven Arabic papers and last thing at night we went down to Midan Tal'at Harb so he could get the English and French ones. He bought me a PC and had me connected up to the Net. I told him that I had made contact with Tareq 'Atiyya and that he was going to help with the school on Tawasi. I did not tell him about Tareq's plans for his land and I did not arrange for the two men to meet.

Isabel called and said she was staying in New York for a while as she had to sort out all the legal matters relating to her parents. 'I'm clogging up a room for you,' she says.

'It's your room,' I say.

'You can move my things if you like,' she says.

'It's your room,' I say again. 'Everything will stay as you left it.'

I know she was waiting for him to go back. When he speaks to her I can hear his voice shift into a deeper and more resonant pitch: the pitch of sexual tenderness. But he is unwilling to commit himself. He goes on about being fifty-five.

'You look wonderful,' I say, 'you act thirty.'

'But I'm not,' he says. 'And I am tired of explaining. If I am to be with a woman she has to be someone who knows it all. Someone who doesn't need to be told.'

'Knows all what?' I ask, although I know what he means. 'Everything.'

'What? Egypt, Palestine, America, your kids, your music, the past, the future? Come on –'

'She doesn't have to know the future.' He grins.

He planned concerts in Ghazzah and Jericho and Qana. They were to be free so he had his manager working to find sponsors. I said he should have one in the Sa'id – and come to Tawasi. In the odd times when he went out alone, I worked on my Anna story. I would not show him my manuscript, but I showed him Anna's journals, her letters, her candle-glass, her white shawl. I showed him the great green flag with the Cross and the Crescent and we unrolled, once again, the length of tapestry that I had found so carefully wrapped in a corner of the trunk; the tapestry that matched his.

'I'm sorry,' he said again, 'I'll bring it next time.'

We clipped the panel to a couple of hangers and hooked it on a high bookshelf: Osiris, seated. You would know him anywhere by his dark face, his shrouded body, the hands crossed over his chest carrying the sceptre and the flail. Above his tall crown, painstakingly woven in curling Diwani script, every diacritic meticulously in place, the single Arabic word 'al–mayyit'.

10 May 1905
My husband lies sleeping and I am so restless with the baby that I cannot sleep. For weeks now I have been unable to lie down but must needs sleep propped up on cushions like an invalid. It is a small enough price to pay for the happiness this unborn child has already brought us but that I am tired and listless for lack of sleep and everyone is constantly telling me that I must build up my strength for the birth.

I am afraid of the birth. I cannot pretend otherwise. My husband has tried repeatedly to persuade me to engage the services of a British physician and he has even – once only, and that in the early days – suggested that I might like to go 'home' to be confined among 'my people'. I have refused both offers and said I could not feel safer or better cared for than I am here in this house. I am determined that I will not countenance any arrangement that might hinder his joy in the occasion. He has much need of joy now for the Entente has cast its shadow widely over Egypt and, though he continues to strive and work for her good, there is that heaviness in the air which betokens the ebbing away of hope.

TOWARDS THE END OF 1904 Anna fell pregnant. My mother surrounded her with tenderness and as for my brother, if Anna had asked for bird's milk he would have brought it to her. We had particular reason to be grateful to her for bringing this new happiness into our lives at this time. For in April of that year, and after Madame Juliette Adams had toured Egypt, hosted and fêted by all the Nationalist Notables and even banqueted by Efendeena,

France and Britain declared the Entente Cordiale, giving France a free hand against Morocco in exchange for letting Britain do what she would in Egypt. For seven months we campaigned and made representations. They came to nothing and the Entente was declared ratified. Then 'Abbas Hilmi broke our hearts by standing with Cromer under the British flag in the court of 'Abdin Palace and surveying the Army of Occupation on the occasion of King Edward's Birthday.

Cairo
12 May 1905

Dear James,
I have received yours of 10 March with the picture of your new house in Chelsea. It looks delightful and if we ever come to England you may be certain of a visit. I am sure your mama is most happy to have you near her.

We are expecting our baby in early June and there is a great fuss being made of me. I am not permitted to make or buy anything for the baby, however, until it is born, as that would bring bad luck. The rules and edicts concerning Fate and the Stars and what acts bring Good Fortune and what bring Bad are laid down by Mabrouka, an old Ethiopian serving-woman who is my belle-mère's childhood companion. Even Sharif Basha more or less heeds her, for she was his nanny when he was a child.

Ahmad is now five years old and is a very handsome little boy. I believe he has a musical gift for he happily spends much time with me at the piano and can already play tolerably well. We have told him I am growing a little cousin for him and he daily enquires how the baby is doing and whether some bit of it has not appeared that he might see it.

Our household is a happy one, although the waves created by the Entente Cordiale are felt everywhere and no one knows where they will end. The Khedive, for one, has abandoned all hope of being a true Ruler and now gives free rein to his cupidity. He tried to engineer a land deal of advantage to himself in Mushtuhur, but Sheikh Muhammad Abdu – as being responsible for Awqaf – put a stop to it. Since then the Palace and its newspapers have mounted a virulent attack on the sheikh and – since Lord Cromer supported Muhammad Abdu in this matter – the attack takes the form of publishing scandalous (and counterfeit) pictures of Muhammad Abdu drinking and consorting with foreign women. It has had the effect of provoking his resignation from the Board of al-Azhar and indeed has made him so ill that it is a cause of grave concern to us all.

I have heard that there is talk in London that Cromer is negotiating with Eldon Gorst that he hand over Egypt to him, on condition that Gorst hands it to Cromer's son Errington in later years. You would think he was the Monarch here. And indeed it seems that he imagines himself so now – although I suppose we have to thank him for putting an end to the al-Arish project in Sinai. But he has lately been touring the Provinces in a kind of Triumphal Progress which sits most ill with people of patriotic feeling.

I had not heard of the al-'Arish project. Once again I enlisted the help of my son in London, and his research yielded the following story. In 1902, Herzl, in his search for a homeland, hit upon Cyprus and al-'Arish as possibilities. He won the support of Lord Rothschild by describing how the new community of settlers would guard the Suez Canal, sabotage the German–Turkish autobahn project and generally keep an eye on Turkey to the advantage of Britain. With Rothschild's support he approached Joseph Chamberlain, the colonial secretary. Chamberlain said he could not give him Cyprus but set up an appointment with the foreign secretary, Lord Lansdowne, to discuss al-'Arish. Lansdowne duly sent a Mr Greenberg, his friend and confidential agent, to speak to Cromer. Cromer commissioned a feasibility study, but eventually decided that the amount of water needed for the agricultural settlements Herzl wanted could not be spared from the Nile – and the laying-down of pipes would interfere with the Canal for several weeks. And so it was that one evil diverted another.

There is nothing for us to do, however, but continue with the works we are engaged in. I work on L'Egyptienne with the other ladies. We have set up a fund to start a hospital. My husband and his uncle have established a school in Tawasi and we have high hopes of the School of Art, and Mustafa Basha Kamel has already started campaigning for a national University. My husband, having resigned from the Legislative Council in protest at their approving the latest Budget without a murmur (indeed, they thanked the Government for the efforts of all the ministries – another effect of the Entente), is working more with Mustafa Kamel now and together with Ya'qub Artin Basha, Hussein Rushdi Basha and some other Notables they have started a campaign for a Graduate Club as a paving of the way for the University.

It is a shame that you have never seen the new Museum, it houses objects of such amazing beauty that alone it would make a visit to Egypt worthwhile. I remember when I first came to Egypt how you spoke to me of the ancient monuments and your regret that the most choice among them had found their way to Europe. I have since found out that your feelings, not surprisingly, are shared by many educated Egyptians, who see in the trade their past being stolen as surely as their present is. It is a source of some sad satisfaction that the French have insisted on the Entente stating that they retain control of the Department of Antiquities, for today the British and the Americans are the gravest threat to the monuments.

Dear James; I have some news that I think will make you happy. I did not tell you of this before, but when you were leaving and were so anxious to secure positions for your staff before your departure, I – knowing of your regard for Sabir and also sensible myself of an affection for him due to his loyalty on that occasion which was to have such far-reaching consequences for me – I asked my husband whether we might not take him on. He refused and I did not press the point, particularly as you then succeeded in placing him in an English household. However, it appears that he was unhappy there. He moved to another, with no better results. A short while ago he presented himself at my husband's offices, and Sharif Basha consented to see him. He has since then entered my husband's employ — in the offices, not in the house — where he is being taught to read and write and some use is being made of his knowledge of English, and it seems everyone is well pleased with the arrangement. My husband commends his intelligence and zeal, and Sabir is happy, for I took occasion, when he once delivered some papers to the house, to go down and see him and he told me so himself. He ended with his hand on his heart and the wonderful phrase: 'Ya Sett Hanim, my neck is for you and the Basha.' And I do believe he means it.

I send you two books: the collection of poems compiled by the late Mahmoud Sami Basha, God rest his soul. And the book which everyone here is reading: Muhammad al-Muweilhi's Hadith 'Isa ibn Hisham. *I hope you enjoy them. At the least they will serve to polish up your Arabic —*

WHEN LORD CROMER TOURED THE provinces in triumph in January of 1905, one month after the death of my uncle Mahmoud Sami Basha, it seemed that our cup of bitterness was full to the brim. Many Notables, seeing that there was no present hope of getting rid of the British, vied to host Cromer on his progress through Egypt. And there were those who came to my brother to advise him to abandon a stance that was sentenced to failure, and to say that were he to be in Minya at the appropriate moment so that the Lord might drink tea in his house, it would be well for him and would be counted in the balance for him against his history, his known views and his marriage. My brother remained in Cairo and Mustapha Bey el-Ghamrawi also removed to Cairo for the duration of the Lord's Progress. And so it was that Tawasi remained unvisited, as did the lands of al-Minshawi Basha and other of the more steadfast Notables.

Al-Minshawi Basha had personal reasons, besides the public ones, that precluded his offering hospitality to Cromer; for it was the Lord's policy of combating any nascent national industry that led directly to the bankruptcy of the Basha's textile factory. Other friends, who had invested in the tobacco and sugar industries, were in similar difficulties, but we were fortunate in that our material fortunes could not be touched by the Occupation and our household was – within the confines of our domestic life – a happy one. Our one concern, in those months, was for Anna and although she made it clear that she lacked no reason for happiness, our sensibilities constantly urged us to compensate her for the absence of a mother or a sister who would naturally have been with her at this time.

21 May 1905
The midwife comes to see me often now, and every time Zeinab Hanim or Layla or my husband set eyes upon me it is 'let us walk around the garden' or 'let us go sit on the roof', so that I have never walked so much nor climbed so many stairs in my life as I do now. Zeinab Hanim shows me exercises that are reputed to ease the birth, Hasna rubs me all over with sweet-smelling oil each day and Mabrouka is scarcely to be seen but she is murmuring incantations and swinging her incense-burner. One of the guestrooms has been prepared as a birthing chamber and the huge birthing chair – which shares certain features with a commode – has been carried into it. There is a bed there too and it will be there that I sleep after my confinement until I may rejoin my husband after forty days.

He looks at me as though unsure what I am making of all this. He tries to ascertain how strange it is to me and whether there is anything that might be done to make it more familiar and more comforting. But in truth it is so strange – strange to such an extreme degree – that it does not matter any more. For my condition itself is strange and wonderful to me. And as I have had no experience of childbirth – either my own or anyone else's – I am content to let Zeinab Hanim and Layla take charge and count myself in good hands.

It is as well that this impending baby keeps us happily busy, for so many things have converged upon us in the last few weeks. Our friend Sheikh Muhammad Abdu grows more ill and there is talk that he should go abroad for treatment. The students from the School of Engineering have gone on strike and are marching about the streets in their military uniforms, and we fear it will not be too long before a confrontation takes place between them and the Army. We have just had word that Shukri Bey and other Notables in Jaffa, Nazareth and Jerusalem have been put under house arrest by the authorities for possession of Naguib Azoury's pamphlet Les Pays arabes aux Arabes. And through it all we hold on to our love and the expectation of the child. At times it seems to me that my baby is being placed in the balance against all the ills of the world. But so far the magic has not failed and my husband smiles to see me grown so big and makes great play of no longer being able to get his arms around me –

Cairo
3 June 1905

My dear Sir Charles,
I am awaiting my confinement daily and although I am in excellent health and spirits and am marvellously well looked after, I have such a sense of imminence that you must forgive me if I show somewhat less reserve than is generally considered proper and write to you today of what is in my heart.

My happiness here is such that every day I am grateful to be alive. And yet, I am greedy. For of all that I have had to leave behind, the loss I am not reconciled with is yours. We cannot come to visit you – will you not come to visit us?

Dear Sir Charles, you were a dear and loving father to me for so many years and you were also my guide in ways which perhaps at the time we were neither of us aware of. Whatever ideas I have of Truth or Justice I first learned from you. Not by direct teaching but from observing the positions you adopted on matters both private and public. My interest in Egypt was first awakened by you and, indeed, I still have the white shawl and the silver-cased coffee cup you brought back in '82.

The Entente has been a heavy blow indeed. Many of the Nationalists had counted France as their ally against the British Occupation. And although my husband has never been one of those who put their trust in France, he sees this new Entente as heralding an age where Britain can do what she will in Egypt with no thought for the opinion of the world.

Now there is nowhere to turn but to British Public Opinion. I have been thinking of Ireland and of how whatever progress the Irish Question was vouchsafed, it only came about because there were people in England prepared to state Ireland's case. It was their good fortune that they were able to state it in English and that there were those among our rulers whom they could count as their friends. This is not how things stand for Egypt, for — besides yourself and Mr Blunt — there is no one to state Egypt's case. (I had, I confess, expected Mr Rennel Rodd to do something.) However, I have come to believe that the fact that it falls to Englishmen to speak for Egypt is in itself perceived as a weakness; for how can the Egyptians govern themselves, people ask, when they cannot even speak for themselves? They cannot speak because there is no platform for them to speak from and because of the difficulties with language. By that I mean not just the ability to translate Arabic speech into English but to speak as the English themselves would speak, for only then will the justice of what they say — divested of its disguising cloak of foreign idiom — be truly apparent to those who hear it.

Well, what if there were someone, an Egyptian, who could address British public opinion in a way that it would understand? Someone who could use the right phrases, employ the apt image or quotation, strike the right note and so reach the hearts and minds of the British people? And what if a platform were secured for such a person? Is it not worth a try?

I know that the case of Ireland is different from that of Egypt. But there are aspects of that difference which are in Egypt's favour;

for surely the interests of Britain in Egypt are not yet so entangled
that they might not be gently pulled apart without harm? There are
no British settlers who have lived for years upon the land. The
number of British officials here – although certainly too large in the
view of the Egyptians – is not so large that their dislodging would
constitute a serious problem. It is merely a matter of removing the
Army of Occupation. And no Egyptian whom I know is not in
favour of economic reform or of paying off Egypt's debts. Indeed
they would be more willing to be guided by Britain in economic and
financial matters if the guidance were that of an elected Friend
rather than an imposed Guardian.

Dear Sir Charles, will you help me?

Oh, if you could see the fields, tall with sugar cane, or purple
and blue with the flower of the kittan. If you could see the
children, making kangaroo-pockets of their galabiyyas to gather
in them the new-plucked cotton. If you could see the ancient
willow trees trailing their hair in the running canals and see
Nestorian monks heading back to their monastery while the call
of the muezzin unfurls its banner in the reddening sky! This is a
land where God is unceasingly manifest.

Forgive me. I ramble and am grown overwrought. Our
beloved friend Sheikh Muhammad Abdu is gravely ill and
we fear for him. Come and visit us when I am safely delivered,
for I long to place my child in your arms –

ANNA WAS DELIVERED SAFELY OF her baby and we
named the child Nur al-Hayah, for she did truly bring
light into all our lives.

When my brother's most beloved friend, Sheikh Muhammad 'Abdu, died three weeks after the birth, Nur al-
Hayah was the one most able to give her father solace. He
carried the baby in his arms, he walked her up and down
when she cried, he attended her bath and wrapped her
tenderly in her soft white towels. From the day she was
born, Nur al-Hayah was beautiful. She had her mother's
fair colouring and her violet eyes, and she had my brother's dark hair. He would sit and gaze into her face and

bend to kiss the tiny foot. And although Mabrouka did her duty and secretly placed the baby's first nail clippings into Abeih's waistcoat pocket to ensure his constant love, it was clear that he had lost his heart to her without the aid of magic. In fact, my father, Husni and Ahmad all fell in love with little Nur immediately, and when I think of her now I see a smiling infant, surrounded on all sides by our love and attention.

October 1905
I am content. If I look at myself with my old eyes, I see an indolent woman. A woman content to lie on a cushion in the garden, in this miraculous October sunshine, watching the stillness of the sleeping fruit trees and the changes of the light. Each thing that happens — and there are things that happen; small things — adds to my contentment, until I would say, as they do here, May God bring this to a good end. I hear Ahmad's laugh ring out from somewhere in the house. My baby stirs on the cushion beside me. I slip a finger into her curled hand and I cannot resist kissing the corner of her mouth. Nur al-Hayah, light of our lives. I think of her father and feel that melting of my limbs as I sense again his breath, his smell, the warmth of his hand gentle on me. I think of his kisses, and how he would pause, his hand on my face, to look into my eyes. His eyes are intent and a small smile touches his lips. I stir and as the pause lengthens I murmur, 'Please.'

'Please what?' he whispers.

'Kiss me.'

'Why?'

I try to raise my head, to reach his lips, but his hand is in my hair and he holds my head back. His mouth is just out of my reach but I feel our breaths mingle.

Cairo
15 November 1905

My dear Caroline,
Has it really been so long since our last exchange? I know it has. And that knowledge was borne most powerfully upon me by the

joy with which I recognised your writing on the letter I received today. I do most happily accept your congratulations on the birth of Nur and your wishes for us both. Had circumstances been different, I would have wished you to be her Godmother – might you not consider yourself so, after a fashion?

You do not tell me much about yourself or the children – five years older now than when last I saw them. I know from Sir Charles that all is well with you, but I would be glad of some proper news.

Nur is the most adorable baby and inspires the most tender affection in everyone around her. For myself I am in love with everything of her down to her tiny pink toes. This will not surprise you, with your experience, but I had not thought motherhood would be so wonderful.

She is smiling now, and I fancy her babbling is the start of words. Sharif Basha says I should speak to her in English. I believe he fears I miss my own tongue for – as I think I wrote you a long time ago – all our conversations here are conducted in French, although my Arabic is now quite usable.

It is true, though, that I use English only for writing and – sometimes – singing. It would be such a pleasure for me to use it in speech to you, my dear friend . . .

Cairo
20 November 1905

Dear James,
Thank you so much for the Tatler. I have been studying the evening gowns with Eugénie, with the result that we shall be visiting Madame Marthe, I think, quite soon! I wear Egyptian dress most of the time now but in the evening, for receptions and soirées, one is obliged to dress in the latest European fashion and I have had nothing made since I grew big with Nur.

Mrs Butcher arrived this afternoon just as Madame Rushdi was leaving and we had a very pleasant time together. She was quite unable to let go of the baby, dandling and petting her all the while. She told me a most amusing story about our old friend Mr Gairdner who, after much trouble, succeeded – as he thought – in the conversion of one boatman. He took the man in and gave him a room and prayed with him constantly, but after three days the man's wife came looking for him and it transpired that the conversion had taken place under the effect of a matrimonial quarrel! Reconciled to his wife, the boatman apologised to Mr Gairdner, thanked him and took his leave, returning home with his wife. Mrs Butcher says Mr Gairdner was quite cast down but has since recovered his normal exuberance and is determined to redouble his efforts in the service of the Church.

My husband urges me to celebrate Christmas in church this year, but I do not believe I shall. Even though Mrs Butcher – I think – would be kind enough to have me sit with her, it would be too uncomfortable. Can you not just see the heads bending towards each other, the ostentatious shifting of skirts and then the staring straight ahead? I would find it impossible to attend to the service or enjoy the singing. It would be more an act of defiance than worship and it seems wrong to taint Christmas in such a manner. I have made a Christmas cake, though, even if without brandy, and we shall have a little tree for Nur.

I have grown quite proficient with the loom and have started on a most wonderful work – at least I hope it will be wonderful when it is finished. It is to be a tapestry six foot wide by eight foot long, made up of three panels, for my loom can only accommodate a width of two feet. I shall use nothing but what the Ancients themselves might have used in the way of flax or silk or dye, and it shall be my contribution to the Egyptian renaissance, for it shall depict the Goddess Isis, with her brother consort the God Osiris and between them the Infant Horus, and above them a Quranic verse – my husband will choose an appropriate one for me in time. I have already prepared a sketch of it and for the colours I will use the deep turquoises, gold and terracotta of the Ancient Egyptians and the deep green that I have never seen anywhere except in Egypt's fields.

Nur al-Hayah lies in her basket and watches me as I work. Ahmad chases the balls of silk, and Baroudi Bey – as a change from his rosary – twines and untwines the silken thread around his fingers. I wish you could see them. I have asked Sir Charles, *but I fear his back now gives him so much trouble that he cannot travel —*

January 1906
'I will plant some trees for her — here,' my husband said. 'As soon as the season is right.' He did not turn as I approached, but drew me to his side and continued with his thoughts aloud. 'Here,' he said, 'I will make a garden for her, with shade, and a fountain where she can play when the world gets hot.'

Even when I sleep, I dream of him and of Nur al-Hayah.

25

The want of gratitude displayed by a nation to its alien
benefactors is almost as old as history itself.

Lord Cromer, 1908

Cairo, 18 September 1997

As for me, my dreams have become a confusion of times and places. I am lying in the courtyard of the old Baroudi house – 'Beit el-Ingeliziyya' as the driver called it – with Nur sitting by my head tugging at my necklace when I think to look in on my sleeping children. With Nur on my hip I go into the house and upstairs to the boys' room in our house in England and there they lie: the older one splayed out like a starfish, open to the world, the younger curved and tensed gracefully, like a diver in mid-air.

And often, while I sleep, I find myself in a house I have never seen while awake. In the dream I know that I have dreamed of this place often and in the dream I am flooded with relief at having – at last – found it. It is exactly as I dreamed it would be: it has a light, open courtyard surrounded by delicate cloisters with graceful pillars of faded pink and in the middle there is a pool. It has an air of comfortable decay: the plaster is peeling a little from the walls and the garden is overgrown. I walk around. I plan how I will restore it, I note the crumbling capitals of the columns, the missing fragments of mosaic in the floor around the pool, the sagging cane chairs with their faded cushions. I love this place. I know that my mother is in her room somewhere inside, happy, not homesick any more. I shall go in to her soon, when I have collected Nur. I stand by the side of the pool, towels over my arms, calling to the child to come out. And we are expecting others too. I know my sons will love this house. I can see my brother's delighted recognition when he sees it. When I wake and try to capture its image in my mind, what I see are the frescoes of Pompeii.

My brother is gone and Isabel is not coming back for a while. Most people I know are still out of Cairo for the summer. I pack my PC, my manuscript, Anna's remaining papers and my grandmother's, and Madani carries them down to the car. I take Anna's woven Osiris off his hanger, roll him up carefully and replace him in his length of muslin. I ask Tahiyya to come up to the flat every three days to water the plants and phone me in Tawasi. I decide, before I set out on the road, to go to the museum. Now that I know what the two tapestries are, I want to go and wander around there for a while. Maybe I will find the paintings that Anna used as her references. But in her letter to James she mentions three panels. Where, I wonder, is the third?

I cross Qasr el-Nil Bridge and turn right and pull in by the Mugama' building. As the parking attendant comes up, I say, 'If I leave my keys, will you try and find a bit of shade for me?' If Mansur were alive I'd have left the car with him.

'How long will you be?' the man asks.

'A couple of hours,' I say. 'I'm just going to the museum.'

'There's no museum,' he says, 'the museum is closed.'

'How is it closed?' I ask. 'We're twelve o'clock and it closes at four.'

'Because of the bomb,' he says. 'They've exploded a bomb there and they've closed the museum. Look.'

Across the square I see the smoke, the people running, the white uniforms of the police.

'When?' I cry. 'What happened?'

'They say someone threw a bomb and killed some tourists –'

'Ya n'har iswid,' I cry. I run. I run across the square, through the bus terminus and on till I am stopped by a policeman.

'It's forbidden, ya Sett,' he says.

'There's been a bomb,' a man tells me. Crowds of people are standing around. A charred bus is smoking. Officers are yelling into walkie-talkies and others are yelling at the crowd. A police officer turns to the man who'd spoken to me and shoves him in the chest:

'Move away. It's not a spectacle.'

The man moves a few paces and mutters, 'Why don't you do your job properly instead of acting brave on us?'

'What happened?' I ask. 'Was anyone hurt?'

'Yes,' he says. 'They've removed them.'

'They say some are dead,' another man says.

'Tourists?' I ask.

'They say Americans.'

'What a disaster, what a disaster —'

'Of course it's a disaster. They won't stop till they've ruined the country —'

'They were Germans,' a woman says. Her make-up is caked with perspiration under the big headscarf. 'All from that bus over there — eight dead. And the driver. God have mercy on them. My heart on their children and their people —'

I stand in the burning sun and think of the tourists on holiday, of Mansur and how I'd never known if he had a wife and children, and I listen to the voices asking questions, answering them, speculating, praying for mercy for the souls of the dead.

'They say it was one man. And they've caught him.'

'They've caught one. But it will happen again —'

The asphalt is so hot it feels like marshmallow under my heels as I walk back across the square. The car is still in the sun and the seat burns the back of my legs and the steering wheel stings my hands. The barricades on the Upper Egypt road will be worse than ever today. Somewhere in the world eight families do not yet know of the grief that has struck them.

I drive. In Tawasi I will be far away from all this. I will see the school working, see my garden and the fields beyond it. And I will be with Anna.

Dear Sir Charles,

You will know by now that the Sultan has refused to vacate Taba and there is a general understanding that he is backed by Kaiser Wilhelm. If Britain should force the matter and issue an ultimatum, it cannot but be war. I am certain that you and our other friends in England are doing everything possible to put the situation forward in its true light and to that end I am sending you an article which sets out the legal and international position with respect to Taba from 1841 when the Vice-Regency of Egypt was granted to Muhammad Ali. Perhaps the Manchester Guardian *or the* Tribune *might print it?*

The general feeling here is very much with the Sultan, not from any love of him, but from a revulsion at Britain tightening her grip yet more upon Egypt. The Khedive is perceived to be with the Sultan, he confers daily with Mukhtar Pasha. But it is known that he is grown closer both to the King and to the Prince of Wales and it is probably only a matter of time before Cromer calls him to heel.

Cromer appears more determined than ever now to show us who is master here in Egypt. In February the students of the Law School went on strike to protest against new regulations very like those operating in the primary schools. They saw these regulations – instituted by Mr Dunlop, the new Secretary of the Ministry of Education – as an affront to their dignity. The Government immediately closed down the School for a week, during which time they negotiated with the students, who returned to their classes on 3 March. On 24 March Cromer appointed Mr Dunlop Adviser to the Ministry of Education – in effect the Minister. This has been a most unpopular and provocative appointment, especially as it is in Education that the Egyptians find themselves most badly served by the British Administration.

You see how politics overshadows everything? Is it so in England? I do not remember it so – except at the end with Edward. But perhaps I was young and unaware. Here nobody escapes its malign shadow except for old Baroudi Bey, who has long since retreated into a world of his own, and our precious little Nur, who every day brings fresh and clear pleasure into our lives. She is taking her first steps now, so precarious and full of courage and adventure, and is a truly blessed child for no one sees her but falls in love with her and she is very generous in her affections and will happily submit to being hugged and petted by anyone. My husband's cousin Shukri Bey el-Asali is visiting us from Nazareth and has for the first time accepted our entreaties that he not open up his family house but stay with us instead. We believe this is due to Nur's having made a complete conquest of him, for she is the first person he asks after when he enters the house and he has infinite patience with retrieving her ball countless times from the fountain where she loves to throw it. As for her cousin Ahmad, who is six, he has appointed himself her guardian and her tutor and allows her free access to his books and his slate. She will be reading at three years old if he has his way. Her most serious affections, though, she reserves for her father: she will hang about his knee, her eyes spaniel-like with devotion, and whatever his business, he has to be home at her bedtime or she will not go to sleep. Bedtime is the one thing I have held to; for here, children are allowed to stay up until sleep overtakes them wherever they may be and I cannot think that is good for them. So I carry Nur off to bed at seven despite daily remonstrances from Zeinab Hanim and Mabrouka. The child is well for it and loves the ritual of bidding good night to all her favourite people and things in the house, ending up at last in her father's arms for a lullaby and a kiss before he lays her in her bed.

I fancy I am going on too much, but if you will not come and see her for yourself you must resign yourself to these detailed bulletins, for the prospect of our ever being able to come to England grows more remote with each event that comes to pass. Mustafa Kamel Pasha will be in Europe soon and he has expressed the wish to see you and Mr Blunt also. It would be good if that can be arranged —

In my old room at Tawasi, with the windows open to the veranda to let in the evening breeze, I remember the day when my elder son was just three months and I was carrying him in a sling against my breast and standing at the deli counter in Selfridges' foodhall. He looked up at me with the serious gaze with which he had entered the world and I put my tongue out at him. When he put his tongue out in reply I almost fainted with delight. When they said their first words, when they took their first steps, when they put on their new school uniforms and picked up their bags, at every point I was filled with wonder and thought, This is the most enchanting phase yet.

In Anna's words I read her love for her child and Sharif Basha's grateful and amazed delight. I see the black-haired little girl, her ears already pierced and set with golden studs, her violet eyes serious, concentrating. She takes one tottering step down into the fountain and the small, plump feet stand on the cool, wet floor. So much to choose from: down on hands and knees again she explores the squares and triangles, the blue and white and red of the tiles, till looking up she catches the glint of sunlight on the spray and stretches a hand towards it.

Her father sits cross-legged by the edge of the fountain, in the rough linen trousers he uses for working in the garden. His shirtsleeves are rolled up, his feet are bare. He adjusts the baby's sun bonnet, then dips his fingers into the water, stirring it lazily, making more patterns for her to see. He glances up at Anna's window and from behind the lattice she smiles down.

I consider whether to go to the school and decide to stay with Anna. Tareq 'Atiyya's men are doing a good job. Two young men with intermediate diplomas, they take it in turns to man the school five nights a week. They help the children with their reading and maths and the village is grateful to them and sends them home from time to time with gifts of eggs, butter or pastry. I ask them veiled questions about changes on the 'Atiyya land and they say no, there's nothing and nobody new. I should call Tareq, or write him a note to thank him.

Dear James,

Thank you so much for yours of 20 April and for all the papers. Is it not amazing that a man who has never been abroad except once — and that to France — and who speaks not one foreign language should be in charge of British Foreign Affairs? I am sure your mama is relieved that you turned down the offer of the posting to Syria — are you at all disappointed that you cannot be in a place where you can make more use of your Arabic? Sir Charles wrote to me what you said about not wishing to be involved in British foreign policy and I imagine the sad events in Natal will only serve to reassure you that you have made the right decision. I believe you can do more good where you are — and remain truer to yourself.

Matters here, thank goodness, can never be as bad as in South Africa, even though Cromer chooses to represent the political unrest here as fanatical in nature. Yesterday al-Muqattam asked if the Egyptian Army should fight on the side of the British against His Majesty the Ottoman Sultan Abd al-Hamid Khan (for half the Fifth Battalion was sent into Sinai), or should it mutiny? In truth we do not know whether to be disappointed that the Sultan has backed down over Taba or relieved that the prospect of war has been averted. The common sentiment was very much for Turkey and I did, in fact, ask my husband whether Turkey's being Moslem had to do with it; he said that in '98 the people were for Marchand in the Fashoda affair and France is not a Moslem state. I do not know how Cromer squares this, for I do not believe he would lie. But he perceives things as he chooses to and if the Government should grant his demand to double the Army it will be very ill received here. He has now taken to promenading the Army through the country in a show of force — and but two years ago he had declared that he could govern Egypt without an army, as he was widely accepted as a friend of the fellaheen!

We would dearly like to spend more time in Tawasi, but for the impossibility of persuading Baroudi Bey to leave his shrine and our reluctance to take Nur away from Zeinab Hanim (and Ahmad too, for where Nur goes he goes), so we continue much as usual and Nur does new things and gives us more pleasure every day. I am working on my tapestry but it is exceedingly slow; I am on the feet of Isis now.

We are planting a magical grove for Nur which is to be completed before she reaches her first birthday. It has an Italian Cypress, a Jacaranda, a Poinciana, a Magnolia, a Persian Lilac and a Palestinian Willow and her own special pool with a fountain. Zeinab Hanim is not happy about the Persian Lilac because of its poisonous fruit, but my husband says that Nur will learn that good and bad can come of the same tree.

I am sending you a watercolour I made of her and Ahmad. The figure reclining in the easy chair is Shukri Bey al-Asali, our cousin from Nazareth. He is most concerned about the situation in the Holy Land, and the loss of Sheikh Muhammad Abdu has been a bitter blow to him for he had counted on his support. He says, however, that the new Mutasarrif of Jerusalem, Ali Ekrem Bey, is known for his integrity and will act honestly on the anti-immigration laws. He has brought with him a most fascinating and disturbing book, Le Réveil de la nation Arabe, *which I would send you a copy of but that it is illegal here and we would never get another. But it is published in Paris and so you must get a copy. I would be very interested to know what you think of it.*

We have had a new addition to our household in the form of Mahrous, a little boy of four who is Mabrouka's great-nephew. The child was orphaned of his mother and on his father marrying again, Mabrouka wished to have him. My husband gave his consent readily for, as he said, she has brought up all the children of the family and it is but fair that she should now have one of her own. He is a little black boy with perfectly delicate features and springy hair and – being fresh from their village near Tantah – is still somewhat shy. Ahmad is not quite sure how he feels about him but I am certain they will become friends in the end.

We are thinking of going to Italy again in September and

perhaps to Paris. If we do, I shall try to prevail upon Sir Charles to meet us there –

Sharif Basha is digging in the garden when Anna comes to him. He is planting Nur's 'magical grove', that collection of brave bedraggled trees, still trying to flower in the new slum in Touloun, where Isabel and I had sat, drawing triangles in the dust.

10 June 1906
He digs in rhythm with Fudeil, the gardener's son: one man rising, his spade describing an arc over his shoulder, the soil scattering from it like a shower on to the mound behind him, while the other swoops down, digging his spade deep into the earth. Nearby, Abu Fudeil, the old gardener, is preparing the young cypress for planting.

'We shall be finished in a minute,' Sharif Basha says.

Abu Fudeil lowers the cypress carefully into the ground and holds it straight while Fudeil and his master gently shovel the loose earth in around it. When they have finished, Sharif Basha lays his spade on the ground. 'Water it well now,' he says, then turns to Anna. 'Why, whatever is the matter?' he asks. He puts his arm around her and as they move away, Fudeil is on his knees patting the earth into place while his father fetches the bucket of water that has been standing nearby.

'I've just received these from London.' Anna holds out some sheets of paper. She is pale and the papers in her hand shake.

'What is it?' Sharif Basha asks again. 'What has happened?'

'James,' she says, 'James sent me this. It is a letter – a copy of a letter – that was sent to Sir Edward Grey. It is a translation. The original, in Arabic, fell into Cromer's hands here in Cairo. It describes a plan for an uprising in August.'

'Uprising? What uprising?'

They have both come to a stop and Anna's hands are on her husband's arm, her eyes searching his face:

'Sharif? You would have told me?'

'What are you saying? What uprising?'

'A nationalist uprising.'

'There is no such thing. Come, read me the letter.' He walks her into the house. 'Come in here. And for God's sake, don't look so frightened.'

They go into Sharif Basha's study. He makes Anna sit in an easy chair and pours her a glass of water.

'Now. Translate for me. Barrington's letter first.'

' "Dear Anna. I am writing in haste because you should have this immediately. This letter was forwarded to the Foreign Office in support of Lord Cromer's request for reinforcements in Egypt. It is meant to be a translation of a letter in Arabic that was given to the Oriental Secretary by one of his native spies. For me it does not ring true but I could be mistaken. Show it to your husband." '

'Now the letter.'

' "To the Branch of the Fair Tree, the Light Rain of the Generous Cloud, the Son and Daughter of the Prophet –" '

'The what?'

' "The Son and Daughter of the Prophet".'

'This is nonsense.'

'Well, if it has been translated from Arabic into English and now I am translating it into French –'

'It is still nonsense.'

'So there is no uprising?'

'Anna, darling. An uprising with what? The army is scattered in the Sudan. The man in the street? The fallaheen? Where is the organisation? Our spirits have never been at lower ebb since '82. And the Porte has just shown it cannot support its own positions, let alone ours. Do you think we are mad?'

'No. No, I know *you* are not mad. But there are others –'

'Give me the letter. I shall have it translated back into Arabic.'

'But Sharif –'

'Don't worry. I shall tell no one how I came by it.

415

Barrington's name will not be mentioned at all. You keep his letter. And thank him on my behalf. And please – look, come here –'

He pulls her to her feet, sits her down on the diwan and sits close by her. He puts his hand under her chin and tilts her face so that she looks into his eyes. 'Do you think I would be part of any plan that must jeopardise all our lives? Do you think I would do such a thing and not tell you?'

'No,' Anna shakes her head but her eyes fill with tears.

'What then? Do you think something like this can be planned without my knowing about it?'

'Yes.'

'Yes?' He is surprised.

'Oh, Sharif!' The tears come flooding. 'People can do things without telling you. You think they won't but they can. It is not only the British who dislike you. The Khedive does not like you, you have turned down government posts, resigned from the Council, you were a friend of Sheikh Muhammad 'Abdu –' Anna's voice is choked with her tears. 'The Turks know that you want Egypt independent from them, and now you are also involved in Shukri's campaign against the settlements in Palestine. The Islamists hate you for your position on education. We *know* there are more radical nationalists who think your way is too cautious, too slow. And there must be people who do not believe you can be married to me and yet have nothing to do with the British, who suspect you of playing a double game –'

'My, my!' Sharif Basha smiles. 'What a popular chap I am –'

'Oh, darling, the people who know you *adore* you, would do anything for you, but you must not discount the others –'

'Anna, listen. Listen, hush –' He kisses her face, he wipes her tears, he holds her close and strokes her hair, her neck, her back. 'Listen, I know it has been difficult for you –'

'No, it has not.'

'Yes, some of it has. I know. And I wish it could have been different. But we have made it worthwhile, have we not? I will not let anything come near us. Tonight I shall find out if

416

there is anything to this letter. And meanwhile, courage, Lady Anna. Go wash your face and don't frighten Nur and my mother. I thought you were never afraid?'

'I am now. For you.'

'There is no need, believe me.'

Ya'qub Artin Basha translates into Arabic:

' "To the Branch of the Fair Tree, the Light Rain of the Generous Cloud, the Son and Daughter of the Prophet —" '

He raises his eyes, looks over his spectacles. 'Is this a joke?' he asks.

'Read, read, mon ami,' Sharif Basha says, lying back in his chair, his legs stretched out, his feet crossed at the ankles, his eyes closed.

' "To the Drawn Sword of the Straight Way, Seyyid Ahmed el-Sherif —" '

'Sayyid Ahmad al-Sharif? Who's he?' Shukri Bey al-'Asali asks. Ya'qub Basha shrugs and continues:

' "May he be always under the protection of the divine eye — fullest greeting and most perfect benediction. May all the odour of these greetings be upon you and may the blessing of God cover you —"'

'The odour?' Sharif Basha opens his eyes: 'Was that the *odour* of — what? Blessings?'

' "Greetings",' Shukri Bey says.

'I think he means "perfumed greetings",' Ya'qub Basha says, frowning at the paper in his hand.

'Well, in that case . . .' Sharif Basha closes his eyes again.

' "What I wish you to understand by this letter is that the bearer and that which he bore have reached us and that your wish is established in our understanding; but we have been able to understand from your messenger verbally only so much as you have declared in your letter. How can one arrive at the planet Souad? To arrive there —" What is this planet Souad?'

' "Su'ad has appeared and my heart today is full of joy",' Sharif Basha quotes.

'Your mood is very clear today, ya Basha,' Shukri Bey smiles.

'I have been working in the garden all day. Planting trees for Nur.'

Ya'qub Basha rustles his papers and continues: ' "To arrive there the summits of mountains must be passed, and beyond, there is death. For the thing which you have conceived is very difficult, and its difficulties are insurmountable even for one who might have greater means than you, and that is a thing impossible. The matter presents obstacles which can be explained neither by direct statement nor by implication. He who would wish to reach it will find many things which are opposed to the Sacred Law, even supposing him to reach it safe and sound. On the contrary, he must stoop and crouch, and even thus he will not attain his end. God is generous and merciful. Inquiry has been made.

' "Is his demand that he should arrive in the night at the stated time, or would he arrive at another moment? God makes him happy who states things openly and clearly. Some say that the time indicated in the Sacred Law is less disadvantageous, so that the principal may enter into the accessory. Is it possible —" '

Shukri Bey starts to laugh. Sharif Basha grins at him and Shukri Bey throws back his head and roars with mirth. Ya'qub Basha frowns at him over his glasses.

'Forgive him,' Sharif Basha says. 'He is but a foolish Arab and afflicted with lightness of the brains. He comprehends not the words of the sagacious —'

'This is not a laughing matter,' Ya'qub Basha says.

'I really — what rot!' Shukri Bey says, wiping his eyes with his handkerchief. 'And that last bit about the principal — did you get that right?'

'Let us have the rest of it,' Sharif Basha says.

Ya'qub Basha adjusts his spectacles. ' "Is it possible for lovers at night to go twice, first giving precedence to their chiefs and then causing others to follow them? Lightness of clothing and food indicates sagacity of mind. He has cast aside

418

the sheet of paper to lighten his steps until he has flung away even his shoes. It is a true saying: (verse) "Why do the camels march so slowly? Are they bearing stone or iron?" '

'Ah, the camels – I have been waiting for those!' Sharif Basha sits up. 'There had to be camels.'

'Rubbish. Rubbish!' Shukri Bey says.

'There is more,' Ya'qub Basha says. 'All in the same vein.' He scans the rest of the letter. 'And wait – "If our journey takes place, the divine power having permitted it, the fast will be preferable in the month of Rajeb, the return being in that month –" In Rajab. Something is to happen in Rajab?'

'What do you think?' Sharif Basha asks seriously. 'Of the letter?'

'It is a nonsense,' Ya'qub Basha says.

'It could not have been written by an Arab,' Shukri Bey says. 'It makes no sense.'

'This is the work of an Englishman,' Ya'qub Artin says. 'An ignorant Englishman who imagines he knows how Arabs think.'

'The Oriental Secretary,' Sharif Basha says, 'Mr Boyle.'

'But why? Why would he write this?'

'Because Cromer has asked for reinforcements of the Army of Occupation and he needs to persuade the Foreign Office of their necessity. So Boyle writes this letter and they send it to London pretending they have got it from one of their spies.'

'I do not think Cromer would do that,' Ya'qub Basha says.

'This letter was sent to the Foreign Office,' Sharif Basha says. 'It is supposed to prove that a revolution is being planned.'

'But it can prove nothing. It is a piece of stupidity.'

'But the Foreign Office will not know that. They will read "camels" and "God is generous" and "odours of blessings" and they will say "fanatical Arabs" and send the troops.'

'How did you get this?' Shukri Bey asks.

'I cannot tell you that.'

'But what can we do with it?'

There is a silence. Then Ya'qub Basha says, 'We can do

nothing. Even if we were to write a – a critique of this, showing how it is not Arabic – I would not have believed Cromer would do such a thing.'

'He probably believes the spirit of it is true,' Sharif Basha says.

'But he knows the letter is not genuine,' Shukri Bey says. 'Unless – do you think Mr Boyle might have not told him?'

'Impossible,' Ya'qub Basha says. 'Boyle is Cromer's creature. He would not dream of tricking him.'

'I think,' Sharif Basha says, 'the only thing we can do is to try to get someone in London to print this – if it is possible to do so without revealing how they came by it. Then we can be ready with a reply.'

'It would be a very esoteric discussion,' Ya'qub Basha says, 'points of language, imagery. We would have to imagine what Mr Boyle wished the Arabic to say and then translate it correctly into English. The problem is too subtle. In a court perhaps you could present it, but to the general public, no.'

'What else then?' Shukri Bey asks.

'We can take it to the Agency and stuff it down Cromer's throat,' Sharif Basha says. 'Bring the revolution forward by a couple of months.'

'But there is no revolution, is there?' Ya'qub Artin says.

'I do not know of one,' Sharif Basha says. 'But with the Army on alert and parading through the country . . .' He pauses.

'Of course, anything can happen,' Shukri Bey says.

'I have spoken to some young men in my office,' Sharif Basha says, 'asked them to find out for me. But I do not believe anyone is planning anything. We would have smelled it.'

14 June 1906
My husband tells me that his enquiries confirm his belief that no uprising is being planned by any section of the Nationalist Movement. Mustafa Kamel Basha is shortly to leave for Europe, once again hoping to arouse public opinion in support of

Egyptian Independence. My husband says there is no reason to expect anything but a quiet summer. Pray God he is right.

Last night when he came upstairs he found me in Nur's room. The child sleeps with her back curved in an athletic arch. He regarded her for a moment in the soft lamplight, and – smiling at me – said, 'Look! She is flying.'

'Am Abu el-Ma'ati comes to see me every few days. He has detailed a young woman from the village to look after me and I asked if she could bring a friend as I was working all day and she would be lonely. So Khadra and Rayyesa come for a few hours each day. They are both newly married and have no children yet. They dust and wash and water the garden. When the meals they prepare sit for days in the fridge, they stop cooking and bring me little dishes of whatever they are eating at home. And 'Am Abu el-Ma'ati comes to see if I have everything I need, to sip tea with me on the veranda and bring me news of our village and the neighbouring lands. I tell him I am writing a history of my ancestors and he says he remembers my grandmother, for he was a young boy when she died. He brings the Qur'an from his house and shows me his name and the names of his father and six of his grandfathers, inscribed one after the other on the flyleaf.

'Soon,' he says, 'the next time my oldest boy comes back from the sea, I will write his name down, then give it to him.'

'May He lengthen your life, insha' Allah,' I say.

'Lives are in the hand of God,' he says. 'I've lived and I've buried those who were younger than me.'

'God give you good health, ya 'Am Abu el-Ma'ati,' I say.

'We do what we can and the rest is with God.' He coughs and takes out his packet of Cleopatra. We are such good friends now that he offers me a cigarette and I accept. If someone else comes along, I will crush it under my chair and wave away the smoke. We speak of the land and how it should be run. The five faddans, the smallholdings set up first by Kitchener and then by 'Abd el-Nasser, are no good, he says. 'At first they seem good and a man thinks he has independence but then he finds himself marching in place. He can't modernise, bring in big machines. And in the end what can he leave to his children? Divide five faddans between them? In the end, still a man eats up his neighbour's land and one ends up rich and the other at God's door.'

'What then?' I ask. 'Cooperatives?'

'Maybe.' He looks doubtful. 'But people quarrel and each one wants to be boss –'

'So what's best?'

'Fifty faddans. At least fifty faddans to one owner is a reasonable size. A good owner who lives on the land and lets people share in its returns.'

'So you are a reactionary, ya 'Am Abu el-Ma'ati?' I smile.

'Never, ya Sett Hanim,' he defends himself, 'but the land is with us in trust. We have to do what's best for it.'

'I hear,' I say slowly, 'I hear there are Israeli firms offering services – agricultural services. I hear they get special concessions from the government.'

'I've heard that too,' he says. 'But up in lands by the Canal, not here.'

'Has no one brought them in here?'

'No, not in the whole governorate.'

'Would you work with them? If they were hired to improve the land?'

'Never. And anyone who brings them in – you'll excuse me – is a fool. Either a fool or an agent. Isn't that how they took Palestine? By pretending to show people how to plant their land? And then they're clever and they take it over. No. We've been working our land for thousands of years. We don't need strangers to show us how to do it.' He looks at me. 'You're not thinking –'

'Never,' I say. 'It's just talk I hear in Cairo and I wanted your opinion.'

'And if we do need strangers,' he says after a moment, 'the world is full of nations with technology. Why does it have to be the Israelis when we know they have us in their sights?'

'Because they underbid everybody else.'

'Then we should ask ourselves why.'

'You're right,' I say. 'I wish they could hear you in Cairo.'

'Each one goes with his own head,' he says, standing up. 'I shall leave you to work. Don't you want anything?'

'I want your safety,' I say.

13 June 1906

I was sitting at the piano with Ahmad at my side and Nur on my knee. Nur had discovered the great sound she could make by banging her little hand down on the keys and I was trying to restrict her to the high notes while her cousin sat at the centre and picked out a melody. I was just thinking that the child is ready for better training than I can give him when Hasna came in all agitated and begged to be allowed to bring in Mahmoud Abu-Domah, a kinsman of hers who – having just arrived in Cairo from their village – had come to visit and bring her news of her family. I gave my permission and a pleasant, open-faced young man came in, Mahrous holding him tightly by the hand. He was clearly embarrassed to be shown into my presence, although the sight of the children did somewhat put him at ease. Hasna was plucking at his sleeve and saying 'Tell my lady, tell her', and it transpires that as he was waiting for his train at Tantah there had come news of trouble in a village nearby between some British officers and the fellaheen. What he had understood was that the officers, shooting at the fellaheen's pigeons, had killed a woman and set fire to the storerooms where the wheat is kept, and the fellaheen had attacked the officers with sticks.

Hasna was much distressed and was all for going there immediately, but both Mahmoud and I persuaded her that such an act would be foolish, especially as – thank God – it was not her village that was in trouble. We have asked the young man to stay with us tonight, for it will please Mahrous and besides I wish my husband to hear his story. What a wicked and senseless business this shooting of pigeons is, and how much harm it does the British in the eyes of the fellaheen!

Shukri Bey is due to leave us tomorrow and we are all sad to see him go, for he is of such a pleasant and sunny disposition that he has been a wonderful guest in our household. He insists that we should go to visit his family in the Holy Land and indeed I should very much like to visit Nazareth and Jerusalem and Bethlehem, which I have sung of so often but never seen. My husband also would like to go, for he has fond childhood memories there. And if Layla and Husni and Ahmad could come too — since Jalila Hanim, Husni's mother, is from Nazareth — we should make a very pleasant party indeed.

Layla is much affected by Shukri Bey's accounts of the settlers. She has started to collect articles about their activities and has asked me to furnish her with anything that I can from English sources.

14 June 1906
The newspapers today carried an account of the events at Denshwai and they are worse than we thought: one of the officers was killed and the case has been taken out of the hands of the District Attorney and will be dealt with by Findlay Basha in the Special Court. A cordon has been placed around the village and two hundred and fifty people have been arrested. Mr Matchell has already put out a statement praising the officers and blaming the fellaheen for the events — and this before any investigation has taken place. Of the fellaheen five are wounded and one is dead.

18 June 1906
This is what has happened in Denshwai. A miltary force on promenade through the Delta were encamped near Tantah. Some officers wished to go shooting pigeons in the village as they had done the year before. They sent a message to the Umdah but did not wait for his permission as they are supposed by law to do. They commandeered two local carriages and went, accompanied by a local police guard. The choice of Denshwai was due to its having large numbers of pigeons, which constitute an essential part of the people's livelihood. When the officers arrived at the village, an elder, one Sheikh Mahfouz, came out to meet them and asked that they do their shooting far from the villagers'

homes, as the law says that no shooting may be done within 200 metres of a house. The officers paid no attention and deployed themselves in different positions, but all within 150 metres of the village. At two o'clock in the afternoon they started to shoot, the people the while watching them from their homes and fields in resentment.

Presently a fire started in one of the rooms in which the just-harvested wheat was stored. Nobody can be certain what started the fire. The fellaheen say it was the shots of one of the officers. Mr Matchell says the fellaheen burned their own wheat as a prearranged signal to attack the officers. But how could such a thing be prearranged when no one knew the officers were coming? The Umdah had been out of the village and indeed only arrived during the incident.

When the fire started, the owner of the house (who happened to be the village muezzin) and his wife ran out and started to beat the two officers closest to their house and to try to disarm them. Captain Porter's gun went off and the woman, Ummu Muhammad, fell. Her husband and the villagers — thinking she was dead — attacked the officers with sticks and tried to wrench away their guns. The other officers, hearing the noise, came to help their companions and all fired shots low into the people. Five people fell, among them the head of the local police, so the police joined the people in beating the officers. Two of the officers ran to fetch help from their encampment, which was some six kilometres away. The others were disarmed and held by the fellaheen, who, when they found that Ummu Muhammad was wounded, not dead, grew calmer, so that some of their elders intervened and protected the officers and returned them safely with their guns to the encampment.

Meanwhile, of the two officers who had run for help, one, Captain Bull, unable to withstand the heat of the June sun, fell by the roadside by the market village of Sirsina. The other jumped into the Baguriyyah canal and swam to the encampment. A man from Sirsina by the name of Sayyid Ahmad Sa'd came upon Captain Bull fainted on the road and, with the help of some villagers and Muhammad Hussein, the market police-

man, carried him into the shade of the small market hall and gave him water. When the English force came into sight, the villagers scattered and hid. Sayyid Ahmad Saʿd hid in the millhouse nearby, where he was found by the British soldiers. Believing he was the cause of Captain Bull's condition, they beat him to death with the butts of their bayonets.

Captain Bull died later in the day and the villagers were to be tried for murder. But he was exhumed and it was found that he had died of sunstroke.

The investigation has ended today and the whole of Egypt waits to see what will happen.

I fear that this will be represented as the beginning of that insurrection promised in that false and wicked letter and will have widespread repercussions.

My husband has volunteered to defend the case but has been turned down by Matchell.

Hasna is going around weeping and little Mahrous is very silent, for although they are from Kamshish they have friends and kin in all the surrounding villages and the whole area is engulfed by the troubles.

20 June 1906
Cromer left yesterday for England on his annual leave. But al-Mu'ayyad publishes a report that the gallows were tested out the day before in the prison store. The Councillor, Charles de Mansfeld Findlay, will be acting for him. I pray and pray that justice will prevail in the Court.

The Court will consist of Boutros Basha Ghali, the Prime Minister; Mr Bond, Vice-President of the Courts; Mr Hayter, acting Judicial Adviser; Colonel Ludlow, Judge Advocate for the Army of Occupation; and Ahmad Bey Fathi Zaghloul, President of the Native Courts. The Prosecution will be conducted by Ibrahim Bey al-Hilbawi, and the Defence by Muhammad Bey Yusuf, Ismaʿil Bey ʿAsim and Ahmad Bey Lutfi al-Sayyid.

My husband says that Boutros Ghali is in a difficult position, as he is acting for the Minister of Justice who is absent. For al-

Hilbawi and Fathi Zaghloul he is surprised, but he says al-Hilbawi has never been any man's friend but his own and Zaghloul considers he has been Head of the Preliminary Court for too long and Bond has been obstructing his promotion to the Court of Appeals. And yet, he says, he would not have thought this of them.

27 June 1906
The sentences have been announced. Four men, Hasan Mah-fouz, Yusuf Saleem, Sayyid Salim and Muhammad Zahran, are to hang. Two, Ahmad Mahfuz and Muhammad 'Abd el-Nabi, the muezzin, are to get Life with hard labour. Ahmad al-Sisi gets fifteen years with hard labour. Seven years with labour for six more men and fifty lashes for eight men. The sentences are to be carried out in Denshwai.

28 June 1906
In the salamlek Ahmad Hilmi's hands cover his face. His shoulders shake and a muffled choking sound rises from behind his hands. Sharif Basha al-Baroudi puts a hand on his shoulder. Husni Bey al-Ghamrawi sits forward, his elbows on his knees, staring at the floor. Isma'il Basha Sabri holds his prayer beads still in his hands. The three men sit in silence. Above, behind the mashrabiyya, Layla and Anna kneel side by side on the hard banquette. They make no effort to wipe away the tears that fall silently down their faces.

'I am sorry.' Ahmad Hilmi wipes his face and straightens his shoulders. 'It was barbaric,' he says. 'Barbaric. The gallows set up in the village, the "bride" next to them, the people herded in to watch. They hang one man, leave him dangling there in front of his family and his people, and tie another to the "bride" and whip him. And again. And again . . .'

There is silence.

'And they call themselves civilised,' he says.

The men do not speak.

'Yusuf Saleem,' he says, 'twenty-two years old. He stood

427

on the platform, turned towards the villagers and shouted, "God's curse on the unjust!" And then they hanged him.'

Layla's hand finds Anna's and the women cling to each other. Isma'il Basha Sabri draws his hands across his face.

'I have filed my report for *al-Liwa*,' Ahmad Hilmi says. 'I recorded the bare facts and begged readers to excuse me any further description, for words can only insult today's events.'

Husni Bey al-Ghamrawi straightens up. 'This will be the end of Cromer,' he says.

'We must make sure it is,' Sharif Basha says.

'Do you think that is possible?' Isma'il Basha Sabri asks.

'Yes,' Sharif Basha says. '*L'Egypte* is read abroad. The *Manchester Guardian* has already taken the matter up. The *Daily Chronicle* on the 20th – before the trial had even begun – carried a telegram saying that Cromer had decided to have the men shot. The *Tribune* too will probably speak up. I am sending a man to Denshwai and preparing a full account of the case. We shall get it published in England. If the case is publicised enough, people will press for questions to be asked in Parliament and the Irish will take it up. The Foreign Office did not want this to happen. They will be embarrassed. Mustafa Kamel will write in France. If need be we will get the friend who furnished us with that forgery of a letter to find a way to make that public – or to threaten to. We may not end the Occupation, but we will get rid of Cromer.'

'And who would you have instead,' Ahmad Hilmi asks bitterly, 'Kitchener?'

'Chitty Bey would do,' Husni Bey says, 'the director of Customs. He was born here and speaks Arabic. He knows us. He is a good financier. We could work with him.'

'And what about today?' Ahmad Hilmi asks. 'The people were not even allowed to bury their dead. The police carted them away. They are forbidden to open their houses for condolences. They cannot even grieve –'

'We will open a house for condolence here,' Sharif Basha says.

The others look at him in surprise.

'I will open the house in Hilmiyya,' he says, 'for three nights, and the Thursdays and the Fortieth Day.'

'That is dangerous, ya Basha,' Isma'il Sabri says.

'It is fitting,' Husni Bey says.

'We do not need to make an announcement,' Sharif Basha says. 'We shall just put word about. We will allow no speeches, no demonstrations. Just the Qur'an and condolences. They cannot prevent that.'

29 June 1906
When he came up to our apartment last night he found me weeping. He took me in his arms and I said the words that came to me:

'I am ashamed.'

'No, Anna, no.' And when I hid my face in his chest and wept, he held me away and said, 'Listen. You must not — ever — feel like this. This is not to do with being British. Al-Hilbawi is Egyptian, and so is Ahmad Fathi Zaghloul. And your Mr Barrington and Mr Blunt are British.'

'I listened,' I wept, 'I heard what Ahmad Hilmi said. I cannot bear it. All those people there tonight, in Denshwai. All those mothers and wives and sisters —'

'Hush,' he said. 'The only way we can bear this is to make it work for us. To make sure it can never happen again. Never. And we shall work for the release of the prisoners. Your friends in London will help us.'

He held me to him so that I could feel the tremor in his chest and he said, 'Will you come to me? I need us to be together completely tonight.' When I looked at his face I saw new and deep lines etched at the corners of his mouth and into his brow.

For three days, for five Thursdays and on 6 August the house in Hilmiyya and the large marquee set up in its garden filled and emptied with men and women from Cairo, from the towns and villages of the Delta and the Sa'id. Sharif Basha al-Baroudi and Husni Bey al-Ghamrawi and other notables stood at the door, shaking hands, accepting condolences. Cups of black, sugarless coffee were drunk in their thousands. And not a sound was heard save for the melodious chanting of the Qur'anic message of hope for both the living and the dead.

. . . some of the leaders have been cowardly. One would
almost say they have betrayed a country that has been
generous to them beyond their wildest dreams. As for me,
I shall stay on course till the end; for I believe that the
fruit of this defence, if not harvested by the first defender,
or the second, will still be harvested by an Egyptian
somewhere down the years . . .

Mustafa Kamel, 1898

17 November, 1997
Tawasi,
Isabel is pregnant.

'I told you it was meant to be,' she said on the phone last night. 'We've been seeing each other – but it was the first time that did it. I'm three months gone. I'm sorry I didn't tell you before but I wanted to be absolutely sure. I promised myself I'd tell you at three months.'

'Isabel, that's wonderful!' I said. Then I said, 'Isn't it?'

'Yes,' she said. 'Yes, I'm madly happy.'

'And 'Omar?' I asked.

'Well.' She hesitated. 'He – actually, he's quite upset. He didn't quite ask if I wanted to keep the baby. He didn't do that. But he is very concerned at the fact of being fifty-five.'

'Give him time,' I said.

'Absolutely,' she said. 'And a lot of space. I've not suggested either of us moving in. He can take his own time. I wait till he calls me – mostly.'

Trapped, I think. He must be feeling partly trapped, partly proud, partly what shall I tell the kids? His kids are grown up – older than mine. Will they be amused? Or resentful? He cannot have told Isabel about his affair with Jasmine yet; she would have told me. He must have put aside his fears – since he was seeing her anyway. But this will bring them all back. Father and grandfather in one – like Rameses or Akhenatun or any one of the great pharaohs. He would not appreciate

432

that. He is a modern man: an Arab–American. And, I tell myself again, he is not her father.

She says she cannot make plans to come back just yet. She wants me to go over. I say, when I've finished. I think I am fairly close. Cromer has resigned and Eldon Gorst has taken over. In the new, more conciliatory atmosphere, four official political parties have sprung into being. The first, naturally, is the pro-British Free National Party with *al-Muqattam* as its mouthpiece. Its slogan is 'The Safety of the Fatherland and the Nation lies in Peace with the Reforming Occupiers', and it is generally despised. Then Ahmad Lutfi al-Sayyid and some of the notables and high-ranking civil servants form Hizb al-Ummah, the Party of the Nation. They establish *al-Garida* as its newspaper and call for gradual independence from Britain, ending Turkish rule, investing in education and industry, and government by constitution. Mustafa Kamel then forms the real Nationalist Party, al-Hizb al-Watani, speaking through *al-Liwa* and calling for immediate independence and a constitutional government within the Ottoman state. Finally the Khedive, acting through Sheikh Ali Yusuf and his *al-Mu'ayyad*, forms his own party, Hizb al-Islah. Its programme is immediate independence and a constitutional government but it soft-pedals on the Turkish ties and floats the idea of an Arab caliphate with the Khedive as the caliph.

And my husband of course will join none of them. The Palace and the British parties are out of the question. He dislikes al-Watani's cleaving to the Ottomans, for he sees more and more of a divergence between the interests of Egypt and those of Turkey. The Hizb al-Ummah would have been the most natural place for him, indeed several of his friends are founding members, but other Parties will have it that the interests of the Ummah's members – being among the more wealthy Notables and Civil Servants – are close to those of the British and there is some talk of Cromer having given the Party his blessing before he left. Were it not for the fact that I am his wife – a fact which renders him perhaps excessively anxious to avoid any whisper of a link to the British — I believe he may have joined it. As it is, he remains a free man and publishes his writings where he chooses and works on those projects on which both the Watani and the Ummah are united.

We are very close now to seeing a School of Fine Art inaugurated. The Khedive has appointed Prince Ahmad Fuad Chairman of the Council for the National University and my husband and Ya'qub Artin Basha are working on its Charter. I believe on the whole that the tally for 1907 has been a good one, with the pardon for the Denshwai prisoners coming, as it does, at the end of the year. I wonder if it is any comfort to the widows and orphans of that village that the brutality committed against them has led to the fall of Cromer and has reverberated across the world? The odd thing is that Cromer was by all accounts most surprised and disappointed when he returned to find feeling in all quarters so united against him and he persisted to the end in ascribing this to the schemings of the Khedive rather than to his own actions. But enough! Enough of politics, as Zeinab Hanim constantly says. Poor lady, her life has been completely governed by the politics first of her husband and then of her son. But she is happy enough now with three children running about the house. She looks at me kindly and says, 'Look at the wisdom of God, my daughter, sending you from far countries to my son after all those barren years.'

How I wish it were possible to say 'Enough of politics', truly and forever. I find myself thinking sometimes of life in London, occupied with nothing more than choosing the day's menu, attending to the children and doing odd things about the house. Perhaps walking in the Park. Perhaps going out in the evening to the theatre or to dinner with friends. And now, in December, I think of Christmas trees and lights and breaking off from shopping to have lunch with a friend. But when I imagine myself in Thurloe Place I see Nur come dancing down the stairs. When I enter the foyer of a theatre it is my husband's arm on which I lean. When I go into Harrods it is to choose a present for him and another for Zeinab Hanim. And when I stop for lunch it is Layla with whom I compare purchases and lists across the table.

AND IF I INTERPRET ANNA'S presence among us as a sign that He willed good for our house, how then do I interpret those other, later events? Events that perhaps found their roots in that very presence. I do not know. I leave that question to other, wiser minds than mine. We lived our lives together and hardly a day passed but we were in each other's company for some of its hours.

The University, as everyone knows, was started in 1326/1908. What many people no longer remember is that in its first year it held special classes for ladies on Fridays. Nabawiyya Musa, Malak Hifni Nasif, Labiba Hashim and I were selected to conduct these classes. And we invited Anna to talk about art and Madame Hussein Rushdi to talk about European history. Anna joked that the hareem had made a working woman of her, for she was constantly occupied in preparing for her classes, writing for the magazine and translating from and into English for my brother. She had information from her friends in Britain and he had a knowledge of Egypt, a clear mind and a gift for logical yet impassioned argument. And then she had a talent for the English style and so each article they published struck a true blow.

Mustafa Kamel Basha's death was a great setback to the country, but for a while it seemed that his work would be continued by Muhammad Bey Farid. My husband worked with him on the affairs of the workers and during 1908 we succeeded in establishing four trade unions. And with the CUP revolution in Turkey and the declaration of the Turkish Constitution and the Ottoman Parliament, it seemed that change was truly coming. The British Government refused to allow Egypt to have a Representative at the Parliament, and at the Army Parade in November the students and the people burst into spontaneous cries of 'Vive l'indépendence!'

And our domestic life was happy. My mother was like a
hen with a great brood of chicks, my father was content to
sit and watch Anna weave her magical tapestry, and
though we were only blessed with one child each, the
children grew up and with them grew their loving affection for us and for each other.

Nur is on her father's knee. She has pulled his gold watch out
of his pocket and is staring at it thoughtfully. Thoughtfully he
regards his daughter. In the silence Layla looks up from her
book and reads her brother's mind:

'May He preserve you for her, ya Abeih, and you see her a
bride. You'll deliver her with your own hand to Ahmad.'

He pays attention. 'How do we know they are for each
other?' he asks his sister with a smile. 'Might they not meet
other people and prefer them?'

'You can see they already adore each other,' Layla says.
'They can't bear to be separated for a day. When they —'

'Bass ya Sett Layla,' Mabrouka cuts in. 'The knowledge of
what's hidden is with God alone.'

'And where have you popped up from all of a sudden?'
Layla asks —

There is a great crying and wailing coming towards the house
and I start up from my vision of ninety years ago as a loud
hammering shakes my door. I run through the hall and fling
open the door. Outside there is 'Am Abu el-Ma'ati's daughter, the midwife from the clinic and other women, a swarm of
children following behind. The women are bareheaded, their
black tarhas hanging round their necks.

'They've taken my father, ya Sett Hanim,' 'Am Abu el-
Ma'ati's daughter cries. 'The soldiers came and they took him
and took the men of the village. Help us, ya Sett Hanim! Who
can we go to? Who can we speak to? God will avenge us —' She
sits on the ground weeping, beating her head with her hands.

'Why?' I cry. 'Why? What happened? Where have they
taken them?'

'Because of what happened in Luxor, ya Sett,' the midwife says. 'They've rounded up the men —'

'What happened in Luxor?'

'Don't you know what's happening? The world is standing on a leg —'

'Sett Amal works all day.' Khadra comes to my side. 'How can she know?'

'They killed the tourists at Luxor. Fifty or a hundred, we don't know. At the temple. And there was a battle and shooting and now the government has turned on the people —'

'They took my father, they took my father —'

'What's our village got to do with this?'

'They've turned on the whole of the Sa'id, not our village alone. War, ya Sett Hanim, war. Seventeen men they've taken from our village. And what are people to do? Where can we go?'

'Where did they take them? The police station?'

'The central police station, the markaz.'

'I'll get dressed and go.'

I run inside and stand in the middle of my room with my heart beating fast. All the things I've read — the things I've heard about what goes on when people fall into the hands of the police swirl round in my mind: the stripping, the blindfolds, the whipping — I sit on the bed and close my eyes and force myself to calm down. When I open my eyes, my mother is looking at me sadly out of her portrait. I take a deep breath and put on city clothes, stockings, a silk scarf. I brush my hair, put on some lipstick and put pearls in my ears. I pick up my bag, then on an impulse I take my British passport from the dressing-table drawer and put it in the bag next to my Egyptian ID card and driving licence.

All the women want to come with me but one woman knows the way to the police station so I take her and Abu el-Ma'ati's daughter and Khadra. My hands are shaking and I grip the wheel tight. I can feel myself starting to cry and I force the tears down and hold myself rigid. As we come to the edge of the clearing around the police station, soldiers run at us with their bayonets, forcing us to stop.

'Halt! Stop! Where are you going?' they shout.

'We are going to see the chief,' I say.

'It's forbidden.' They surround us. Boys, nervous and angry.

'What's forbidden? We want to go into the markaz.'

'I told you it's forbidden.'

I open the door and get out of the car. 'Listen, you and him,' I say and am amazed at authority in my voice. 'There's nothing called forbidden. This is a police station and I am going in to see the chief. And if you don't make way immediately right now I shall call Muhyi Bey the Governor on the mobile and turn your day black. I'll have you sent to Tokar.'

'Ya Sett Hanim, we have orders –'

'What orders? One of you go in and tell the chief Amal Hanim al-Ghamrawi is coming to see him and I'm coming in right after you.'

'But cars are forbidden to come near the markaz.'

'I'll leave the car here. And if something happens to it I'll bring you a catastrophe.'

One of the soldiers heads for the markaz and I start to follow. The women open the doors of the car but the soldiers push them back.

'No natives.'

'Natives? These people are your people.'

'Impossible,' the soldier says. 'I'll be shot.'

'Ma 'alesh,' I say to the women. 'Wait for me. And lock the doors from the inside. And none of you come near them,' I say to the soldiers.

In his office the Ma'mur stands to greet me. He is a big man, fortyish, thickset with a black moustache. He looks harassed and is perspiring heavily in the cold November night. Two men in civilian clothes are sitting in armchairs to one side of the room. I shake his hand, say my name and sit down.

'I have come to Your Excellency regarding some people from our village —' I begin.

'Which village?' one of the civilians asks.

'Tawasi,' I say. 'Some soldiers came to the village today and collected the men. I have come to see what can be done for them.'

'And what is your concern with this affair?' the man asks.

I turn to him; he has pale grey eyes and he is looking me up and down. I do not know what he is, is he Police or Army or Intelligence? Is he superior to the Ma'mur? He has to be, to cut in like this.

'Tawasi is on my land,' I say, 'and the fallaheen are my responsibility. The women came to my house and asked for my help.'

'We have a state of emergency,' the Ma'mur says.

'Because of Luxor?'

'Yes, because of Luxor. They killed sixty people there. Tourists.'

'And what has Tawasi to do with Luxor? These are a peaceable people —'

'We have to collect all suspects,' he says and I hear a trace of weariness in his voice.

'But why should people in Tawasi be suspects?' I press 'These are people living and seeing after their work. You collect them from their houses at night —'

'Everybody is a suspect.' Pale-eyes speaks again.

'So you'll collect all the men of Egypt?'

I watch him flush.

'And the hareem too if we have to,' he says.

'Ya-fandim —' I turn again to the Ma'mur — 'have any of these people done anything to arouse suspicion? Have you found anything in any of their homes —'

'I told you: we have a state of emergency.'

I am silent for a moment, then I try again: 'How long will you keep them?'

'Nobody knows. It depends.'

I turn completely towards the Ma'mur. I will him to look up and meet my eyes.

'Your Excellency the Ma'mur,' I say, 'among the people you are holding there are some old men. Respectable sheikhs. Why would you want these? Let them go and the village will calm down and tomorrow God will do what is right for everybody. And your favour will hang around all our necks.'

'Nobody will leave tonight,' Pale-eyes says. 'Tomorrow they will be interrogated and after that we shall see.'

I look at the Ma'mur but his face is closed. 'You heard what the Basha said,' he says.

As I stand I feel the tears well up behind my eyes and I am so angry that I point at the notice hanging on the wall above their heads. 'You see this?' I say – it reads "The Police in the Service of the People" – 'I think it would be more honest if you removed it.'

I drive away from the clearing but I am weeping at the wheel. I know what the men will be going through and the women know it too. They are all crying softly. I see the rope around 'Am Abu el-Ma'ati's neck, the blood trickling from the corner of his mouth into the fine wrinkles of his chin. I wince at the blow that lands on his face, on the back of his neck: 'ya *kalb* ya ibn el-*kalb* –' I have to, *have* to stop myself imagining worse –

Back at the house Khadra decides to stay with me. It is ten o'clock. I call Tareq 'Atiyya and his wife or one of his daughters answers me.

'Good evening,' I say, 'I am Amal al-Ghamrawi. May I speak to Tareq Bey?'

He comes on the line: 'Amal! Hello! You've seen the disaster at Luxor?'

'Tareq,' I say and I start to cry.

'The Governor,' I say when I've finished explaining. 'He can get them out?'

'Yes,' he says. 'I'll call him in the morning.'

'But they'll be in there *all night*.'

'Listen. I know what you're thinking but nothing is going

to happen to them tonight. The police have other jobs in hand and these are small fry. Believe me. We'll get them out tomorrow.'

I send Khadra to the village. 'Tell the women I've spoken to Cairo and insha' Allah tomorrow good will happen. Stay there and don't let anyone get rash. Tomorrow, before sunset, if the men are not back I'll be there to bring you news.'

How can I sleep? How can I work? Anna's world seems a world away. Or does it? I mess about on the Net getting details and versions of the killings at Luxor. I phone Deena in Cairo and she tells me they have news of several villages suffering like Tawasi. 'We can take up the case,' she says, 'but pulling strings is faster. Let me know what happens.' I hope the men are asleep. Small fry, wretched and cold, but asleep. I send e-mail to my brother and he phones me.

"Atiyya will get them out,' he says, 'he seems to know what he's doing –'

'It's so wrong,' I say.

'Yes, of course it is,' he says. 'But you're doing everything you can.'

'They wouldn't listen to me,' I say. 'If you'd been here they would have listened to you.'

'I'll come over if it'll make you happy,' he says.

'No,' I say, 'no.' What would he do? He probably could not even do what Tareq is doing. He's lived abroad all his life. He doesn't have the connections. 'No,' I say again, 'I'm just being – you know how I am.' I lighten my voice: 'Tell me what's happening with Isabel.'

'I've told her,' he says.

'What? About her mother?'

'Yes.'

'How did she take it?'

'She was stunned, I guess. She thinks of Jasmine as old, you know. It mainly made her see how old I am.'

'You're not old. You were massively younger than Jasmine.'

'Well, but, it put me in that generation.'

'Did she ask if I knew?'

'Yes. I said I'd only told you very recently. Anyway, she's argued herself around it now. She's decided that it's further proof that she and I were meant to happen.'

'So it's like you got it wrong the first time around.'

'Yeah. I was in too much of a hurry. I didn't realise my real mate hadn't been born yet.' The familiar laugh is back in his voice. I decide not to ask if he no longer thinks he might be her father.

'Will you come over soon?' I ask.

'As soon as I can,' he says, then adds, 'There's nothing stopping you getting on a plane, you know.'

I walk through the empty house. I go out on the veranda where I had sat with 'Am Abu el-Ma'ati and I look out across the fields towards the village, missing – tonight – seventeen men. I end up in Isabel's room in front of the portrait of my great-uncle Sharif Basha al-Baroudi. 'You see? You see, ya Sharif Basha?' I say, and the tears well up once more into my eyes. And his dark eyes look back at me and behind them lie el-Tel el-Kebir and Umm Durman and Denshwai and it seems to me that he does indeed see and I want – oh, how I want to be in his arms –

18 November 1997

At eleven there is a knock on my door. I open and Tareq 'Atiyya is there.

'What's this?' I say. 'You've come yourself?'

'I thought it would be better. I am going to the markaz. Do you want to come?'

At the markaz we find that the message from the Governor has already filtered through the several necessary layers.

'We will finish our procedures and the men will be sent home,' the Ma'mur says. He looks even more haggard and drawn than he had last night. 'So we do not need to hold you up,' he says.

'There's no holding up,' Tareq says easily. 'We shall drink a cup of coffee with you till the procedures are finished.'

The Ma'mur rings for coffee.

From the car we count seventeen men climbing into the police box. There are no ropes round their necks, but their galabiyyas are torn and bloodied and their heads are bowed. My chest is tight with tears and anger as we follow the box all the way to Tawasi.

'Khalas. Nothing will happen now,' Tareq says as he veers away from the road and on to the track leading to the house. He follows me in and when I start to say 'I'll make you some tea', the great lump in my chest dissolves and I hold on to a chair and weep. After a moment he comes over and gathers me into his arms, and against his chest I give way to my pain as he holds me and strokes my head and pats my back.

'It's over now,' he says. 'Khalas. They're home and no one will come near them again.'

'But why did it have to happen? How *could* it happen?'

'The emergency laws. Luxor —'

'But these are people who have nothing to do with anything —'

'They're home now.'

'And they were beaten. Did you *see* what they looked like?'

'They're home now, ya Amal.'

'And the other people?'

'What other people?'

'The people in the other villages. The ones whom no one got out.'

'Are you going to mend the universe? What you could do, you did.'

'All I did was call *you*. You did everything.'

'Khalas, it's over.'

'What would I have done without you? What if I didn't know you? If I hadn't been able to call you —'

'Yes but you do and you can.'

'And you drove all the way. You must have set out at five —'

'Six.'

443

'Ya Tareq, I don't know what to say to you −'

'Nothing. Here, let me look at your face. You do this to yourself? Go splash your face with cold water. Do you have any cognac?'

'Cognac?' I start to laugh. Cigarettes with 'Am Abu el-Ma'ati and cognac with Tareq 'Atiyya. Here in Tawasi.

'What's so funny about cognac?' he asks.

'Nothing,' I splutter and rush into the bathroom, where, washing my face, I start to cry again. I hear myself make small sobbing sounds like a child. I stand up straight and breathe deeply, in, out, in, out. I stare out of the window. I make myself think of his wife answering me on the telephone.

When I emerge from the bathroom, he says, 'You look terribly pale. Did you not sleep last night?'

'Not much,' I say.

I make tea and take it into the hall. With the glass in his hand, he looks around. 'How many years is it since I've been here?'

'Don't even try to count,' I say.

'You have nothing to fear,' he says. 'You shall never grow old.' In the face of my silence he continues: 'It's true. I've told you before. You grow more beautiful each time I see you.' He smiles, puts down his glass and leans back in his chair comfortably, his legs stretched out. 'I wish I could have seen you last night at the markaz, telling them off.'

'Don't,' I say. 'I must have been comic.'

'You must have been magnificent −'

As I stand, he reaches up and catches my arm above the elbow. He pulls me down, his eyes look questioningly into mine for a moment, then his mouth is on my mouth and his hand is tight in my hair. When I can breathe, I whisper 'My back', and he pulls me down to kneel on the floor while he bends over me, his kisses on my face, his hands cupping my head. 'Amal,' he breathes, 'Amal −'

I hear the knock on the door and scramble to my feet. Khadra and Rayissa are there, beaming, carrying two large

444

trays covered with white napkins: 'That you both might have lunch.' They smile.

'May your bounty be increased,' I say. 'We'll have it on the veranda in the sun.'

They lay the food on the table, stealing glances at him.

'Are the men all right?' he asks.

'El–hamdu–l–Illah,' Khadra says. 'And the village rejoices and kisses your hands.'

The women cover their smiling mouths with the edges of their tarhas and ask, 'Will you be needing us now?'

'Yes,' I say, 'stay awhile.' And they vanish into the kitchen.

'You coward,' Tareq says, and I shrug.

'Perhaps it's best,' he says. 'This is the Sa'id, after all. My, this is a festive lunch.'

At the door he says, 'I'll stay at my place tonight and leave for Cairo in the morning. You have my mobile number?'

'Yes.' I nod.

'And the first thing you do – right now – is get some sleep. Before you try to do any work or anything.'

'Yes,' I say.

'And Amal, you can't hide in Tawasi for ever.'

As he drives off, the women join me at the door.

'The Basha has his eye on you, ya Sett Amal,' Khadra says.

''Abd el–Nasser abolished titles,' I say. She tosses her head.

'A Basha is a Basha with a title or without. And this one has his eye on you.'

'What are you saying? I'm an old woman,' I say.

'Lies! You are like the moon and any man would lose his mind over you.'

'I've known him for a hundred years,' I say.

' "The near one is more deserving than the stranger",' she says.

'And he's married,' I say.

'So what?' Rayessa says. 'A man has a right to four.'

We watch his car disappearing into the distance.

'So I would marry a married man?' I ask.

'And why not? Since he has the means and will make you live and keep you happy? This is a Basha, ya Sett Amal, and he wants you. Look at him – the live image of Rushdi Abaza –'

'So I steal a man from his hareem? I destroy her life?'

'And why should her life be destroyed? She's in her house and you are in yours. And if she doesn't like it she can say so and she has her children and her apartment and her alimony. And he doesn't look like a miser.'

'And when *your* husband comes and tells you he's taken another wife, you won't change your words?'

'I'd slit his throat and drink his blood,' Rayissa laughs.

'The clever woman looks after her husband,' Khadra says, 'fences him in.'

'Thank you very much for the lunch,' I say. 'May your hands be saved. I'm going to rest now, and later I will come to the village, to greet 'Am Abu el-Ma'ati and the others.'

'Why don't you wait till tomorrow, ya Sett Amal?' Khadra says. 'Today the village will be upside down –'

'You think so?'

'It's better,' Rayissa agrees.

'Fine,' I say, 'I'll come tomorrow. And now I'll go and sleep for a while.'

'Happy dreams,' they call out after me, giggling.

I dream I am holding on to Sharif Basha al-Baroudi. I kiss his face, his eyes, his shoulders. I lie by him on the great bed in my grandmother's room and I sob with relief at having found him. He holds me and lets me kiss him, slightly amused at my passion. 'Thank God you are not my father,' I say over and over. Against his chest I feel I have come home.

I wake up embarrassed. Sad to be alone. I walk through the rooms of the empty house. In the village, the men are in their homes. Tareq 'Atiyya is in his house, a few kilometres away. But it is not him I want. I stand in front of Anna's painting, I look in on her garden and watch Sharif Basha as, with his back to me, he plots out a sheltering garden for his child. I school myself to work and open Anna's papers. Anna, my friend, who wrote all this down for me and now writes of Abu el-'Ela, my favourite bridge, the bridge they are tearing down even as I read:

Cairo
15 October 1909

Dear Sir Charles,
Today is the first day of the Eid and there are festivities all round. We have just come back from seeing the wonderful new bridge at Bulaq. It is a most amazing construction, designed by Monsieur Eiffel and built in Chicago and then transported here to lie across the Nile at the other end of the island from Ismail Bridge and form a link between the new quarter of Ghezirah and the old Port area of Bulaq. They say it is 200 tons of iron, but it is so intricate and airy that it seems as light as a bridge in a fairy tale. All of Cairo is turning out to see it and – as is usual now whenever there is a gathering of people – cries of 'Vive l'Egypte' and 'Vive l'indépendence' are to be heard and it is all most exhilarating.

We have been following the news of Dingra's trial for the assassination of Sir Curzon Wyllie; the papers printed his statements in court and before his execution and there is no one here who speaks a word against him. Al–Liwa came out on the morning of his execution with an eulogy which has already earned it an official warning, and a whole spate of fair to middling poems about him have started to appear. From this you may judge the strength of feeling there is against Britain. The Government has seen fit to reissue the 1881 decrees to muzzle the Press so that publications, theatre performances, reviews and public meetings have become subject to criminal law without appeal. Any student taking part in demonstrations, writing articles or giving news to the Press is to be expelled. Our Friday ladies' classes at the University have been suspended and we have news that Gorst is preparing a White paper that will permit him to deport people without trial. All this is causing great commotion and public protests. My husband has written an article about these measures which I have sent – in English – to James

Barrington and I pray that you take the matter up with your friends in Parliament.

Our friend Muhammad Farid Bey (Mustafa Kamel's successor at the Hizb al-Watani) is much pleased with the events of the Egyptian National Congress and his meeting with Keir Hardie. We have hopes that Labour may prove more sympathetic to Egypt's aspirations than the Liberals have so far proved. Farid Bey has caused great uproar by revealing, in al-Liwa, the plans to extend the Suez Canal lease by sixty years. It lends strength to suspicions that the Government has misspent a substantial portion of the Reserve Fund and seeks to recoup its losses by selling the lease of the Canal for four million pounds payable over four years. A meeting of several Notables of the Assembly was convened at our house two nights ago and they are determined to fight this measure.

We entertained an American gentleman by the name of Benjamin Gordon at Hilmiyya last week. He is visiting here with a view to writing a book about the Jews in Egypt and Palestine and had a letter of introduction from Sharif Basha's old friend Maître Demange in Paris. My husband introduced him separately to Cattaoui Basha, the head of the Jewish community in Cairo, and to Benzion Bey and other prominent Jewish notables. Then we had him and his wife to dinner at Hilmiyya.

I found when I spoke to him of our fears regarding Palestine that Cattaoui Basha and the others had all expressed similar sentiments, fearing that the settlers' activities are bound to cause a rift between the Jews on the one hand and the Christians and Moslems on the other. We furnished him with details concerning the activities of Mr Rupin in the Palestine Office in Jaffa (which is really a colonial office organising the purchase of land which from the day of its purchase is never to be allowed to pass into non-Jewish hands), of Dr Jacobson, who is now the permanent Zionist Representative in Istanbul, and of the transfer to Beirut of Ali Ekrem Bey, the Mutasarrif of Jerusalem, and many other matters. I am not sure, however, whether he has a clear difference in his mind between Jewish families emigrating to live in Palestine as subjects of the Ottoman State, and colonising *settlers retaining allegiance to their countries of origin. We are sending him to Shukri Bey in Nazareth and hope that what he sees there, on the land itself, may bring matters home to him.*

My husband has decided that I should be able to meet foreign visitors, especially English-speaking ones, as they all come wanting to find out about political conditions and what the Egyptians think; he feels that together we can give them a true and sympathetic account of these things and so help to inform public opinion in their countries, as they are mostly people with some influence. This breaks the social custom of segregation and so we only do it in secret and in Hilmiyya so that our household is not affected. We have a few trusted servants in attendance, chief of whom is Sabir, who used to work for James Barrington, and who has become my husband's eyes and ears in various places as he has kept up his old connections at the Agency and other households.

I understand that Cromer is still pulling the strings at the Foreign Office with regard to Egypt. Can you tell me if this is true, and what the extent of his influence is? I was most amused at your tale of Lady Cromer turning suffragette in opposition to the Lord. He surely deserves an insurrection in his own castle. It seems hard, though, that women should be jailed in England for their political opinions. They are bound to get the vote one day, so why does the Government not make a gift of it to them now with grace and spare everybody a deal of trouble?

Tawasi,
20 November 1997

I wait till after sunset prayers, then I walk along the edges between field and field, across the mud bridges over the canals and into the village. The women call out greetings and invitations from inside their doors and I reply but make my way to 'Am Abu el-Ma'ati's house. We sit opposite each other on the Istambouli settles in his mandarah and I say:

'Praise God for your safety.'

'By the grace of your hand,' he says, placing his own hand on his heart. He is washed and shaved and is wearing a clean brown woollen galabiyya with his grey shawl round his neck and his cudgel resting by his knee. His 'imma is white as snow but his eyes are dim. I hardly know what to say to him.

'Am Abu el-Ma'ati,' I say, 'I know people in Cairo, a small organisation of progressive lawyers and journalists. Good people. They can raise up a case for us.'

'Against the government?' he asks.

'Against the police. Unlawful detention, ill-treatment –'

'Ya Sett Hanim, leave it with God.'

'Ya 'Am Abu el-Ma'ati, what happened was wrong –'

'Yes, it was wrong. But it is over, by your favour.' He shifts uneasily. He wants me to stop talking about it.

'But how can we guarantee that it doesn't happen again?' I ask.

'Nobody can guarantee anything. Can anyone guarantee his own life?'

'Ya 'Am Abu el-Ma'ati, if each one when he gets home says "al-hamdu-l-Illah" and then he stays quiet, what will make the government stop treating people in this way?'

'And if I don't say al-hamdu-l-Illah, I spend what remains of my life running between lawyers – and the government puts its eye on our village and it becomes a vendetta. Like this, the matter is over. And we are neither the first nor the last village to have this happen to it. And this is not the first nor the last government to terrorise the people –'

The television in the hall speaks of yesterday's atrocity and as I leave I pause to watch the image of tens of wooden coffins laid out on the sand.

I walk through a village humming with normal life. The small store spills its bluish light on the dust road, two men sit with their nargiles in front of the counter, children play at the edge of the light. But somewhere out there I know there are men, young men, unresigned, who boil with anger and swear to avenge their villages and their people. When I think of them my blood runs cold and I clench my fists in the pockets of my coat, bow my head and hurry quickly home.

The telephone is ringing as I open the door and I rush in and get to it before the third ring. An old game I've always played: I hear it ring and the thought forms itself in my head: if I don't get to it before the third ring, something will happen to the children – and I rush forward even as I chide myself for thinking ill near them, for dragging their wellbeing into my stupid games.

'Alo?'

'Sett Amal?'

''Am Madani!'

'How are you, ya Sett? How is your health?' He is shouting into the mouthpiece. I hold the receiver a little way from my ear.

'El-hamdu-l-Illah. How are you, ya 'Am Madani? How are the children? And how is their mother?'

'She's up in safety, el-hamdu-l-Illah. She brought us a girl.'

'Alf mabrouk, ya 'Am Madani. Girls are good.'

'Girls are tender,' he says, 'their hearts are compassionate.'

'It's known,' I say. 'And what have you named her?'

'Hanan,' he says, and laughs.

'May her arrival bring you good fortune, insha' Allah,' I say.

27

Dieu m'est témoin que je n'ai fait que du bien à mon pays.
Boutros Ghali Basha, 20 February 1910

*What sad, sad events we have had here! Poor Boutros Ghali
Basha is dead and Ibrahim al-Wardani is sure to hang for it.
The most his Defence can hope to establish is that it was Milton
Bey's surgery that killed the Prime Minister rather than
Wardani's bullets, and so get the sentence commuted. But there
is very little hope of that. Husni and other gentlemen of al-Hizb
al-Watani were arrested and later released. All their houses have
been searched. But Wardani is steadfast and insists that he acted
alone and for the good of Egypt. He calls Boutros Basha a traitor
and cites his signing of the Soudan Convention in '98 and his
presiding over the Denshwai trials as evidence. He denounces
him for the Government's repressive measures over the last year
and again for being behind the plan to extend the Suez Canal
lease. All are acts for which the Prime Minister was indeed
nominally responsible, but being a man who had chosen public
service, working for a government so trammelled and circum-
scribed — my husband knew him well and is of the certain opinion
that he was no traitor. He says his plans for tax reforms put
forward in the '80s remain a byword for judgement both humane
and astute. But he was a peaceable man by nature and overawed
by British might, and he was pushed forward at every turn by
Cromer and then by Gorst, who will now make a Coptic martyr
of him. Wardani did not once mention religion, however, but
politics and politics alone. He is a clever and sincere young man:
an orphan brought up by his uncle and educated in Lausanne
and London, and he was Secretary to the National Congress in*

Geneva last year. He owns a pharmacy near the police station in Abdin and was very active in the Trade Union Movement. It is a thousand pities for — as my husband says — now the country has lost two men it could ill afford to lose. It is heartbreaking to think of Boutros Basha's last words — and to believe that he meant them.

IN FEBRUARY 1910, AFTER THE assassination of Boutros Basha Ghali, Muhammad Saʿid Basha took over the premiership and within days he had invited my brother to call on him. Abeih Sharif declined and suggested instead that a meeting could take place at the Club or at the home of one of their mutual friends. They met at the home of Ismaʿil Basha Sabri and the Prime Minister invited my brother to join the Cabinet, offering him the Ministry of Justice. Abeih Sharif responded that he was honoured but that as long as there was a British Adviser to the Ministry and an Army of Occupation to support the Adviser, he could not accept a post in Government. And my opinion at the time was that he was correct in his refusal, although Husni Bey expressed to me the misgivings of his heart for, he said, a man who stands alone, refusing to belong to any faction, is standing without cover. It became known that Muhammad Farid Bey had in his turn also refused the ministry and the following year he was sentenced to six months in jail for writing the introduction to al-Ghayati's book of verses and, having completed the term, he was effectively banished from Egypt, never to return.

But at this time, in the early months of 1910, my brother was working without rest to strengthen the resolve of the Assembly against extending the lease of the Suez Canal, and had it not been for his efforts and those of Ismaʿil Basha Abaza and Muhammad Farid Bey, the thing would have passed. As it was, the Assembly stood firm and the extension was rejected.

Demonstrations swept through Cairo and Alexandria and the Provinces expressing support of the Assembly's decision and we hoped that this triumph would lend weight also to the efforts of the several Coptic and Muslim notables who were working to strengthen our country's national unity in the face of the assassination of Boutros Basha.

Eldon Gorst was, naturally, not happy with the Assembly's decision and it was rumoured that he wished to leave Egypt but that Grey could find no one who would take his place.

All this gave us hope, and it was in this hesitantly optimistic atmosphere that we heard of the impending visit of Colonel Roosevelt, the former President of the United States of America –

Cairo
22 June 1910

Dear Sir Charles
We are not at all surprised by your report of Mr Roosevelt's speech about Egypt at Mansion House. The speech he delivered here in March was similar – but the more offensive for being at our invitation and in the University. There had been high hopes of him, as his Nation stands for Democracy and Liberty and has not (yet, in any case) sullied its hand in a Colonial endeavour. However, some remarks he was said to have made in Khartoum caused Prince Ahmad Fuad Basha, as Chairman of the University Council, to go and visit him at Shepheard's Hotel and to remind him that the Rules of the University forbade the introduction of political speech or debate within its halls. Mr Roosevelt assured the Prince he had no intention of discussing politics and then proceeded to instruct a packed hall of the Egyptian élite that it would take 'generations' before they learned to govern themselves and to admonish them for religious fanaticism!

You can imagine what a turmoil this threw the country into. Even the Reform *and the* Journal du Caire, *the newspapers of the Foreign Residents – being anxious that Egypt not be represented as in a state of chaos for the harm that would bring*

*to their businesses – were up in arms demanding apologies. The
Hizb al-Watani held a large meeting on the same day and some
thousand people marched on Shepheard's Hotel waving the
Egyptian flag and crying 'À bas les hypocrites!' and 'Vive la
constitution!' and the next day the Hizb al-Ummah held a
meeting in one of the larger cinématographe halls and Ahmad
Bey Lutfi el-Sayyid took occasion to remind Mr Roosevelt that
Egypt had attained her maturity a few thousand years before
America came into being! All in all it is very sad – not so much
in itself, but as a new disappointment to the Egyptians and
further proof that the Nations of the West hold one system of
values dear to themselves while denying it to their fellows in the
East. It is a hard lesson to learn for a people who, for the last
hundred years, have read our philosophers and admired our
institutions and have aspired to a system of government like our
own – and it must necessarily strengthen the hand of those who
would turn their faces completely from the West and hark back to
the golden days of the Caliphate. You yourself say that Egypt's
best hope now is to cleave to Turkey and hope she is strong
enough to withstand the designs of Europe.*

*Your account of Grey's speech in the Commons, responding
to Roosevelt's, and going back on three and a half years of
conciliation in declaring openly that a policy of coercion is now
to be used in Egypt, chills me to the heart. And not one word
for Egypt from the Radicals. I know Gorst is disappointed –
but what did they all expect? Surely the only possible end for
a policy of conciliation would be the granting of a Constitution
and Representative Government? Gorst knows the feelings of
the people here and he led some of them to believe that he was
their friend – that he was more sympathetic to their cause than
Cromer had been. Naturally they formed political parties, and
the Press spoke up – and what everyone demands is an end to
the Occupation. And Gorst and the Foreign Office behave as
if they have been betrayed – as if they thought that the
Egyptians would be happy with the British Government
patronising them and allowing them to play at parliaments
and are disappointed that they still want them out. It makes*

me mad. I should not be surprised if there were an agreement between Grey and Roosevelt, that the latter's speech was set up for Grey to introduce his Indian-style system of detentions and deportations for Egypt. After all, as you have said before, Roosevelt is the only foreign politician Grey takes to, because he can speak to him in English.

I have put John Dillon's recommendation before my husband and he approves the wisdom of it and thanks you. He is gone tonight to see Isma'il Basha Abaza and will propose to him that the Assembly protest publicly at the coercion laws that are being passed over their heads. It is said also that the Khedive is most angry at the decrees that are being put out in his name – and with the death of the King whom he regarded as his friend, he might yet embrace the National Cause. Dillon and Keir Hardie are now our only hopes in the House.

We are removing to Abu Qir on the North Coast for the summer. I fear my husband is overworked and hardly spends any time with little Nur, and she minds this terribly even though she has Ahmad (who is grown into a fine boy of ten. He has learned the whole of the Quran by heart and has a clear genius for the piano) –

Throughout this story, I have not been able to see my father in the child described by Anna and by Layla. Now, suddenly, I recognise him: *He has learned the whole of the Quran by heart* – and he would recite passages from it in a low voice, simply for his own pleasure, as he worked in the garden, here in Tawasi. But I had never seen him touch the piano that stood in the drawing room in our house in Hilmiyya. And now I see again the look on his face, the pride and the regret in his eyes when 'Omar played for us on his visits back from the States. And now I look again at his portrait here in the hall, standing behind his mother, looking straight at the camera. How did he, then, imagine his life would turn out?

– even though she has Ahmad and Mahrous to play with. Sharif Basha minds even more, though, for he is most conscious of the

passing of the days and but the other night exacted from me a
promise that, were his time to come before Nur is grown up and
firmly set on a path of her choosing, I should return to England
and take her with me. I said nothing could happen to him, and
indeed Baroudi Bey is seventy-five and still well though he has
not half his son's constitution. But he was serious, for he said her
life here would be too difficult if he were not near her to smooth
her path. I did not argue the point for it was but a theoretical
discussion, but I resolved that we would go to our summer house
and away from all the politics and the spies and unpleasantness
in Cairo. The sea and some good riding and building sandcastles
on the beach with Nur should clear this dark mood –

Connecticut, February 1998

Isabel raises her eyes. Beyond her table and the window, the garden and the trees are grey in the early morning mist. She shivers. The wrap has fallen from her shoulders. She feels behind her and draws its warm folds up, over her bare arms and across her chest. She shivers again as she pulls it close. She holds it to her with one hand, while with the other she takes off her glasses and pushes the hair back from her face. She lays the glasses down on the table and stands up. From outside the window comes an answering movement: a grey shape unfolds from the wooden deck, shakes itself and lollops softly towards the door.

'It's OK, Honey. Honey, Honey,' Isabel croons as she opens the door. She cannot bend easily now, but she crouches, and allows the dog's wet muzzle to settle into her hand.

'Breakfast, breakfast,' she whispers as she scratches his ears and pulls his head back. They stare into each other's eyes.

'Yes,' she says, 'yes, I miss him too.'

Scattered on the table behind her are seven love letters.

Tawasi, One hour later

'I needed to talk to you,' she said.

'I'm here.'

'I got the last of my mother's papers, the ones that were in the bank.'

'Yes?'

'His letters are here. I've read them.'

'Whose letters?' I ask, even as I see him seated across the table from me in Zephyrion, hear him say 'Imploring and arguing, you know the kind of thing . . .'

'Omar's letters. To my mother.'

'Oh . . .'

'He was in love with her.'

'Isabel. You knew that.'

'I know.' She sounds dull, flat.

'Well then?' I sound practical, brisk.

'It's different. When you actually read the letters.'

'They were written thirty-five years ago.'

'She kept them. She was talking about him before she died.'

Thank goodness he had told her, I am thinking. He could have not told her. And then she would have got the letters —

'It feels spooky being in this place, *his* place, without him. And with these letters.'

'Leave. There's no need for you to be there. What's the time with you now? Heavens! It's five o'clock in the morning. What are you doing up?'

'I couldn't sleep. I got them yesterday afternoon.'

'Isabel, this isn't right. You're pregnant. You need your rest.'

'I know, I know. Listen. How are things with you?'

'Arwa Salih is dead.' I say it before I can stop myself.

'What?'

'Arwa Salih,' I say. 'Do you remember?'

'Yes. The beautiful woman who we met at the Atelier. She's dead?'

'She killed herself. She published a little book about how hopeless everything was. Then she killed herself.'

I am still stunned by the news. By the violence and decisiveness of her act. She had gone up to the roof of her

460

building and thrown herself down to the pavement, the parked cars, below.

'That is so terrible,' she says.

We are silent and I hear her dollars ticking away.

'Yes,' I say. Then I say, 'I've been thinking, maybe if she'd had children –'

'Yes,' Isabel says.

Abu Qir, August 1910

We are become children again. We take no newspapers, we discuss no politics. The only question that occupies us is whether we should return to Cairo in time for the Ramadan fast, or wait until close to the Eid. We swim and build sandcastles, we collect shells and polished stones. We chase balls and play cards. Mahrous proves an excellent hand at Gin Rummy, and Nur can now play Snap passably well and is particularly enamoured of the Seven of Diamonds, being so transported with happiness when it is dealt to her that we contrive to slip it among her cards for the pleasure of hearing her triumphant laugh.

Baroudi Bey would not be moved and he became so distressed when Hasna tried to pack my loom that I told her to leave it where it stood. Perhaps he thinks if the loom stays there it is a guarantee of our return. The School of Art is two years opened and I am halfway done with the third panel of my tapestry.

Layla and Zeinab Hanim take it in turns to come to Abu Qir and Husni Bey comes when he can, but Ahmad stays with us all the while. We have had a small piano installed for him and when Layla is here we have exquisite music, my husband turning out (I discover after five years of marriage) to be possessed of a rich baritone and a love of the dramatic which he disguises by pretending he only mocks.

We read novels and linger over the sunsets and later, with the house asleep and our casement windows open to the sea air, we spend the sweetest hours of these wonderful days together. And in the daytime, when I watch him climb out of the sea under the blazing sun, with Nur on his shoulders and Ahmad and

*Mahrous on either side, the love I feel for each inch of his body is
an exquisite ache in my heart.*

Tawasi, March 1998

Tareq 'Atiyya appears on my doorstep.

'I was wrong,' he says. 'You *can* hide in Tawasi for ever. But
don't, ya Amal. It's a waste.'

'Itfaddal,' I say. 'Come in.' I hope I don't show how pleased
I am to see him.

'You're reading the newspapers on the computer! How
civilised Tawasi has become,' he says.

I give him a look. 'Tawasi has always been civilised,' I
say.

'I'm joking,' he says, 'joking.' He looks at the screen, scrolls
down. 'So you know everything that's been happening?
There's a revolution against the American ambassador.'

'Well,' I say, 'he's asked for it. The first thing he says when
he gets here is that the trade restrictions can take effect against
our medicines without waiting for the grace period –'

'That wasn't exactly –'

'Then he meets with the Islamists while his Congress is
accusing us of discriminating against the Copts and his
administration is planning to bomb Iraq again –'

'Why are you so embattled?' he asks.

Khadra comes in with the tea tray. She throws the edge of
her tarha over her hand before she shakes Tareq's hand.

'Marhab ya Basha. You've brought light to the village.'

'It's lit by its people, ya sett Khadra. And how are you and
how are all the people?'

'El-hamdu-l-Illah, they kiss your hands and pray for you.'

'Nobody's bothering you?'

She laughs. 'Nobody dares come near us.'

'And how's the school?'

'Working. And your young men are correct to the limits of
correctness.'

'And the kids are studying?'

'They're studying, ya Basha.'

462

'Good. Tell them to get smart. The country needs people to develop it.'

'We'll tell them, ya Basha,' she laughs. 'Do you want anything else?'

'No, thank you,' I say, 'but I'll need you in a little while.'

'I'm staying,' she says.

'So,' Tareq says when she's out of the room and I am pouring his tea, 'tell me. How long are you going to stay here? Seriously.'

'I'll stay till I've finished my – finished what I'm doing.'

'Those papers of your grandmother's?'

'Yes.'

'Is it a good story?'

'Yes. I think so.'

'How long?'

'I don't know. I like it here. I'm comfortable here.'

'Why particularly?'

I look at him. 'In Cairo, I'm in my flat. And all this big stuff is happening and I feel I should do something about it but I can't. Here it's manageable. So tell me I'm naïve.'

'A small oasis. A stable island in a sea of change. Is that what you think?' He sits back and smiles at me.

'Have you been to your place?' I ask.

'Yes.'

'What are you going to do about it?'

'I'm still thinking.'

'Tareq, would you turn people off the land?'

'Yes, and burn their crops too.'

'Are you serious?'

He sits up, annoyed. 'No, I'm not. But you take everything so much to heart. If land is to be viable, it has to pay.'

'Yes, but can't it pay just a little? Why does it have to keep paying more and more? I don't understand all this growth business – surely growth can't be infinite, can it?'

'Look,' he says, 'I'll make you a deal. I won't hire our cousins if you'll come to Greece with me for a week.'

'What?'

463

He looks at me.

'You can stuff your land,' I say. 'Tie it up with ribbon and hand it over to the Israelis for free if you like.'

'You are beautiful,' he says.

'Stop it,' I say.

'No, truly. Look I haven't come here to quarrel with you. I won't hire them if it means that much to you. I'll find someone else. Amal?' His eyes are gentle. 'I came to see how you were, and if you needed anything. And because I missed you.' He leans forward and puts out his hand. 'So can we be friends?' When I hesitate he says, 'It's all right. I know Khadra is in the kitchen.'

Cairo
1 October 1910

Dear Sir Charles,
We are returned from Abu Qir very brown and healthy and quite renewed. It is such a beautiful place with white sands and the water so clear you can see the lines that separate each shade of colour, from the palest green by the sand to the profound blue of the far distance.

We spent the entire month of Ramadan there and it was quite beautiful to sit down to our simple iftar just as the sun completed its descent into the sea. I was put in mind of that journey I made – so many years ago – into the Sinai, living so close to Nature that everything you do is determined by her and each passing minute is felt rather than made use of.

I thought of you often, for it seemed to me that the peace and wholesomeness of the air could not but be of benefit to you. I still wish you could be persuaded –

How often, I think, has Anna wished to bring everyone she loves together under one roof? For almost ten years now she has thrown herself into her Egyptian life, but in several early letters to Caroline Bourke she has repeated her invitation to come to Cairo, and in her letters to Sir Charles that invitation is almost a constant refrain. Here in Tawasi, I reflect on my

English life and I find myself wondering if there is some sense in which this, Anna's Egyptian life, will only be fully real to her once it has been linked with her older one, witnessed by someone she has known and cared for from her earliest days? She never says this, or even hints at it, in letters or in her journal. In Egypt she met a man she could love and married him, she had his child, she found a place within his family. She also found a cause. But she cannot speak her own language, cannot see her own people – and they cannot, or will not, see her. Does this cast a doubt over her life – make it seem provisional? And is this part of the reason why she adopts Egypt's cause with a more and more relentless fervour?

Cairo
16 November 1910

Dear James,
Mr Rothstein's book – which we have just received – is excellent and shows a complete understanding of how matters stand here in Egypt. His discussion of the land of the Delta being ruined by overwatering should give pause to the most fulsome in praise of Cromer's Public Works. We shall have it translated into Arabic, and even if it contains nothing that is new to the Egyptians, it should serve to remind them that not all Englishmen are their enemies. Keir Hardie's declaration for 'Evacuation and Revolution' at the Brussels Congress has given us much heart – but it remains to be seen whether he takes up Egypt's cause in the House.

Shukri Bey al-Asali is involved in a great campaign in Palestine to prevent some 2400 acres of prime land adjacent to his estates in Nazareth and Jenin being sold to the Palestine Land Development Company. The vendor, Elias Sursuq, a Syrian Christian, is a great friend of the Mutasarrif of Beirut, who has jurisdiction over the entire district, and Shukri Bey has therefore had the Police raiding his house more than once.

Police raids are an experience that I have been spared, thank God. As my husband has chosen not to take up membership of al-Hizb al-Watani, we are not subject to the raids and arrests

465

*that beleaguer our friends who are Members. Any action against
our house would of necessity be a specific one, and since Sharif
Basha is meticulous in doing everything according to Law – and
Law still rules in Egypt – we are, I believe, safe on that front.*

*Dear James, I read my letter and for a moment I wonder at
myself and at the distance I have travelled since those quiet years
in England. I wonder, what if Edward had not gone to the
Soudan? What if Sir Charles had not come to Egypt in '82 and
so impressed me with his stories? How much is our life governed
by the lives and past actions of others? But I shall not tire you
with these thoughts. They are more suited to a fireside chat, and
that is something we are not likely to enjoy for some time –
although I do yet hope that all my husband's and others' work
should not go unrewarded and that by doubling and redoubling
our efforts we shall indeed see the day when we all breathe a freer
air –*

As Anna lifts her eyes from the letter, I see Mabrouka come
into the haramlek.

'You will make yourself blind with all this writing,' Mabrouka scolds. 'Blind,' she repeats, shaking an admonishing
finger. 'May evil stay outside and far away. What's all this
learning useful for? You and Sett Layla, always writing,
writing. Does anyone eat this writing or drink it? Does it
bring up the children or plant joy in any heart?'

AT THE SAME TIME OUR concern was growing for the
situation in the Holy Land. The victory of Japan over
Russia in '05 – a victory in which Egypt, or the Arab
countries in general, rejoiced as showing that an Oriental
nation could repulse the attack of a European one – that
victory, or rather the Russian defeat and the persecution
that followed it, had caused a great new wave of some
100,000 Russian Jews to descend on Palestine. And
although half of them left again, the remaining 50,000
needed land to settle. After Herzl's death the new leadership of the Zionists was younger and more aggressive.

466

Weizmann declared that although it was necessary for the Zionists to keep their case before the world, the Charter they sought would be worth nothing unless they had already settled large portions of the land. Their policy would be immigration, colonisation, and the education of their own people in their ideals. Our friends and family in Palestine were living in the midst of this. They fought each instance of land transfer, but the decision was always in the hands of the Government in Istanbul, and the Turks needed money.

Towards the end of 1910, when the people of the Hauran rose up against the Turks, complaining of the Capitulations and of the failure of the Government to protect them in the face of the Zionists' activities, and the Turkish Government sent Sami Pasha al-Faruqi to quell them, our cousin Shukri Bey al-'Asali wrote an Open Letter to Sami Pasha describing how the Palestine Office targets prime land and organises its purchase by the Land Development Company on behalf of the Settlers, the funds being loaned at 1 per cent by the Anglo-Levantine Banking Company. How a condition of the purchase is that the land can never be sold or rented to a Muslim or a Christian. How the Settlers never mix with the Nationals or buy goods from them, but in each village and colony they set up their own central committee and school. He wrote that they fly their own flag and have their own anthem and their own postal service. They do not become Ottoman subjects but turn to their own Consuls for all their affairs. They teach their children martial arts and fill their houses with weapons and Martini rifles. Is it any wonder that the villagers are fearful and the notables disturbed?

This letter, and my brother's introduction to it, I translated into French and Anna into English, and we sent it to Mr James Barrington to use his good offices to get it published in the West.

Tawasi, March 1997
My computer pings and I've received an e-mail from Isabel:

Amal, Hi,
About those letters: It will be all right. God, I
must have sounded bad the other day. I was very
confused. I have read them over and over again
and now I feel as if they were written to me. It's
not just that I've gotten used to them. It feels
more real than that. Does this sound crazy? If
people can write to each other across space, why
can they not write across time too? And after
all, she was my mother. He is not my father,
though. I am totally definite about that. I
know Jonathan was my father. I have suggested
that we do a DNA but Omar does not want to. So
that's fine by me. Amal, I do miss you and I would
so love to sit with you again on your balcony and
talk as we did before. You are very sweet and
generous to keep my things for so long. Do feel
free to move them if you have to. But I like the
idea of them there, in your flat in Cairo, waiting for me to come back. How is Anna doing? No,
don't tell me. You can tell me everything when we
are back on that balcony with our cold drinks in
our hands and your neighbours' TV flickering
away. Tell Deena I'm so sorry about Arwa Salih.
    Love, Isabel.

18 November
We have just heard the news of Tolstoy's death. He has lived to
a good old age and has achieved as much as a man can hope to —
and yet his death saddens me. I have derived more enjoyment
from Anna Karenina *and* War and Peace *than from any other*
novels that I have read.

28

'Deux phénoménons importants, de même nature et pourtant opposés, qui n'ont encore attiré l'attention de personne, se manifestent en ce moment dans la Turquie d'Asie: se sont le réveil de la nation arabe et l'effort latent des Juifs pour reconstituer sur une très large échelle l'ancienne monarchie d'Israel. Ces deux mouvements sont destinés à se combattre continuellement, jusqu'à ce que l'un d'eux l'emporte sur l'autre. Du résultat final de cette lutte entre ces deux peuples représentant deux principes contraires dépendra le sort du monde entier.'

Négib Azoury, Paris, 1905

Cairo, 20 October 1911

'The whole area stands together or falls together,' Shukri Bey says. 'Omar Tusun is right to call for volunteers to fight the Italians in Libya. The Libyans themselves have requested it.'

'Kitchener will not allow them to go,' Ya'qub Artin Basha says. 'He will find a way to stop them.'

In the midst of the men a black upright stove sends out its heat. On the glowing holes at the top Ya'qub Artin has carefully placed some chestnuts, each with a neat incision in its side. The men are ten years older than they were at the beginning of this story. Ya'qub Artin is a little plumper but as sleek as ever. Shukri al-'Asali and Sharif al-Baroudi are both still tall, broad-shouldered men, but their hair is more shot with white, the lines around their mouths and in their brows more pronounced. Of the two, it is now Shukri Bey who gives off more nervous energy, more anger:

'Sharif Basha? You have been silent all evening?' he prods his old friend.

'Ya'qub Basha is right,' Sharif Basha says. 'It is all arranged – since the Entente.'

'France takes Morocco and the Italians' price is Libya,' Ya'qub Artin says. 'Germany and Russia will divide up Persia. Britain has the biggest prize in Egypt, but she is also arming the Arabs in Sinai –'

'And we will go to the Zionists,' Shukri Bey says bitterly.

'You might not.' Ya'qub Artin picks up a chestnut with his

silver tongs, examines it and lays it down carefully on its other side. 'You just won a battle against them in Parliament.'

'I lost the Sursuq case.'

'But you forced Çavid Pasha to resign.'

'It was shameful. He is a Dönme, and as minister of finance he has been borrowing from the Zionists against crown lands in Palestine. The government is so indebted to the Zionists it is practically in their pockets.'

'Money, money,' Artin Basha says softly, 'always money. 'Abd el-Hamid at least used to turn them down.'

'They say he is so ill-tempered in his exile, all his hareem have left him.' Shukri Bey smiles briefly.

A chestnut pops and Ya'qub Basha picks it off the stove with his silver tongs, laying it on a plate to cool down. He turns over two of the others.

"'Abd el-Hamid did not need money so badly,' Sharif Basha says. 'The Turks are beleaguered on every front.'

'So,' Shukri Bey says, 'we shall sit back and allow them to carve us up?'

There is a silence.

'What about the killings?' Shukri Bey says again. 'The thousands killed in Morocco and Libya? The people turned off their lands in Palestine? The French atrocities in Algeria?'

'These have become commonplace,' Sharif Basha says, 'and will become more so if there is a war between the Europeans.'

'An Alliance between them would be even worse for us,' Ya'qub Basha says.

A war is bad and an alliance is worse. And one of them has to happen. This is a race to subjugate the world – each nation using the tools it masters best: France, brute strength; Italy, terror; Britain, perfidy, false promises and double dealing; the Zionists, business schemes, blackmail and stealth. And Egypt? What is Egypt's strength? Her resilience? Her ability to absorb people and events into the pores of her being? Is that true or is it just a consolation? A shifting of responsibility? And if it is true, how much can she absorb and still remain Egypt? Sharif Basha looks up at Nur's trees, taller than him now, and sturdy after five short years. His daughter and the light of his eyes. When she hugs him she pats his back as though he were in need of comfort. How he wishes he could protect her! Turn her loose into life as he releases her into this garden: free but lovingly watched over. And what of Ahmad? And Mahrous? Already they are climbing out on the roof of their school to shout 'el-Dustur ya Efendeena' at the windows of 'Abdin Palace. Will they too spend their lives in battle, caught up in events not of their making? Using all their energy, all their intelligence, to ensure that things do *not* happen? 'But, my love,' he hears Anna say, 'you misrepresent yourself again. Look at all that has been achieved: the university is there. Education for women is moving fast. The School of Fine Art already has one brilliant graduate: Rodin himself has agreed to take young Mukhtar into his studio. Look at the articles you have written, the people you have defended. Look at your people in Tawasi —'

COULD WE HAVE LIVED OUR lives ignoring politics? The Occupation determined the crops that the fallah planted, it stood in the face of every industrial project, it prevented us from establishing our own financial institutions, it hampered our wishes for education, it censored what could be published, it deprived us of a voice in the Ottoman parliament, it dictated what jobs our men could hold and it held back the emancipation of our women. It put each one of us in the position of a minor and forbade us to grow up. And with every year that passed we saw our place in the train of modern nations receding, the distance we would have to make up growing ever longer and more difficult. It sowed distrust amid our people and pushed the best among them either to fanatical actions or to despair. And in Palestine we saw a clear warning of what the colonialist project could finally do: it could take the land itself from under its inhabitants.

Could we have ignored all this? And what space would have been left for our lives to occupy? And what man with

472

any dignity would have consented to confine himself to that space and not tried to push at its boundaries? And what woman would not have seen it as her duty to help him? My brother had pushed at boundaries for thirty years with every legal means available to him. He campaigned against repressive laws and defended Egyptians against them. With Anna at his side he met foreign visitors and hoped to influence them. His voice, after the death of Mustafa Kamel, was the only voice from our part of the world to address the powerful West. But in that year, the first year of the second decade of this century, I sensed a growing distance between him and his work — a distance of the emotions.

Sharif Basha glances up at the haramlek. Behind Anna's lattice her light is on. She is writing her letters, her journal, waiting for him. He crosses the courtyard towards his father's shrine. He would like to spend more time with Anna in Tawasi. The weeks they have spent there and in Abu Qir have been among their happiest. In Tawasi you keep hold of the things that matter: the land and the people. And he is lucky to have land. Land that he can leave to Nur and to her children, to keep them rooted and in touch with the things that matter. Land that they can go to when the world gets too much.

Mirghani is asleep behind the door but his father is not in his bed. Sharif Basha finds him seated by the tomb, leaning his head against the cold marble.

'Kheir, my father?'

There is no reply.

'Could you not sleep?' The old man does not answer and his son asks again: 'Could you not sleep?'

'The time for sleep will come,' Baroudi Bey says softly.

Sharif Basha lowers himself to the floor by his father and takes his hand. 'Are you worried about something?' he asks.

'God is forgiving and merciful,' the old man whispers.

Sharif Basha sits in silence, his father's frail hand clasped gently in both his own. When his father whispers again, he leans close to catch his words.

'He was no traitor,' the old man says, and his son knows he speaks of 'Urabi.

'No,' he says. 'God have mercy on him.'

'They betrayed him,' the old man says. 'De Lesseps betrayed him.'

'God have mercy on him too,' Sharif Basha says, 'all this was a long time ago.'

'God forgets nobody,' Baroudi Bey says. 'His mercy is vast. And He forgets nobody.'

'Recite "Say He is God, the Only One," and ease your mind,' Sharif Basha says. 'Come, lean on me and I will walk you to bed.'

The old man leans his head against the tomb and closes his eyes.

A rustle at the door and Zeinab Hanim hurries in. She is in her dressing gown and carries a spirit lamp in her hand.

'Whatever is the matter?' she cries, and Mirghani springs to his feet. 'Why are you both sitting here by the tomb like this?'

'My father could not sleep,' Sharif Basha says. His father's hand holds tightly to his.

'Get up, ya Baroudi Bey,' she says. 'You will surely get piles sitting on the cold floor like this. You too, ya habibi, get up. Get up.'

Sharif Basha helps his father to his feet, and with his mother lighting the way, he walks him back to his cell, past Mirghani sitting dazed on his pallet, and sits him down on the bed.

'I'll get Mabrouka to make you some aniseed tea, to help you sleep,' Zeinab Hanim says.

'No,' her husband says, his voice plaintive, 'I don't want aniseed. I want something cold.'

'We shall get you some tamarind.' His wife turns to Mirghani.

'Water will do,' the old man says, and Sharif Basha pours him a glass from the jug on the chest of drawers. When he has drunk it he looks up at his wife. 'Stay with me, ya Zeinab, don't leave me.'

474

'Yes,' she says. 'Whatever you want.'

'Stay with him where?' Sharif Basha looks at the narrow bed.

'Leave him to me,' his mother says. 'You go to your wife now. It is late.'

When he goes in to Anna, he says, 'I looked at your loom. It is empty?'

'I have finished the tapestry. It took long enough.'

'Where is it, Anna? Can I see it?'

'Mabrouka and Hasna are stretching it and sewing on the backing. When I have stitched it together I shall exhibit it for you.'

'So what shall you do now?'

'You know what I would really like to do?' Anna puts her arms around her husband's neck.

'What, my love?'

'I should like to paint you. But you never sit still long enough.'

'Khalas ya Setti. I shall sit.'

'Truly?' Anna looks up at him in surprise. She had not thought it would be so easy.

'Yes. I shall sit in Nur's garden and watch her play and you can paint to your heart's content.'

I DO NOT SAY THAT he was losing heart, rather it was as if he had managed to climb above the mists of our daily concerns and had seen the chart of his life in its just proportions. 'You are young,' he said to me, 'and you have time.' But for himself, he wanted to slow time down. Ahmad was eleven and Nur was six. I used to look at them and pray that their childish affection, so strongly rooted, would green and flower and last them through their lifetimes.

'If you suck your thumb you'll have protruding teeth and no one will marry you,' Hasna says.

'Ahmad will marry me whatever I do.' Nur takes her thumb out of her mouth for long enough to say the words and puts it back in.

'A girl with a hard head,' Hasna says.

'Let her be,' Mabrouka says tenderly. She holds out her arms and Nur comes into them, snuggling, thumb in mouth, against the warm breast, taking in the same scent of orange blossom her father had breathed in half a century before. Mabrouka's hand cradles the child's head, strokes her hair. 'The name of the Prophet guard and protect you,' she whispers. 'May He write down happiness for you wherever you go.'

20 October 1911

. . . it is an incomparable blessing and joy to know that I have eased my husband's burden and that in the darkest moments of these last ten years he has turned to me and he has found comfort.

If it were possible I would say I love him more now even than I did at the beginning. It is as though my heart and soul grow and expand to make room for this love. Or as though as I perceive each new aspect of him – or as he changes, my love grows to encircle and hold what I see.

And yet I do not know what to make of his recent mood for I have, of late, seen some intimations that lead me to fear that he may be losing heart. He continues to defend cases vigorously, but he no longer seizes on opportunities to place his cause, the cause of Egypt, before the public. He has said, on two occasions, that he would like to spend more time in Tawasi, or perhaps travel abroad. But I own I cannot imagine him leading the life of a private gentleman. For all the happiness that I would have in private times with him, there would be the sadness of knowing that he has relinquished the one essential purpose of his life –

Tawasi, 15 July 1998

The headlines on my computer read: Security Council demands Israel cancel Project Greater Jerusalem – European Parliament rejects report on Islamic Fundamentalism threat –

Beirut demonstrations demand release of Arab prisoners from
Israeli jails — Algerian journalists in protest demonstrations —
Israeli reservists refuse to confront Palestinian civilians —
Famine in Sudan — Bomb alert in American embassy — 3
killed in fundamentalist confrontation in Upper Egypt.

Isabel's e-mail reads:

```
Amal, Hi!
The doctors say it's safe to travel with Sharif
now so we are coming over on the 17th. He is so
adorable I cannot wait for you to see him. Omar is
starting his tour but says he might come to Cairo
but he will let us know. I shall go to your apart-
ment and call you from there. Don't worry about
me, Tahiyya can sort me out, I'm sure.
    Love,
    Isabel.
    I can't wait to see you. Omar has given me some
fabric to bring to you. He says you know what it
is.
```

My brother's e-mail reads:

```
Dearest, all's well that ends well. It hasn't
ended yet though, has it? The baby is fantastic
and Isabel is a devoted mother. He has your eyes
-- our eyes, I suppose. Can you tear yourself
away from your fallaheen for me or will I have
to come to Tawasi and play the 'umdah? I'll let
you know when I'm coming over. The kids are de-
lighted with the baby. Relief.
    Much love w' mit bosa --
```

Khadra comes in pale with morning sickness. She tells me 'Am
Abu el-Ma'ati is not well. In the evening I go to see him. It is
the first time I enter beyond the mandarah and into his
bedroom, where I find him propped up in a big brass bed.

477

'It's a small thing and will pass,' he tells me, but he has to pause for breath.

'Have you seen a doctor?' I ask.

'Yes, the doctor came and wrote him a medicine and we got it,' his wife says. She shows me the medicine: a painkiller and an antibiotic.

'What can I do?' I ask.

'Nothing, ya Sett Amal, may He keep you safe. He is not in pain and his breathing is easier now.'

I sit with him for a while in silence. When I leave I press the gnarled hand lying on the green cotton counterpane. His son insists on walking me home.

Cairo
25 October 1911

Dear James,
We had your Dr Ginsberg to dine last night at Hilmiyya with Husni and Layla. This is the first time that Layla dines in mixed company in Egypt and her brother and husband are taking some risk by permitting it, but we all got on very well for Dr Ginsberg is indeed a most charming gentleman and you did not exaggerate the breadth of his learning and his grasp of affairs. He and my husband – as you suggested – will write two articles, each giving a kind of summing-up of the political situation today, from their respective points of view. And if Mr Blunt should write the third and they should all be published together, this conjunction must surely have some effect on the public mind.

It was not all solemnities, however, for Dr Ginsberg told Jewish jokes and Husni and my husband Egyptian ones, and I heard Sabir as he poured the coffee mutter 'May God bring this to a good end' for there is not generally so much mirth round our dinner table.

My husband speaks – privately – of turning his back on politics and public affairs and leading a private life with me and the children. I do not believe that is possible. I think he would grow restless and weary. And yet there is justice in his view that events have become too large, that almost nothing that can

478

happen within Egypt — short of another assassination — will
change how things go for her now. What a small place the world
is become and how interlocked its interests!

The picture you send of your mama and her garden is
exquisite —

Cairo, 2 August 1998
In Tawasi we sat on the veranda as we had done a year ago —
old friends now, and sisters. The doors were open into Isabel's
room, where her baby lay on my grandmother's bed, barricaded with pillows, protected by the mosquito netting and
watched over by Sharif Basha. He touches me to the heart. I
had forgotten how downy their heads are, how delicate their
ears, how soft their skins. I had forgotten their scent.

I had not been able to go to Cairo, for 'Am Abu el-Ma'ati
died on the day of Isabel's arrival. He died quietly and easily,
with his forefinger outstretched, with his children and grandchildren around him, with his wife moistening his lips with
wet cotton wool and his son's name inscribed on the flyleaf of
his Qur'an. God was generous to him, for he died in the
morning and so he was washed and prayed over and buried
before the sun set. And in the evening the people of all the
villages surrounding us came to Tawasi to shake his sons'
hands and sit with his wife and daughters and speak of his life
and invoke God's mercy on him while the chant of the
Qur'an washed over the houses and the planted fields and the
still canals.

And Isabel had not been able to wait, for it was a Friday,
and I said I would have to stay in Tawasi till the first Thursday;
so I turned, once again, to Tareq 'Atiyya, for I could not see
her on the train or braving the barricades in the back of a
Peugeot taxi with her baby. And Tareq had sent a car and a
driver and she and I had hugged on my doorstep and even
though the village could not rejoice, with 'Am Abu el-Ma'ati
dead just the day before, the women still came round in the
afternoon before they went to his house for the Second Day
to congratulate her and to see the baby and bring him gifts,

and every one of them said, 'And where's the Basha? He lets you travel like this alone with the child on your arm?' And I wondered how many times, over the coming years, she would hear this phrase.

'They'll really let him have it when he comes, won't they?' Isabel said. She is happy and appears settled. She is still in love but no longer in pain. She has him now – in part, anyway.

We sat on the veranda and she told me, once again, of Jasmine's death and we wept a little, together, for both our mothers, and then for our fathers too. And I told her Anna's story so far and we wondered over the distance that had been placed between the two branches of our family when Anna and Layla had been like sisters and Nur and Ahmad had loved each other so much. And she told me of 'Omar and how he had never yet said he loved her but everything showed that he did. And he had come with her to the hospital but could not bear the delivery so paced outside the room like an expectant father in an old movie. And when he had come in he had held her tight and whispered, 'I was so afraid for you.' But when the nurse gave him the baby and he held it and looked into its eyes, she had seen a completely new look come over his face and she knew he belonged to little Sharif for ever.

I packed my computer and Anna's papers. Isabel came with me to the Thursday, and on Friday morning we put everything in the car. We agreed that she would sit in the back seat and hold Sharif since I did not yet have a baby-seat. We kissed Khadra and Rayessa and said we would be back soon and try to bring the Basha with us, and I remembered I had not packed Anna's green flag. So I ran back in and fetched it, which was just as well since after the third barricade the temperature gauge teetered towards the red, and we decided we would not wait for the car to start smoking, but we would stop and let her cool down, then fill the radiator from the massive firkin of water we had brought with us, for we were women who learned from our mistakes. Once again we spread out our rug and sat by the roadside – but this time we had the baby. So I rooted in the car and found the flag and we pushed three sticks into the earth and spread the flag over them, and the baby lay on the rug with his mother on one side of him and me on the other and above his head the green and white flag of national unity.

And as we sat there, Isabel told me she wanted to make sure my brother knew that she understood his work and what it meant to him – not just the music, but the writing too. She had created a home page for him and linked it with several information sites, and now his articles went across the world and into cyberspace the moment they appeared in the paper.

Cairo, 26 October 1911

«Put simply, the East holds two attractions for Europe:

1. An Economic attraction: Europe needs materials for its industries, markets for its products and jobs for its men. In the Arab lands it has found all three.

2. A Religious, Historical, Romantic attraction to the land of the Scriptures, of the Ancients, and of Fable.

This attraction is born in the European while he is still *in his home country*. When he comes here, he finds that the land is inhabited by people he does not understand and possibly does not much like. What options are open to him? He may stay and try to ignore them. He may try to change them. He may leave. Or he may try to understand them.»

Self-evident, Sharif Basha thinks, laying down his pen. So self-evident as to be hardly worth saying. But Anna does not think so. Anna, when she sees a wrong, cannot rest until it has been put right. Besides, she wants to make him happy. Not just happy at home, but happy altogether. He knows she imagines a day when the shadow within which their life together has been lived will be lifted. And she still has confidence in public opinion; that if only people can be made to see, to understand – then wrongs can be undone, and history set on a different course.

«The last two options are harmless, but they are never chosen – unless it be by individuals. The first two, when linked to large movements of people, to Colonial Enterprise, are of untold harm.

As to the first option, it may be safe to suggest that the more the Colonialist wishes to ignore the inhabitants, to deny their existence, the stronger the historical or religious ties he claims to the land. This is what we are witnessing now with the Zionist Colonial enterprise in Palestine. I say Zionist rather than Jewish, since there are many Jews who, seeing the Zionist project in its true colours, have been at pains not only to distance themselves from it but to warn other of their co-religionists against it. They have done this at no small cost to themselves.

And for the second, the Romantic European can lend himself without too many pangs of conscience to a Colonial Enterprise such as the one we have been living with in Egypt for thirty years – the one that is beginning in Morocco and Libya. He speaks of the White Man's Burden, of his duty to help 'primitive' nations fulfil their potential, his duty to civilise them. He is intrigued by the image of himself as a Reformer – a Saviour. He feels righteous as he 'protects the peace', 'supports the legitimate sovereign', 'ensures the safety of the religious minority' or the Europeans.

There is also a kind of attachment that comes from a satisfaction with the European's own image of himself in the East, an image different from the one he has of himself in his own country and among his own people. Certain aspects of the European's personality which find no outlet in his own land, he allows to flourish while he is in the East.

Thus the new economic ambitions of Europe in the East find a good use for the old feelings of Europe towards the East.

Seen in this light, every question is answered and all

the pieces fit into place: the Treaties between the Powers according them 'free hands' in the countries of the East. The aggression of France against Morocco and Italy against Libya. The cooperation between finance and politics in the project of displacing the Palestinians and creating – in the heart of the Arab lands – a state not merely friendly to Europe, but European in substance and Colonial in ideology. Europe simply does not see the people of the countries it wishes to annex – and when it does, it sees them in accordance with its own old and accepted definitions: backward people, lacking rational abilities and subject to religious fanaticism. People whose countries – the holy and picturesque lands of the East – are too good for them.

And what of us Orientals? What of our responsibility in all this? We in Egypt have been proud of our history; proud to belong to the land that was the first mother of civilisation. In time she passed the banner of leadership to Greece and then Rome, and from there it reverted to the lands of Islam until in the seventeenth century it was taken hold of by Europe. For the last hundred years, we have tried to find a place for ourselves in the modern world. But our attempts have collided with what Europe perceives as her interests.

There have been those among us who have been so dazzled by the might and technological wizardry of Europe that they have been rather as a man who stands lost in admiration at the gun that is raised to shoot him.

And our hands have been tied by the presence in our countries af an earlier Imperial Master: the Ottoman Turk. And it was in the weakness of the Turks and the turbulence that attended each country's attempt to rid herself of the rule of Constantinople that the European Powers saw their chance to take control of our lands.

The Colonialists' response – if response there is – to this article, will be to say that it does not express a general view. That its author is an Anglophile or Francophile or a -phile of some sort that renders him not representative of the mass of his people. To this I say that there are many others who think and speak as I do. And that this body of men and women bears the same relationship to the fallaheen of Egypt and the Arab lands as your Honourable Members to the farmers of Somerset or the factory-hands of Sheffield whom they represent in your Parliament.

If there are elements of Western Culture in us, they have been absorbed through visiting your countries, learning in your institutions and opening ourselves to your culture. There we have been free to choose those elements that most suited our own history, our traditions and aspirations – that is the legitimate commerce of humanity.

Our only hope now – and it is a small one – lies in a unity of conscience between the people of the world for whom this phrase itself would carry any meaning. It is difficult to see the means by which such a unity can be effected. But it is in its support that these words are written.»

Cairo, 2 August 1998
'The Internet,' Isabel says, lifting little Sharif against her shoulder, patting his back. 'I am serious. The potential is incredible. Look at all the action and information groups on it. The speed with which you can get a piece of news out. The freedom from control. Have you seen all the postings in support of the civilians in Iraq?' The baby burps and she turns her face slightly to kiss his head.

Cairo, 28 October 1911
Sharif Basha puts Anna's translation into an envelope and seals it. Tomorrow it can go to Barrington. The Arabic will come out in *al-Ahram*, under his own name, as a letter. Anton el-Jmayyil will see to it. The French will appear in *Le Temps*,

when Ginsberg and Blunt have done theirs. For him, he is finished. He stands, pushes back his chair and stretches. Anna looks up from her book.

'Ça va?' she asks.

'Yes.' He nods.

'You are supposed not to know English, but you always read my translations?'

He smiles, shrugs. 'An old habit; I read what will come out under my name.'

'You think I might misrepresent you?' Her answering smile is mischievous.

'Only with the best intentions. I am a lawyer, after all.' He sits down heavily on the sofa next to her. He lifts her book and looks at the cover. 'Are you reading *War and Peace* again?'

'I like going back to things I know.' She puts the book aside. 'You see more in them the second time.'

'A pity we can't do that with life,' he says.

'What would you do differently?'

His face clouds for a moment, then he answers lightly, 'I would walk up to you in the Costanzi and say, "You do not know it yet but you are in love with me . . ."'

Anna laughs as she reaches for his hand. 'We would have had an extra fourteen months.'

'Or you might have run away – and we would not have had this.' He eases a lock of blond hair from the grips that hold it down, fingers it, lets it spring free.

'We could never have not had this,' she says, 'it's impossible. What would life have been? This is forever.'

'Amen,' he says, smiling into her eyes.

'That's what Mabrouka always says,' says Anna, leaning back, 'but she says "Ameen". Is it Arabic?'

'Yes.' Stroking the smooth neck, the soft skin behind the ear.

'When I was a child I always wondered what it meant,' Anna says.

' "Amn" is safeness and security and "amana" is to believe – to become secure in your belief. When someone says something and you say "Ameen", you are saying you believe in what they've said and also that you wish to secure it.'

'I love you when you explain things seriously.'

'You weren't listening.'

'I was. But I was also thinking how sweet you are.'

'Sweet, yes. That's me. Anna, you are a frivolous woman.'

'You know, when Nur is serious she looks just like you.'

'I see *you* in her all the time. She is the most beautiful child. These eyes, Anna, these eyes –' and now he gathers her close and his lips are on hers and there is that familiar feeling, miraculous in its constancy, at first like the strains of music heard from far away, then coming closer and closer till Anna pulls her head back and says, 'Shall we go upstairs?'

'Yes,' he says, 'yes. But I have to look in on my father. Wait for me in bed.'

He stands, pulls her to her feet and pats her off in the direction of the doorway. Then he steps out into the cold courtyard.

29

Perchè, perchè, Signore,
Perchè me ne rimuneri così?
Tosca

Cairo, 8 August 1998

My brother is conducting in Sarajevo, in the ruins of the National Library. I have seen photographs of it: the high ceiling and all the central floors collapsed, the marble columns rising from the edge of the abyss to support the charred scalloped arches, the atmosphere dreamy with the smoke of one million Ottoman books gone up in flames. And now, in the midst of it all, I see my brother, intense and concentrated. The moon and the stars shine down on him and his orchestra. His arms are raised, the baton poised in his fingers. A flick, a spreading of the arms and the music soars up like a great voice from the heart of the earth.

He should be here in a couple of weeks. I have copied out Sharif Basha's article for him. I have a mind to suggest that – with a few small amendments – he prints it again, now, under his own name. I see him coming through my door and I know how tight I shall hold him. I imagine him with Sharif in his arms, tender, rueful, amused at himself. Will I have finished Anna's story by then? I know I am close to the end and I have slowed down. I don't want it to end.

My brother has sent his panel of Anna's tapestry with Isabel. We unfolded it and hung it up from the bookcase: Isis, mother of every king, queenly in poise, on her head the cow-horn crown and the sun-disc of Ra. Her arm is stretched out, but her hand is missing. Isabel is delighted that she has carried her namesake from 'Omar to me.

'I told you it was meant.' She laughs. 'Isn't this a sign?'

'I thought you were rational,' I say.

'I am.'

'What about your millennium?' I ask as I watch her smooth a dab of Bonjela on little Sharif's gums.

'He'll be two,' she says. 'Imagine that. Two in the year 2000.'

'I found you something for your paper,' I say. 'Listen':

If we could shrink the Earth's population to a village of 100 people, with all existing human ratios staying the same, it would look like this: There would be 57 Asians, 21 Europeans, 14 from the Americas and 8 Africans. 80 would live in substandard housing. 70 would be unable to read. 50 would suffer from malnutrition. 50 per cent of the entire world's wealth would be in the hands of only 6 people. And all 6 would be citizens of the United States.

Isabel fastens the fresh nappy round Sharif's waist. 'No!' she says.

'Are you going to finish your course?' I ask.

'Of course I will,' she says.

'Is there a time limit on it?' I ask.

'Oh, Amal —' she begins and then interrupts herself. 'I bought you a book. How could I have forgotten? I found it in a second-hand bookshop. It's about your Mr Boyle.'

Boyle of Cairo (printed by Titus Wilson & Son Ltd, 28 Highgate, Kendal: 1965) is Clara Boyle's memoir of her husband. Isabel is delighted at my obvious pleasure as we study the photograph of Harry Boyle, looking just as I had imagined him, with a long, straggly moustache and a crumpled collar, and there is even a photograph of Toti.

Cairo
31 October 1911

Dear Sir Charles
I hear from James Barrington that you have not been too well. It is very naughty of you not to tell me yourself. I should so much

like to come and see you – and my husband says I must. He speaks of travelling to Europe, of giving Nur her first proper Christmas. I own I do love the idea – but then thinking about it creates a kind of unease in my mind, I cannot quite tell why.

You must tell Mr Winthrop to prepare a list of any medicinal herbs that he may need. If we do come for Christmas I can bring them with me. And if we do not, I shall find somebody – Mrs Butcher perhaps, or one of our Hilmiyya guests – to carry them.

Al-Ahram has published an article by my husband, setting out most simply the state of relations between the West and the East as he sees them today. It should appear in English and French soon, accompanied by articles from Mr Blunt and Dr Ginsberg, and I have hope that it may yet make an impression upon the public mind.

Nur is grown into such a beautiful child, you would love her immediately. I see a great deal of her aunt, Layla Hanim, in her. In her vivacity and her frankness and her readiness to laugh. But when she is thoughtful, I see her father –

Cairo, 10 August 1998

The ironing-boy comes up loaded with our pressed washing, Tahiyya and two of her children keeping an eye on him. When I bring out my purse and pay him, the older child, a little girl, says shyly: 'You've got pictures of the pharaohs.' She points at Anna's two panels hanging from my bookcase.

'Yes,' I say. 'Do you know who they are?'

'Isis and Osiris,' the child says while her mother covers her mouth with her hand and laughs.

'Bravo,' I say. 'Did you learn that at school?'

The child nods and retreats behind her mother's skirt.

'She's very intelligent,' Tahiyya says. 'But she's naughty like the jinn.'

'She doesn't look naughty,' I say.

'That's just because she's shy in front of you.'

Isabel comes out of her room carrying the baby. 'Who is a jinn?' she asks.

'This one,' Tahiyya says, nodding at the child. 'Give him to

490

me, ya Sett Isa –' holding out her arms – 'let me carry him for a bit.'

'And are you lacking children?' I ask as Isabel hands over the baby. Tahiyya starts to dandle him and the baby crows and chuckles.

'I've got another root for you,' Isabel says to me. 'I had it all prepared and then I forgot: "j/n".'

'Tell me,' I say.

'Well, "jinn" is a spirit, and "janeen" is a foetus and "jinan" is madness. So what's the common theme?'

'Let's look it up.' I reach for *al-Mu'jam al-Wasit* from the bookcase between Isis and Osiris. Tahiyya's little girl says:

'Why have you put them so far apart? Weren't they married?'

'There's a bit missing,' I say. 'The bit in the middle.'

'That would be their child,' Tahiyya says.

'Yes, and it would complete the aya. See –' Above Isis's head is inscribed: "It is He who brings forth –" Osiris stands facing her, above his head "– the dead". ' "It is He who brings forth the living from the dead," ' I recite. This must have been the verse that Sharif Basha chose for Anna to weave.

'But they were infidels,' Tahiyya says. 'Did they know God?'

'Ya Tahiyya, is there anyone who does not know God?'

'True,' she says. 'True, true,' she says, making it into a song, dandling the baby. I turn back to the dictionary but the phone rings and Isabel takes the book from me. It is Tareq 'Atiyya.

'Have you recovered from your journey?' he asks.

'Yes, thank you,' I say.

'And how does it feel to have a baby in the house?'

'Wonderful!' I laugh. 'Especially as there's two of us.'

'There would always be two with a baby,' he says.

'No, no. Two mothers. We take it in turns to wake up nights.'

'You sound good. It's great to hear you sound so happy.'

'And 'Omar is coming next week. He is in Sarajevo. Then he goes to the West Bank and 'Amman. Then he comes here.'

'We must all have dinner,' he says.

'That would be great,' I say.

'Amal?' he says.

'Yes?'

'When the world has settled and you are a bit more free, I want to sit and talk with you.'

'What shall we talk about?'

'You don't know?'

. . .

'Amal?'

'Tareq, I'm not the one who's not free.'

'I need to talk to you. Later. I'm just – putting down a marker now.'

'All right,' I say, 'we can talk.' We can talk, I find myself thinking, but it will come to nothing.

When I go back to Isabel, she says:

'The common theme is concealment. "Jinn" are those which are hidden, and "janeen" is a diminutive hidden one.'

'And "jinan"?'

'From "junna" – his intellect became concealed. And "al-Jannah" – Paradise, the place that is hidden –'

'Of course,' I cry. 'Oh, and Isabel, listen, "junaynah", garden, is little paradise –'

'That's just too neat,' Isabel says.

'But what about "jund", soldiers, and "janub", south?' I wonder.

The buzzer goes and Tahiyya says, 'Madani wants me downstairs.' She collects her children and hands me the baby. 'Don't you want anything?'

'Your safety,' Isabel and I both say.

It is more difficult to get down to Anna's remaining pages with Isabel and the baby in the house. Is this true, or do I make it so because I do not want to arrive at the end?

Cairo, 12 August 1998

Isabel has taken Sharif to show him off to Ramzi Yusuf and his wife, and I leaf again through Clara Boyle's memoir, looking

492

at the pictures, reading a paragraph here and a sentence there. Suddenly I am arrested by a phrase I have come across before: 'How can one arrive at the planet Souad?'

An hour later I am still sitting with the book on my knee and, on the table in front of me, the letter Anna had in such agitation given to her husband as he planted the young cypress tree for Nur back in 1906. Oh, how angry I am, and how I wish I could tell him! 'If people can write to each other across space,' Isabel had asked, 'why can they not write across time too?' But how do you write to the past? Once more I read Clara Boyle's words, written in 1965:

About 1906 there had been some disagreement between Lord Cromer and the Foreign Office in connection with a point of policy to be followed in Egypt. Lord Cromer had sent a dispatch to London, which had had no effect.

As a last resort Harry then submitted a paper which was to give a true picture of the workings of the oriental mind; it was supposed to be the translation of a letter which had reached him secretly, and as such it was transmitted to the Foreign Office. Only Lord Cromer himself knew the truth – that the original letter was written by Harry Boyle himself. Such a letter might indeed have come into his hands at that time, but as he needed it at that exact psychological moment to make his point, he did not hesitate to use his knowledge of the oriental, for what he meant to say was to the benefit of the Egyptians and towards better understanding.

The original paper, typed by Harry laboriously with two fingers, is still in my possession. As will be seen, there is all the picturesque, flowery language of the East, transposed into equally picturesque English . . .

This letter was to serve as a warning to the Foreign Office of general dissatisfaction among Egyptian people and notables. It was supposed to convey the plot of a big Nationalist rising, giving all particulars about the time, the strength, the manner of conducting the revolt against

British rule. Every single sentence, almost every word, has a double meaning. Harry must have had great pleasure in writing this letter. Although he invented the 'translation', he did not invent the spirit of it which served as a graphic illustration of the situation. Lord Cromer was delighted to have this letter at hand to drive home his point, and he sent it to the Foreign Office informing the authorities that it had come to him through one of Harry's secret contacts.

Again I check the letter quoted in the book against the letter on my table. They match word for word. Tomorrow I guess I shall be triumphant in my find. But now, all I want is to be able to rush back and tell him, show him the book, say, 'Look! You were right.'

Cairo, 15 August 1998
Sharif is restless and I hold him against me and walk him up and down. Up and down, past the screen, and the bookcase, and the tapestry, and the sideboard, and up to the mirror on the far wall, then back again. I am still thinking about Harry Boyle's letter. About his wife's confidence – not in some long-ago forgotten time, but in the Sixties, in the Sixties when *I* was alive – her confidence that he had put his finger on and had actually expressed 'the workings of the oriental mind' – *my* mind. Up and down I walk the baby, up and down. His weight against my chest soothes me, his breath on my neck comforts me. I wonder if Denshwai would have happened had Enoch not written his letter and his Lord not sent it. I wonder if that is why Cromer left Egypt just before the trial – having tested the gallows before he went. All the British officials in Cairo must have believed an uprising was imminent. Only Boyle and Cromer knew the truth. So Cromer leaves Matchell, de Mansfeld Findlay, Hayter, Bond and Ludlow to deal with what he knows they will see as the beginnings of a people's revolt. He hopes that when his leave is over and he returns to Cairo, the unrest that had shown itself

there since the Entente, since Taba, will have been cowed and he can come back once more as the 'friend of the fellah'. But it had not worked – and he had lost Egypt. Is that why in a two-volume book published in 1908 in which he lists practically every detail of his Egyptian rule, Denshwai is never mentioned?

And as for the Egyptians, Fathi Zaghlul was promoted to undersecretary for Justice after the trial but was booed wherever he went; Ibrahim al-Helbawi spent the rest of his days trying to atone – the portraits of him in later life are portraits of a haunted man. And Boutros Ghali paid with his life.

Sharif is fast asleep against me, but I don't want to put him down. Does all this matter now? After ninety years of Boyle's letter and thirty of his widow's commentary? Anna would have been incandescent.

Isabel comes into the room. She is in a pink towelling robe and is rubbing her hair dry. She hangs the towel round her neck, flings her hair back from her face and sees us.

'Oh,' she cries. 'I want to take a photo of you. Do you know, I have not taken a single photograph of Baby. I left my camera here. But you look so great together, you with your cheek resting against his head like that. Just walk, walk – while I get the camera.' She runs to her room and comes back with her bag, looking puzzled.

'Amal,' she says, 'what's this? Look! It was in my bag.'

Hanging half out of the big holdall is a fat, oblong bundle wrapped in muslin. I've seen one like it before. I know what it is before we open it.

I untie the ends awkwardly, working with one hand, while I hold the sleeping baby against me with the other. We roll out the fabric and a hint of orange blossom comes into the room, and there is the infant Horus, small and naked and still with his human head – on which rests the hand of Isis, his mother. Above him, two words: 'al-hayy min –'. The Living from –

5 November 1911

Sharif Basha's prayer beads hang from his right hand. With his left he leafs through a pile of sheets on a low bookcase in Isma'il Sabri's study. On each sheet a photograph is pasted.

'I see you are interested, ya Basha?' Isma'il Basha Sabri is seated in a deep easy chair, a chequered blanket in pale cream and blue spread over his knees.

'We know so little about them,' Sharif Basha says. 'Long ago, in the days of Mariette Basha, I wanted to go on a dig.' He turns to smile at his friend.

'Maybe you will yet.' Isma'il Sabri smiles back. 'I hear you are planning a sort of retreat from public life?'

Sharif Basha, who has turned back to the photographs, stiffens. 'And where did you hear that?' he asks lightly, picking up the sheets, rearranging them into a neat pile.

'Talk travels,' Isma'il Sabri says, his eyes steady on his old friend's back. 'Is it true?'

Sharif Basha turns. 'Do you blame me?' he asks – and it is a real question.

Isma'il Sabri shakes his head. 'I would have urged it, but I thought you would not listen. I thought you would say, "He is grown ill and fearful" –'

'You would have urged it?' Sharif Basha is surprised. 'Why?'

Isma'il Sabri makes a small ducking gesture with his head. 'You have stood too much alone. Particularly in the last few years. I have felt –'

The door swings open and Ya'qub Artin Basha hurries in followed by an apologetic sufragi who has not had time to announce him. 'Look!' Ya'qub Basha waves his newspaper. 'Unrest in the Balkans, and Turkey needs money to quell it –'

'Ya'qub Basha!' Isma'il Sabri holds out his hand. 'You will excuse me –'

'No, no. Your excuse is with you, my brother.' Ya'qub Artin grasps the seated Isma'il Sabri's hand and pumps it, then advances on Sharif Basha. The sufragi leaves the room quietly, closing the door behind him.

'You have been looking at our ancestors, I see,' Ya'qub Basha says, eyeing the pile of photographs at Sharif Basha's side. 'Our friend the poet here has been urging me to get the history of the pharaohs taught in our schools. What do you think?'

'A good idea,' Sharif Basha says.

'We do not know very much about them, though,' Ya'qub Artin says.

'Enough for schoolchildren,' Isma'il Sabri offers.

'It would be interesting to find out more,' Sharif Basha says.

'Ah! The magic of the past!' Ya'qub Artin sits down heavily in an armchair opposite Isma'il Sabri. 'So much more attractive than this present.' He throws his newspaper down on the large, marble-topped coffee table that stands between him and his host. 'There will be more massacres by the Turks and more money borrowed from Europe to fund them.'

'We are heading for war,' Isma'il Basha Sabri says, 'a big war.'

'*They* are heading for war,' Sharif Basha says from his position by the bookcase. 'It is not our war.'

'But we will suffer,' Isma'il Sabri says.

'We suffer anyway.'

'True, mon ami,' Ya'qub Basha says. 'But since when are you so fataliste?'

Sharif Basha shrugs. 'I am going to go up to Tawasi for a while,' he says, 'for the winter. These pictures you have here – I want to see the temples for myself. I want to take my family to Luxor, to the Valley of the Kings.'

'I wish I could come with you,' Isma'il Sabri sighs.

'Come,' Sharif Basha says simply. 'We will look after you.'

Why should they not travel? Take things slowly. Enjoy their time together. Ahmad can come with them. And Mahrous too if he wishes. It will be a good education for the children. His parents will be looked after, Layla and Husni are in Cairo. And his mother can come to Tawasi when she pleases. He will move Sabir and his family into the house. Sabir tells him

Kitchener likes him even less than Cromer did, although he has never met the man. Time was when he would have found some satisfaction in that. Now he does not care. Muhammad 'Abdu is dead and Qasim Amin is dead. 'Urabi is dead. Even young Mustafa Kamel is dead. Died in agony with cancer eating at his stomach. And what is it all for? A millimetre by millimetre struggle while the world sweeps by like a hurricane.

Sharif Basha paces the garden of the quiet house in Hilmiyya. They have carved out a life, a good and happy life even if overshadowed by larger matters. Perhaps it is time to set that life free. In the summer he can take Anna to Europe. And if he feels distaste at the thought of Italy, of France, he shall school himself not to think of their politics. He and Anna can take pleasure in the music, in the paintings, in the food. They can go to Palestine and visit once again the olive groves of his childhood in 'Ein el-Mansi and pray in al-Aqsa: once for himself and once for Muhammad 'Abdu. They might even go to England. Why should she not have the pleasure of going home just because of his sensitivities? People would stare? Let them stare. He would wear his tarbush in the park and outstare them. Let her have the pleasure of showing him her countryside, her Lake District, her museum with the paintings that had brought her to him. They could call on Blunt, visit Barrington. He might get on well with Sir Charles. She should have the joy of watching Nur play in the places where she played as a child. There is no need to have the whole world poisoned. He pauses under the sycamore that spreads its branches up to his bedroom balcony. Twenty years he lived in this house alone. And now it has become their hiding place. Where they have foreign guests to dinner and entertain together. And when the guests have gone and they are alone, she stands close by him on the balcony and he hears the rustle of the sycamore and remembers the nights he paced here, longing for her – and afraid.

He enters the house and strides through the halls to the street door, where Sabir is waiting for him.

'I am going home,' he says.

'I shall accompany you, ya Basha.'

They step outside and a hire carriage draws up. Sabir tries to pull up the hood but it is stuck. He climbs up on the box by the driver.

Sharif Basha leans back in his seat. He will be in time for Nur's bath. And then a quiet dinner with Anna. She does not believe that he will be happy with a quiet life. But he will; after almost thirty years of fighting, he is ready. And she? Will she be happy? She had adopted Egypt and adopted his cause. The one woman in all the world who was meant for him – and God had sent her to him. Had her kidnapped and thrown into his house. Sharif Basha smiles to himself as, once again, he sees Anna, in a man's shirt and trousers, sitting – obstinate and determined – in his mother's haramlek. What if he took her back to Sinai? Showed her the coral, this time? A whole world beneath the surface – and all you had to do was put your head in the water and open your eyes. She would enjoy that. Would she have been happier in a different life? Useless to wonder. She seems happy with him. But he could have given her more. Not more care or tenderness, but more of the ordinary things of life. She loved so many things: people and trees and painting and music and cooking. A woman who was always busy but carried a great and restful stillness always around her. Sometimes he just entered her and lay with her, not moving, just resting. And he had taken her in joy and in passion and tenderness, in sorrow and in despair. She was his sea to swim in, his desert to gallop in, his fields to plough –

'Move a bit faster, will you?' he says to the driver.

15 August 1998

It is evening and I am watching the news on television when Isabel comes into the living room.

'He is asleep,' Isabel says.

I smile at her. Another crisis burgeoning between Iraq and the United States. Not between Iraq and the United Nations –

'Amal,' Isabel says.

'Yes?' I half turn towards her.

'I know how it came to be in my bag.'

'How?' I say.

'She put it there.'

My heart sinks. 'Who put it there?' I ask quietly.

'The woman in the mosque. Umm Aya. She put it there.'

I look at her and I feel a growing anger. I have no better explanation, but I am angry all the same.

'You still don't believe me, do you?'

'No, I don't.'

'So what do you think happened?'

'I don't know. I don't know, Isabel. But I cannot –'

'Listen,' she says, leaning forward, her eyes huge, 'I've been going over it. As I was leaving, I was going to forget this bag. I had put it down somewhere inside. On the bench or on the floor. And it was open, I'm sure of that, because I had been using the camera and I hadn't closed it. And as I was leaving, she came towards me and handed it to me. She said, 'Don't forget your things.' And she smiled and hugged me. And when she handed it to me the zipper was closed.'

'And you didn't feel that the bag was heavier?'

'No.' She pauses. 'But I always find this bag heavy.'

'And you never opened it again?'

'No, I didn't. I was getting ready to go. I didn't take any more pictures. And I left it here with you.'

'I don't know,' I say, 'I don't know.'

'Well, where else would I have got the thing?' she asks. 'And why would I lie? I might as well think *you* put it there. The bag has been here for months.'

'I didn't put it there,' I say.

We sit in silence.

I WILL NEVER KNOW HOW she knew. I heard her cry before I heard the wheels, the shouts, the loud battering at the door. I was in the courtyard. We had been in Nur's room, she and I. Anna still bathed her last thing at night – as the English do. Nur was out of the tub, warm and rosy.

She would not put on her pyjamas but kept wrapping herself in the big, white bath towel. We unwrapped her and she wrapped herself up again. It turned into a game. We would pull at the edges of the towel and ask, 'What's this? What's this that we have found? Is it a monkey? Is it a gazelle?' And she would fling off the towel, laughing with delight: 'It's a girl, it's a little girl!' and wrap herself up again. And again. And again. Then she said, 'I want my doll.' We looked for the doll and I remembered she had been playing with it in the courtyard in the afternoon. I called Hasna but she must have been in the kitchen. So I went to look for the doll. And that is why I was in the courtyard. The doll was there, lying by the fountain, and as I picked it up I heard Anna's cry. A great, long cry that rang through the house and sent a shiver through my body and brought Ahmad running from the garden. 'No,' she cried – and it was an English 'no'. I looked up and she had burst out of the house – she was running along the courtyard, stumbling. 'No . . . No . . .' And then I heard the sounds outside. The wheels, the shouts, the stamping and then the banging at the door. I ran, and she was there – pulling at the heavy door as Fudeil and Mirghani came running out to help – to pull the door open. And then the men's voices saying one thing: 'El-Basha, el-Basha   '

They carried him in. My brother. Three men carried him in. And there was a small, bent old man limping after them, holding my brother's stick and his tarbush, while the horses stamped and neighed and reared outside with no one to hold them.

They carried him into the salamlek while Anna hung on to him. She had stopped screaming but she was still saying 'no' – holding on to his arm, saying 'no, no' and shaking her head. She was refusing it, turning it away, sending it back, this thing that had come to us.

'Hush,' he said. I heard him and my legs went weak with relief. A turn, a heart attack, a slight stroke, any-thing, but he was alive. He was alive and saying 'hush', and when they laid him down on the diwan and she fell to her knees beside him, he raised his hand and put it on her neck.

I did not understand it at first. What had happened. Till the men stood back and I saw the stains on their clothes and I went rushing to him – and Nur came faltering into the room following her mother's scream – still naked, trailing her towel behind her – and saw her father lying on the diwan, his eyes closed, and ran to him. I saw the blood spreading on the diwan under him and caught hold of the child. And Mirghani came to me and said, 'I shall go fetch Husni Bey' and Anna said, 'Get the doctor. Get Milton Bey and Sa'd Bey el-Khadim. Quickly.' And she was on her feet and unbuttoning his shirt: 'Can you turn over, my love? Can we turn you over?' Nur wriggled out of my arms – 'Papa is hurt,' I said, 'he's hurt' – and she was kissing his face and trying to get to the wound: 'Shall I kiss your hurt away?' He opened his eyes. 'Kiss my cheek, ya habibti, and go put your sleeping clothes on.' Fudeil had brought the medicine box and Anna was pulling out bandages and bottles and cotton wool and as they were turning him on his side he saw her holding the lengths of bandages and he said 'Are you going to tie up your hair again?' and closed his eyes. She cut his shirt, and she was speaking to him all the time as she bathed his wound and staunched it with cotton wool and held her hand tight over it. I came close and said 'Abeih?' and he opened his eyes and said 'Layla? They've done it – the dogs –' and I said 'Who ya Abeih? Who?' and he said, 'There are plenty of dogs. Don't be afraid. Send for mother. And put Nur to bed. And see to Sabir.' Sabir's wound was in the shoulder. He had thrown himself over my brother when the shots rang out.

My mother was at the wedding of Mustafa Pasha Fahmi's youngest daughter. I sent for her. I put Nur to bed and made Hasna stay with her. She was no use downstairs and kept calling, 'Sidi! Sidi el-Basha!' I told

Nur her father was fine and her mother was looking after him and he just needed to sleep. Coming down the stairs I leaned on Ahmad, but my heart had been wrenched loose and was stumbling and banging itself against the walls of my chest. I could only draw my breath in short, shallow pulls. I was whispering 'ya Rabb, ya Rabb' continuously. I put water to boil and I said to Ahmad, 'It is a wound, just a wound, Khalu is strong and the doctors are on the way', but fear was a tight band round my chest and my heart kept banging into it.

As I went downstairs I heard the galloping outside. All night the horses were galloping to and from our house, and as I went into the salamlek Milton Bey hurried in, already opening his bag.

Three bullets. Two in his stomach and one in his back. Milton Bey and Sa'd Bey said they would have to take them out and Mirghani went upstairs to bring the boiling water and Husni came and they lit a spirit lamp and they said Fudeil and Mirghani and Sabir should stay and we should leave. Ahmad would not leave his uncle's side. Anna and I went outside into the courtyard and stood close by the wall. And we prayed and prayed and his first clenched cry of pain threw Anna into my arms and we held on to each other crouched by that wall until Husni came and said, 'They've done everything they can. They will wait outside if you want to go in.'

Milton Bey and Sa'd Bey stayed all night with us. At first he was not conscious, then he came to and spoke with Husni. Then he spoke with me and he told me – he told me what a good and gallant brother tells the sister he knows would give her life for him.

Then he spoke to Anna, who was kneeling on the floor at his side.

'Anna, listen to me.'
   'I love you.'
   'Anna, listen. You have made me –' He stops.

'Please don't talk. Please, please, don't talk.'

'Be quiet. Be quiet and listen. We have been good together. Yes?'

'Yes,' she whispers, 'yes.' The word catches in her throat. 'I have been so happy with you. So happy.' She is kissing his hands, rubbing her forehead into his arm, rubbing herself into him.

'I want you to live your life −'

'I love you, I love you −'

'I know. Hush. You have to be brave now. For Nur. Remember your promise.'

'This is my home.'

'This *was* your home. Because of me. I don't want her to have to fight so hard.'

'I want to stay.'

'No. Anna. It won't do. It only worked because of me.'

'You are so arrogant −'

Sharif Basha raises an eyebrow and gives her a look and she puts her hands in his hair. 'Oh, please,' she begs, 'please, try −'

'Bring her up − like you.'

'My love,' she says, 'oh, my love, my love . . .'

OUR MOTHER CAME INTO THE room and he lifted his eyes to her. 'Mama?'

She bent over him, reached for his hand. 'Sharif. Habibi. Ibni. What happened?'

He raised her hand to his mouth. 'Pray for me, ya Ummi', and his sigh was like when he sat down in the entrance hall and took off his boots after a long ride on a hot summer's day. My mother put her other hand over his eyes and said the shahada for him before her legs gave way −

Dawn breaks and the sun comes up on a house of keening women. Their voices rise from the salamlek, loud with anguish, tailing off into despair: ya habibi, ya habibi, ya ibni ya habibi, my son, my brother, my beloved, ya habibi.

*   *   *

504

AND AS FOR ME, A hundred – a thousand times a day I think of him. I think I'll ask Abeih this, or Abeih will laugh so when he hears that. I wait for his step when I hear the sound of wheels on the gravel. When the coffee runs low I think we had better get – then I remember. I see him in a turn of Ahmad's head, in the look he has started to give me – and I catch my son to me and hug him and kiss him and turn him away before he can see me weep. He has grieved for his uncle and taken the parting from Nur very hard and asks whether he might not go to study in England.

Anna writes to us often. With news of Nur. For herself she has no news, she says, only news of Nur. She paints. And she looks after her old kinsman – Sir Charles. And her garden.

My father is in his shrine. We do not know whether he understands what has happened. My mother is grown very quiet. She prays a great deal. But Ahmad and Mahrous can still make her smile.

Mabrouka has grown into an old woman overnight. She sits by the door of my father's shrine, where Anna's loom used to stand. She mutters incessantly, whether the Qur'an or spells we do not know. On the day after my brother's murder she rolled up Anna's tapestry in three bags of muslin. One she gave to me 'for Ahmad', she said, 'and his children after him'. The other she gave to Anna for Nur. I do not know what she did with the third. The loom itself we carried into the shrine for my father would not allow us to remove it. Sometimes he sits at it, threading a ball of silk as he used to watch Anna do. But he has made nothing.

Sabir is heartbroken and blames himself. But he threw himself over my brother and was wounded in the shoulder. What more was there for him to do?

Husni is very tender and very good to me. They have not yet found out who did it. They say it could be Coptic fanatics in retaliation for Boutros Basha's assassination.

They say it could be Muslim fanatics for my brother's position on women's rights and because he married Anna and was known to wear her image on a chain round his neck – and so that the Copts would be blamed. They say it could be British agents to get the Copts blamed and increase the divisions in the country and rid themselves of a national leader. They say it could be the Khedive out of spite – and not fearful of consequences, since Lord Kitchener would be glad to see my brother dead. They say it could be bigger people than all these. They say – they say. My mother has stopped listening. Husni says my brother's last orders were that nobody should be allowed to make use of his murder.

Husni says there will be war. And that will be our chance to get rid of the Occupation. He says I should try to organise some more lectures for women at the university. He says I should start a new magazine and get Anna to write for us from England. And Juliette from France. He says Abeih would have liked that. El-Basha would have liked that, he says.

El-Basha. My brother. Sometimes I open the partition curtains and peep through the mashrabiyya into the salamlek, as though I might find him there, as though maybe if I wait, if I wait long enough, the great doors will swing open and there he will be, handing his cane and his tarbush to Mirghani, his head lifted to listen for the sounds of life, for the sounds of us women inside, here, in the house.

Tuesday 2nd Safar 1332
[agreeing with] 30 December 1913

An End

And so I beg the darkness:
Where are you, my loving man?
Why gone from her whose love
Can pace you, step by step, to your desire?

Song, Egypt, 1300 BC

And so he dies. And Amal, who has known the ending all along, yet has loved him like his mother, like his sister, like his wife, mourns him with fresh grief. She reads and rereads Anna's last entry:

> *I have tried, as well as I could, to tell her. But she cannot – or will not – understand, and give up hope. She waits for him constantly.*

She scans the page and the pages beyond it, willing Anna to write more; to write to her again. But there is nothing. Anna's letters to Layla, where are they? And what of Nur? And Ahmad, her own father? And Mahrous? There is nothing more. Amal finally has to close the journals. She smooths down each sheet of each letter and cutting and arranges them neatly in files. But she has not the heart to bury them back in the trunk. They remain in her bedroom, on the table by the window. Her brother will want to see them.

She goes to the family mausoleum in the City of the Dead. A special visit for Sharif Basha al-Baroudi; the old resident sheikh chants Suret Yasin especially for him.

Cairo, 21 August 1998
He holds Amal's eyes as he feeds. He sucks hard and fast on the bottle, his hands curled into fists, pumping from time to time

with effort. His face is clear and open, his eyes hold hers. When the teat folds with the pressure and she eases it out of his mouth, he protests and wriggles for the moment that it takes to fill with air, then gasps with eagerness when she touches it once again to his lips. He sucks a few times, then lets the teat lie idle in his mouth. And then the decisive push with the tongue and he turns his face away, interested once again in the light and the moving shadows. Holding him close against her shoulder, patting his back, Amal walks around the room crooning to the baby until two deep burps tell them both that all is well.

Amal lowers Sharif into her arms and looks at him. He gazes back at her with wide-open black eyes. 'So? You don't want to go to sleep yet?' She shakes her head at him and he stretches out a hand. Her older son used to do that: wake up at three in the morning, feed and then fuss until she put him in his chair and sat opposite him, chatting, singing, playing with him. 'Let's go and change your nappy, then.' She holds him to her and walks down the long corridor, quietly past the room where Isabel lies sleeping and into her own bedroom. She lays him down on the bed and plants a kiss on the sole of each soft foot. 'OK, son of 'Omar al-Ghamrawi. Don't you dare pee on my bed.'

Later, she stands by the window. The glass is closed but the shutters are open and she lowers the baby's feet to the table, holding him upright against her so he can look out at the stars. The day is the twenty-ninth of Rabi' al-Thani and the moon is nowhere to be seen. Tomorrow a crescent so thin as to be almost indiscernible will rise once more into the sky, but for tonight, all is blackness. The baby stamps his bare feet against the table, against Anna's journals, against the files. He looks down and, following his gaze, Amal picks up the bronze statuette. In her hand, the cat sits erect: the front legs straight, the back a graceful slope from the pointy tips of the ears to the tail curled gracefully round the haunches. 'This belongs to your cousin,' she says. 'Yes, yes, you don't know it yet, but you have cousins and a brother and a sister. Lots and

lots of people, and they're all going to love you *so* much –
and it's too heavy for you to carry so don't even try.' She
moves the cat away from the baby's reaching hand and bends
to place it under the table where he will not see it. As she
straightens up, his attention shifts once again to the table: to
the shiny black oval pebble. 'Your papa gave me this,' she
says, holding it out on her palm, the baby safely enclosed in
the circle of her arm. 'Yes, he did,' she says, 'we were walking
on the beach and he found this and gave it to me.' The little
hand stretches out and feels the stone, but the fingers slip on
the shiny surface when he tries to grasp it. The feet kick
against the table and the eyes lift to Amal's. 'And he gave me
lots of other things,' she says to him as she brings her face
close to rub noses gently. She lifts him up against her chest
and starts to walk around the room. 'He played with me
when I was little and helped me out when I was big and he's
been my bestest friend and bestest brother – well, *only*
brother – and he's your papa too, and he's brave and he's
handsome and he makes music,' she sings softly as she walks
and rocks the baby, 'wonderful music . . .' She rocks the
baby.

She lays the sleeping child by his mother and places a long
pillow at his other side. Asleep, Isabel stirs and places a hand on
Sharif's leg.

The light from the newly opened pharmacy downstairs
spills out on the road. Men are unloading cartons off a van and
carrying them into the new supermarket. Down the road the
small grocer's shop is still open. The young men sit on the cars,
their hands in their pockets, their feet kicking rhythmically at
the bumpers. Warda's voice and the drums and castanets
surrounding it swirl around them: 'I've stopped loving
you/Loving you/So don't love me/Take back your heart/
Oh your heart/And set me free –'

In the living room Amal picks up the newspaper she has not
had a chance to read. Monica Lewinsky and her blue dress
take up two pages. Sudan should not be partitioned. Clinton

vows to avenge America on Ben Laden. Albright threatens action against Iraq. Torture in Palestinian jails – she folds the newspaper and throws it into the big wastepaper basket. *It is very hard*, Anna had written a hundred years ago, *not to feel caught up in a terrible time of brutality and* we – Amal edits – are *helpless to do anything but wait for history to run its course.* She puts the tape her brother had brought back from Ramallah into the tape player, stretches out on the sofa under the ceiling fan and lights a cigarette.

'I have a ship
In the harbour
And God's forgotten us
In the harbour –'

They have not heard from 'Omar since he left Sarajevo. In the soft light of the table lamp the iced hibiscus tea is as red as blood. Will he stay long enough to read the story? To imagine Anna with her? Anna, on the boat back to England: *The child sleeps. Nur al-Hayah: light of my life . . . She waits for him constantly . . .* And Layla. Amal had wept over Layla's last pages. She had her husband and her son, but her brother, her beloved Abeih Sharif, had been snatched away from her. And Anna had taken her daughter and gone. Did they live in England? How did Nur meet her Frenchman? Did she and Ahmad never meet again? Did Anna decide that Nur would leave the East behind her for ever, would keep her world in one place – or was it the war that decided for her, for them all? And the old Baroudi house grown silent once again – would 'Omar want to see it? Isabel would surely want to take him there –

'My pipe in my hand
And a fur on my back
Filled with silver
Filled with cash –'

On the wall Anna's tapestry, still in three pieces, hangs from the makeshift batten Madani has rigged up for it. Yet again Amal wonders about that middle panel, about Horus. Where had he come from? She tries to put the question out of her mind. She reminds herself of Harry Boyle's letter – of how that had been a puzzle for Sharif Basha and his friends, and how she had stumbled upon the answer ninety years later. But once more she goes over the possibilities. She had not put the panel in Isabel's bag. She is sure, at least, of that. But could Isabel have done it? And if so, when? And where had she found it? In the trunk before she brought it to Amal? But when they had gone through the trunk together and found the Osiris panel, Isabel would have said. She would have said, 'Oh, there's another one. I left it in New York.' Could she have found it later, in New York among her mother's things? She still would have said. Why should she hide it? No. Isabel was surprised to find it in her bag. Amal is sure of that. Or is she?

'I have a ship
And God's forgotten me
In the harbour
Come, little flower
Come with me –'

Amal has intuition. She has imagination. Does she still believe that every question has an answer? She goes again over Layla's words: 'Oh the day after my brother's murder Mabrouka rolled up Anna's tapestry in three bags of muslin. One she gave to me "for Ahmad", she said, "and his children after him." The other she gave to Anna for Nur. I do not know what she did with the third.' Layla had given the Isis panel to Ahmad and he had given it to 'Omar. Anna had not given the Osiris panel to Nur. Or if she had, it had still ended up wrapped inside her trunk and been passed down to Jasmine. What had Mabrouka done with the third?

They have not yet told 'Omar that it has appeared. It seems

too strange a thing to mention casually over the phone. They have thought perhaps they should surprise him. Stitch the whole thing together, iron it, and have it hanging there for him to see.

'Come, little flower
Come with me
I mean you well
And my heart is whole –'

When would he come? When would he call? Isabel is not worried, but she has not known him long enough. She does not realise what a solitary figure he now cuts. Beloved by many, hated by many, but essentially solitary. How else could he have ended up – living where he lives, doing what he does – except alone in that no-man's-land between East and West? For her it has been different. She has not had a public life. She has concentrated on the boys, and she has translated novels – or done her best to translate them. It is so difficult to truly translate from one language into another, from one culture into another; almost impossible really. Take that concept 'tarab', for example; a paragraph of explanation for something as simple as a breath, a lifting of the heart, tarab, mutrib, shabb tereb, tarabattatta tarabattattee, Taroob, Jamal wa Taroob: etmanni mniyyah / I've wished / w'estanni 'alayyah / I've waited / 'iddili l'miyyah / I've counted . . . Amal catches herself falling asleep and considers whether she should go to bed – or would the baby wake and get her up again immediately? She cannot wait to see 'Omar with him. She has grown used to worrying about her brother over the last few years. She worries, and then he phones. He will phone soon. She looks up at the tapestry. Tomorrow they can stitch it and have it ironed. They can put little Sharif in his bouncer seat under it. He would look at it as Nur used to look at it when she was a baby, lying at her mother's feet in the courtyard watching the balls of silk jumping on their threads. Once more Amal sees Anna sitting in the sunshine, working at her loom, old Baroudi Bey beside her, his eyes on his rosary, the baby in the basket, the sounds from the house drifting into the courtyard. She sees Sharif Basha coming through the doorway, pausing to take in the scene and to feel his heart flood once again with love. She sees Anna take each finished panel from the loom. Mabrouka holds one end and the two women roll the length of cloth carefully between them. She sees Sharif Basha lying on the diwan in the salamlek and she sees hands draw a white sheet over him and she hears the sobs of the men and the keening of the women. She sees Mabrouka in her room, tying wrappings of muslin around three long rolls of cloth, weeping, pausing to dash away the tears that blind her, muttering, muttering all the while. Amal makes out a few of her words: 'from the dead come the living', 'the branch is cut but the tree remains'. Mabrouka weeps and wraps and mutters, 'The precious one goes and the precious one comes.' The tears make their ragged way down the lines on the old face. 'The Nile divides and meets again,' and again, and again. 'He brings forth the living from the dead' – the baby's cry sounds through the house and the sudden fear that seizes Amal's heart is so strong that it jolts her off the sofa and to her feet.

'Omar!' she cries out loud. 'My brother . . .!'

The battered trunk, ransacked of its treasure, sits by the wall. The old journals, emptied of their secrets, lie on the table. Beside them are the pages, neatly stacked, in which Amal has written down the story of Anna and Sharif al-Baroudi. Next door, Isabel sleeps soundly. Sharif is cradled in Amal's arms as, once again, she makes her way with him down the long, dark corridor. She holds him close, patting his back. Whispering. 'Hush, my precious,' she whispers, 'hush . . .'

Abeih: title of respect for an older brother or male relative (feminine: **Abla**). Turkish.

Abuzeid: an epic ballad describing the life and deeds of Abuzeid al-Hilali.

afandiyyah (also effendis); plural of **afandi** (effendi or efendi): an urban (Western-) educated man (see **Basha**).

ahlan wa sahlan: welcome. Literally '[you are among] your people [and on] your plain'.

akhi: my brother.

al– (and **el–**): prefix meaning 'the'. 'Al-' is formal, while 'el-' is colloquial.

al–hamdu–l–illah (also **el–hamdu–l–Illah**): thanks be to God.

alf mabrouk: a thousand congratulations.

Allahu Akbar: God is the greatest.

'am: uncle. Specifically father's brother. Used as title of respect for older man.

amrad: a man who has no facial hair.

'Antar: an epic ballad of the love story of 'Antar and 'Abla.

Aqsa: the Aqsa mosque in Jerusalem. Islam's third holiest shrine (after the Ka'ba in Makkah and the Mosque of the Prophet in Madinah).

aragoz: a Punch and Judy show.

'arbagi: driver of a cart. Derogatory.

Ard, el–: *The Land*, a 1970 classic of the Egyptian cinema by Yusuf Chahine. Based on the novel by 'Abd al-Rahman al-Sharqawi, it shows the peasants uniting with a religious leader and a patriotic city lawyer to take issue with unjust irrigation laws.

'asr: afternoon. Also the name of the third of the five prayers of the day.

Assiuti chairs: a particular type of wooden armchair with reclining back originating in Assiut in Upper Egypt.

awqaf (plural of **waqf**): an endowment or trust. Most great Muslim institutions in Egypt, such as hospitals, schools, libraries and mosques, are established upon endowments, or awqaf, which come under the supervision of a ministry of that name.

aya: a verse from the Qur'an, a sign demonstrating the existence of God, also a woman's name.

aywa: yes.

Azhari: a graduate of al-Azhar, the thousand-year-old religious university in Cairo.

Bahawat: plural of Bey (see **Basha**).

balah el-Sham: a sweet pastry (literally dates of the Levant).

Balfour Declaration: Arthur Balfour, British foreign minister in 1917: 'His Majesty's Government looks with favour upon the creation of a national homeland for the Jews in Palestine . . .'

barakah: blessing or grace.

barsim: a green plant similar to clover. Used for feeding cattle, donkeys, etc.

Basha: Ottoman title, roughly equivalent to 'Lord'. Can be placed at the end of a name or in the middle. The titles in use in Egypt – and all countries subject to Turkish Ottoman rule – were 'Efendi' (an urban person with a secular education and wearing Western dress – although not Western himself), 'Bey' and 'Basha' (Turkish: Pasha). The last two were conferred formally by the Khedive in Egypt or the Sultan in Constantinople. The Khedive, alone, was known as 'Efendeena' (or Our Efendi).

The Arab titles, acquired through attaining a degree of learning, were 'Ustaz': master; and 'Sheikh': head or principal.

bass: Stop it! Enough! Probably from Italian 'Basta!'

Bey: see **Basha**.

b'iftikarak . . .: What good will it do you to remember?

brawa 'aleiha: bravo (on her).

Coptic calendar: the most extreme persecution of Christians in Egypt took place in the reign of the Roman emperor Diclidianus. The Coptic Church adopted the year of his ascension, AD 284, as the beginning of a new calendar: the Time of the Martyrs.

corvée: forced labour – employed for large national projects like digging the Suez Canal, but also for work on the Pashas' or the Khedive's lands.

courbash (kurbaj): the whip. Normally made of rhinoceros hide.

Dar al-Kutub: the National Library of Egypt.

Dönme: a member of a Judaeo–Islamic syncretist sect.

Dustur: Constitution.

el- and **al-**: prefix meaning 'the'; see '**al-**.

faddan (also feddan): a measure of area used for agricultural land in Egypt. Roughly equivalent to an acre.

Fadilatukum: form of address to a sheikh who holds a religious position. Similar to Your Grace. Literally 'Your Virtue', from 'fadeelah': that by which one person is preferred (f/dd/l) over another.

fallah (also fellah): peasant. Feminine: **fallaha**. Plural: **fallaheen**, from (f/l/h) to till the land. The root also means: to be successful.

fantasia: fantaziyya, a display of extravagant joie de vivre (as in 'what's all this fantaziyya' to a child wearing fancy ribbons in her hair). British travellers used it specifically as a name for an event of Bedouin horsemanship.

fasakhani: a shop that specialises in salted fish and roe.

Firman: an absolute decree issued by the Ottoman sultan from Constantinople.

galabiyya: long, loose robe worn by peasants and traditional people of Egypt.

Ghezirah (also **Gezira**): island. Also a district of Cairo which is an island in the Nile.

gibba (also **djibbah**): traditional long garment of satinised cotton, usually white with thin black stripes, worn by men of religion under the quftan.

habara: a woman's cloak.

habbet el–barakah: a seed, the oil of which is widely used for medicinal purposes. Recently found to have a good effect on the immune system.

habibi: my darling, my beloved — masculine (feminine: **habibti**).

hadith: discourse.

hanim: Turkish for 'lady'.

haraam: it is sinful, it is pitiful, it is arousing of compassion, it should not be done.

haraam 'aleik: literally 'it is a sin upon you', used as 'please don't say that' or 'you should not do that'.

haram: the root h/r/m denotes a sacred or inviolable space. The haram of a mosque is the space within its walls. The haram of a university is its campus. The haram of a man is his wife. A man is referred to as the 'zawg' or 'the other half of the pair' of his wife.

haramlek: the area in a house reserved for women.

hareem (also harem): women, from h/r/m: sacred.

hasal kheir: 'good has come about', to be said when something not so good has happened but has ended without too much damage. Equivalent: 'it's not that bad'.

hayawan: animal.

hayy: alive.

ibn: son.

ibni: my son.

Ibrahimiyyah: large irrigation canal from the Nile.

iftar: literally 'breaking the fast'. Used for breakfast on normal days and for the sunset meal during Ramadan.

'imma: turban.

ingelisi: Englishman; feminine **ingeliziyya**.

insha' Allah (also **inshalla**): if God wills. Used as 'I hope' or 'let's hope so' or 'I wish', etc.

'Isa: Jesus — a name common to both Muslims and Copts.

'Isha: dusk or early evening. From 'a/sh/a: to become unable to see. Also the name of the prayers performed at dusk – the last of the day's five prayers.

Iskindiriyya: Alexandria

ismallah (ism Allah): the name of God (protect you).

itfaddal: please go ahead, please come in, please sit down. Literally 'do [me] the favour' (as in Italian per favore). Feminine: **itfaddali**.

izzay el–sehha?: How are you? Literally how is the health?

Jama'at (Islamiyyah): (Islamist) groups. General name for several factions of Islamist activists in Egypt who believe in armed opposition to the state.

jinn: supernatural beings. Generally naughty, can be evil.

kalb ya ibn el–kalb: (you) dog, you son-of-a-dog.

kattar kheirak: (may God) increase your bounty. Literally 'increase the good that comes from you', used as 'thank you'.

Kesh malik: Cringe, King! Warning before checkmate.

keteer: a lot.

khalas: literally 'it's finished', used also as 'done' or 'agreed'.

khali (also **khalu**): my uncle – specifically my mother's brother.

khamaseen: winds that blow in March and bring the desert sands into the cities.

khatibet akhuya: my brother's fiancée.

khawagaya: a foreign (European) woman. Masculine: **khawaga**.

Khedive: title of the ruler of Egypt from 'Abbas Pasha in 1849 to the Sultan Hussein Kamel during the First World War.

kheir: (may what has happened/the news be) good.

kittan: flax.

kufiyya: scarf.

kufr: disbelief. **Kafir**: an unbeliever (in Islam, Christianity or Judaism, the three religions of the Book).

kunafa: a sweet pastry.

kuttab: traditional elementary school which teaches reading, writing and the Qur'an.

la hawla wala quwwata illa b-Illah: there is no power or strength but with the support of God. Said when matters go beyond what you can help. It is a kind of 'I am absolved of responsibility in this'. An expression of helpless sadness as one watches matters get out of hand. Also of exasperation as an opponent refuses to see sense.

la hawl Illah: short, ungrammatical version of above.

lalu: childspeak for **'khalu'**: my uncle – specifically my mother's brother.

lek yom: your day will come (when you will be defeated).

lessa: not yet.

ma'alesh: never mind.

mafish: there is no[ne] . . .

magzub: one drawn (to God) by religious fervour to the extent that he separates himself from all worldly matters – and (the worldly) part of his mind. From g/z/b: to pull.

ma'mur: chief of police (of the markaz).

mandarah: a room slightly apart from the house to receive male visitors who are not of the family.

marhab: welcome.

markaz: centre. Also central police station (of the district).

masha' Allah: literally 'Look what God has willed!' Used to express admiration without being thought envious or activating the evil eye.

mashrabiyya: the ornate wooden screen that protects the privacy of the balconies in traditional houses.

mawwal: a traditional form of folk song, usually narrative, performed by one singer to the accompaniment of a rudimentary string instrument (a rabab). It is roughly equivalent to the English ballad, but relies heavily on verbal play, the lines often ending in a pun.

mayyit: dead.

misa' al-khairat: Oh evening of many good things!

mutasarrif: governor (Ottoman title).

n'har iswid: (Oh) black day.

Nahdet Masr: the Renaissance of Egypt.

nazra: a look.

'oud: lute.

Qaroon: historical (or mythological) character reputed to be fabulously rich.

quftan: traditional long garment of wool or heavy cotton, in a dark colour, worn by men of religion over the gibba.

Rabb: God – although the specific name of God is 'Allah'. So: Allahu Rabbi: Allah is my God.

Rabi' al-Thani: a month of the Arab year. The Arab year has twelve months. But since the months are lunar (the full moon falls on the 14th day of each month), it is shorter by eleven days than the Western year.

ruq'a: the informal Arabic script used for personal letters, drafts and notes. Ruq'a is also the piece of paper on which the writing is done. Possibly: writing done on a scrap – rather than the formal 'naskh' (copying script) done on a formal folio.

Safar: the second month of the Arab year.

sahara: desert.

salamlek: part of the house where men can move freely (as opposed to the haramlek, where they can only go by permission of the women).

'Salamu 'aleikum ('alaykum)'. ''Aleikum as-salam wa rahmatu allahi wa barakatuh.': 'Peace be upon you.' 'And upon you peace and the mercy of God and His blessings.' Traditional greeting and response upon arrival and departure. Spelled differently according to level of formality in speech.

Sallim silahak ya 'Urabi: surrender your arms, 'Urabi. Used for when an opponent is in an impossible position – as 'Urabi was in Tel el-Kebir. Chess terminology: Wazir: [Prime] Minister. In the West the Queen; the Elephant is the Bishop, the Horse is the Knight and the Fortress is the Rook.

sanduq el-dunya: Literally 'the box of the world'. A peep-show. Putting your head beneath a black hood and your eye to the peephole, you could see the seven wonders of the world or the Eiffel Tower etc.

Satir: One of the names of God. Literally He who shields, covers, protects.

Sattar: One of the names of God. Emphatic form of He who shields, covers, protects.

sayyid: master, also used as 'mister'.

sayyidna: our master, used to a sheikh.

sebertaya: small stove lit with **seberto** (spirits, alcohol).

sett: lady.

Settena Maryam: Our Lady Mary.

setti: my lady.

shahada: the creed. 'I bear witness that there is no God but God and that Muhammad is his prophet.' From sh/h/d: to bear witness. This is the first of the five essential bases of Islam and what a Muslim will say in extremis, such as at the moment of death.

sheikh el-mestakhabbi, el-: the hidden sheikh (kh/b/a: to grow faint; kh/bb/a: to hide (transitive); makhba' is a hideout, an air-raid shelter)

Shobbeik lobbeik, khaddamak bein eidek: the traditional opening line of the jinni of the lamp. 'Lobbeik' is a variation on l/bb/a; to respond. 'Shobbeik' is there for the rhyme, although it is also a variant on 'What's the matter with you?' in Levantine dialect. 'Khaddamak': your servant, from kh/d/m: to serve. Bein: between. Eideik: your hands.

shwayya: a little.

si: shortened version of **sidi**.

sidaq: money given as pledge of marriage. Normally given by the man to the woman, the lesser part on the signing of the marriage contract, the greater held back as the woman's insurance against divorce.

sidi: my master (abbreviated from **sayyidi**) used in secular context.

Southern Lebanon Army Militias: army created and funded by Israel from right-wing Lebanese militias.

Sublime Porte: a title for the Sultan (al-Bab al-'Ali).

sufragi: a male attendant. From Turkish 'sufra': table (laid for dining), one who attends the 'sufra' – a footman.

suhur: late meal eaten to prepare for the next day's fast during Ramadan. Can be any time from two in the morning until just before the rising of the sun.

sura: a chapter of the Qur'an.

Suret Yasin: the Chapter of Yasin. A favourite chapter for reciting for the dead as it tells of God's mercy and of paradise.

syce: groom. From Arabic 'sayis', root: s/a/s, to tame (siyasah is politics, siyasi is both a politician and a tactful person, musayasah is coaxing).

takht: literally 'a raised platform' and by metonymic transfer the musical ensemble to accompany a singer. It consists of a lute, a qanun (a kind of small horizontal harp), a tambourine and a tabla (drum). The musicians are all seated.

tarab: explained in text, **mutrib**: one who causes tarab, **shab tereb**: a gay dog, a young blade; **tarabattatta tarabattattee**: tra-la-la; **Jamal wa Taroob**: a Lebanese singing couple who were in vogue in Cairo in the Sixties; **etmanni mniyyah**: make a wish; **w'estanni 'alayya**: and give me some time; **'iddili l'miyya**: count to a hundred . . .

tarbush: fez.

tarha: headcover of black chiffon used by traditional women. If worn in the house it is white and shows great piety.

tayyib: good, very well, OK.

Tewfiq: the Khedive of Egypt in 1882 during the 'Urabi Revolution.

Tokar, I'll have you sent to: a common expression of threat. Tokar was a distant province in the Sudan known for its harsh climate and conditions. When the Sudan was under Egyptian/Turkish rule, an officer or civil servant who incurred the displeasure of the authorities was posted to Tokar – there to live a miserable life and die an early death.

Toshki: a huge irrigation project, inaugurated in January 1997, to create another main branch for the Nile at Toshki, slightly south-west of Aswan.

Toubah and Baramhat: Coptic names of the months corresponding to January and April. Fallaheen, in their dealings

527

with the land, still work by the old Coptic calendar as it most accurately corresponds to the specific climate of Egypt.

'umdah: the headman of a village. In 1997 a law was passed making it possible for women to hold the position of 'umdah.

umm/u: mother. In traditional society a woman, rather than being called by her given name, is called **umm** followed by the name of her oldest child. Similarly a man is called **abu** (father of) followed by the name of his oldest child. This is considered more respectful than using the given name.

ummi: my mother.

'uqal (also **ugal**): the black cord circle worn on the crown of the head over a kufiyya.

wa (also **we** and **w'**): and.

w' mit bosa: and a hundred kisses.

wadi: valley [of].

walla ma: or not. Derogatory, dismissive, 'it makes no difference' – like the use of the prefix 'shm' in Jewish-American parlance.

waqf: a trust.

ya: vocative instrument – optional if the vocative phrase is at the beginning of the utterance, obligatory if it is in the middle.

Yafa: Palestinian coastal town. English: Jaffa.

ya-fandim: sir (abbreviated **ya afandi**).

yakhti (**ya okhti**): my sister.

yalla: hurry, let's go.

yama: an indication of great quantity, as in 'yama I told him, but he wouldn't listen'.

ya'ni: an interjection. Literally 'it means'. But used like 'you know' and 'almost' and 'so-so'.

Yasu' al-Masih: Jesus, the Christ. Specific to Christ, as opposed to 'Isa which is Jesus as a common name.

zaffa: wedding procession.

zagharid: ululations, joy-cries, celebrating a happy event. Made exclusively by women. Singular: **zaghruda**.

zarafa: giraffe.

Isma'il Basha Sabri's poems:

'Take your fill . . .':

Tazawwada min al-aqmari qabla ufuliha
li-dhulmati ayami-l-furaqi wa tuliha

to:

A-anta razinun ayyuha al-qalbu fi ghadin
ka'ahdika am sarin wara'a humuliha?

'Leave off your coyness . . .':

Khalli sududak we hagrak
W-itfi lahibi we wagdi
Sa'it wisalak we urbak
aghla min el-'umr 'andi
laglak hagarni manami
we fik gafeit kulle saheb
we lagl urbak we waslak
sahibt gheir el-habayib

529

A NOTE ON THE AUTHOR

Ahdaf Soueif was born in Cairo and educated in Egypt and England. She is the author of *Aisha*, *Sandpiper* and *In the Eye of the Sun*.